"The war won't last forever, Sadie.
I'll be back before you know it and we'll be together."
He smoothed her hair from her face and traced his
thumbs over her lips. "Did I tell you I bought us that
farmhouse in the country you've had your eye on?"

She gasped, forcing her quivering lips into a smile,
grateful for his well-timed fantasy. "You mean the one
with the pond and the weeping willow?"

"That's the one." He kissed her nose. "With the
barn and more land than you can see from the porch. I
already dug the holes for the fence posts." Now he
kissed her lips while cradling her face.

"Not bad for a city boy." She pulled back to crinkle
her nose. "Tell me more."

"We can teach the kids to ice skate on that pond,"
he said.

"Oh, there will be kids?"

He nodded, stone serious, his laugh creases now
white lines marking each and every wonderful trace on
his flushed face. "A bevy of girls like you. We'll be
blessed with a house full of them—"

"Unless they happen to be sons. To help in the
fields."

"Fields? But I'm just a city boy."

Praise for Carolyn Menke

"A sweeping, romantic debut that brings the war-time forties to vivid life in this Titanic meets Philomena tale—fast-paced, tender, and real."

~RITA award-winning author Gwyn Cready

~*~

"Menke's writing is so lovely, you will want to wrap yourself in her words and savor each moment you spend in Sadie's story. *RETURN TO ME* will tug on your heart strings and take you on a journey back in time."

~Dana Faletti, author of the Whisper Trilogy

~*~

"A timeless tale of love, loss, and sacrifice that will equally break and warm your heart, as you cheer for the beautifully complex characters until the very last page."

~Lori M. Jones, author of Renaissance of the Heart

~*~

"I loved this heartwarming, sweet story of love and all its obstacles. In *RETURN TO ME*, Sadie Stark and James Pasko's accidental meeting ignites passion that takes them by surprise. These dynamic, likeable characters and their tangled life sucked me into the book, right back in time to World War II. Heroics, secrets, longing, loss, and hope all meld to keep the plot tight and compelling until the very end. ...wrought with warm moments and cold choices that threaten the idea that love really is enough. Wonderful writing, beautiful imagery and a lovely happy ending—what else can a reader ask for?"

*~Kathleen Shoop, award-winning author of
After the Fog and The Last Letter*

Return to Me

by

Carolyn Menke

Return to Me

Cover Art by *Kim Mendoza*

The Wild Rose Press, Inc.
PO Box 708
Adams Basin, NY 14410-0708
Visit us at www.thewildrosepress.com

Publishing History
First Vintage Rose Edition, 2015
Print ISBN 978-1-5092-0314-7
Digital ISBN 978-1-5092-0315-4

Published in the United States of America

Dedications

For my parents, who first taught me how to love.
And for Stephen, for proving it's possible.

Chapter One

Springhaven, 1972

Sadie set her buttery tart pie on the windowsill to cool. She folded her husband's misplaced glasses, and walked them out to his favorite reading spot on the front porch.

A billow of dust parachuted behind an unfamiliar green Ford Pinto barreling up their lane. The tires crunched across gravel near the portico that sagged like their swayback mare, and Sadie re-pinned a stubborn wisp of hair that had escaped her carelessly twisted bun at the nape of her neck.

The Pinto puttered to a stop.

A young woman peeled her toned thighs from the vinyl seat and eased to the ground. After studying a piece of paper, she cocked her head up, catching Sadie's gaze. Then she hoisted a bag of groceries in her arm the way a mother lifts a child.

"May I help you?" Sadie didn't recognize this woman, although her gait was oddly familiar.

"Yes, I hope so." The woman shifted the bag and shaded her eyes. Her puckered cheeks were the color of a ripened peach. "I stopped at the market asking for directions. Ruth Dalton directed me here, and asked that I bring your groceries. I hope that was okay."

"Thank you." Sadie took the sack from the woman

as they met on the porch, wondering why she was here. Was she looking for someone who'd once stayed at Springhaven? A breeze sucked the checkered curtains to the screens and then released them to tinker with the chimes as the women stared at each other for an awkward moment.

"I'm looking for Sadie Stark." The woman tucked back a shock of straight dark hair, bundled like sheaves of grain.

Sadie Stark?

Confusion rippled through her mind because nobody had called her by that name for some time. Sadie set the groceries down on the wide-planked floor. As she studied the woman's face, she nervously twisted her filigree wedding band that had become too loose to stay put, but too tight to work over her knuckle.

"Well then," Sadie said, her flesh prickling with goosebumps. "You've come to the right place."

"You're Sadie?" The woman's voice cracked.

"I am."

The woman stifled a cry and reached into her jeans pocket. Nestled in the palm of her hand was an old black lighter with a name etched into it—all the evidence Sadie needed to know who she was.

The woman's voice was steady and strong. "This lighter belonged to—"

"Yes. I know," Sadie said.

"You remember?"

Sadie dipped her head and covered her mouth with quivering fingers. "Not a day goes by that I don't think of it…"

Chapter Two

Pittsburgh, 1942

James Pasko dodged a streetcar to cross Penn Avenue. As he loped to the other side, he adjusted the pack on his shoulder that held his military enlistment papers. Pittsburgh's Union Station, looming before him, was shrouded in snow the color of dirty dishwater. A bleak gray sky, polluted by the fiery steel mills in his hometown, wouldn't dampen his spirits. He'd enlisted, and now that his brother had made it back from the war alive, it was his turn to fight for their country.

He surged faster through the crowds, tilting and turning and rerouting his blistered steps to avoid being swallowed up in the tearful goodbyes around him. It wasn't until he reached the box counter and purchased his ticket to Fort Dix that he allowed himself to fully catch his breath. Although James didn't like to draw a scene, he couldn't help but feel a little disheartened at the flurry of activity. Nobody had come to see him off.

Ticket in-hand, he found the train and chose a seat at the back of the car, where he could keep his eye on passersby. He adjusted his Army-issued cap. Through the grimy window, he studied the strangers, catching the subtle yet telling nuances of their body language, and concocting stories about these people as if they were characters in a book. The pot-bellied bum in overalls was a bootlegger's son that still made rye whiskey. The plump woman that smelled of mouthwash to hide her liquor had stolen the plumed hat off the display window at Horne's when the sales clerk wasn't watching. The pink-cheeked slip of a girl whose soldier's hand rested on her belly in the moment before they kissed goodbye, was expecting his brother's baby.

But what was this? A young woman strolled toward the first-class car. James inched closer to the window. She carried a hatbox pressed to her chest, a clutch tucked under her arm, and a suitcase handle gripped with a white-gloved hand. Playing his game, he imagined her to be the new governess for a family in New York. No...too well-to-do, not to mention pretty. He tilted his head to consider why this dark-haired beauty was traveling alone. Bobbing and dodging strangers who grazed her cashmere coat, her eyes glazed with an empty lifeless stare he didn't like. The lonely expression didn't fit in with the fur-trimmed lapel speckled with snowflakes. Perhaps she was a widow, who had lost her husband in the war. It was possible, except then she'd likely have the hand of a child in hers, leading their way to an uncertain future. No, James decided, this young lady with her chin held high, exuded a willfulness he didn't often observe in his Depression-strapped part of town.

James threw open the window for fresh air, and maybe for a closer look at her. When she fixed her attention on him, warmth spread from his shoulder-to-shoulder, sweat dampened his forehead, and he couldn't peel away from that endearing crinkle between her delicate brow, or the beauty mark gracing her upper lip. She had the face of a screen star.

He blinked at the blinding light of flashbulbs sparking all around the platform. An entourage of media reporters moved in a mob around Governor Stark as he approached the young lady. The governor. Of course. That's how James knew her. Nostalgia crept up the back of his neck as he realized this girl was related to the governor. He'd nervously shined the newly elected official's shoes years earlier, while she had watched nearby. James still felt the soft satin ribbon that had fallen from her hair; he'd kept in his trouser pocket after she had gone.

Despite the commotion, her eyes never left his. The stale reek of train travel and cigar smoke gave way to a memory he had of her lemony candy breath and that raspy voice. James couldn't have been the first man taken by her beauty, but she flushed and looked away as if unused to the attention.

The spell had broken. Had James imagined it all like he did with the bootlegger's son and the lady hat thief? He didn't think so.

"Always a pleasure to visit the nation's greatest producer of steel!" The governor shook hands with someone while posing for another picture, this time with his arm around his wife. A small group of well-heeled travelers hovered nearby.

Out of the corner of his eye, James spotted a boy approaching the group.

"My clutch!" The young woman dropped her hatbox and suitcase on the platform, spilling the contents, and setting in motion a collective confusion. The thief took off with her purse, his oversized jacket flapping at mid-calf.

James bounded from his seat to the vestibule

railing. When the boy drew near, James leaped off and tackled him. A second boy, the thief's accomplice, it seemed, jumped on James' back—pummeling him in the ribs, head, and face, allowing the first boy to scramble away. Pain seared across him, but he wrestled free and continued. In McKees Rocks, known in Pittsburgh as "The Rocks," he and Paul had fought their way across schoolyards and to the steel mills and back.

The chase was on.

The boy boarded an adjacent train car. He crossed through it to the other side. James followed. He dodged boarding travelers and a blue-suited conductor announcing travel times and destinations. The commotion grew more chaotic as stragglers clambered onto packed cars.

Slowed by the crowds, but not dissuaded, James gained on the small thief. The boy was equally determined and perhaps growing more sure of the importance of the stolen item.

A conductor threw his hat at the thief, missing. Another well-intentioned bystander tried to take him out with a cane. When James was finally close enough to grab him, the boy tossed the clutch under the tracks.

A police officer seized the boy.

"All aboard!"

James hunched over, gasping for air, his dripping blood marking the platform.

"Board your train, son. I have him from here," the officer said.

James ran to the edge of the tracks and saw the clutch just out of reach.

"Go on, before you get your head chopped off."

"Sir?" James asked the man with the cane. "May

I?"

Seemingly amused by the scuffle and perhaps eager to help in the spirit of young love, he handed it over.

James, lying prone, used the cane to grab the girls' purse the way a shepherd hooks his lamb, dragging it closer to the wall, and scooping it up by the handle, carefully lifting so it didn't fall down into the hole. When he pulled it out, victorious, a small audience applauded his efforts.

He held the clutch overhead for the crowd to see. Then he wiped his brow with the back of his sleeve and strutted off to deliver the object to its rightful owner.

But the whistle had blown.

Wheels were in motion.

Steam shot into the steel-colored sky.

James sprinted, now trapped between train lines. He found an opening at last and ran along the platform to get back to where he started, his temples throbbing from the rhythmic clicking of the steamers.

The last car in the train pulled away. He saw her through the observation window, perhaps training her eyes to find him? She pressed her white-gloved hands against the glass.

He waved his arms, shouting at the receding car, even though he doubted she could hear him over the deafening noise. Even if she had, what could she do?

And just like that, she was gone.

Chapter Three

Sadie's ice cubes clinked in time to the surging click-clack of the steam locomotive. She peered around the dining car, complete with gleaming brass light fixtures, polished mahogany, and white linens, and wondered what ended up happening back in Pittsburgh. Did the soldier catch the thief?

Traveling with her governor uncle often caused a scene, drawing beggars and dishonesty, and perpetuating her belief that people outside their circle couldn't be trusted. But something felt different this time. Not in all of her years of traveling had she seen someone act so brave and chivalrous without hesitation. She felt a stirring in her core that a complete stranger, someone she'd never even met before, would leap off and miss his train to chase down a petty thief.

"Shameless, some people are," Henry said. "So desperate for a handout that they make fools of themselves."

Still shaken by the incident, she peeled off each dirtied glove from Pittsburgh's soot, and wondered if Henry meant the pickpocket or the soldier. The soldier, unlike Henry, had at least tried to help. Henry wasn't the type to lay down his jacket over the mud puddle for her, although it was times like these that she wished with every fiber in her being that he was or could be.

"I'll buy you a new one." He cradled his snifter of

Four Roses bourbon. His breath smelled of burnt vanilla.

She forced a tight smile. The engraved compact inside her clutch that had belonged to her mother could hardly be replaced. He knew that. A waiter catered to nearby men playing cards. Their laughter rumbled through the smoky air as they puffed cigars and gulped Manhattans.

"Come on, doll. Let's talk about something else." Henry studied her over the top of his pear-shaped glass as he took another swig. Everything about him exuded confidence, from his grease-darkened red hair, which he had slicked back and parted like Spencer Tracy, right down to his expensive wingtip shoes.

"Okay. Are you ready for second term at school?"

He groaned. "I meant let's talk about us." He dipped his head toward her face, the husky tone in his voice putting her on edge.

"I can't help but worry."

"What are you driving at?" He reached out, palms up, veins bulging in the underbelly of his forearms.

His rocky scores for starters. A war-deferred status that depended on his staying enrolled. But mostly, whether they had a future together.

She rested her hands lightly on his.

"You want to talk about school? All right." He squeezed her hands gently. "Our first party is at the end of the month. You'll come, won't you?" His forehead vein bulged along with his renewed enthusiasm. He cocked his head to the side. "The guests like to see the bottles their liquor comes from, so I'll line them all up. Only the good stuff, you know."

"Sounds like you aspire to tend the bar rather than

pass it."

He tilted his head to the other side as if trying to decipher whether she was teasing. "I'll pass the bar all right, and when I do, I'll be set. Your uncle will take care of me, doll. Especially with you as my wife." He narrowed his eyes, the same color as the bourbon in his belly, then half-stood, half-leaned over the table for a kiss, sealing her fear. He expected her to help his political career, no matter what. Forget her aspirations.

"Unless you fail out first."

"Sadie Stark." He covered her hands with his and rubbed her bare ring finger with his thumb. "No one will let that happen to me. Ever."

Let that happen? "And if it does? You'll be drafted." She tried to keep her voice down.

"You worry too much, doll." He brushed a thumb along her chin, seemingly pleased with her concern.

She stared out the window at the passing scenery. Clumps of snow clung to the evergreens, a stark contrast to the ice-encased branches of the deciduous trees. Yesterday she'd forgiven Henry's flirting with a buxom bridesmaid at the Mellon wedding, the one he'd quickly grown bored with—or, rather, would have grown bored with had she overlooked his wandering eye.

"You're my girl," was all he'd said to assure her, through a one-armed hug that was anything but remorseful. Sadie worried that she too, one of these days, would lose her luster in his eyes, when his chase was over, his conquest won. What about when she was cranky, old, and wrinkled—would he love her then?

The question wasn't whether he'd leave her. He admittedly needed her connections to secure his career and she had no doubt he'd continue to need them to maintain it. The question was whether she'd ever feel emotionally secure despite it. Not that it was his fault really. It would take a bigger person than Henry to fill the void that had been created when her mother walked out. A bigger man. One who would chase down a runaway vagrant, maybe? Her lips flittered up with a rush of excitement.

When she imagined the soldier's rough hand caressing her face the way Henry had, a deep stirring pulled at the pit of her belly. The intense sensation was like strings stretching across her chest, swelling inside her like an ocean's cresting sea.

Sadie wondered if a man as selfless as that solider who'd sprung to action before her eyes would ever openly flirt in front of her as Henry often did. For as much as she tried to put the idea out of her head, she couldn't stop replaying the scene—the way he tackled the thief and chased on was as clearly etched into her mind like a picture show. She remembered the deep boom and echo of the uniformed man's voice as he tackled and wrestled the pickpocket right there on the dirty platform, throwing punches. Her skin heated through her blouse at the idea of it all.

If only she could see him again and thank him. Not just for his kind gesture, but for the flood of emotions he'd awakened inside her. Maybe for the chance to know who he was.

As the steamer chugged along, surging and lurching and bouncing her corkscrew curls, it occurred to her that perhaps he'd left something on the train. A piece of luggage under his seat that held some clue. If she found any piece of information leading to his identity or whereabouts, maybe she could find him. She had to try.

Seated across from her, Henry shook out the pages of the newspaper while nipping the end of a cigarette between his thin lips.

"Will you excuse me?" She pushed to a stand. "I'm not feeling quite myself."

Henry's eyebrows shot up while he checked her over the top of the newspaper. "What? You still shook up by that scuffle at the station?" He set down the paper and winked, pinching his cigarette between his pointer and thumb to flick the ashes. "You just need to relax. Take a nap, baby."

Sadie narrowed her eyes. She'd learned to pacify Henry in her own quiet way. "Motion sickness, I think," was what she said, when in fact she couldn't wait to search under the seats of the train car where she'd first seen that broad-shouldered soldier lock eyes with her through his open window.

On her way out of the dining car, Sadie hovered near the table where her aunt and uncle dined with Henry's parents. Uncle Edward had worked with Mr. McAlister during Mellon's term as Secretary of the Treasury.

"What is it, dear?" Aunt Bea asked, her pale, powdered face creased in agitation at Sadie's interruption.

"The soldier who jumped off the train," Sadie said as casually as possible. "You don't suppose he left luggage behind, do you?"

"Did he not get back on?" Aunt Bea asked. "Well, someone will take care of it."

"The least we can do is make sure he gets his

belongings back. If there are any, I mean."

Uncle Edward dabbed at the corners of his mouth with a napkin, turning his attention to his niece. "What's this about, Sadie?"

"It's nothing," Aunt Bea answered for her, dismissing Sadie with a wave of her jewel-ridden hand. "Go on, eat your meal before it gets cold."

Had the McAlisters not been present, Sadie was certain her aunt would have asked whether she'd mingled with the wealthy, eligible bachelors at the Mellon wedding.

"Looking lovely as always." Mr. McAlister winked at her as she excused herself.

Sadie found the car where the soldier had been. She glanced around uneasily, not wanting to draw attention. When she approached an empty seat in the back, the person next to it happened to be asleep. She maneuvered around him and sat, sweeping her eyes up and down the aisle.

When nobody seemed to be watching, she reached under the seat, brushing against something soft. A pack. His? Her heart pounded against her blouse dampened with the sweat of anticipation. She swooped, grabbed it, and made her way to the vestibule area between this car and the next. Nobody stopped her, but an old man wearing dark sunglasses in the far corner smiled a toothless grin and nodded.

She ducked into a bathroom to catch her breath, locking the door.

She did it!

Inside the pack she found a pocketknife, cash, military certificates, and paperwork. She slid her hand farther into the pack and felt a small piece of thicker card stock. His military identity card. It smelled like the inside seam of a worn library book. She inhaled with a smile.

"James," she said softly, unprepared for the way his chiseled features unnerved her. She grazed her thumb along the typed name of the 6'2, hazel-eyed soldier, born on May 6, 1922 in McKees Rocks. She'd once met a boy from McKees Rocks. But he was just a boy. When she stared into the eyes of this soldier, she saw a glimmer of recognition. Could it be him? *What were the chances?* Sadie sank her teeth into her bottom lip. Her scalp prickled at the idea that she'd met this fellow before and that the powers that be had placed them like chess pieces where they'd find each other again. As if they were connected by some invisible thread. No, not a thread—a rope, woven by something more than happenstance. She frowned at her childish fabrication. But her curiosity traveled to the pad of her fingertip that traced the ink forming his signature.

James Pasko.

A knock on the door interrupted her reverie.

"Just a minute, please." While she stuffed everything back into the pack, another knock sounded, this time louder and more urgent.

"Shake a leg, will ya?"

She fled from the bathroom, colliding with a porter. "Excuse me, miss. Can I help you?"

"A soldier left this on the train."

"Very well. I'll take it." He reached for the pack she wasn't ready to relinquish.

"Sir?" She hesitated. Of course it would appear odd to everyone—not the least of all, to Henry—if she returned to the dining car with a stranger's belongings, but she couldn't let it go. "Will you drop it off at the next stop?"

"Naturally, miss. I'll take it now."

"Okay." She stalled, hugging the pack to her chest. "How will I know he receives it?"

He pursed his lips before he spoke. "We have our ways."

"On second thought, maybe I'll just mail it to him. I'm certain his identification's inside."

"Does this belong to someone you know?"

"Not...yet."

"I need to take that from you, then." He grabbed for it, and, realizing she couldn't play tug-of-war with the porter, she left, her pulse amplified in her ears. She wanted to get back to the dining car before Henry came looking for her.

Almost immediately she regretted not including a note in the pack asking that James let her know he received it. Her telephone exchange at the governor's mansion? If only she were better able to think on her feet.

Distracted, she bumped into an older woman hunched over like a mole, her baggy eyes popping out from under a headscarf. The woman extended her frail arms and said hoarsely, "Have you seen my boys?" Her quivering fingers gripped Sadie's arms. "Have you?"

"No. How old are they?" She glanced up and down the aisle for young runaways.

"None of them were supposed to leave me."

"Of course not."

"War or no war." Her face contorted and she jutted her lower jaw forward.

Sadie's smile faded. A friend apologized and

redirected the woman by her elbow.

But her words had sunk in. Sadie knew she'd been sheltered—people were dying overseas while she and her surrogate family dined well, traveled for pleasure, and went about their business. Although her uncle had been close with the people, and going away to school had opened her eyes to their financial well-being, she was embarrassed to admit how often she forgot the way the rest of the country lived, the way she may have lived had she not fallen into a world where she didn't belong.

She found her seat next to Henry. Purling cigar smoke mixed with frying food brought on a fierce nausea. She clawed into the seat, bracing for the feeling to pass. *Don't look out the window. Look straight ahead.*

Sweat formed on her upper lip. "Henry," she whispered. "I think I'm going to be sick."

Henry shook out the newspaper and glanced her way. He held up his glass to offer her a sip, his go-to for everything.

She flared her nostrils at the waves of nausea and very wisely forced herself to the ladies' room just in time to vomit in private. She missed the toilet, splattering the carpet, the velvet curtains, and the edge of the metal sink, heaving uncontrollably.

Chapter Four

James held the clutch in his work-calloused hands, tracing the smooth leather with his thumbs. The army expected him at Fort Dix, but he wanted to return her belongings himself. Then again, what would a girl like her—a girl with the world before her—want with a penniless steelworker from The Rocks? She'd probably forgotten all about the scuffle at the station by now, and was safely on her way home. He'd lost his golden chance to see her again when he missed that train.

His officer's orders were clear—report to basic training in three days. The ticket collector could mail it to her. He frowned, knowing he was acting as childish as a bedridden lad stuck listening while the kids played kick-the-can. But as he turned to find the office, he paused. How would he know if she received it? What if the man in the booth kept her clutch and the contents inside it for himself? Or the postmaster gave it to his wife? These people didn't care. They probably found piles of lost or forgotten items on trains every day; this item would most likely be buried among the rest. James couldn't bear the thought of what this beautiful woman would think of him if he didn't see this through. Maybe he was as poor at the pickpocket who stole from her, but he wouldn't have her thinking he'd been out for himself. He had to return her clutch himself.

Even if she didn't care.

Even if it was only for the chance to see her face one more time.

He found a public washroom, tucked her purse snugly inside his coat, and cleaned up. The cold water stung his face with every splash, but he continued until the water ran clear of rust-colored dirt and gravel mixed with blood. At last he peered into the mirror, grimacing at his reflection. The cuts and bruises would heal and recede, eventually disappear. But the face staring back at him—the inherited face of an immigrant factory worker—*that* would be with him always.

****

While James stood in line at the ticket counter checking the schedule for the next train out, he reached for his wallet out of habit and felt his pocket empty. In his flustered state, his first irrational thought was that someone had stolen his wallet too. And then he remembered that he didn't have one nickel to his name because his pack, including all the cash the Army provided to cover his meals and other expenses until he reached Fort Dix, was stowed where he'd shoved it—under the damned train seat. Yes, the sum total of what he was on paper—which wasn't a whole hell of a lot—was headed off to Philadelphia without him.

Her ticket, however, was right here. He had no choice but to use it. And conveniently, it led him to her destination: Harrisburg. James figured he could find the governor's mansion easily enough. But he wasn't sure the guards would admit a man off the street, so he'd have to be clever.

Curiosity got the best of him. Inside her purse was a vial of perfume. The scent took him back to the way she smelled of sweet, cool sheets hanging out to dry. A silver-plated compact mirror was engraved with the letter A. He rubbed his thumb along the raised wreath border and then up and down the rib of each stripe. Had it belonged to a relative? A cousin? Maybe it was one of many. Or maybe it held a story like the ribbon that had fallen from her hair and the hollow, empty look in her eyes. What had happened to her since they last saw each other, and who was the woman she had become?

He had to know. He would find out.

On the train, James' questions settled like a rock in his empty stomach, and the exhaustion of everything cloaked his shoulders with a heavy, sleepy stupor. Gazing out the window at the winter scenery blazing by, he was reminded of a train ride he took with his mother when he was a very young boy. He couldn't recall where they were headed, possibly to visit a sick relative. What he remembered first was the porter who passed his seat with a fruit-laden tray. He had longed to sink his teeth into the waxy skin of one of those apples, imagining its sweet juice in his mouth. He suspected his mother couldn't afford a sandwich from the box, or a piece of fruit, and rather than call attention to this fact by asking her to buy either for him, he clutched his grumbling stomach.

While his mother napped, young James had wandered off to investigate and found himself in a dining car full of men playing poker, lured by the rich aroma of garlicky seasoned meats. One table was empty, crumpled napkins on top; he spied food on a plate. Without thinking, he grabbed a chicken leg and took a bite. He was onto a second bite when someone noticed him and pointed. The strangers roared with laughter.

Humiliated and unable to swallow the mouthful of food, he dropped the chicken right there on the plush maroon carpet and ran off to hide in an empty sleeper car.

He wasn't alone. Muffled sobbing came from the corner where a girl his age was huddled. It was the same girl with Governor Stark.

"Hi," he said softly. When she didn't respond, he reached out and cupped her rounded shoulder that was the size of his bedroom doorknob.

She peered up over red-rimmed eyes that crinkled between her delicately thin brows causing him to waver. Maybe she wanted to be left alone, he considered, although having a little sister, he knew a few things about girls. He guessed she'd want company and until she asked him to leave, he wasn't going anywhere.

"Are you hurt?" He leaned down.

She hastily wiped at her eyes pushing stray hair from dampened cheeks and straightening her back. "Sit with me, if you want."

When he hesitated, she said, "You shine shoes, don't you?"

"When I have to, yes." A jolt of warmth filled his cheeks at her upturned lips in response. He quickly wiped his mouth when she was looking down to create a spot for him, hoping there wasn't any grease from the chicken. Then he joined her on the floor. The rhythmic motion of the locomotive vibrated from the sleeper car rug all the way to his eardrums, humming and itching and tickling.

As he was trying to think of something clever to say, she pointed to his temple. "Did you know you're bleeding?"

Heat flooded his cheeks as he dabbed his finger on the spot and cringed at the sticky droplets of fresh blood. What every girl liked to see, he thought miserably, wiping his hand on his pants. "Sorry, last week my brother and I got into it. I must have knocked it open."

"What happened?"

"I followed Paul to town. In the alley, I found money."

"How much?"

"A nickel and a penny."

"What did you do with it?"

"Bought candy, of course." He grinned at the recent memory. "When I got back to my house, Paul was sitting on the porch empty handed. He'd been headed to the picture show with his girl but lost a nickel and a penny."

"Did you tell him?" she asked in her cute, raspy voice.

"It was too late to give it back, even if he could prove it was his. But I definitely let him know how much I enjoyed the candy."

She wrinkled her nose when she giggled. "Then what happened?"

"We wrestled around in the yard until our mother threatened the belt for ruining our clean clothes." He touched the cut again to check if it was still bleeding. It seemed to have stopped. "Something tells me you've never been threatened with the belt."

She smiled and shook her head. "Since you like candy...here." She pulled a striped stick out of her coat pocket and broke it in half.

They peeled off the wrappers and sucked in silence. He stole a glance at her, taken with that cute beauty mark on her upper lip. He'd never known a girl like her before, and he found himself drinking in every detail.

He took a chance then and dug into his pocket for her hair ribbon. When he pulled it out, she frowned. He'd made a mistake.

"That's mine. Where did you find it?"

"I found it on the curb the other day when I shined the governor's shoes."

"And you kept it?" She took it back, a hint of pleasant confusion clouding her gaze. She melted into a smile. "You know what? Keep it. For good luck." She pressed it back into his hand.

Before either could speak another word, a conductor opened the door to look for tickets.

"I should go." James left without saying goodbye. He thought maybe he could sneak back to her, but never got the chance.

His mother never knew about the encounter with the girl on the train or the chicken leg, for that matter, but she sure found the sticky last bit of candy in his trouser pocket while doing the wash and gave him the belt. He grinned at the vivid memory of his sore backside that had smarted for a week at least—it was the only time a whipping had been worth every lash.

Soon he'd see her again. He was eager to know the woman she'd become, but apprehensive at the same time. They'd made a connection that day on the train— would it be like that again or had he imagined it to be greater in his memory than it really was? Would she even remember him?

He stretched his elbows back against the horsehair upholstery and accidentally bumped the sleeping passenger beside him. The man sat up, cocking his hand like he was about to strike.

"Easy, buddy," James said.

"Jesus, I'm sorry." His beady eyes darted around. "You on your way there?"

James nodded.

"I could of guessed. They love 'em young." He chuckled sadly. "After a certain age you boys aren't daring enough. They need you to be eager to fight. Do anything for a thrill." He looked around with crazy eyes as if someone was watching and he needed to be unseen. "I was there," he whispered, squinting his eyes. "In the foxholes, we learned to grab our knives at every little noise. Sorry. I guess I'm one of the *lucky* ones sent home."

James detected sarcasm, then noticed the man's slack coat sleeve.

"I was just a kid when I left. I'm so changed now." He rubbed at his face with one hand then curled his mouth down like a trout. "You involved with someone?"

James shook his head.

"Good. It's better that way. My son's nine months old and I've never held him."

James didn't ask why, remembering the vet's lost arm, not daring to look there again.

"At first, when her letters slowed, I figured she was busy with our baby. Then her letters stopped coming altogether. I guess she couldn't handle being apart. And old Seymour came sniffin' around, helpin' fill her loneliness. She swears the baby is his, but I know better." He looked away.

James thought about his brother's girlfriend who sobbed on his shoulder the day Paul left in his army greens. Not two months later, he saw her at the picture show under the arm of a war-exempt factory worker who made bomber parts. James hadn't told Paul.

Not all girls were like Paul's girlfriend, though. He'd seen just as many who stayed behind and waited. And waited. Like the girl walking toward his train car along the platform. He was willing to bet she'd wait. Not that he'd want to put her through the endless waiting and worrying. Even if he ever had the right to.

"My brother..." James said. "He's been with the Army's 84th Infantry Division for the past year." He recalled the evening the telegram came, days before Christmas. "His last mission ended badly."

The vet closed his eyes.

"He's wounded, but coming home. Honorably discharged."

Another memory flooded back: of his mother dropping the garland she'd been hanging at their boarding house when he'd read the telegram to her.

"I'll pray for him." The vet made the sign of the cross. "God bless him."

They traveled in silence for the rest of the trip. Soon he'd get his chance to fight. He'd heard enough reports to know how his countrymen were faring, watched the injured come home, seen the toll it was taking on helpless folks stateside. He was eager to get over there and do his part. Like Paul had.

The war would change him. It already had.

The vet had been right about a lot of things, but mostly that he was better off without any attachments at home. Yet, as he looked out the window while they passed traces of small town rural America, all he saw was the lovely face of the dark-haired beauty looking for him to return, her white-gloved hands pressed to the glass.

And for the first time in his life, he had a purpose all his own.

Chapter Five

At the governor's mansion, Sadie curled her hair into finger waves for her date with Henry. She'd settled on a butter yellow knee-length rayon dress, perfect for swing dancing or jitterbug, instead of the full and boxy blouse and Vera Maxwell skirt that her aunt had selected for her. Yet all she could think of was seeing James again, wondering if he was in fact that same attentive boy who'd leaped to action at Union Station and saved her clutch. She certainly hoped so.

"I understand Henry plans to visit you at Bryn Mawr." Aunt Bea raised her eyebrows, sipping tea from the loveseat in Sadie's dressing room. "He'd be a lovely date for the school dance."

"We'll see," Sadie said, her mind stubbornly stuck on James and his smoldering slate-colored gaze. "I'm thinking of taking a break from Henry." She sneaked a peek at her aunt in the mirror's reflection and shuddered at the older woman's curled lip. Aunt Bea's beady-eyed stare pierced through Sadie's back like twin daggers.

Sadie tried to explain. "I mean to focus on my studies. I really don't have time to date anyone right now."

That part was true, sort of, although lost on her aunt.

No sooner had the words trickled out of her mouth

she wished she could rewind the reel and swallow them. Her aunt's nostrils flared. Why the sudden interest in her social life? She certainly didn't want her aunt to think she was ungrateful—she'd never wanted for anything material. Sadie noticed in the mirror that a splotchy rash had flared on her chest. She steadied herself on the vanity as she fastened the bangle bracelet around her wrist.

"Don't be foolish, dear. Henry can marry any girl he wants. You're lucky he's even looking in your direction." Beatrice clinked her cup onto its saucer and placed the coupling on the sill. "If you don't cater to him, dear, he won't expect much. That's how I started with Edward."

Sadie wouldn't respond, desperate to get out from under her aunt's critical eye without disappointing her further.

"Hats? Gloves? Bangles won't do. Let me give you something of mine." Aunt Bea flitted off to fetch what she deemed necessary.

She hadn't the faintest idea how girls Sadie's age shopped, scouring Montgomery Ward's catalog for cotton dresses on sale for 98 cents. Girls like Sadie's college roommates. No, Beatrice had the good fortune of keeping all of the finest stores afloat, particularly the milliner in town, whose watery eyes gleamed every time they entered the shop.

Sadie rushed to the large wardrobe closet and quickly packed the hats—each costing more than a month's rent at her college rooming house—that she'd chosen for her friends. She smiled while thinking how Ruth would adore the burnt orange travel hat, made of felt with beaded appliqué. The kelly green tilt hat matched Betty's eyes. For Maria, Sadie had selected a black-winged hat with cascading veil that suited her Italian flair. None of these friends had their tuition paid for like she had. They worked to cover their expenses, which could never include hats like these.

Aunt Bea returned with jewelry. She handed Sadie a pair of Cartier earrings and then draped a carved orchid pendant on her chest, inspecting the effect with eyes framed by well-manicured eyebrows. Sadie held up her hair while her aunt fastened the necklace behind her. The middle-aged woman smiled while fondling the pearl necklace that cradled in the hollow near her collarbone. "As I was saying about Henry, dear, if you play your cards right, you could do very well. Isn't that what you want for your future?"

"I suppose." Sadie wondered if that really was true. If a life with Henry was to be her future, why did she feel so empty about the prospect?

****

The bells on the door jingled as a bevy of girls blew into the club with a wintry gust. They swooned over Henry while strolling past the booth.

"Ladies." Henry tipped his head politely, grinning, his gaze lingering longer than necessary.

"Some of your recent party guests, I presume?" Sadie asked through a slow burn of jealousy.

"You'd know if you'd been there."

As soon as the girls passed, Henry pouted, grumbling about the brass band canceling because of the expected snowstorm.

"No live music." He untwisted the pocket flask cap that he'd been having a love affair with since they arrived. He poured a dram into his Coca-Cola.

When the waitress leaned over to deliver their cheeseburgers, Henry peered down her blouse and proceeded to make eyes at every pretty patron who passed their booth. He even winked at a cigarette girl displaying her wares.

As the evening progressed, he grew more agitated, and more compulsive about nursing from his flask, skipping the Coca-Cola altogether. At one point when Mary and Ray joined them, he moved to sit next to Sadie, wrapping an arm around her waist and pulling her in for a liquor-tinged kiss, never taking his eyes off the dance floor.

"Henry, slow down," Sadie said.

"Slow down? I'm just getting started." He took one more pull on the flask, tucked it away, and patted the slight bulge. "Excuse us ladies, but Ray here and I need to take matters in our own hands. Let's get this joint hopping, band or no band."

Henry pushed himself from the booth then draped his arm over Ray's shoulders. "And let me tell you how to serve the perfect martini. Drop an olive into a glass. Pour the cocktail over it. Twist a thin slice of lemon rind above the glass to let one drip of juice fall in…" His voice trailed as they walked away.

Rage rolled from under Sadie's blouse. She clenched her jaw against it, then grabbed her purse. "Let's go powder our noses," she said to Mary.

Inside the ladies room sitting area, Sadie collapsed onto the chaise. "What are we doing here?"

"Powdering our noses?"

"One minute I'm fine and the next I'm jealous of girls goggling over Henry—my Henry. Why does he have to be so doll dizzy? Aren't I enough?"

"He's a man. That's what they do. You don't think he's on active duty, do you?"

"Fooling around? No, he wouldn't do that." At least she didn't think he would, but what did she know? "I just wish he'd ease up and save something for me. Is that too much to ask—that he only has eyes for me?"

"He doesn't mean anything by it. Look, Henry's up and down. At least he's not boring. So he's moody. What man isn't?" Mary pulled her up by her upper arms. "Let's go dance. I'm feeling a little khaki wacky. Did you see the service men here tonight?"

Sadie had, but there was only one service man on her mind. She realized, as she applied a slick of red lipstick at the mirror, what a phony she was being, wanting Henry to focus solely on her while she couldn't erase the vision of James.

When they reached the booth, Henry had taken over the jukebox, playing songs that had the entire club on the dance floor, moving to the lilting Swing rhythm. Sadie had to admit the call of the trumpets and saxophones weighted by the double bass and drums had her itching to dance, despite her earlier frustration with Henry.

When she and Henry danced, and his sole focus was on her, she felt happy. She moved in time to the jaunty beat, feeling the tug of his grasp as he spun her around the floor. The strength of his pull and his pleasant grin kept her moving under his spell, distracting her enough that she didn't notice the crowd had cleared a space just for them until the song ended. But before she could catch her breath, as soon as another song started, he dropped her hand to spin two other girls at once. And there before her eyes was the downside to his charismatic draw.

It wasn't for her alone.

Maybe she should have vied for his attention. But instead she found herself looking for the clock and wiggling her toes inside her shoes that now pinched, feeling like she'd aged about ten years in ten minutes. She shrank to the edge of the dance floor as patrons coupled off around her, switching up partners. Ladies linked arms to swing dance together. Henry was in a huddle of men at the far corner, probably emptying the contents of his flask, if he hadn't already.

A gang of uniformed men elbowed and shoved each other playfully toward her. In the center was a portly fellow with ears that stuck out. By the time his buddies dragged him in front of her, Sadie stepped forward to spare him more agony. Maybe she wanted to make Henry jealous for a change.

"Hi." She rocked from her toes to her heels with her hands clasped behind her back.

He stuttered, "M-may I have the next dance?"

"I'd be delighted!" Sadie led him onto the floor, casting around to locate Henry.

Before she knew it, her butter yellow dress was spinning to gold as the stuttering soldier with big ears twirled and swung her body around. Who knew? Breathless and bouncy, they jitterbugged all over the floor.

Sadie heard the rip before she saw it.

"Your uniform…" Sadie stopped to turn him so she could assess the damage. Straight across his back, he'd torn his seams. She assumed it would be costly for him to repair. "I feel terrible. I could sew it for you, if you'd like."

Sadie wasn't sure if he heard. Her voice was drowned by the roars and hollering and back slaps of the enlisted friends who crowded about.

Henry appeared out of nowhere, his jaw twitching and eyes blazing like a possessed bull, grumbling incoherently. He grasped Sadie like a rag doll by her forearm and pulled her away, seething through his clenched teeth as if it were *her* fault.

The enlisted man stopped Henry with a hand on his chest and took his eyes off Henry for one second to ask Sadie, "Is this souse bothering you?"

Henry threw the first punch.

The two men tumbled to the black and white checkered floor, arms punching and kicking, body parts akimbo. The escalating excitement of onlookers generated so much noise that Sadie couldn't even hear her own cries to stop them.

Henry landed on the bottom, all of his varsity wrestling expertise dulled by his drunkenness. A jumbled mess of men then jumped in to break up the fight. All except the owner, who hung back. Somehow, and not too surprisingly, since Henry was the club's best customer when he was home from school, the enlisted man was the one escorted out the door.

Sadie stood there as Henry thumbed out cash and tossed it at him. "Here, buy a new one, this time with pleats in back!"

Chapter Six

When the train slowed into Harrisburg, the veteran next to James elbowed him awake so he wouldn't miss his stop. James, disheveled and famished, staggered off the train and across the platform to the window box to ask about his pack.

"Nothing's been found, yet. Check back tomorrow. Next!"

Fresh snow blew from every direction, paralyzing downtown Harrisburg. Cars spun out, swinging their taillights in perfect pendulums, forming snow angels with their back tires. Folks huddled around bus stops awaiting buses that probably wouldn't come, their backs to the blistery wind like a herd of wild horses on the open plains. James slipped on the icy-coated sidewalk, catching himself awkwardly.

It was a struggle to move, and James hunched over, his stomach cramped from lack of food and liquids as he passed decorated shop windows closed for business. An eerie bleakness settled over the town. He would look for a hotel to stay the night and find the governor's house first thing in the morning. It wouldn't do to appear on their doorstep at this time of night, unannounced and with no place to go. Inside his coat, he felt the shape of her clutch against his chest. It was the only thing keeping him going.

A light shone from the portico of a corner hotel.

With any luck, his pack would surface by morning and he'd have the money then to pay the owner. Inside the cool foyer he rang a bell on the counter. A woman's heels tapped along the hardwoods.

"Sorry, mister." She eyed him up and down and then smiled. "Really, I am." Then she pointed to a "no vacancy" sign that had burnt out. "If they can't accommodate you next door, I'll work out something here." She winked.

The next inn and the one after that were full. James couldn't find a room anywhere. His original plan crumbling, he hitched a ride. He'd do what he came here to do, and worry about a night train out if the line was even running in this weather.

"Where to, son?"

James steeled his voice. "Can you take me to the governor's house?" He could do this.

"Son?"

"The governor's house?"

"You have some business with Governor Stark?"

James nodded, hovering over the window.

The man leaned over and opened the door. "I'm heading that way. You can ride with me."

Moments later, James' breath puffed into the dark air as he stepped from the truck. The stale scent of the musty train station clung to his clothes. And before him, looming grand and austere was the Second Empire Victorian home on Danbury Lane.

Her home.

Now he had to get inside. The driver lingered, illuminating his path to the gatekeeper's window with the Chevy's headlights. James rapped on the glass with his raw knuckle, shivering in the darkness, prepared to do whatever it took to gain access to the governor's mansion and at this hour. But how could he explain why he'd come? Saying he was a friend of the family seemed off. That she was expecting him was presumptuous. That he had to be here was the truth, but nothing they would believe. Would they? James didn't like this feeling of being in a corner, of wanting something so badly. As the guard slid open the window, James cleared his throat and clasped his hands.

"Evening, sir. I have a delivery for the governor's...daughter."

"That right?" The man's feet were propped up and he smirked while holding his cigarette between his lips. The guard beside him was reading a book. "Well that sure is something, mister. Because the governor has no daughter."

"Only a niece," the other guard piped in.

James clenched his teeth together flexing his jaw against the shivering that wracked his weary body. Damn, he thought, shifting his weight and peering at the well lit home in the outside chance someone might see him through the window. Maybe she would see him? A vision of her white-gloved hands on the observation car window stirred his next move. He hadn't come all this way to get to her to let this be it.

"I have orders to hand deliver it." James folded his arms across his chest.

"Orders, eh?" the throaty voiced guard responded, chuckling and erupting in a productive cough. "Now I've heard it all. Why don't you just hand it over, son? The governor and his family will not be disturbed at this hour."

James squinted and stepped forward. His eyes

flicked to the wrought iron gate. It wouldn't be hard to scale, not for him. He'd scaled plenty of fences during back alley scuffles, and he was prepared to do what he had to. Then again, alarming the family wasn't exactly the way to impress her.

"Hold on now, what's this all about, Al?" the other guard said after studying James. "Which branch are you in, son? I got a nephew in the Navy." Pride softened his withered features. A smile pulled the skin taut across knobby cheekbones.

James saw his chance and seized it. "Army, sir." What the hell, he'd go with the truth. "The governor's niece was robbed in Pittsburgh. I got back her purse. Now I plan to hand deliver it to her."

The men exchanged looks. "Let him in," the man with the nephew grunted, pushing some button. "Watch yourself," he told James. An armed guard swung open the gate.

James shook the men's hands through the window and saluted the man in his truck, hardly believing this had worked. It almost seemed too easy. Then he forged up the snow-covered drive to the mansion, his empty stomach twisting every step of the way.

The idea of seeing her again filled his weary body with new energy. He admired the tall white pillars as he hurried up the snowy steps taking them two at a time. Then he rang the bell while smoothing his crumpled uniform that his little sister had pressed that morning, embarrassed by the bloodstains.

The double doors opened and an older Negro woman kindly asked, "May I help you?"

James hesitated. "Ma'am, I believe this belongs to"—he held out the clutch, unsure of her name—"the young lady of the house?"

"Please, come in," she said with a broad smile, eyeing the purse in his hands. "You're looking for Sadie."

Sadie. James followed her into the foyer and removed his hat. Lively banter floated from the other room. As the maids cleared empty cups and dessert plates from the velvet-draped parlor, the group discussed the weather.

"Be a gentleman, Bailey," the woman told the miniature schnauzer who snorted at her ankles. "No barking." Then she interrupted the dinner party with an authority that probably came from years of service. "Excuse me, Governor, this man has come to return Sadie's bag."

The governor approached James, clearly impressed. "What's this, Nanny?"

Now the whole party gathered near the foyer to hear this mystery visitor explain the object in his outstretched hand. "At Pittsburgh's Union Station, sir," James said. "A boy stole it from her."

"Ah, yes, yes," Beatrice Stark said. "How lovely of you!" She fingered her pearl necklace and smiled. "Margaret, this is the soldier I told you about. I'm Beatrice Stark."

"Nice to meet you." James shook her cool, slender grip and then awkwardly held his hat in his hands. "It was no problem, ma'am, just trying to help a lady."

"Sadie will be delighted. How on earth did you catch that vagabond?" Margaret asked.

"Margaret...really," said the man with her. "Look at him and tell me you're surprised, a strapping young man like himself."

"Well." The governor extended his hand for a proper handshake. "Mister…"

"Pasko. Please, call me James." They shook hands.

"All right then, James." He withdrew his wallet. "Allow me to give you something for your troubles."

"No, sir. I can't accept that."

"Please." He fingered the bills, pulling out a few more for good measure. "A good deed should not go unrewarded."

James wasn't about to take money, as if he were a paperboy delivering the news. Seeing Sadie would be reward enough.

Nanny broke the awkwardness. "James, where are you headed?"

"Fort Dix, ma'am. For basic training."

"Good for you, son, for doing your duty," the governor said.

Nanny's eyes softened. "I'm sure your folks are terribly sorry to see you off." She patted his hand.

"Not at all, ma'am. I'm ready to go. Proud to do it."

"When do you shove off?" Margaret's husband asked.

"After basic training I'll be a replacement in the Infantry Division. Probably two months' time."

"James, why don't you stay the weekend? From the looks of it…" The governor gestured to the whiteout through the window. "It could be some time before you're able to go anyway."

"I really shouldn't impose."

"We insist, dear, and will not take no for an answer," Beatrice said. "I'll have a maid make up a room for you on the third floor. Dolores?"

"Please, join us in the parlor for an update on the weather," the governor said as the group began heading that way. "Care for a brandy?"

Nanny said, "He'll do no such thing until he eats. Must be famished." She pulled him along toward the back. "Come with me now and I'll get some of Cook's braised duck into you. You like duck?"

"Yes, ma'am. Thank you very much."

Margaret added, "And you can return the clutch to Sadie yourself! She and Henry will be so pleased." She winked at Beatrice in reference to the union. "I do hope the kids get back soon. I don't know what we were thinking agreeing to a date tonight." She placed her hand on Beatrice's forearm as they walked away.

In the kitchen, James stared at the artfully arranged plate of sliced duck, fanning out across a bed of mashed potatoes and baby carrots. Without savoring any of it, he robotically cut, stabbed and lifted each piece, dripping with sauce, to his trembling mouth. He worked over the savory bits, letting his mind wander.

Sadie was with Henry.

He wasn't surprised, really. Of course she was involved with someone. The last thing he wanted to do was spend even one minute watching them together. He'd finish the meal, leave the clutch with Nanny and escape out the back door through the butler's pantry. Then he'd make his way back to the main street where someone, maybe that woman at the inn, would take mercy on him, although it wasn't in his nature to accept a handout.

Then again, he had the feeling he wouldn't get very far this time of night and in these conditions on foot. He was stuck here at least until the snow cleared and he located his pack.

And by what miracle did he have a chance with Sadie, anyway? He had no money, no schooling, no job. No well-connected relatives. He couldn't even offer himself, since he'd already done so to the U.S. Army.

Although it had been his idea to eat in the kitchen, the grandest of all kitchens, now that he was seated here, surrounded by working-class servants, their very presence made it impossible for him to pretend he wasn't one of them. Because he was one of them, through and through.

She was not.

He scooped up the last bit of mashed potatoes smothered in a savory sauce and swallowed. Then he pushed the plate away, wiped the spot clean with his napkin, and placed her clutch before him. He stared at it for a long time, deciding what to do next.

Until now, Nanny had busied herself with attempts to help the kitchen staff put away dishes and glassware, more of a hindrance than a help really, and he'd found her efforts endearing. Her pride in this household and her puttering reminded him of his Ukrainian mother and the way she'd kept busy while remaining at the attention of his steelworker father—who always ate his dinner late, seated alone at the table.

Now she stared at him with a pursed-lipped stance, arms folded across her chest. "You're in love with her. Our Sadie." Her lips stretched into a smile.

James shook his head. "I don't even know her."

"You're here, aren't you?" She patted his shoulder and swayed away, coating the air with melodious laughter as thick and rich as molasses. Then she hummed, and the sound lingered after she'd disappeared down the hall.

****

When Sadie and Henry entered the mansion, removing their snow-dusted wool coats and wet boots, they learned the local weather advisory deemed the city in a state of emergency, and everyone was invited to stay through the storm. Maids hustled to procure clean linens and turn down beds. Sadie peeled off her gloves and rubbed her hands together to warm her numb fingers.

"Let's warm you up by the fire," Henry whispered, draping an arm over her shoulders. He'd sobered up since the fight, riding the entire way there with his window open.

"We can play cards in the library," she suggested.

When they entered the darkly lit room, Sadie was startled to see someone already there. A man, reading in the high back leather wing chair near the stone hearth. A man in uniform. Her pulse throbbed out of her ears, bursting and pulsing like a big brass band.

He'd come!

She blinked rapidly. Her voice caught in her throat. Beside him on the dark mahogany desk under the library lamp's soft glow was her purse.

Her next reaction was relief that he was okay, followed by joyful confusion. She resisted looking too pleased, for Henry's sake, but was betrayed by a burn in her cheeks from the knowledge that James had come here for her. In a snowstorm.

"And you are?" Henry asked, glaring.

James stared at Sadie. "I figured you'd be missing this...Miss Stark," James said shyly, standing to hand her the item that had led him here. "I owe you a train ticket, by the way."

"But how..." she said. "When...are you okay?" For all she knew, he may very well have come for some favor or another. But she didn't care—she was just glad he'd come.

"I'm fine." He set down the book he'd been reading. "Better than fine. Warm." He rubbed his hands together, grinning.

Sadie saw out of the corner of her eye Henry sneering at James. She hadn't meant to hurt him—she'd been too enthralled with the scene playing out before her to even think about anything or anyone else. Now she saw her error.

But—it was definitely James! One look in his deep-set kind eyes and her mind was catapulted back to the day they'd shared stories on the surging, steam train floor.

She picked up the clutch and peeked inside. Her mother's mirror was there. She'd been right about him, she thought smugly. And he hadn't even known how important the mirror was to her.

"We'll have to travel with you more often." Henry shook James' hand. "Henry McAlister. You seem to know Sadie."

"We haven't met, officially."

"You could have mailed it and saved yourself the trouble." Henry grasped Sadie around her waist. "But we're thankful, aren't we, darling?"

She shrank, desperate to disassociate from Henry. The last thing she wanted was for James to think they were an item. Of course, they were an item. *Why were they an item?*

"Are you staying out the storm?"

Please sweet Jesus, let him be.

"It appears that way." James grinned, his eyes the color of the mansion's slate roof, worn smooth from nature's elements. She could swim in those eyes.

"Well..." Sadie boldly stepped away from Henry's hold. "For what it's worth, I can't thank you enough, Mister..." She extended her hand to carry out the pretend greeting, as if she didn't already know the last name that had played on her lips, testing it out with her own.

"Pasko." He pressed her hand to his warm mouth, blurring the space around them. "At your service."

Chapter Seven

That night when James washed up for bed, he splashed water on his face and patted the scrapes along his jaw. The chase and detour in his trip were well worth it to see Sadie's pleased bewilderment in the library. He'd caught her watching him, too. And more than once she'd shrugged off Henry's advances.

But it didn't feel right.

He climbed into bed, ruminating. The irony, that a missed train had led him here. To her. Yes, she was already involved with someone else. And the way that factory worker had burrowed his way into Paul's girlfriend's arms like a cunning weasel had turned James' stomach. But what really mattered was what Sadie wanted. That's what he intended to find out.

The governor's mansion had lost power a few hours earlier so the room was dark but for candlelight. Outside, the snow fell steadily, white tornado-style swirls lifting from the ground while the wind blew against the windowpanes.

Someone rapped on the door.

"Sorry to bother you." It was Nanny, illuminated in the dark hallway by a single candle in her hand and his Army coat draped over her arm. "Here." She handed the coat to him. "It cleaned up awful nice. And Miss Sadie needs extra blankets I can't reach. She needs someone…tall."

"Thank you." He followed the old woman down the servant's back staircase to the second floor and into the first room on the left.

Inside Sadie poked at a fire while kneeling in her nightgown covered by a kangaroo cloak with wide, deep pockets. "Oh," she said, standing. Her eyes widened with surprise, her cheeks flushed with color. Obviously this had been Nanny's idea to bring them together.

"Got a helper," Nanny said then left them.

James was so taken with Sadie's face in the glow of the fire that he barely got his words out. "You're...cold?"

"No. I mean yes! We keep extra blankets up there." She pointed to an armoire. As he pulled down a stack of neatly folded quilts, she closed the bedroom door and pressed her back against it.

"Look..." James handed her a blanket, unsure what to do next. He was about to apologize for even coming to the mansion, but before he could, footsteps approached in the hall. Her eyes grew wide again and she placed a finger to her lips.

"Baby doll?"

"Just a minute." She shepherded James to the far corner, past the armoire. She opened the door to the large wardrobe closet. He understood her concern and, still holding the bundle of blankets, backed into the closet and let her close the door on him.

James couldn't see what was happening, but adrenaline heightened his hearing, every sound magnified. Her door creaked open; Henry walked into the room, and gave a heavy groan as he collapsed on her bed.

"Baby, I've been thinking."

"You're drunk."

James pictured the stocky red-haired Irishman sprawled on the bed. It turned his stomach.

"Henry, you need to leave."

"Shhh. Nobody will know I'm here. Can't I warm up by your fire? You can warm me up."

"No."

James held his free arm over his head, flat-palming the door, ready to burst out of the closet and strangle the leech by the throat. He cursed himself for hiding here, appearing cowardly, but he'd done it out of respect for Sadie. He didn't want to cause any trouble.

"The only person who has to leave is Pasko. What kind of name is that anyway? What family does he come from? Nothing, that's what. He needs to pack up and go. I'll tell him myself."

"Pack what? Go where? Have you looked outside lately?"

"Not my problem. What's it to you, anyway?"

"My God, Henry. Have you no compassion?"

"It's true then. I saw the way you were watching him."

"I appreciate what he did for me."

"How about what I can do for you?"

James heard the pop and crackle of a disintegrating log collapsing in the fireplace. He pressed his cheekbone to the door, unsure if he could handle much more of this. Was she interested in him? Had she not been able to put him out of her mind the way he'd wrestled with her in his fantasy over the years? He wasn't sure, and he slumped his shoulders while shutting his eyes.

"Henry," she said. "It's late. I'm tired." James heard the twist of the doorknob and the whine of the hinge. "Good night."

"Sadie, how many times do I need to get on my knee? You want me to beg?"

James cringed on Henry's behalf. Did the man have no pride? Then again, this was Sadie and James imagined she'd brought more than one sorry soul to the brink.

"Of course I don't want you to beg. And please, for the love of God, stop talking to my uncle."

"I thought you wanted his blessing."

"I do, but not like this."

"What are you waiting for? Just think, after we're married, no more sneaking around. No more dates cut short by curfew. And you can quit school."

"I love school."

He wasn't listening to her.

"We can be together. You can be free of your aunt..."

"Henry," she pleaded.

James wondered if she stopped Henry because he was spilling their intimate secrets.

"You need to leave, *please*." Her tone was tough to hear.

Was she only keeping Henry at bay because James was a silent third party, or was this how she really felt? Henry's intentions were clear. He wanted to marry her. The parents knew and approved. Henry offered an escape from a situation she had confided in him about, one that was not ideal, for reasons James couldn't imagine.

What could James offer her? His confidence

47

crumbled like that log on the fire as he realized Henry may be a better match for her after all.

Henry grunted like a spoiled child and shuffled to the door. "Only if you promise to dream about me tonight."

Pathetic. James opened the door a crack just in time to see Henry embrace her and kiss her forehead.

After Henry was gone, she whispered, "I'm sorry you had to witness that." She held a candle, standing before him in the doorway to the wardrobe closet. She entered the dark space with him, saying, "I want to show you something." Their bodies brushed against each other, sending a current of warmth across him. She reached behind and clicked open a latch on a small half-door revealing a narrow staircase leading up.

"My secret hideout." Her face was aglow with flickering candlelight.

"Sadie, I don't think we should—"

"You have to come see this." She won him over with a luminous smile that flickered her eyes with a promise of mischief.

Against his better judgment he followed her up the stairs while manipulating the stash of blankets he was still holding, the candle she handed him, and trying to maintain his balance along the narrow steps, deep enough for the balls of his feet only. At the top of the stairs they entered a musty, cool attic with an A-frame ceiling and dormer windows to one side. On the far end was a circular window. They settled on a blanket James laid out in front of the window. He draped another blanket over her shoulders like a shawl.

"Isn't this view amazing?" she said. Her voice, James noticed, was as cute and raspy as the last time they'd met.

"It's breathtaking." His eyes never left her.

"James," she continued, oblivious. "Who do you think has looked out this very window?" She spoke with a familiarity that put him at ease.

"A maid on break?"

She shook her head. "They don't come up here."

"An unwanted visitor eavesdropping on lovers?"

Her smile faded. "We aren't lovers. And you are very much wanted here."

"He's in love with you."

She looked away. James wanted to ask if she was in love with Henry, but feared what she'd say.

"People plotted their escape route from this spot, James. People running for their lives. This house was part of the Underground Railroad, a safe house. I researched it at the historical society library. It's possible this attic once sheltered runaway slaves on their trek north."

She spoke with such fervor that he instinctively inched closer, unable to deny a selfish need to touch her, or just be closer physically. They could plot their own escape from this window—ride horseback through the woods to the river where they'd tie up their mounts and embark on a boat or maybe a train? But then what? He was scheduled to begin basic training in a matter of days.

He followed her gaze out the window. The downtown area was out of view, but he remembered during the drive here that on the other side of the woods, a river led to the city. There were no neighboring houses to speak of, except for a few cottages he assumed were home to the groundskeeper, and the like. He peered down at the treetops surrounding them, heavy with clumped snow, snow swirling around, but all he could think about was the smell of smoke in her hair that hung loose around her shoulders.

"I know who else has seen this view." He studied her. "An artist looking for inspiration."

Her full attention on him made his pulse quicken.

"I have a confession to make," he said, sheepishly. "I peeked inside your purse. I saw the compact is engraved. And I know your name doesn't begin with the letter A…"

Her smile faded as she inhaled deeply, her neck muscles protruding.

"I'm sorry. I didn't mean to—" He kneeled, wanting to reach out to her.

"It's okay. Nobody has asked me about her before." She sounded more surprised than upset, to his enormous relief. "I found the compact years ago, while playing in my uncle's office. He explained it had been a gift for Audrey, and that I should keep it now. When he showed me playbills starring her name in various roles, a photograph slipped out."

"Of?" He relaxed back down and propped one knee up, resting his arm on it.

"A young woman posing for a camera on a picnic blanket like this." She leaned onto her hip, placing both legs to one side. "She wore a white blouse with full sleeves and eyelet around the scoop neck collar. I've studied that picture for clues of who she was."

He reached out and clamped her cold hands between his. "Your mother?"

She nodded, but pulled back and hugged her knees

that were drawn up to her chin. "Not much to go on."

"What do you remember about her?"

"I remember she wore Chanel No. 5." A crinkle appeared between her eyebrows as she spoke. "One moment she'd been rocking me on her hip while I rested my cheek in the crook of her neck. The next moment, she was gone. All I have is that single memory. A memory that would have faded had Nanny not kept her perfume for me."

"How old were you?"

"Maybe two? And when the perfume ran out, Nanny let me play with the bottles. Expensive French ones. I used them as vessels for my potions during bath time. Masque Rouge's held *magic*." Her face livened with childlike recall. "And one dousing of Arlequinade's and I'd turn invisible, although never long enough to escape bedtime." She snapped her fingers, a smile playing on her lips.

"What happened to her?"

"My aunt said she ran off with a playwright. To New York. She wanted to be a star and he promised to make it happen."

"Why did they keep this from you?"

"It wasn't a secret, exactly. I've always known my mother couldn't keep me, but the details surrounding her absence were hazy. It wasn't until I was older and found the compact that I wanted the full story. I still remember when I confronted Nanny about what my aunt said. She twisted a rag in both hands and said, 'Oh chile...dear sweet chile. I wish it ain't true that your mama left. Wish it ain't...'" Sadie said in Nanny's twang. "I suppose they were waiting for the right time to tell me."

She stood up. At first he feared he'd ruined their time together, probably his only chance to be alone with her. But she rearranged the blankets and sat in front of him Indian style. "So, what I really want is for you to tell me your story. Start with where you live."

He was reluctant to abandon their conversation about something so important to her, but following her lead, answered her question. "McKees Rocks."

"Were you drafted?"

"No. I enlisted. My brother Paul was one of the first to deploy right after Pearl Harbor. I wanted to go with him, but our mother and little Anne needed me. So I waited."

He hadn't revealed this to impress her, but apparently he had from the way her facial expression softened as she reached out to squeeze his arm.

"What about your father?"

"We lost him in a mill accident years ago." He looked up trying to remember how many years it had been.

She stared at him and then dropped her gaze to her hands in her lap. "I am so sorry."

"I quit school to take Paul's job at the mill. And taking in boarders helped."

They sat in silence, watching the candle flicker. James swallowed hard while trying to think of something interesting to say. Unlike his brother, who had an easy way with women, and who drew them in with his one-dimple smile, James had been ill-equipped to connect. When Paul used to be out on the town, James had been the one to stay home and help their mother, peeling potatoes for her stews and reading to her when her eyesight worsened.

"But you would like the boarding house—it's historic like this."

She raised her eyebrows, the light casting a strange shadow on her face.

"The original owner was a professor. A scientist. When Anne was probably five, she told me about her new friend named Norah."

"An imaginary friend? She must have been lonely."

He nodded. "Boarders came and went. Most were mill workers, struggling poor folks like us. Rarely were there kids for Anne to play with."

"But Anne had Norah."

"I asked Anne about Norah: 'Where does she sleep? Where is she now? I want to meet her.' Then strange things started happening. A boarder's watch, which I had been accused of stealing, appeared on his pillow that night. Dirty dishes stacked in the sink one night were clean and put away on the top cupboard shelf—out of Anne's reach—the next morning. A piece was missing from the freshly baked pie on the sill."

When she shivered, he said, "We should warm you up by the fire."

"I'm okay. Go on."

He took off his coat and wrapped it around her anyway, then draped the blanket on her again. Paul would have turned this situation into something romantic, but James didn't quite know how to do that. Besides, Sadie seemed interested in his story and storytelling was something he knew how to do.

"One night after all the boarders were in bed, I couldn't sleep. I went to the kitchen and poured myself a glass of wine." He failed to mention the wine came from a discarded bottle a boarder left by the trash. "I wrote a story for Anne."

"You're a writer?" She drew his coat tighter around her shoulders.

"I don't make a living at it," he said modestly, although he suspected he could. His mother had encouraged him. But James had never pursued a writing career out of fear his father would consider it indulgent and impractical. Or worse, his father would be right.

"What do you write about?"

"People mostly." He eyed her reaction, feeling uncomfortable discussing something that seemed to have such little value. "The people I worked with in the factory...the butcher flirting with the new maid, the school children skipping through the playground. I write about the boarders who come and go. Whatever inspires me."

You. He'd written about her.

"That night, I was writing a story about a boy who saw the future and wanted to stop it from happening. And while I was writing, she appeared out of nowhere."

"Who?"

"Norah. I know how it sounds. But she was real to me. She floated into the kitchen."

"Were you scared?"

"Not at all. She glowed like an angel under a hooded cloak and carried a doll. Her skin as pale as the dead, bluish almost."

"Did she speak to you?"

"No. We stared at each other for a while and then she vanished."

The candle flickered, illuminating her big eyes.

"Now I've scared you," he said.

"No...but *this* is what I'll be dreaming about tonight." They laughed at her reference to Henry.

"Are you cold?"

"I'm fine," she said through chattering teeth, still sitting Indian style. The attic was drafty, and she appeared more than chilled despite his jacket and blanket.

He realized his chance to kiss her was rapidly disappearing. "Let's warm you up downstairs by the fire." He stood and helped her up with his outstretched hand. "Wait," he said more gruffly than intended, a note of desperation in his voice. If only he could stop time and stop the future from happening, like the character he'd written about. He may have been unable to hold onto this moment, but he wouldn't let it elude him. He boldly cradled her face in his hands and kissed the spot where her forehead crinkled.

"Do you remember me?" he asked.

She lowered her chin toward her chest, then peered up at him with those doe eyes. "I have a confession to make also. After you missed the train, I went to find your pack."

"You did?" He noticed for the first time how flecks of orange and gold colored her eyes.

She nodded. "I saw your military ID card and your birthplace tipped me off."

"So you knew. And here I thought I was the only romantic fool here." He pulled from his pocket the ribbon that he still carried around.

"James! I can't believe you still have that." She reached out to touch it. "Has it brought you good luck?"

"I'm here, aren't I?"

She cocked her head at him, still grinning. "This is

55

the most romantic thing anyone has ever done for me." She grazed her finger over his scar near his temple. "This and the whole chase at the station. I've been waiting for the right time to tell you. Keep the ribbon."

He melted into her, closing his mouth over hers, feeling her hands migrate to his shoulders and cling to him as he explored her lips, moving his weight into it, letting all of the fear and trepidation fade away. The attic spun around them as he murmured her name into the soft places along her neck and behind her ear—satiny soft—losing himself in her splayed smoky hair as he gently lay her on the blanket, supporting her with one arm around her and the other slipping down to the curve of her lower back. Again he murmured huskily, "Sadie…Sadie…I found you…"

Chapter Eight

James wasn't in the guest room when she crept by the next morning. Fear shot through her, panic set in. Last night, after a maid returned to her room to draw a bath, she'd had to sneak him down the secret stairs and out the door, naively thinking they had today together. Now it was daylight, no chance to speak with him privately or at all as his bedroom was vacant, bed covers pulled taut and tucked neatly.

Surely he hadn't left without a goodbye?

Sadie bit her bottom lip, chafed from the roughness of his unshaven skin against hers when they kissed in the attic. Standing in the bedroom doorway, she replayed the way he touched her lips gently at first and then fervently—sending a deep stirring across her chest.

She hurried down the back stairs into the kitchen to find Francois, the cook, preparing breakfast for the full house, which she knew from past observation was not an easy task, especially given the imposed rations. A few of the guests were down there along with her aunt, greeting each other, grateful for the heat, which was back on.

James wasn't one of them.

"He certainly is a hard worker," Nanny said, probably recognizing Sadie's panic-stricken face. She gestured to the window. "Been up since dawn."

Sadie peered through the wavy, glass-blown

windows at the men shoveling snow from the driveway. The ripply waves distorted her view, but there was no mistaking the broad-shouldered man clearing the snowfall alongside Alfred and Joe, the driver and stable hand. She melted into a smile.

"Looks to me like he's eager to be on his way." Henry trickled down the backstairs, still pale and disheveled from his bender the night before. He clamped his arms around her waist.

She broke free from his hold to help Nanny arrange the buffet. When she was finishing up, James slipped inside. Nanny directed him to the fire.

"Well," Aunt Bea said with a flourish, entering the room. "The weather looks like it will break soon."

Sadie panicked. Her chest restricted when she tried to breathe. Although she liked to think otherwise, the weather was the only thing keeping James. Their time together would end. And soon. But not until he found his pack and military papers. That bought her some time.

"The roads are still impassable," Uncle Edward said as they took their seats. "We might as well enjoy being inside and warm, now that the heat's back on." When a server brought around coffee, Uncle Edward added, "James, how about if I place some calls to expedite you getting your missing luggage back."

Not too expeditiously, Sadie hoped.

"So, James," Henry said. "Tell us the name of the lovely lady you leave behind. Surely there is one?"

Sadie's armpits prickled with jealousy as she strained to hear his response.

"There is someone I'd rather not leave."

Sadie fumed with jealousy. She realized how little

she really knew of James Pasko.

"So…" Henry said. "You engaged?"

"No. I wouldn't ask her that, given my situation."

"What if she's not around when you return?"

"Henry!" Sadie couldn't take this line of questioning any more. "Isn't this a little personal?"

"It's okay," James said. "She's a remarkable woman. And waiting for me would be her decision, ring or no ring."

She'd heard enough. She wasn't sure who she was angrier with—James for deceiving her or Henry for eliciting what she couldn't bear to hear and enjoying it. She could tell from Henry's smug look that he'd accomplished what he intended.

"You know what." Henry patted his forehead with his napkin. Sadie noticed his hand was a little shaky. "If we're going to be cooped up all afternoon, I'm gonna lie down." He leered at James while he stood, tossed the napkin on the table, and leaned over to gruffly kiss Sadie's cheek.

A thrill rippled over her. Now she'd have James all to herself. But she had to be careful.

****

Aunt Bea blocked Sadie's way on the landing. "Watch yourself, dear. You don't want Henry to get the wrong idea."

"What do you mean?"

"I don't think it's right to upset Henry with the idea you're interested in this James." All of a sudden heroic James from the train had been demoted.

"This James?" Sadie said as they climbed the rest of the stairs.

Aunt Bea was on a mission. "I suppose a little

healthy competition never hurt. You know, when I was your age, I had boys lined up around the block. You just have to be careful you pick the right one."

"Of course you're right," Sadie lied.

"Henry's a fine young man. Maybe a bit hot-headed and thick, but he'll settle down for you, provide the life of your dreams."

When they'd reached the room, Sadie sat at the vanity to powder the sheen from her face.

"It's just that you have everything a girl in your position could ever want."

A girl in her position?

"And I'd hate to see you throw it all away. You know, by making the same mistake your mother made."

They were fighting words, but Sadie wouldn't let the woman antagonize her. James was still here, even if he did have a girl back home, she thought wistfully, unable to believe it was true. Her chest fluttered as she ran a brush through her hair.

Chapter Nine

Sadie scanned the dining room then filled a couple of small plates and sneaked to the kitchen. Nanny looked up from her plate with her eyes only, still chewing, a rust- and maroon-colored headscarf tied snugly.

"Library is where I seen him last."

Nanny had already started on Francois' main course and emptied the china teacup in one swallow.

"Thank you, Nan." Sadie leaned over to kiss her forehead, inhaling her familiar earthy scent that carried a hint of onion. She'd been helping in the kitchen again.

When Sadie reached the library holding their plates, she called out "James?" and entered.

He was studying the *Times*.

"I'm sorry, did I disturb you?"

"No...please come in." He set down the paper, smiled at her, and eagerly took the plate.

"I was right, you are hungry."

"Famished. Thank you." He melted her with those simple words, his lingering eyes stirring a swirl across her belly. They stood in awkward silence.

"Where's Henry?"

In daylight she was able to see him more clearly, and those eyes the color of an overcast sky or brewing storm at sea.

"In bed. Probably still recovering from last night's

bender." She pushed the thought of Henry from her mind. "Would you rather eat in the dining room?"

"Would you care to?"

They laughed at their absurd formality.

"How about here?" He motioned toward the game table in the corner by the window.

"Wait a minute." She handed him her plate and untied the silk scarf that covered the gap between her two-piece cream-colored suit. Then she draped it over the table. He hesitated, hovering with the plates.

"It's okay, I have plenty of these," she said carelessly and then regretted it. Most women couldn't afford silk, which was needed for parachutes in the war. How easily she'd forgotten.

As they took their seats, she nibbled on a cracker. His proximity made her self-conscious of her every chew, every swallow, and her appearance in the stark lighting. She ran a tongue across her teeth to check for stuck bits of food and took a shy peek at his freshly shaven face.

"When do you have to leave?"

"Trying to get rid of me?" He grinned.

"No." Her cheeks warmed. "I mean, not just yet. We need you for the next catastrophe."

He wiped his mouth with a napkin and let his smile grow.

"Today's Sunday. You can't leave today because of the blue law." She shrugged with mock sympathy.

"What's keeping me from leaving tomorrow?"

As if on cue, a young maid interrupted them. "Excuse me? Delivery for Mr. Pasko," she announced, pressing James' pack to her pert breasts, smiling at him as if they were the only people in the room.

James leaped up and thanked her. The demure maid, oblivious to Sadie's presence, blushed and offered a little too eagerly to put it in his room for him before leaving. Seeing this interaction made Sadie wonder if she too appeared too available—just another able-grable.

"Does having your pack change your plans?" She bit and held her bottom lip under her teeth.

"Well, I'm expected at Fort Dix for training. I need to leave first thing tomorrow."

Her thoughts spun out of control. He'd need the good part of a day to travel from here to New Jersey, which meant they only had the rest of today to be together.

"I have something I want to give you." She retrieved a box and handed it to him. "To thank you."

"What's this?"

She smiled, gathering her skirt in her hands, pleased with his surprise.

He opened the box to reveal stationery inside. And a writing journal tied with a string.

"For letters home." *Letters to me.* "I would have chosen something else had I been prepared," she said of the flowery trimmed set. "I know you can put the journal to good use."

He seemed overwhelmed while pulling out the journal, untying the string and thumbing through the crisp untouched pages. "Thank you, Sadie." He set it down. "Living here must be quite the life. I'd live in this room, if I were you. I bet you do."

"Now you have me figured out." She was teasing; in truth, she loved that he was trying to get to know her and feared he may stop at any time because of Henry.

"I'd never presume that. But I am observant." He squinted and crossed his arms on his chest, pretending to analyze her.

"That's right, you're a writer. Tell me then. Where will life lead me?"

"It's not where life will lead you." His stare heated the space between them. "The question is, how will *you* lead your life?"

"Go on."

"First you'll eat your food." He cast an eye on her full plate.

She picked up a cracker and smiled. "Hmm..."

"Tonight you'll pack for second term."

"Oh?"

"Yes, you're sensible. You're in college, after all, which means you're intelligent. At least I hope."

"Is that so?"

"Or you're terribly dull, admitted to college on your uncle's name, and running from an overbearing aunt. Either way you want to be ready to catch that first train out in the morning."

"Definitely the first scenario. What makes you so sure I'm leaving tomorrow?"

"You may not be. You may leave Tuesday or Wednesday or Thursday for that matter, but if you leave tomorrow with me, we could share a car to the station. You'll need an escort, right?"

"No. I've traveled on my own before. And then?" She found herself on the edge of her chair, taking in his scent of fresh soap and sandalwood. He leaned in, too, and spoke in a deep, tender voice that she could fall into if she weren't careful.

"You'll resume classes. You like history and

economics." He cocked his head to get a better read on her. "I mean science and math. You want to be a teacher. Or follow your uncle in law."

She narrowed her eyes, pretending to contemplate that.

"So you can make change happen."

"Not bad." Sadie did want to be a teacher.

"You'll marry the love of your life." James raised his chin to better study her. "And have lots of babies together."

She crossed her eyes in mock surprise.

"And travel the country speaking on behalf of women's rights," he continued.

"So *serious*. Don't I have any fun? Besides how could I leave the love of my life with all of those babies?"

"They'll join you."

"Naturally."

"Naturally." His closeness caused her throat to constrict and light perspiration to pinprick her upper lip, despite the blustery cold outside the library window.

"How will we feed all those mouths?" she mused.

"The family show, of course. You all sing and dance."

"That's where you're way off. I can't sing. And I'm a real dead hoofer."

"Come on now. Do you know the polka?" His eyes sparked.

"I don't know about this..."

"Say, my grandma taught me when I was this big." He held his hand to his knees in obvious exaggeration.

"I don't think you've ever been that small." A smile tugged at her lips. "Fine. But don't say I didn't warn you."

James stood abruptly, bumping the makeshift table and tipping his plate and fork, which careened across the hardwood. They lurched simultaneously to catch them and bumped into each other.

"Are you okay?" he asked, holding her at the shoulders with both hands.

A jolt shot across her body at his touch. "I'm fine," she said. They stood facing each other.

"Hold on." He moved their plates to a side table. Then he took her silk scarf and tied it around her waist, searing her exposed skin with his hot touch.

"Give me your hand." He took her right hand in his left one, not waiting for a response. He held it high in the air. "Put your other hand on my shoulder, like this." He placed her left hand above his shoulder, which she couldn't help but admire. He put his other hand on her back below her shoulder blade and along her bra strap. She awaited his next direction like a marionette subject to her puppeteer.

"The polka has four counts to the measure. It goes like this: one and two, three and four; one and two, three and four. Got that?"

She nodded, giggling out of nervousness.

"You'll start by going backward with your left foot. The basic step is twice on your left and then switch to your right foot. You'll be doing a quick little half-step."

"Wait a minute." She shook her head.

"Don't over-think it. Just go with it and let me lead you."

"Don't we need music?" she stalled.

"I'll count. Ready?"

She nodded again, completely smitten and in awe over this near stranger who had taken center stage in her life practically overnight.

"Five, six, seven, eight…" he said slowly. Then faster, "…one and two, three and four; one and two, three and four." They traveled around the library in a circle. Despite her clumsiness, he never broke hold, keeping them in unison and to the beat.

"Am I doing it?" she asked, mystified and afraid to look away from his intent eyes for fear she'd trip or step on his feet.

He nodded, smiling. "Hippety hop, to the barbershop, to buy a stick of candy."

His eyes bore into hers as they glided around the room. "Okay. Now that you've got the basic step, let's add a right turning basic and you'll really have your boots on." He beamed.

They danced the polka again and this time he turned her as they went and she felt in tune with a man for the first time in her life. She had done the jive and jitterbug with Henry and boys she barely knew, but this was the first time a dance connected her with her partner.

The late afternoon sun warmed the library with golden shafts of light. She absorbed the visceral beauty of their moment together, wishing to suspend it in time, the way she often wished the sun would hover longer at the horizon.

Taking her off guard, James suddenly planted his feet and cradled her face in both hands, tracing her burning cheeks with his roughened thumbs. She froze, pressing her eyelids closed, feeling a light tingle teasing up and down her spine. They should stop. But yet, as he gently pressed his full lips to hers, they melted together, opening and closing, his mouth asking, hers answering. He pleaded with his kisses, then nipped at her lips, along her throat, and in the soft hollow under her jaw. Her fingers wandered up to his shirt pocket and then around to his back, dipping into the muscular ridge along his spine and splaying across shoulders that turned her knees to mush. His hands traveled down to her waist, resting there before venturing to the curve of her hips. They were like explorers approaching unchartered sea.

Nanny burst in the door, stealing the moment. As they released each other, Sadie seized the closest chair to steady herself.

"Gracious! You're still in here?" Nanny had her feather duster in one hand, a rag in the other. Uncle Edward preferred the new maids to do the cleaning— after all Nanny was like family—but she stubbornly insisted on keeping busy.

"Nanny," Sadie said, patching over her awkward recovery. "James taught me to polka. Watch." She took hold of James as they had in their formal dancing position, delighted by the apple redness spreading from his collar to his cheeks. "I'm ready."

"James, I hope you don't need all them toes."

"She's a natural, really," he responded without taking his eyes off Sadie's. "Five, six, seven, eight...one and two, three and four; one and two, three and four."

"Lord almighty! She can *glide*!"

Sadie smiled with everything she had, mirroring James. The sun's last flaming glow lit his face. They dovetailed together like the corners of her dresser drawer. In the next instant, the golden light dipped away. So too did her sinking realization that another day with him would soon pass. Had she relished each second spent with Henry as she did with James? Or was it the unusual circumstance of having James here that had inflated her longing?

The moment was officially lost when a maid barged in. "Henry's asking for you, Miss Stark."

"Now?" Sadie released her hold on James.

"Yes." She dared Sadie with her narrowed eyes that traveled from Sadie to James and back.

"I'll see you later." James had regained his composure but nothing could erase their wanting.

"And Mrs. Stark asked me to hold off pressing your clothes. She says you will wait to leave with Henry."

Was the maid her aunt's spy? It didn't matter, whatever that woman had cooking. Nothing could dampen the cascading thrill still fresh in her lower belly. Spy all she wanted, Sadie thought smugly. She had nothing to hide.

Chapter Ten

Sadie paused at the door till her eyes adjusted to curtain-drawn darkness of the bedroom. She made out the shape of Henry's body under the blankets, facing the wall, and didn't want to disturb his sleep.

He rolled over. "Hey doll," he whispered, reaching out. "Where have you been?"

She moved to the bed, settling on the edge beside him and dodged his question with one of her own. "Are you feeling all right?"

"Been better. Been worse. I think it's the flu." His face was pale and his eyelids swollen. He branded her thigh with a heavy, hot hand.

She removed his hand to hold it. His touch was familiar and comforting like a worn blanket from childhood, but void of the sparks James elicited with a single glance in her direction. She wondered if the excitement and wonderment James aroused would wane in time or turn into something even more meaningful than she had experienced with Henry.

"Stay with me and we'll go back to school when we feel like it," Henry said, lying supine, dark circles under his eyes causing him to appear aged and weak.

"That's easy to say when your parents help you out." The words betrayed her attempt at civility. She wasn't sure where her underlying annoyance with him came from, and why it came out like this, bringing out the worst in her, and she was ashamed by it. Perhaps by pleasing him all these years, she had begun harboring a resentment that was growing harder to disguise.

"Is that what you think of me?" His face contorted, the vein in his forehead bulged. When she remained silent, he added, "That's why you won't marry me, isn't it? I'm too great a risk?" He pulled his hand away like a pouty child.

"Henry."

"It is."

"I worry about you," she softened, not wanting to upset him further. "Because I care about you." It wasn't a lie. She felt strongly about Henry because of their history and wanted him to be happy. Before James, she had thought her reservations with him had to do with being young and having unfinished goals, such as finishing school. Now she had a sinking feeling her hesitation was more than that. But she couldn't be sure.

"You really do want to finish school?"

"Henry, listen to me. This is important. Yes. I do. Want to finish school. And you need to finish, too." She searched his face for a sign that he understood, hopeful that for once, he would put aside his own needs and see the situation from her point of view. But how could she fault him for loving her and wanting to make this commitment to her? Most girls in her place would be overjoyed.

"When do you have to leave?" He massaged her hands and furrowed his brow.

"Tomorrow."

"Tomorrow?"

"I still need to pack, but yes."

"What about me? I barely had any time with

you…alone." He pulled her upper body down on top of him. She recoiled from his foul breath; obviously he hadn't had time to clean up. Was that gin she detected?

"Henry!" she pulled away and smoothed her top. "Have you been drinking?"

"Just a little something to take the edge off. When will I see you next?" He propped up on his elbows. "How about the weekend I get back?"

"I don't think that will work. The start of the semester is always so hectic, getting into a new routine. You understand." Here she went with the excuses again.

"Doll—"

"Henry," she interrupted, stepping to the window. The snow-covered stable in the distance looked peaceful and calm, the complete opposite of how she felt. She smoothed her skirt with clammy hands, her throat thick. "I think some time apart may do us good."

"If you're waiting for me to finish school and get a decent job, you don't have to worry about that. Your uncle will help and—"

"Listen, Henry." She turned to face him, but stayed far enough away that he couldn't touch her. "I'm not sure I'll ever be ready to marry you."

Not only was she not ready, she shied away from the public scrutiny her uncle's role as governor brought into her life, the same political future Henry sought.

A grin spread across his face as he shook his head. "This is what my father warned me about. All the best girls play hard to get." He sat up and motioned her to come closer. Color was returning to his cheeks as his excitement grew. "Sadie Stark, I am not giving up on us."

She smiled meekly, realizing he wasn't in the right frame of mind to fully digest what she was saying. "You should get some rest."

"Can't you postpone your trip, doll—until I feel better?" He did his best to appear the vulnerable man-child Nanny accused him of being.

"No, Henry. I can't."

He flopped back in the bed. "You exhaust me." But he seemed satisfied.

Relief washed over her that once again she had avoided the final blow that their break-up would cause. She supposed it was like watching a beloved suffer a terminal illness, knowing the situation would only worsen, praying for the ultimate outcome to arrive sooner rather than later if only to spare him from prolonging pain. She knew he'd find someone else quickly and easily—someone who was better suited for him.

"I better go pack." She pecked his tepid cheek and left. But there was something that flickered in his eye—a determination—that terrified her. There was no denying a man like Henry.

Chapter Eleven

A faint light illuminated the stable yard in the distance near the kennels where Governor Stark's hounds yowled, anticipating their next meal. From the stone walled patio, James inhaled the smell of burning wood that emanated from the mansion's many chimneys. He rubbed his cold hands and jammed them into the pockets of his Army coat.

The salmon-streaked sky reflected off freshly fallen snow—a canvas of varying shades of pale-pinkish orange. His first urge was to run through the powder and pelt snowballs the way he and Paul had loved to do. A good snowball fight was what he needed to release the tension building in his chest. Instead he used his bare hand to sweep the accumulated snow off the stone wall that lined the courtyard patio.

It seemed like yesterday that he and Paul had parted at the station for the last time. He remembered his brother climbing aboard and waving to the crowd gathered to see him off, his girlfriend front and center. Even in the end, Paul had the glory of being first.

He wished Sadie were here now, enjoying the view of the sky's fading light beside him, pressing her warm body to his, like she did during their dance, their bodies moving together as if meant to. He wanted to kiss her again like he had in the attic, touch her unbelievably soft skin and run his hands through her hair—get lost in her. It was selfish to want her, to want to be her lover, yet he refused to let go of the fantasy.

"Nice night." Gideon McAlister crunched across the hard-packed snow toward James, puffing on a cigar, cradling a scotch glass in his free hand.

"Evening, sir." James stiffened.

"The Starks host a great shindig out here every summer," he said, his speech slurred. "Independence day. Shame you won't be around to see it."

James shifted and kicked the snow with his boot.

Drifts of snow blanketed the courtyard around them, on display through an impressive row of French doors. The patio was dark in contrast to the inside glow of chandeliers where the others mingled and sipped their cocktails; Martha Tilton crooned "A Stranger in Town" in the background.

"Let's cut to the chase, shall we. What'll it be?" He gulped down the last of the golden liquid and turned to face James.

"Nothing for me," James said.

Gideon McAlister chuckled. "A drink's not what I meant. Look…" He pointed at James while cradling the glass. "I know about men like you. I know what you're after."

James was confused. That tightness in his chest had returned and was growing as he guessed where this conversation was headed.

"I'm going to be completely frank with you, Pasko."

"Please do." James turned to face him square-on.

"You don't belong here. It was fine to play in the big house for a bit, but seeing you lurk makes me sick. Makes Henry sick. Governor Stark may not admit it, but he tries to keep the people at arms' length. You understand. If he were to give one bum a handout, the whole state would be at his back door, like stray dogs. We know you came here for a reason. I'm gonna make this real simple for you." He reached for his wallet. "Just take this and your stuff and go to town. Nobody has to know why you left," he said as if doing James a favor. "Go to The Rusty Nail on the Square. Tell Rusty I sent you and he'll set you up even though it's Sunday."

James silently raged; Gideon McAlister had hit on his insecurities. A stray dog. An imposter. But he was wrong about James' reason for coming here. He raised his hands in surrender, to diffuse the heated moment.

Misinterpreting his gesture, McAlister said, "You greedy son of a bitch."

When James shook his head, the inebriated man understood. "Sadie's a nice girl. But if you hadn't noticed, she's taken."

"Really? Is that according to her?" James' blood heated his core.

"And believe me, you aren't worth her trouble." He sniggered. "What kind of name is Pasko, anyway?"

James resisted the urge to punch him. One shove and he could knock the pompous man off his feet. He pictured Gideon in the snow, a baffled look on his insipid face, his glasses askew. But what would that prove? Nothing worthwhile. Instead, he tolerated a chuckle from Gideon and a smirk that faded into the darkness enveloping the patio.

Through clenched teeth, James said, "I don't want or need your dough. Never did." He headed back inside.

Careful not to be noticed, he took the back

staircase two steps at a time to his room to get his pack. The confrontation with Gideon had cemented his decision to leave. He felt trapped here—trapped by his inability to be the man he wanted to be for Sadie. The drunk had been right about one thing. It was time to carry on. He had to get out of here before he saw her again and had to explain. It was a mistake to have come and interrupted her life. He knew running off was cowardly, definitely not what Paul would have done, but it was better this way. She would soon forget him and their kiss in the attic, their interlude in the library. She was better off without him and the sooner he made that possible for her, the better.

****

"Going somewhere?" Governor Stark asked as James passed the heavy molded office door with his pack slung over one shoulder. Seated alone, he held a pipe in one hand and reclined in a leather chair flanked by framed oil paintings, lamp glow, and herringbone.

At first glance, James saw the governor's public persona: decisive and unyielding, unweathered by the strain of a prominent career, but when James said, "Sir?" and tentatively stepped in, the governor transformed before him, exhibiting a private persona punctuated with laugh lines and the telltale wrinkles of a life well lived. *Grandfatherly* came to mind.

James stood on the edge of an oriental rug, probably worth more than his family's home, and took in the rich mahogany paneling that threatened to swallow him whole like the whale did to unsuspecting Jonah.

"Have a seat, son." The governor raked a hand through his thick salt and pepper hair.

James sank into a leather armchair warmed by the blazing fire opposite the governor. The formality of their private meeting had him concerned. Had Gideon spoken with him already? What lies had he told? That he found money in James' pack upstairs—money James accepted as a bribe to leave? Of course the governor would believe Gideon over him. James set down his pack half expecting with foolish paranoia the governor to search it right then and there.

"Do you have any idea..." The governor simultaneously lit and puffed on his pipe to get it going. James stiffened. He looked for escape points in the room. "How...*extremely* impressed I am with you, son?"

"Sir?"

"Let me back up. You're familiar with the War Council, I take it?" Governor Stark crossed his legs, obviously at ease, which allowed James to breathe, but not let down his guard.

"Yes, sir," James said. The War Council was the organization the governor had created to better correspond with citizens on war issues.

"Last week I received a summary of pending action on petitions." He held his forehead as if to stifle a headache. "I receive *countless* letters from citizens asking for help with war-related issues, son." He sucked on his pipe again and the sweet tobacco smoke swirled around the air. Dread filled James, bearing down on his shoulders. Gideon must have gotten to the governor about something. Did the governor think James came here with a hidden agenda?

"Yes, sir," James said. "I can imagine."

"Complaints of favoritism on draft boards, requests

for exemptions from rationing, the list goes on and on."

James shifted uncomfortably. He knew part of the governor's role was to be a liaison between the public and the government. Governor Stark was nearing the end of his second consecutive term in office and dealing with the war couldn't be easy.

"But do you know what my favorite letters are? The bright spot in my day?" the governor asked.

"No, sir." James couldn't tell if he was being facetious or not.

"Letters from folks like you."

"Me, sir?"

"Yes, James. Honest, good people like yourself who volunteer themselves for the armed services."

"Thank you, sir." James spoke cautiously, wondering if this was a test.

"Not only that, James, but for you to go out of your way to help another citizen—my dear Sadie—is commendable."

James' thoughts turned to the heart-stopping beauty he kissed in the attic and danced with in the library.

"Are you familiar with mounted foxhunting?"

"No, never had the opportunity."

"You would like it. The aim is to ensure a long chase, and the longer the better." He puffed on his pipe, reclining. "I've got a registered pack of trained foxhounds on the property. Used to be the master of foxhounds." He took a swig of brandy from a glass on the side table.

"That sounds like a real honor, sir," James said, although he still thought fox hunting was unfairly weighted on the side of the hounds and riders and a sport for the wealthy.

"Do you still hunt?" James asked.

"Oh yes, yes. I have Sadie to thank for that. Well, when my old bones allow it. Care for a brandy?"

"Yes, sir," James conceded. He had stopped drinking regularly after seeing the ghost at the boarding house though, at times, he still indulged.

The governor crossed the room, took out a second brandy glass, and poured the alcohol from a crystal decanter. "Sadie started hunting on a pony. This," the governor said, raising his bushy eyebrows, pointing a finger at James, "happened after much campaigning on her part. Years of it." He chuckled and sauntered back with James' glass. "I relented at last."

James took the glass from the governor, swallowing more than the sip he intended, the alcohol burning as it went down.

"Now that she's in college, we won't get to hunt together." He took a sip of the brandy. "Hunting is a lot like life, James. You will understand this, being a young man with your life before you. When you hunt, you have to think ahead, anticipate the unexpected. Of course that's harder for an old man like me to do. When you become my age…" He chuckled, patting his sunken chest. "You have more life to reflect on. Regrets, James. Anyway, the hunt is about thinking ahead and being hopeful. You understand?"

"Yes, sir." A lightness spread across him as he related to the man Sadie admired, who was paramount in her life, therefore important to him, too. Whether he felt relaxed because of his company or the alcohol, he couldn't be sure, but at last he released some of the pent-up frustration that had consumed him earlier. He was curious about something. Had the governor alluded to his regrets to make James aware of his own?

He took a swig of brandy and set down the almost empty glass, with his hand covering the top.

"Let me ask you, James. How will your family fare when you deploy? Are you married?"

"No, sir."

"Are your parents in good health?"

"My mother gets by. My father passed..."

"I'm sorry to hear that." He shifted in his seat. "Siblings?"

"I have a sister and brother, sir."

"No dependents?"

"No, sir."

"Very well. I'll make sure your family is taken care of, James, throughout your absence. You have my word."

"Thank you, sir. That's very generous of you. I appreciate everything."

"Don't mention it." The governor stood, signaling an end to their conversation. James stood, too. "Anything else I can do for you?" the governor asked.

James had an overwhelming urge to confide in him about his feelings for Sadie. Would he be as impressed with him then—impressed enough to give his blessing? No, he shouldn't push it. He wasn't pedigreed like Henry with the financial security, advanced education, and the ability to provide for her. How could he compete? He shuddered over bringing Sadie back to his poor part of town, having her struggle like his mother did. His life wasn't an easy one, and he wanted far more for her. But after the war, when he made something of himself, everything would be different—

if she waited that long. For now he was content with the gifts he had been given, time with Sadie and the governor's respect.

"No, sir. Thank you for hosting me this weekend." They shook hands.

"Here." The governor handed him a black crackle lighter. When James hesitated, he said, "Take it. You never know when it might come in handy."

"Thank you, sir." He realized the man wanted to give him something, and, when he turned it around and saw that it bore the governor's insignia, probably one of a kind, his chest swelled.

"Well then, Nanny tells me you and Sadie are heading in the same direction tomorrow. Allow me to send a driver to the station and take care of your ticket. It would please me immensely to know Sadie is in good hands. Bound for New Jersey are you?"

"Fort Dix, sir. But a ticket won't be necessary. You've been too generous already. And tonight..."

"I insist, James. Please, allow me this."

"Thank you, sir."

"So you'll depart first thing tomorrow?"

James hesitated, wondering if the governor had been more strategic than nostalgic during their fireside chat in suggesting he escort Sadie. "Yes, sir."

"And James," the governor said just as he was about to leave the room. "I'm sure your father would be very proud of you."

His sentiment caught James off guard and he savored the man's approval. "Thank you, sir."

James stepped outside for fresh air. Standing in the cool nighttime peace, he ignited the lighter with his thumb and watched the flame flicker.

Chapter Twelve

Sadie pretended to focus on her filet if only to occupy her eyes, which had already betrayed her one too many times to peek at James across the dining room table. After slicing her fourth tiny piece of meat without eating any, Aunt Bea placed a hand on her arm to stop her. "Everything okay, dear?"

"I'm fine," Sadie said.

"Have you heard a word I've said?"

She hadn't. Not with James sitting across from her, his hungry eyes meeting hers. "Yes. Go on."

"In February," Aunt Bea said. "Starring Hepburn & Tracy."

"What's it called?" She gulped her ice water.

"Sadie, I just told you it's the opening of 'Woman of the Year' at Radio City in New York. I wondered if you and Henry would like to go. I could arrange for tickets." She pursed her lips.

Sadie forced a tight smile and sat up tall, her eyes straying to James, who fixed her with a worried expression, his eyebrows furrowed. She wished she had the nerve to mouth "meet me in the library."

"Thank you." She patted her mouth with her napkin. "If you'll excuse me…"

She felt James' eyes on her, the lovely tension between them palpable.

"Sadie." The governor caught her attention. "I was

thinking that James should accompany you back east tomorrow. And..." He stopped suddenly and frowned.

She followed her uncle's strained look to where Henry appeared, dressed in the expensive suit he had worn during their recent date, his ashen face cleanly shaven, but dotted with perspiration, and his red hair slicked back and parted on the side; its waviness appearing unruly rather than charming. Although dark circles remained under his eyes, his presence was cause for celebration.

"Henry, my boy!" Mr. McAlister bellowed. "Take a seat."

"Yes, come join us, dear." Aunt Bea gestured to Patty to add a place at the table.

"Are you hungry?" Mrs. McAlister asked.

The party seemed almost unified in delight. Almost. Sadie rooted to her chair, unable to move or speak, and James looked as bewildered as she. How grateful she was to be alone in her thoughts. No matter how public her life was as the governor's niece, her thoughts would always be her own.

Henry beamed, displaying an air of importance while addressing the crowd. "I spent all day laid up in bed thinking about one thing only. I must be dreaming right now." He suppressed a grin. "I think my real body must be at the morgue or buried in a snowdrift. How else can I explain this euphoria?"

"He's gone mad," the professor said, met with chuckles.

"Mad, yes. Call it what you will. I realized something." He maneuvered to behind Sadie's chair, placing his heavy hands on her shoulders. "This wonderful woman right here," Henry said, causing her chest to heave. "Is the reason I got out of bed tonight."

Sadie tensed, gripping her napkin, peering at the astonished looks frozen on everyone's faces. James lowered his fork onto the decorative edge of the china.

"And, I hope she will continue to be the reason I get out of bed every day."

The women gasped. The room seemed to be closing in on Sadie, restricting her breathing. She touched her damp forehead briefly and forced a smile in response, lifting her eyebrows up curiously at Henry. He pulled back her chair so they could face each other before lumbering down on one knee.

"My love…" He looked up with hopeful eyes, his forehead vein bulging.

"Henry," she pleaded, her voice desperate, nausea snaking up her belly to her throat.

She had to stop him! How could he think this was a good idea? She felt caught in his snare. She replayed their last conversation together when she had visited him in the bedroom that afternoon, trying to deduce what gave him this idea. Was he really so out of touch with her feelings or was he forcing the issue on purpose? Choosing this forum strategically?

"Now wait a minute." He squeezed her hands gently. "I know what you're going to say. I know you want to finish school and I want that for you, too. Why can't we be engaged *while* you finish? We can get married this summer and you can join me in Philadelphia while I finish law school. I will study harder than you've ever seen me study."

She opened her mouth to protest, but couldn't formulate a single intelligent thought.

He forged on. "I know why you were unsure

before. Lying in that bed all day gave me clarity. I give you my word this time that starting today I will focus on our future first and foremost."

She wanted to stop the words from coming. Empty promises.

"The way I feel about you..." he said, but fell short. "I can't wait any longer."

More gasps escaped the women around the table. Even Nanny poked her head in the room.

"Henry..." Sadie felt railroaded. He was saying all the right things, but to the wrong girl.

"From the moment I laid eyes on you, I knew. I knew I was in the presence of an angel, someone too righteous for words. You have always been too good for me. I know you deserve more." He grinned, too arrogant to mean it. "But I need you in my life. Don't you see?" He squeezed her hands again. "Doll?" He wiped his forehead with his sleeve while still clinging to her hands the way a boy might tug on his mother's skirt for her attention. "I can't live without you."

"Don't say that," she whispered, even though she suspected their captive audience could probably hear her swallow over the silence he commanded with his performance. She wanted to run from the room—run from the life that he was chiseling into stone.

"Why not say it? It's true. I will report it on the front page of the paper, shout it from every corner of town if that's what it takes to make you see!"

"Henry, can we discuss this in private?"

"No. No more hiding and delays." There was no turning back now.

"Henry..."

"I can't promise I'll be perfect. I'm not perfect. But

I promise to love you and take care of you the best I know how."

A strange rush of emotions surfaced. She was angry, for how could she object to him now? And she was riddled with guilt as she glanced around at her aunt and uncle's faces and the McAlisters—all eager for her to go along with the plan that had been laid out for some time. And what about James? Would she ever see him again? He'd leave her within hours.

At some point she began drowning in the roomful of expectation. She felt on stage, having forgotten her lines, awaiting the curtain's close so she could recede into obscurity and free herself from this charade. She needed time to think. But there was no time.

Henry pulled out a small black box from his pocket and opened it. Inside was a substantial diamond solitaire. Oh God. This was actually happening.

"It's set in platinum," Henry said.

"Divine, dear! Simply gorgeous," Aunt Bea said of the sparkling diamond. You would think a man had landed on the moon.

"Well done, son," Gideon McAlister added.

"Sadie Stark…will you be my wife?"

Did she have any choice? While awaiting her answer, nobody came to her rescue. Nanny disappeared through the swinging door. She couldn't bear to look at James. The others' silence, which she interpreted to be their agreement to this treaty of sorts, a pact between bodies of land wealth not lovers, only added to her waffling. Yet surely they weren't all wrong about Henry? Had she built up James in her mind too much? She was behaving like the fickle, ungrateful person she accused others to be. Every second she hesitated cast a dark shadow across Henry's face that broke her. She couldn't stand her own cruelty; she simply wanted the moment to end.

"Put it on at least." Henry pulled the ring from the box and held it to her, pouting like a child who insisted on his way.

"Yes! Yes! Does it fit?" Margaret McAlister said. Obviously she had been in on this.

Before James had come here, she'd wanted to fall in love with Henry. Nanny had once said arranged marriages worked. Was it possible to develop feelings for someone if you had an open heart? She reluctantly allowed Henry to slide the ring on her trembling finger because she couldn't come up with a reason why she shouldn't.

Everyone clapped and cheered as Henry drew her up into an embrace, his eyes squeezed shut, and kissed her. "I will make you so happy, baby doll! Just wait!"

The tiny bit of peace she clung to fell apart when she saw James watching them. One look at his wounded eyes cut the air from her lungs. His confusion reflected her own.

She hadn't been strong enough to trust in the possibility of them. What did James think of her now? This realization washed over her so completely that she nearly fainted into the welcoming, victorious arms of her imperfect fiancé.

Chapter Thirteen

Like hawks circling prey, Aunt Bea and Margaret McAlister descended on her in the foyer of the governor's mansion the next morning, desperate to set dates for the bridal shower and wedding. A knot formed in her stomach.

"Beatrice, there's plenty of time for that later. Let them be on their way," Uncle Edward said. "They'll need time to purchase tickets. You never know how long the line will be at the station."

James shook hands with the men while Sadie doled out perfunctory pecks on cheeks. Her last embrace was saved for Nanny who whispered, "Engagements were made to be broken," as she propelled the pair out the door.

Sadie turned toward the Bentley. James had already loaded all her luggage and stood holding the door for her. Always the gentleman.

"Call me the minute you arrive, doll." Misty-eyed Henry took her gloved hands and rubbed his thumbs across her tautly covered knuckles. He rested one thumb on her ring while drawing her near for a kiss.

She slipped into the warm refuge of the Bentley that promised to whisk her away with James. Although escapism wasn't the answer, perhaps any physical distance would ease her dread over what she'd done, help her to get used to the idea. However, she suspected as long as she bore Henry's ring, the claustrophobia would follow, no matter how far she fled.

The silence between them during the drive nearly broke her.

****

"Here we are." James guided her toward the first class train car with a warm hand on the small of her back that sent sparks across her belly.

She tugged on her freshly pressed cream-colored suit and secured a pin on her feathered pillbox hat as they boarded. A porter stowed their luggage in the designated overhead racks. When James handed her the Hermes bag with her school papers and books, she pretended they were newlyweds on their honeymoon— he, the doting husband who inherently knew she would need something out of *that* bag and she, the lovely recipient of his attentiveness, the efficient wife who had already tipped the porter. Wasn't this harmonious coexistence the goal of every couple? How could she vacillate from not wanting to be married days ago, to wanting that very union now? Ah, but the answer to that was easy. It was all in finding the right man.

Sadie took a seat, and James, after only the slightest hesitation, continued standing. She suspected why. Sunlight reflected off the diamond like a prism, casting rainbow specks of light inside the train car, twisting her knot of guilt again. When she peered up, she saw that he wasn't hesitating over where to sit at all; he was asking a man in a fedora one row up to close the window. For her? She'd forgotten about the soot when selecting her suit and her seat, but the possibility of dirt on her clothes was a welcome worry compared to everything else. Still, she couldn't help but melt over

James' thoughtfulness. The man lowered and locked the window, securing the leather strap over the metal stud.

James took the drafty window seat beside her, the heat of his body warming her to the core, causing her to feel even more disgusted over falling into Henry's trap. She squeezed her eyelids closed and bit her bottom lip, willing the haughty reminder on her finger to disappear. If only she could explain to James the way her family— her aunt in particular—had pushed her toward this. She didn't care about the McAlister fortune. And James couldn't possibly think she did. Could he? The worst part was the look on his face when she let Henry slide the ring on her finger. Cowardly, she was. She needed to tell James the truth. After she worked up the courage.

"So, you're really going to marry him?" James blurted, confusion crossing his features as he glanced at her hand.

So much for easing into the situation.

"You don't think I should?" *Please, give me a reason. Anything.*

"You tell me."

She sighed and lost her hands in the folds of her skirt. "I always knew Henry would propose. For as long as I remember, everyone expected it. I shouldn't be surprised, and yet…"

"If you had doubts, why didn't you tell him no?"

"I never said yes."

"But you're wearing his ring."

That she was.

Passengers bustled past them, smelling of cigarettes and body odor, stowing luggage and scrambling for seats. Truthfully, she might have been sure about Henry had James not come along when he had, emotionally derailing her from taking the next logical step in the evolution of their relationship. A step both of their families had encouraged. Something even she had once anticipated because she wanted to please Henry, who, for all of his faults, did seem to love her to the best of his abilities. At least she thought he did. Was it fair of her to silently judge Henry's indulgent lifestyle, not unlike her own privileged upbringing? Perhaps his greatest flaw was that he was too familiar? Or, was it possible that James was her excuse to escape a life she'd never felt worthy of having? Maybe James was her fantasy, so unattainable that he appeared the more attractive choice.

"So, you're in love with Henry?" His accusing tone surprised her.

Of course it was clear now that she couldn't possibly love Henry. No, she loved James, whose eyes the color of river rock bore into hers. Her lips trembled ever so slightly. Engulfed in his cloud of direct questioning, words escaped her.

An elderly couple hovered in the aisle next to them, the plump wife out of breath, fanning herself next to her balding, button-down husband.

"Tickets, Stanley?" She extended her head like a turtle peeking from its shell, a wattle of neck skin dangling.

"Oh!" He patted his coat pockets, checking each one, and reached inside to his breast pocket. "Here they are, Myrtle. Right where I told you they were."

"You did not. You said I had them."

"Did I?"

"Yes, you did." Myrtle then smiled apologetically at James and Sadie. She sighed while settling across from James, facing him. "What a pretty, young thing she is," she told him, curiously peering at Sadie over glasses perched on the tip of her button nose.

"We're not—" James said.

"—together," Sadie added.

"No?" She raised her pencil-drawn brows while looking at Sadie's telltale ring and then chuckled. "Well, maybe not yet. Have you set a date?"

James patted Sadie's hand. "Miss Stark is rather noncommittal at the moment."

The quizzical look on the old woman's face rippled into a confused smile.

"What Mr. Pasko means is, I can't wait to be married, but I want to make sure everything is right."

"By everything she means the right man," James added.

Sadie shot him a look.

Myrtle sniggered. "He's funny. Truly!" She lingered, a big-toothed smile frozen on her heavily made-up face, obviously waiting for them to further entertain her. "So, just travel companions for the time being."

"Yes." Sadie's heart ached. Henry's ring weighed her down like an anchor mooring a boat to the ocean's bottom. Pressure cloaked her shoulders the way Henry's clammy hands had felt the previous night. Why couldn't someone else be the bearer of this responsibility, the cause for the bridal frenzy at the mansion right now—freeing Sadie to explore what she and James might have together?

She slipped back to that fantasy, imagining her husband was the rugged soldier beside her. The train lurched into motion. As they departed from the

Harrisburg depot, she squinted at the blinding whiteness outside the window.

"When I was a little girl," she told James, stealing a sidelong glance while he looked out the window, too, memorizing every curve of his face. "I used to say sunshine is God's happiness. Rain is His tears. The wind's His anger."

"And the snow?" He stole her breath with his smoldering gaze.

"Falling snow means the angels are proud."

He covered her hand with his. She struggled to swallow.

"Very poetic, dear," Myrtle said, ruining the moment.

James probably thought she was nothing but a pampered child, a plaything to be tossed about at someone else's will, easily impressed with something as mundane as the weather.

James whispered, "Snow-covered earth means a new beginning."

She melted into a puddle of happiness, clinging to the feeling, knowing full well how inappropriate it was to be enamored by a man other than her fiancé. She panicked at the thought of living out the rest of her days without James in her life, without belonging to each other. She struggled to think clearly.

"Tell me," James said. "What's your favorite subject in college?"

"Umm…" She collected herself. "Art history, probably." She opened her Hermes bag and withdrew a book with worn corners and a spine so loose it flopped flat when opened on her lap. As she flipped through the glossy pages, a postcard stuck out. And another.

"I got these at the museum with Ruth."

"Postcards?"

"Of my favorites. This is Matisse's 'Blue Pot and Lemon,' which I adore. But my favorite is 'Open Window.' I don't have a postcard of that one yet."

When James leaned in for a better look, closing the space between them, his thigh bumped against hers, sending a jolt of warmth up her leg.

"This one's interesting. May I?" When he cocked his head, she spied the small scar above his eyebrow. She remembered the story behind it that James had told her that day they'd met on a train ten years ago. That she knew even one of his childhood stories pleased her.

She nodded and held out the postcard. "That's a Prendergast."

"The people seem mute. Why?"

"He was deaf. His work has a silent quality about it, doesn't it?" She hesitated, unsure if she should continue or not, if he was just being polite and pretending to care. She sensed he did care. "What I love about Prendergast is how he captured fleeting moments in time." She thought about their own fleeting time together.

"What happened to him?"

"He spent a lot of time in Venice. See how he mastered the rippling waves? He died about twenty years ago, alone. His life well lived, influenced by the place he loved."

"Not if he fell in love with Venice instead of a woman. Better to be influenced by the people you love, I always think."

His stare blurred the space around them, causing a deep swirl across her. They were positioned so intimately, she pretended to study the postcard, when really all her attention couldn't help but be used up by his scent of fresh soap and leather and warm breath on her face. Trembling ever so slightly with the anticipation that he might kiss her, she closed her eyes and tilted her face toward his.

A snore escaped Myrtle. James suppressed a smile, sharing in one glance with Sadie her exact sentiment. The fact that they could share a reaction in unspoken terms—finding the humor in it, even—caused another pleasant tug in her stomach. A girl could get addicted.

"Ruth and I want to see the real art at the Metropolitan in New York." She rambled to escape his penetrating gaze. "Ruth's my best friend at Bryn Mawr. She found us the cooperative house on Prospect."

"*You* live in a cooperative house?"

"Why is that so hard to believe?"

"Are you serious? You really don't see yourself, Sadie, do you? At least not the way the rest of the world does."

She knew what he meant; she was fooling no one. "My aunt has an opinion on where I live, which is partly why I chose it." See, she had a rebellious side. Although not, apparently, when it mattered most.

Stanley had put away his paper and closed his eyes, too. His head hung down like a forgotten toy, awaiting the hands of a child to bring him to life once more.

"I bet your uncle is fine with whatever decisions you make." He paused and turned to face her. "I have a confession to make. Last night I considered leaving the mansion…"

He'd almost left her?

"…and your uncle convinced me not to."

Sadie forced a swallow. Although she wondered why her uncle would do that, she could guess at the reason. He intrinsically understood her. But she was stuck on the fact that James had even considered leaving. How could he have done that?

"I can tell you one thing," James said. "You mean the world to him. Did you know he offered to take care of my family while I'm gone? I think he feels that any friend of yours…well, let's just say he's a good man." He pulled the lighter from his pocket. "He gave me this."

Her pride swelled. Encouraged by his confession, she leaned in, eager to continue their confiding. "You know so much about me and my family. Tell me about your parents. Your mom must be terribly upset with you leaving," Sadie whispered. "And with your father gone…"

"Pop was a good man. Hard worker, fair, kind, but he was angry," James said. "My mother, always the diplomat, kept things calm. When Paul started drinking, Pop had this fury about him. I thought he hated Paul. I feared for my brother."

She was taken aback by his candor. It wasn't the conversation she was expecting; it was better. His honesty swept her away. "What happened?"

"Let's just say the more a father loves his son, the more he hates the drunk inside him."

Her thoughts flickered to Henry.

"You know what I think?" he asked. "Anger isn't the opposite of love. Hate is. Pop was angry when he saw Paul destroying himself, but he never hated him. It took me a while to figure that out."

They sat silently for some time, shifting in their

seats, at last with privacy since the elderly couple was sleeping.

"One hot day, my mother dressed us in church clothes to take a train trip without Pop, something we'd never done before. Well, I'd done only once."

The time they'd met?

"My mother seemed rushed and too preoccupied to answer any of our questions. She riffled through drawers and dumped clothes into the open suitcase on her bed. She sent us out to wait on the porch step while she finished. We didn't get far. A neighbor stopped over to borrow sugar for a pie. She and our mother spoke with hushed voices. The next thing I knew, we were told to go to the neighbor's house that was perched on a rocky cliff overlooking train tracks and the Ohio River. Much like ours. Later that night, back home, we ate a quiet supper and went to bed. The next day the suitcase was stowed back under my parents' bed, our clothes neatly folded and put away. I suppose running away is never the answer."

"Did Paul stop drinking?"

"After Pop died, yes. He had to. It was either that or answer to me. And even after he cleaned up, we each struggled to be man of the house."

"Your father never got to see Paul redeem himself?"

"I think he has." James looked up. "At least I hope so."

The train chugged steadily on its course. If only she could stop the train, stop time so she and James could exist like this together indefinitely. She fantasized about James turning to her and saying he wanted to spend the rest of his life with her. That he wanted her to break off the ill-timed wedge Henry had driven between them and wait for him to return from the war. And when he returned, they would be married.

But she knew even if he felt this way, he'd never ask that of her. Even if she wasn't engaged, she doubted he'd ask her to put her life on hold for him—hadn't he told Henry that? But why not? Women all over were waiting for their men to return from the war. It was what they did. She could do it, too. Unless he hadn't really meant what he said and he'd already asked someone else to wait for him. That woman back home, perhaps?

She would rather gamble on their potential future, and risk angering her family in the process, than say goodbye to James without him knowing how she really felt. If only she had the nerve to tell him.

"You know," James said. "Losing Pop made me realize I don't want to live with regrets. I never got the chance to tell him how much he meant to me."

"I'm sure he knew."

James was silent. He flat-palmed his hands together as if in prayer. "Let me ask you something," he said quietly. "Is it right to forgive easily and give someone a chance to change their ways?"

"Of course. Don't you think so?"

He nodded but didn't meet her eyes.

Did he think she should give Henry a chance to…what? Turn into the man she wanted him to be? Would he ever make her feel the way she felt with James?

He continued. "And if someone put himself in front of you and said he would take the fall for you rather than let you fall, is there nothing you can't ask of that person? Knowing someone feels this way about you, you can face anything in life, right? Isn't this the greatest show of love?"

"It is," she said.

"Pop used to say, 'if you have your health, you have everything.' He was wrong. Without love, you have nothing." He rubbed one hand along his jawline. "About your mother…"

She was caught off guard by his sudden change in topic, and then it slowly sank in that he had been working up to this all along. "Yes?"

"You said she moved to New York."

"I did."

"So, she's out there somewhere." The way he clenched his jaw and squinted ever so slightly told her he would not back down.

"Maybe. But if she wanted to see me, she would have come for me."

James took her hands and rubbed them tenderly. His hands, although roughened, held a warm strength as if made to protect her.

"Have you ever tried to find her?"

"No." Even she knew it was unfairly self-righteous, but she didn't think she owed anything to her mother. "I know you've suffered loss in your life, too, James. Losing your father. Losing your childhood too soon. Becoming the financial provider for your mother and sister, not knowing if your brother would return from war. It's too much for me to fully comprehend. But at least none of it happened on purpose. Your father didn't vacate your life willingly." *Like my mother*.

He shook his head. "When you love someone, but you can't give them the life they deserve, you do whatever you have to so they have what they need. Maybe that's what your mother was doing."

She watched the vast white farmland pass through the window.

"I bet she wonders about you."

She remained silent. The idea of her mother thinking about her was oddly comforting, yet made her feel worse.

"Nobody's perfect, you know," he said.

"I don't need perfection. I just want honesty."

"Then go find her." He leaned closer.

Her throat tightened and her head threatened to escape her body and float to the velvet ceiling of the train car.

"Sadie, don't waste your time out of fear."

The only sounds were muffled conversation around them and the click clacking of the train and the occasional squeal of the wheels against the rails. When Myrtle appeared in the aisle, Sadie realized she hadn't even noticed that she'd left.

"Are you two lovebirds having a quarrel?"

Their unified silence gave them away.

"Now, now." Myrtle patted Sadie's thigh. "My Stanley and I have had our share of ups and downs. Right, Stanley? Whatever it is, I am sure you two can work it out. We stuck it out and look at us now." Her face lit up as she stretched her mouth into a wide smile, saggy neck skin dangling to the rhythm of the train's motion. She elbowed Stanley awake and reached out her shaky hand, palm side up, cradling a tiny white pill.

By the way Stanley gazed lovingly at Myrtle, it seemed he could still see in her a youthful beauty, and Sadie guessed theirs had been a marriage of true love.

They hadn't married because it was expected, coexisting in thinly disguised satisfaction like her uncle and aunt, perhaps because they'd never known anything different by which to compare?

In any case, Sadie felt very alone. She didn't want to think about her mother and the deep-rooted fear that she'd left her because she wasn't worth the trouble. What mother didn't want her own child? But the more pressing issue weighing on Sadie was how she'd ever be able to forget James and go back to the way things were with Henry. No amount of time or absence could erase what James had awakened inside her.

Suddenly, marrying Henry seemed worse than a death sentence.

****

Sadie stared out the window at the passing scenery. She was running out of time. Soon the train would stop at her station and she'd have to leave James. She thought everything had been progressing between them back at the governor's mansion. Before Henry's proposal. Then again, what had she expected James to do? Deny the ring on her behalf? She had to take responsibility. But there was the unanswered question of this woman James had alluded to that first day in the mansion, the one he'd rather not leave, that had her flustered. She needed answers.

"Why did you return my clutch?" she blurted out.

James seemed thrown by her directness. "Because it belongs to you."

"You could have mailed it."

He opened his mouth and closed it. "I wanted to be sure you got it."

"You said there's someone you're leaving. Who is

she?"

"She…" He trailed off, his eyes downcast.

"Are you in love with her?"

"I am," he said with a hint of a smile and then made eye contact. Was he enjoying this?

"You're in love with her?" she asked. Surely he couldn't mean that.

"I am. You know how I know? I put her wellbeing before my own." He looked smug. Sexy smug, irritatingly so.

"You don't know the first thing about love."

He cocked his head at her.

"Do you make a habit of running around kissing other girls?" Sparks of jealousy ignited her body, prickling her armpits.

"Of course not."

"Or should I ask: do you make a habit of the pursuit?"

"Sadie." He frowned, fueling her anger. Why would he seem remorseful unless she was hitting on the truth? "Hold on, now."

She wouldn't be swayed. "Let me get this straight. You act all noble, saying you would take a fall for this woman—"

"That's true."

"—yet you've been flirting with me from the moment you stepped foot in the governor's mansion. How is that putting her first?"

"There's something I need to tell you."

"I don't know why I thought you were different, James Pasko. You're not. You're just like the rest of them. You wouldn't know love if it hit you over the head." She hesitated, wanting to shake him into action.

"I only hope my uncle made your 'good deed' worth your while. At least you got a free ticket out of it."

"Which I wouldn't have needed had I not missed my train for you. Do you really think that's why I went to the governor's mansion? For a reward?"

"I don't know what to think."

"Please, hear me out."

She wasn't done. "Does she have a name?" Her chest heaved. She felt ridiculous over the accusing outburst, but adrenaline had taken over. All restraint and good judgment—gone. "Are you planning to marry her?"

"That's for her to decide. If she—" He reached for her hands.

She withdrew as if burned by a hot stove.

"Sadie, listen to me. Here me out. I—"

"Don't say another word." Her voice quivered. Of course she wanted him to say something. To stop her. And when he didn't, her anger fueled the dramatic departure she'd already set in motion. She couldn't let go of her pride, so she gathered her things and stood, dropping her book, which James picked up for her. She snatched it back and stuffed everything into her Hermes bag.

"Good day," she said and fled their row.

The man in the fedora one row up was all too happy to accommodate her. As she situated herself and her school bag away from the man she desperately loved, she fought back an onslaught of emotion. She pinched the sting at the bridge of her nose.

****

The way the man in the fedora devoured Sadie with his eyes made James' skin crawl. From his vantage point, he saw the back of her head and her profile when she turned to take in the view as if nothing out of the ordinary had just happened. His pulse pounded out of his chest in frustration.

He looked out the window to see what she must be seeing. Vast farmland silenced by snow and peppered with livestock, weathered barns and grain silos, naked trees. The whiteness, only broken by an occasional home, stretched on for what seemed like endless monotony. The train passed a lone oak tree, its finger-like branches twisting and twining together like unified antlers or lovers' figures entangled with lust. He imagined he was with her under that very tree, on a hazy summer day, and there was no war, no pending marriage, no clock threatening their time together. They had etched their initials into the bark, gone for a swim, and now made desperate love under the canopy of leaves.

But enough with the fantasy. He needed to act fast. She was about to get off the train and he might never see her again. What he wouldn't give to have his brother's confidence right now. Paul would have been beside her, his arm around her, whispering in her ear, making her laugh, telling her the truth. It had never mattered that Paul was more consumed with being loved than he was in loving another. By the time women saw through his veneer, he was already onto the next girl.

Even a row away, her anger was palpable. The tension between them was as thick as Pittsburgh's smog, as steady as the streetlights that burned there all day, and as inevitable as the soot that turned white gloves gray.

James pulled out his journal and scribbled a note to her:

I'm sorry I upset you. From the moment I saw you at the train station in Pittsburgh, I was drawn to you. I couldn't stop thinking about you. I selfishly followed you to Harrisburg. You're right; I had an ulterior motive. But I had no idea you were involved with someone else. Forgive me.

While writing, he felt Myrtle's eyes watching him. He ripped the page out, folded it quickly before he could change anything and scribbled her name on the front. Myrtle took it from him and tapped her shoulder.

"Go easy on him, dear."

Sadie's shoulders straightened as she read the note.

The conductor announced the next few stops, the first of which was hers. James watched her helplessly thinking of the zillion other, better ways he could have worded that note. At last she responded and passed it back by way of Myrtle:

Go on.

James wrote underneath her delicate script:

Henry loves you. He has a bright future. You have a bright future together. If that is the life you want, I respect that and will let you walk off this train without another word. I promise. In time you'll see what I see. You were raised in the same world as Henry, not me. We're not as alike as you think. Was it a mistake for me to go to the governor's mansion? What if, without meaning to, I'm changing your life for the worse— leading you off course?

He passed it back to Myrtle who seemed excited about helping to repair their feelings, eager to assist with their back-and-forth note passing. Sadie hunched over. Soon she passed back a response:

And if I don't want this life? What then?

Please, be realistic. Your family would never accept me. I would always be an outsider, bringing you down. You deserve much, much more. If I even return from the war, that is. Remember how I said when someone loves you so much, they know when they're not enough, and they must let go? The way your mother did? I won't stop you from having the best life possible.

He passed the note. This time she crumpled it into a ball.

Anger stirred in his chest. She didn't need him to complicate her life any further. He may survive the war, but in what condition? He had seen the wounded return to their wives and children in McKees Rocks, crippled and broken, unable to work and provide for them, placing a burden on their family indefinitely. He would rather die alone than place that hardship on her.

But what the hell was he doing? He might be an expendable enlistee from Pittsburgh—not even a real soldier yet, with no money, no schooling—but God did he love this woman. He'd fallen in love and if he continued to withhold his true feelings, or worse—continued to allow her to believe a lie—he was essentially no better than Henry, deciding for her what was best, instead of allowing her to reach her own conclusions.

As the train slowed into the station, he hoped it wasn't too late. Would she even look his way again?

"Your stop, dear?" Myrtle asked Sadie.

"I'll get your luggage." James leaped up.

"No." Her voice was distant and cold. "I'll manage just fine." She gathered her belongings and tugged on her gloves, appearing to be in a race to be done with it all so she could get off the train and hurry back to her life before him. Damn her stubbornness.

"Good luck," Myrtle said. "You'll make a lovely bride."

When the train came to a complete stop, passengers stood to put on coats and hats and retrieve bulk items from overhead, blocking James at first. He pushed past to get her suitcase and bags for her anyway, accidentally bumping the man in the fedora. "Watch it, buddy," the man said, scowling.

"I'll carry this for you off the train," James told Sadie.

"I said I'm fine," she replied, jaw set, not looking at him at all while ripping the suitcase handle from him.

Look at me, look at me, James thought.

Despite being raised with a sister, or maybe because of it, James was the first to admit he'd never understand the inner workings of a woman, and especially when she was hurt or angry. He knew the value of keeping quiet during these times. But he couldn't let the best thing that ever happened to him crumble apart when they were so close to being right. Maybe if he'd been assertive back at the governor's mansion, she would have had reason to reject Henry's proposal outright and they would not be saying goodbye now like this.

"James, dear, *we* can use a hand." Myrtle tugged on his coat sleeve, tearing him away from the inertia he'd been battling as Stanley moaned about his hernia while reaching his frail arms up to the netted area that held their suitcase. James reluctantly turned away from Sadie to help Stanley bring down his suitcase. Most of the passengers were gone at this point, eager to be on their way, and the conductor's crackling voice urged departing passengers to move on and remaining passengers to take their seats.

"You would think more of first class, wouldn't you?" Myrtle chuckled about the lack of assistance, her hand lingering on James's bicep.

During this time, Sadie vanished. She had been there one minute, close enough that his cheek would have brushed along the net veiling of her hat had he pulled her to him one last time, and inhaled her scent of clementines and cinnamon, and the next minute, just like that, she'd evaporated, in the same dramatic way she'd described the parting of her mother. James looked desperately out the window. He caught a glimpse of her light-colored dress in a sea of dark suits.

Frantic to stop her, he threw open the nearest window and leaned out, bellowing. "Sadie! Wait!"

She kept walking along the platform, either unable or unwilling to hear him.

"Stop, Sadie!" he boomed, his throat vibrating scratchy and raw with the force of his cries, clawing at his throat to be heard over the roar of the commotion around them and the whooshing and spitting of the trains. He needed to get out there. He flew to the train car door, expecting to fling it open. What was this? No door handle on the inside. The central locking mechanism! Damn first class.

James' fist pounded the door. The window wouldn't budge. He bounded over the seat back to the closest window and threw it open, waving his arms madly. "Sadie Stark!"

A porter had delayed her to load her belongings on

his cart. She spun to face him, one gloved hand anchored on her hip in agitation.

"It's you!" he cried with his every fiber. "You're the one I hate to leave." People were turning to stare. "I lost you once—I won't lose you again!"

At that, something registered because she dropped her Hermes bag like a sack of potatoes and ran toward him, reaching for him as the train spit and hissed. "Your timing is lousy, you know that," she howled breathlessly but was beaming. She covered her mouth, but he saw the crumpled smile. "I expect a letter tomorrow!"

"Where do I send it?" The train edged into motion.

"Prospect. I miss you already."

"I miss you more," was the last thing he choked out before the train had snapped their connection the way telephone operators click a switch. His last words may have been lost to her, but nobody would stop them now. He'd spend the rest of his life proving himself to her if that's what it took.

Chapter Fourteen

Sadie plunked her tray of corned-beef hash and overcooked vegetables on the cafeteria table and slipped onto the bench across from Ruth, her best friend since Philosophy 101. "I think, therefore I am," had been Ruth's quirky introduction, quoting Descartes, and Sadie had instantly liked her.

"There you are!" Ruth said. "I've been looking for you all day."

"I've been so busy I can barely catch my breath."

"So, who're you taking?"

"Where?"

"To the school dance."

"It's tonight?" Sadie was in a fog. She had completely forgotten about the Snow Ball. Or was her subconscious at work?

"I asked Jack," Ruth gushed. Jack was a first-string starter on Haverford's basketball team. When she wasn't slouching, Ruth stood a head taller than every other girl in the room and was eye level with the boys. Except for Jack. Sadie thought they'd make beautiful offspring together. Ruth feared their future brood would be freakish and gangling.

"I'm not going." Sadie told her, diving into her corned-beef hash then spitting it out. She'd have preferred a peanut butter sandwich—anything but Spam or cafeteria food—but her lab work on campus had run

Carolyn Menke

late and she'd needed to confide in Ruth, who had returned from break later than expected, about Henry and James.

"What's eating you?" Ruth asked.

The seats around them filled. Her update would have to wait. "I feel scatterbrained lately. Overwhelmed. I guess that's typical at the start of the term."

"Too busy on a Friday night to take a break for the dance?" Ruth pursed her lips, not buying it. With the war going on, finding a date was challenging. Bryn Mawr students tended to date boys from Haverford or the University of Pennsylvania, a short train ride away.

"If only you were as diligent about your social life as you are with your studies," Ruth said.

"And besides, I have kitchen duty," Sadie said. Kitchen duty was the chore their housemother assigned. The girls did all of the prep, cleaning and wash to offset their room and board, not that Sadie couldn't have afforded more. She had her reasons for choosing this lifestyle at school. The ability to work for something made her feel less of a burden on her aunt and uncle.

And Sadie reveled in the off-campus privacy, away from the scrutiny that came with being the governor's niece.

"Now I know you're looking for an excuse. Whatever the cook needs, it can wait."

"And risk a demerit from bluenose?" she said halfheartedly of Louise, their housemother.

"I can help you," Ruth offered.

"It's too late anyway."

"Why? Because you don't have a date? Lemme buzz Jack and ask about George."

"Oh no. Definitely no!" She tore off a hunk of bread and spread it with butter. Now would be a good time to tell her about the diamond ring hidden in a cigar box in her closet. Or, of her encounter with James, the thought of which filled her with warmth. James had awakened senses she never knew existed, a feeling so new and fragile she hesitated to tell anyone about it, for fear that speaking of what they had together would cheapen it all. But she could trust a friend as close as Ruth. She'd wait until they had privacy.

"He digs you. And he's no dead hoofer," Ruth said about George. "It is a *dance* after all."

"George who?" Betty, with the long, toned legs joined them across the table. "Lemme guess. Another flat tire who carries a torch for you? Like Henry?"

"Henry and I are—"

"I'm taking Frank." She shifted the focus back to herself. "The army trainee I told you about who's taking courses near here. He's a real gas, that Frankie."

Gaggles of sorority girls buzzed about the hall swapping names of dates and describing dresses, bringing the noise level to maddening heights; matching the chaos of last month's panty raid by the boys at Haverford.

"Ladies!" Emily Prescott-Jenkins interrupted. The statuesque blonde tapped a spoon to her water goblet. As Tradition Mistress, she often used this forum to grandstand. "I have a few announcements to make. First, curfew tonight will be extended…"

A roar exploded from the hall followed by applause.

"…only until midnight. Also, preparations are underway for Hell week. If you haven't picked up the schedule for your courses yet, please do so." Emily rattled on.

Sadie gazed around the dining hall. The sororities were seated together as usual. The pretty one in the center, the bookish one in the corner, and the ritzy girls across from the pretty ones. As the governor's niece, Sadie had been a top pick by the sororities before she even stepped on campus. The upper class sisters had courted her relentlessly like hounds chasing a new scent. A bawdy pair of Kappa Alpha Thetas had whisked her off one night to a Haverford party, breaking the cardinal rule of interacting with a potential pledge prior to formal rush. The Tri-Deltas had bought her gifts and Phi Mu bribed her with the answers to old exams they kept in secret archives for sisters only. When a creepy Haverford senior walked her home from a dance, a Delta Gamma had rescued her, warning her to avoid that boy because he'd dropped his last girlfriend when she became pregnant.

Uncle Edward had advised her against rushing a sorority. No, he forbade it. Any organization that was exclusive, he reasoned, was not one with which she should associate. She'd named all the organizations he associated with only for political reasons, but he had been adamant on the subject, which meant there would be no swaying him. "You'll understand someday," he said, and that was that.

In the end, Uncle Edward had done her a favor. To choose one sorority was to dismiss the others. By graciously declining them all, she hurt no feelings. She was a free agent, not to be judged based on which Greek letters she donned. She would stand on her own merits, fall on her own mistakes, belong to no one.

She wondered what advice her mother would have offered, given her current predicament. Had she married for love? Sadie definitely had questions. Maybe James was right to urge her to find her mother. She indulged in her fantasy of the mother she had constructed long ago, suspecting her fantasy mother was far from the real woman who deserted her.

"I have one final announcement to make," Emily told the student body, clinking her spoon to her glass for attention.

After taking a last swig of milk, Sadie decided to clear her tray and sneak out before the masses. Since their train ride last week, James had written twice, and she couldn't wait to get back and check her mail cubby at the house.

"Congratulations to our very own…"

Sadie stood with her tray, ready to slip away.

"…Sadie Stark, on her recent engagement. On behalf of the entire student body, I wish you the very best, Miss Stark, in this delightful endeavor."

She almost spit the milk out of her mouth. She happened to be standing, which drew more attention, as if she wanted it. Heads turned to gawk and examine her like a chemistry experiment gone awry. Applause filled the air, ricocheting around the hall, followed by murmurs of approval. Sadie wondered how Emily had known, then remembered she dated one of Henry's fraternity brothers.

She took her seat to allow the excruciating moment to pass. Conversation resumed around her. Ruth and Betty looked dumbfounded, their mouths hanging open, eyebrows furrowed in disbelief.

"Is it true?" Ruth asked.

Her prolonged, sheepish silence was answer enough.

Betty took her hand to look for evidence, of which, there was none. "When were you planning to tell us?"

"And who is it?" Ruth asked.

"Henry?" Betty almost choked on her hash.

She bit her nails. "Okay, I'm sunk. Can we get out of here?"

"I, for one, am insulted Emily knew before us," Betty said.

"Seriously, Sadie, what's going on?" Ruth demanded. "Oh my God, are you pregnant?"

"No," she said. "Come on, let's go."

The girls gathered their things. Ruth wrapped her navy wool coat around her lithe, willowy frame, tucking her short auburn hair under a hat. Betty donned a poncho style coat she had received for Christmas. As they descended the steps outside the dining hall, she instinctively tensed against the cold, tying her headscarf securely against the wind, and picking up the pace.

"I want all the details tonight." Betty veered off toward admissions where she worked as a stenographer to help cover school expenses.

Ruth stared at Sadie expectantly. Students filed out of the dining hall, flowing around them like water rushing past rocks. Groups of girls wove by the ivy-covered buildings of Collegiate Gothic architecture. She saw the pristine, snow-laden campus with fresh eyes. It was the first time she'd noticed the ivy in winter. Did it not die like deciduous vines, losing foliage and leaving behind a tangled mess? A mess, like her life.

"Come on. Let's walk and talk." Sadie linked arms

with Ruth.

As they passed the library, Ruth dropped off to return a book. Traffic from the nearby Main Line magnified in the wind.

"I'm listening," Ruth said.

"Henry proposed in front of everyone at dinner. I didn't want to hurt him by saying no—"

"Sadie!" Ruth shook her head.

"He said he would change for me. Everyone was staring at me, expecting me to accept."

"So, you were guilted into it?"

"I know how it sounds. I never meant to make things worse, but I know I have. Aunt Bea and Mrs. McAlister already booked a string quartet and took my measurements for a custom gown." She bit her bottom lip and paused. A carload of sorority girls drove by beeping their horn.

Ruth pulled her in for a hug.

"But, I met someone."

Ruth pulled back. "What? How?"

She bit her lip again. "He chased down a boy who stole my clutch. Then he hand-delivered it to my house. It was so…" She grabbed Ruth's arms and displayed a dreamy look on her face. "…romantic."

"But you're engaged to Henry."

"I know."

"Who is this other fellow?"

"James Pasko. And he isn't just some other fellow. He's like Jack is to you. Do you think it was fate that brought us together?"

"Sounds more like bad luck. Are you sure he wasn't looking for a handout?"

Sadie's face clouded over. "Yes, I'm sure. James

wouldn't do that." She stubbornly turned to take the steps up, disappointed that Ruth would even suggest it. Ruth stopped her.

"I'm sorry," she said.

Sadie knew her friend had her best interests at heart, and her uncle's prominence did cause people to treat her differently.

"Well, do you think it was fate?" Sadie asked again, needing encouragement now more than ever. If it were fate that brought James into her life, maybe fate would keep him there.

"Until you make the unconscious conscious, it will direct your life and you will call it fate." Ruth quoted Jung.

"Real original."

"What are you going to do?" Ruth asked.

"I never should have accepted the ring. I've made a huge mistake."

"Come on, let's get you inside."

They'd reached their three-story brick house. Sadie was finally warm from the long walk, just in time to become overheated as soon as they entered. Inside, Connie, a second year music student, played piano in the wood-paneled foyer for her friends who were practicing a skit for Hell Week. "Welcome back," Connie sang, not lifting her eyes from the music sheets.

"Didn't see or hear a thing," Ruth said.

Sadie's eyes flickered to her mail cubby. She recognized James' handwriting immediately, and crouched before her bounty like a squirrel holding a newfound nut. Then she took the stairs two at a time, tearing open the envelope with shaking hands, her cold cheeks hurting from the smile that spread across them.

Chapter Fifteen

Every muscle in James' body seared with pain as he rolled off the cot on day nine of the mandatory eight-week basic training. His state of general soreness was punctuated by a wound in his shoulder, compliments of the barbed wire infiltration course yesterday. Pete Langley looked at James, slapped James' good side and said, "Buck up, Shakespeare."

James was too tired, hungry, and spent to tease, let alone speak. Instead, he grunted his response. Even his fingers hurt as he struggled to lace the canvas legging of the field boots issued at orientation. Worse than the boots, the Army-issued uniform made of wools and herringbone-twilled cotton didn't keep him warm or dry.

"They're made to last," Langley said.

"Unlike us," James said.

"Hurry up, Butch. Move it," Langley warned the kid on his other side.

Butch pulled a thin blanket all the way to his chin, too rosy and unaffected by puberty to deserve to be shot at in combat. "Shhh, will you?"

Langley yanked the covers back to reveal Butch in the fetal position, obviously unconcerned about being on time. "Shit boy. You're gonna be late to your own funeral."

The men had to follow orders but they picked their

own friends. James met Langley on day one. The lanky, lean soldier from the Bronx bunked next to him. James and Langley had stood out among the new batch of trainees because of their stature, and James liked his straightforwardness.

His other friend was Butch. Butch was sloppy and floundering, breaking tension with wit, and although he was most likely to buckle in fear, he proved his loyalty to the men and therefore earned their respect. Besides, Butch's stepfather had lied about his age so he could enlist sooner, and although Butch never said it outright, the implication was that his old man wanted him gone. James felt sorry for the kid.

Dying was never far from any of their minds, but Butch talked of the future with optimism. His cousin had enlisted at the start of the war, became wounded, was granted an honorable discharge, and sent home. Purple Heart in-hand, the local hero drew attention from girls, even the prettiest one who had remained single.

"I hate to break it to you," Langley said. "But there are easier ways to get laid."

"You just wait," Butch said. "Girls love a hero."

Later that day at the barracks, James withdrew a piece of the stationery Sadie had given him to compose a letter to her. He brought the paper to his face, closing his eyes while inhaling her sweet scent still on it. In his mind's eye he saw the flush of her cheeks and felt her delicate puffs of breath on his skin that night in the attic. Sadie could bring a grown man to his knees. The good Lord knew she'd brought James there.

Dearest Sadie,

How are you getting on? I'm fine here, but miss

you. You asked what it's like on base. They work us hard, and they're training us to do it all, so you shouldn't worry. Promise me. My Drill Sergeant goes by the name of Carr. He has the eyes and sagging jowls of a basset hound. Can you picture that? I'm sure his underbite made for play yard teasing, toughening him up. You know the saying about our flaws also being our assets? Anyway, he's a head shorter than me, but somehow still stings my face with his spit. Don't get me wrong, I give him the respect he deserves. Sadie, please don't worry about me. I've made some good friends in my squad. Just eager to get on with it.

Frank Sarnicki ripped the sheet from James' hands. "Lookie what we have here." Sarnicki sneered, holding it up for everyone to see.

"A regular Shakespeare," Jimmy O'Reilly said.

"Whatcha writin'—a sonnet to your Juliet?" George Miller chuckled.

Some of the men were playing cards and smoking nearby. Others were reading magazines or just resting on their cots. Obviously Frank, George, and Jimmy wanted to establish a pecking order.

James stood up and held out his hand, head cocked, giving Frank a chance to do the right thing. He knew it was good-humored teasing. "At least I have someone to write to other than my mother." He towered over his new Italian friend. "And I like the nickname, thanks."

"What's with the flowery shit you're hiding?"

"I'm not hiding anything." James snatched back his paper. "This was a gift. It's personal. Let's keep it that way."

Langley stood next to James, shoulder to shoulder. He and James dwarfed the other three. "You fellows need something to do?"

"Nah, just bored." George slumped onto his cot.

"Do something productive. Shut your pie hole and sleep. That goes for you gazoonies, too." Langley motioned to Jimmy and Frank who weren't the brightest stars in the sky.

Chapter Sixteen

Sadie bubbled with girlish joy as she belly-flopped onto her bed, tearing open the latest letter from James. She tugged the folded paper free, then agonizingly savored the delicious tug in her belly as her eyes scanned his opening line.

My dearest Sadie,

I can't stop thinking about you. Will you send me a picture? Of course I can't get a vision of you out of my mind, believe me, but a picture is, if nothing else, proof to the fellows how lucky I am. They wouldn't believe me if I tried to put it into words. But a picture!

Squealing, she rolled onto her side, drawing up her tingling legs, and drowning the page in the yellowed glow of the lamplight to better illuminate James' artfully formed words. She needed every single one of those words like she needed every breath in her lungs, probably more.

Last night Jimmy convinced George to pull a good one on Frank. They'd been to the slop shoot and stumbled into the barracks with their big plan. Are you ready for this? They gathered up all of his clothes out of his bunk and dumped them where the Red Cross women were setting up the next day. He had to go get them in his long johns.

Sadie's flesh twitched with envy over those darn donut girls! She knew they were just Red Cross volunteers, and was grateful that they might brighten James' morning, but wouldn't she give every hair on her scalp to trade places with one of them. She tortured herself by picturing one of the ladies accidentally—or intentionally—brushing her fingers along James' arm while handing him a steaming cup of coffee. She sighed and read on.

What happened next might surprise you. Butch stepped up and took the blame for it. Carr probably knew the scrawny kid from Iowa couldn't have been involved, at least not on his own, but he ordered good ol' Butch to scrub the stockpots and grease pit anyway, which reeked something awful. The stench clung to him for days. I have to hand it to Butch, poor kid.

"Oh, Sadie." Betty waltzed into Sadie's room to look in her long mirror while she held her dress across her chest. "Be a dear and zip me, won't you?"

"Which shoes should I wear?" Connie modeled one of each.

"Which one feels better?" Sadie asked while zippering Betty, and wanting to get back to James' letter. Connie stared at her as if logic were beside the point.

"Shake a leg!" Sue pounded on the bathroom door. "You've been in there forever, Dorris. You'll turn into a prune!"

Sadie was back on her bed, eyes trained to the letter.

I need your smile here. You know you could light up the whole base?

Sadie swooned, hugging the letter to her chest as she smiled at the ceiling, swimming in the lush simplicity of his longing. A picture. A smile. Not to worry. He asked for nothing. She wanted to give him everything. These feelings engulfing her from the tips of her toes to the crown of her head were unlike anything she'd felt before—if only she could bottle it up and drink it in.

She quieted the pitter-pat of her pulse with a hand on her heart as if reciting the Pledge of Allegiance, feeling the rise and fall of her chest that responded on its own accord. Then she reached to her nightstand to withdraw the very first letter he'd sent and reread it. She'd memorized every word on the paper that was worn from her handling, but reacted to each line as if seeing it for the first time, every time.

Dearest Sadie,

How are you getting on? I'm glad you're back at school where you belong. They had us run wearing full field gear. Boy, was I a sight. I'm glad you didn't see it. You asked what it's like on base. Well, there's no question they work us hard, but we'll be that much better off. Please don't worry.

Here was one obvious thing she couldn't give him, square here on the page. She'd never stop worrying about him. She read another letter.

Remember Carr? And those pranks? He makes us pay for them. All of us. But it's bringing our squad together. I trust these fellows with my life.

Sadie couldn't help but giggle. Of course it wasn't all prank after prank during basic training, but his hint at camaraderie gave her comfort that he wasn't alone. She saw his eraser marks and the smudges left by the original words, wondering what he'd felt the need to change.

Sadie, I've made some good friends in my squad.

Just eager to get on with it. I miss the sound of your voice, but I hear you singing to me in my dreams.

Yours, James

Louise called Sadie downstairs as one by one the doorbell sounded and the dapper fellows arrived in the foyer, smelling of cologne and hair gel and looking anxious to leave despite Louise's stubborn insistence to take a picture of each couple. Sadie dragged herself around when all she wanted to do was draw a hot bath and reread James' letters.

Sadie fetched vases for all the flowers the dates brought, leaving no time for her to feel sorry for herself that James wasn't taking her to the dance. Last to leave were Ruth, Connie, and Betty, who beamed with the fresh glow of powdered youth and bantered among themselves to release nervous energy. She felt a pang of regret when she closed the door on the last of them.

She faced the stillness of the empty, dark house, imagining how handsome James would have looked tonight had he been her escort instead of bunking down hundreds of miles away.

Familiar sounds were magnified: the chimes of the mantel clock, the creak of the floor boards as she crossed over, the whistle of Louise's teapot on the stove. After fixing a cup of tea for Louise and carrying it to her room upstairs, she decided to tackle kitchen duty, which involved prepping for the next day's meal. Meat and butter were scarce, and everyone, herself included, was sick of Spam. She craved carrot and raisin sandwiches, but the bread would turn soggy if she made them now. Instead she chopped vegetables for a stew.

She thought about her mother. What advice would

she have given Sadie throughout the years? Did she cook special meals like Maria's mother? Mend her own clothes? It was too late for this wistful thinking, yet she couldn't help but speculate how different her life might have been.

The doorbell rang.

Ruth probably forgot her key. She was so absent-minded. Or maybe Betty wore the wrong coat. Before Louise slapped either girl with a demerit, Sadie rushed to the door and flung it open, unprepared for the sight before her.

"Hi baby doll." Henry cocked his head to one side, a devilish grin on his face, his arms open wide. "Gimme a kiss."

"Henry? What are you doing here?" Sadie hid her bare left hand behind her. His ring was still tucked away in the cigar box in her closet.

"Not exactly the reaction I was hoping for. Sorry I'm late." Undeterred, Henry wrapped his arms around her waist. Although not tall—Henry was exactly eye level with her when she wore heels—he had a presence about him she used to find attractive. She'd seen women's heads turn when he entered a room and had swelled with pride in these moments, feeling more important herself when by his side. But Henry thrived more on the attention of others than on her affection. She was merely along for the ride.

Henry leaned in for a kiss; his thin, cold lips doing little to retain breath tinged with gin, his hidden flask pressing against her chest. She responded with a peck and slinked out of his grasp, hurrying to retrieve her camel-colored cashmere coat off the rack before Louise discovered Henry and began a motherly barrage of

127

questioning.

"Let me grab my coat," she told him over her shoulder.

Henry entered the vestibule and rubbed his gloved hands together. "What's the rush? Ah, you missed me, huh, doll?"

She forced a smile, buttoning her coat quickly and wrapping her neck with the red scarf he'd given her for Christmas. He didn't even notice her scarf, or if he did, he didn't say anything about it. She guessed Mrs. McAlister had purchased it for her. It wouldn't be the first time Henry enlisted his mother's help. Would Mrs. McAlister choose their address and name their firstborn, too?

"Baby." Henry grimaced. "You really need a new coat. That thing has seen better days."

"I like this coat."

"That's right. It was hers," he said. After a few strides, he added, "You know what I think? I think it's her loss that she left, not yours. You don't need her." He slung an arm around Sadie's shoulders. "You never needed her. And especially now. I'll take care of you, baby doll."

How could he say that? That any child never needed her mother? Even now that she was grown, she still needed a mother in her life, in some ways more now than ever. Further, she certainly couldn't deny the curiosity James had dredged to the surface along with the feelings she had worked so hard to ignore. What if she did find her mother and the woman rejected her again? She could do without learning the details of some lusty affair with a sleazy playwright, the way her aunt had described the desertion.

She didn't expect anyone to understand, least of all Henry. But then again, hadn't James encouraged her to seek the truth? She thought maybe it was because James, as a writer, had a need to capture authenticity in life. She liked that he required honesty of everyone. Even her.

"Besides," she added. "The coat's a classic."

"Say, you sound like a man talking about his outdated wardrobe. I'm giving you an excuse to shop. What girl doesn't want that? I'll buy you a new one."

On the sidewalk, he pulled her in for another kiss on the lips, which she narrowly dodged by turning her face. He kissed her cheek instead.

"Everything okay?"

"Yes, it's just that I think I'm coming down with a cold." It wasn't entirely untrue. Just mostly.

"Where's the dance?"

She turned him away from campus, toward Lancaster Avenue. The last thing she wanted was to attend the dance and have to continue this charade in front of everyone.

"You need a stop at the bar first? All right then. I like being spontaneous. Makes life more interesting," Henry said. Never in a rush for anything, he draped an arm around her again, threw back his shoulders, and swaggered along with his usual aimless gait.

Snow fell as they approached the Main Line, sprinkling the striped restaurant awnings and parallel-parked cars. Henry's hot breath puffed before them. She veered left toward her favorite sandwich shop where Ruth worked.

"Let's get a coffee." She almost added, "and talk," but decided she wasn't ready for a serious conversation about their future right away. As far as Henry was concerned, their relationship had never been better. The wedding plans were developing, a guest list drafted. Unbelievably, the engagement was shielding her rather than adding pressure, occupying Henry with a false sense of security. Meanwhile, James' upcoming deployment weighed heavily.

"Coffee? It's early, doll. How about we stop in here before heading to the dance?" He turned her toward a bar causing her to lose footing on the sidewalk. He caught her and said loudly for the benefit of the ladies passing by, "Always sweeping you off your feet." The ladies smiled at him and gave her a suspicious once-over.

Inside the bar, it didn't take long before Henry was buying rounds for the throng of patrons, and trying to pour something into her Coca-Cola from his monogrammed flask. He led the inebriated group through the chorus of Louis Jordan's "What's the Use of Getting Sober (When You Gonna Get Drunk Again?)." The men slapped his back, conversed loudly and laughed like long-time friends. Even the bartender looked to Henry first, thanks to his generous tipping. Glassy-eyed ladies, some of them sorority girls she recognized, swarmed Henry, whispering to him God knew what. He seemed amused and completely unaware of her.

Sadie was tempted to leave, but didn't want to walk home alone. If only she had never answered the door to him. At the same time, she did owe him an explanation. As much as he had disappointed her with his lack of sensitivity, she wasn't being honest with him. There was a side to her that she was withholding, that she was afraid to examine; the one James believed existed through an absentee mother.

Henry bumped into a friend from Haverford, dressed in a suit and loosened tie. Sadie recognized his date, Bette Marshall, from chemistry. The threesome made their way toward her.

"Here she is, John, my fiancée," Henry said by way of introduction.

"Shame on you for letting her sit alone." John helped her up from the chair. "Nice to meet you. I think you know Bette." He gestured to his date.

"Yes, hello." She tried her best to appear upbeat.

"If the fellows aren't already blinded by that diamond ring I put on her finger—" Henry took her left hand to show off his latest gift. His face fell at her bare finger. "Sadie, you lost your ring!"

A lie came to her quickly. "No, it was loose. I took it to the jeweler to be sized."

He scowled, looking more than a little disappointed. "But it fit when I put it on your finger. My mother got the measurement from your other ring."

"It's the cold weather—makes all of my rings loose." She smiled apologetically.

"Congratulations." Bette saved her from further embarrassment. "How wonderful about your engagement. Let's have a toast. John? Shall we?"

"Yes, a toast!" John lifted his pointer finger to catch the eye of the bartender—who, like a vulture ready to pick a carcass clean, had already positioned himself and his glass tip jar near Henry.

****

Before long Henry was too drunk to walk her home, let alone get himself on the train downtown.

131

John offered to take them back to Bette's place on Warner Avenue where Henry could sober up before heading home.

With Henry's arm slung across John's shoulders, John supported his weight as they left the dance and made their way down the snow-covered sidewalk, toward the car. Henry shuffled his shoes through the accumulation. She almost slipped on the snow, making a skid mark with her heeled boot, and Bette helped her. She realized Henry hadn't changed like he promised; he'd fallen back to his old ways. How could she depend on a man who continually needed others to bail him out?

She'd rather be dropped off at her house than deal with Henry right now, but at the moment she was his fiancée, ring or no ring on her finger, and at the very least, she was his friend.

"Where to?" John asked in the rearview mirror.

"To Bette's please, so I can help him."

"Suit yourself." John shrugged and pulled away, placing his arm around Bette's shoulders.

At Bette's apartment, Henry collapsed on a chair and ran his hand through his thick red hair. Then he grabbed both arms of the chair saying the room was spinning. John and Bette disappeared into another room with wine glasses and a bottle of merlot. The scratchy music from a record player drowned out whatever was taking place behind Bette's closed door.

Sadie knelt before Henry, tugging on the heels of his shoes one at a time to pull them off, and sighing heavily. She stood. He grabbed her by her elbows to draw her to him, then hugged her around the waist.

"I'm sorry," he said, surprising her.

She was used to alcohol making him obstinate and rougher than usual, not remorseful. "Let me get you a coffee." She pulled away.

"Leave it," he growled. "I just need to sleep it off." He drew her down to sit in his lap. Although he was clammy with dried sweat from his antics at the bar, she kissed his forehead the way a mother comforted a child worn from activity. Once again they had fallen into their comfortable pattern of Henry over-indulging and Sadie standing by his side, consoling him. She saw a glimpse of their future and didn't like it. She tentatively rested her cheek on his head.

"I would be lost without you. You know that, doll?" he mumbled, his hand on her thigh. "You know why I love you?" He spoke each word carefully, as if trying not to slur. "It's because you love me for who I am. You take me for just me, not what I can do for you or who I might become. Everyone tonight at that bar…" He sighed deeply. "They're not my friends. They just want to use me."

She listened. Another part of their pattern unfolded now. He confessed further, sulking, and she listened patiently, making no judgment outside her own thoughts. She used to think this was what real love was about: tolerating and accepting a person unconditionally. But tonight she didn't want to be the passive observer.

"I used to think that way, too. But Henry, give yourself more credit," she said. "You underestimate people."

"How so?"

"Look at John. He didn't have to offer us a ride. There are people in this world who want to be your friend, not use you. And I think you hide behind your money." There, her thoughts were exposed the way a wart broke through the skin after festering under the surface.

Henry was silent, brooding. He pulled out a cigarette from his coat pocket, packed it and lit it. The crinkle of burning paper glowed in the dimly lit room. He inhaled deeply then forced smoke through his nostrils in a steady stream. It dispersed before them— unseen but still out there, like her implied message.

"Why did you come tonight?" she asked.

"To see you, doll."

"But we haven't spent any time together all night."

"I tried…"

"Henry, you say you want to change for me, that you want to be a better man. I want you to do it for yourself."

"You're right," he said. "Money never worked on you. I know you don't care what size diamond you have. That's more for me and I know it. Tell me something, doll. What is it you want?"

She sighed. How did she tell him she wasn't in love with him? That she never really had been, not the kind of love that would sustain them. That she wished to be free of him, but because of their history together she felt obliged to protect him. Instead she said, "Just sober up, Henry." Sadie stood, clenching her fists.

"Are you saying I can't make you happy as I am? Why the hell not?" He took another long drag on his cigarette, holding it between his thumb and middle finger, squinting at her as he exhaled.

"I have to go." She looked for her red scarf and cashmere coat.

"Wait! I'm trying here, baby." He grabbed her wrist.

"I'm leaving. I shouldn't have brought it up."

"Don't." He placed his burning cigarette on an ashtray beside the chair. "Don't leave me. Love me." He wrapped his arms around her waist like before, his hands on her like a familiar lover.

She bristled and wiggled free. "You're drunk. Let go of me." She then realized she liked that he was drunk. It gave her an excuse to walk away like she had every time before. Had she inadvertently encouraged this? Maybe so, maybe not. He knew how she felt about his lifestyle even though she had ignored his rash behavior in the past and allowed him to feel justified. But maybe his drinking was a convenient crutch on her part to keep her distance.

"Fine," Henry slurred with a wave of his hand. Then he went pale white. He grabbed a nearby trashcan and heaved into it, the vomit splattering the insides like canned tomatoes being dumped into a saucepot. She rushed to the kitchen for a dishcloth, which she ran under cool water, twisting out the excess. She hurried back to him, placing the cold, damp cloth on his forehead. He was slumped back in the chair with his eyes closed. A snore and foul stench erupted from his mouth. At last he had passed out. Relief washed over her. Sadie stubbed out his cigarette, threw on her cashmere coat, and left. Her duty, for the time being, was done.

Outside the bitter cold air slapped her face, stinging her eyes, and cutting to her bones. She walked in the direction of Lancaster Avenue making fresh prints with her boots in the snow-covered sidewalks. Damn Henry for making her so vulnerable out here, alone at this time of night. The streets were quiet and void of activity, eerily so. She rounded the familiar corner onto Prospect, stopping outside the row house where she lived when her fingers found a folded paper in her pocket. A letter from James she'd forgotten she'd put there.

My dearest Sadie,

I'm almost done with training. I just got the furlough paper. I'm coming to find you. I never told you this, but I feel like ever since I met you years ago my course had been set. Weeks before I saw you at Union Station, I'd reported to the downtown Pittsburgh office next to the federal building for my physical exam. They gave me two choices next because the uniforms weren't ready. I could either go home for a couple weeks and then pick up my uniform or stay there for a few days and get my uniform sooner. If I decided to stay, I was told I'd have a two-week furlough to wear the uniform. Since I lived nearby, I went home and waited.

That decision saved my life.

I found out yesterday that the other men who chose to stay were denied their promised furlough and were instead shipped out immediately to North Africa. They didn't make it, Sadie.

I went on to meet you.

Now she remembered why she'd placed this note in her pocket, away from the rest. It was the one that sent shivers up and down her spine. She knew he meant to tell her the story to comfort her, but the reality was, nothing eased her fears.

Remember, sweetie, to look for the moon. That moon you see is the same one I see. No matter what separates us in time and place, we have the moon.

The moon. She enjoyed this warm glove of comfort, but her fluttering smile dissolved as God's quiet judgment weighed on her in regard to Henry. She knew she had to return Henry's ring and the sooner the better. Why hadn't she already? She was hurting him more by her slices of the truth—or whatever she called them—he needed the whole truth and nothing but. And more than that, she owed it to James.

She observed the darkness of her friends' windows as she made her way up the last stretch of sidewalk. They were probably home from the dance by now, washed up, and asleep in their warm beds, dreaming of their boys doing the jitterbug. If only her dreams could be so simple. She would have to wait until morning to tell Ruth what happened.

The porch light flicked on and Louise appeared in the window, her face puckered in anger.

She does care. Sadie smiled in spite of herself.

After climbing the steps, and rushing through the open door with her head down, she bolted upstairs taking two steps at a time and flung herself onto her bed. Still wrapped in her mother's cashmere coat, with James' letter buried in her fist, she imagined his body close to hers again, folded into his embrace to block out all the things that scared her to her core. That lurking fear, clouding her senses and coloring the whole thing murky, wouldn't let her breath come evenly. It was only a matter of time before James deployed and she could only guess at what dangers lay ahead. She clung to the hope she'd see him again, and all she could do now was wait.

Chapter Seventeen

"Ready," Langley said.

James looked through his spotting scope while positioned behind Langley. He'd already called the direction of the wind using the grass and trees. Now he focused on the target. "Send it."

Langley fired.

James saw the trace of the bullet despite the darkening light. "You hit it. Like you do every time." When Langley didn't respond right away, James teased him. "Did you doubt yourself?"

"I'm only as good as my spotter, which means I never doubt myself."

James grinned. Sniper and spotter, they were a team.

When they finished practicing, James scribbled in the logbook while kneeling on one knee.

"Tell me, what's it like?" Langley said as they packed up and made their way back to base. "How you see the world, I mean...being colorblind."

"Just like you do." James adjusted his pack on his back while they walked. He didn't want to be thought of as special or more important than anyone else. They were all important.

"Come on," Langley said. "Squads have gone down because of their spotter alone. And those who have stayed alive, well, let's just say I'm glad you'll be on my side and not on the Jerries." He used the derogatory name for the Germans.

Not long ago, James had been like the rest of the men, lumped together as trainees, learning how to handle his gun, practicing with range estimate. None of it had been difficult, particularly finding the targets. Then again, he wasn't like the other men.

"I guess you could say I see patterns that you can't. It's as hard for me to explain as it would be for you to tell me what you see. Does that make sense?" James asked. "Don't think I'm lucky. It's a trade-off. I'm told I can't see all the colors you can. But then again, you never miss what you never had."

He thought about Sadie then. If they'd never met and fallen in love, would he be less afraid to die?

"But our night training. You see better than me," Langley said.

It was true. Not only had James' colorblind ability to see pattern recognition elevated him to icon status in the spotter realm, his improved night vision made him a highly valued commodity. His colorblindness helped him to locate targets others couldn't readily see. Even the long shots.

"Did you know Carr had me take more tests?" James asked. Now was as good a time as any to tell him. When he'd enlisted they said he'd temporarily be assigned to an infantry unit. James had worried that his unit would deploy before he got his transfer. The transfer had come through.

"I heard." Langley looked up at the sky while they plodded through the brush. "You'll be great up there, James. Just promise you'll look me up when this is all over."

"Will do." James choked on the words. He had mixed feelings about the transfer. He'd grown close to his squad; they all depended on each other. But he was willing to do whatever it took, serve where he was most needed. And besides, who wouldn't want to fly in a B-17 bomber? He was eager to experience flying, and the Boeing Flying Fortress was as good as any chance to try it.

His legs suddenly felt heavy with dehydration, his shoulders weary with fatigue. No matter how fit or well-toned, at the end of the day, his muscles twitched with overuse, ready to give out. Only one thing kept him going. But she would soon be an ocean away.

"What's in store for us?" James asked Langley as they neared camp. Langley pulled out a pack of Lucky Strikes and James flicked on his lighter.

"I'll tell you what. Enough running and push-ups to make everyone cry." He eyed James while taking a long drag. "Except for you." He blew smoke out the side of his mouth. "I'm guessing you can do a three-mile run in under—"

"No, I didn't mean what's in store for us here." James redirected Langley to his original question. "I meant over there." He tilted his head.

Langley narrowed his eyes with another drag but didn't respond.

****

The darkness at Fort Dix was everywhere. It was dark when James woke and dark when he hit the cot. The winter sky let little light through to indicate the earth's rotation; it was just business by the clock. Military time. James reverted to the sleep cycles of a newborn, void of circadian rhythm to differentiate day from night and the ability for independent reasoning or free will.

Some of the men had no direction prior to enlisting. The military gave them new purpose. As the days turned into weeks, the individual men morphed into a singularity that provided security. Whatever turn of events that brought each of them here had taken a temporary back seat to their common goal.

But at the end of the day, everyone did need something. Whether it was to escape the poverty of the streets, make a grandfather proud, or attract a pretty girl back home, each soldier had his reason for being there and his reason for needing to survive.

James had Sadie.

He had everything—everything to lose.

Chapter Eighteen

At the break of dawn, James propped his pack behind his head, settling on the military convoy. He and Midge had hitched a ride. Before long, they reached Philadelphia and stopped to let men off and reload.

"There's my boy!" Midge's cigar-smoking father slapped his son proudly on the back. They embraced while his mother squeezed his cheeks and crumpled into a crying fit into her handkerchief. The elder Hodge was surprisingly tall with long limbs; the two seemed diametrically opposed, but happy as father and son could be. James forced a smile in their direction even though inside the boy in him burned to recall a time when his own father had shown him such pride.

"James, is it?" Mr. Hodge shook his hand. "I've heard all about you. You must join us. Marion can make up the couch—"

"I'm roasting a chicken, James, with all the fixings." Marion Hodge dabbed her puffy swollen nose. "And our Sue will be at the table." She winked.

"Honey." Mr. Hodge chuckled. "Let him be. Can't you see he's off to see his girl? I know that look in his eyes."

"Thank you." James smiled downward. "I do need to be on my way." He shook hands with everyone, smug with thoughts of who his dinner partner would be tonight.

His calves twitched with a burn to get moving to her. As he traveled out of town on foot, he hitched a few rides to get himself up Lancaster Avenue. His hamstrings gave and stretched with every step the same way he gave in to his wanting for Sadie. He practically ran the last few miles through the snow-dusted sidewalks, past gauzy veiled cars, storefronts, and along a wintry stretch of road.

As he neared a busy corner, a bustling sandwich shop caught his eye. A group of satisfied customers burst out the door, one man lit a cigarette by cupping his hand around the flame and sucking in his cheeks. James entered to get out of the cold and catch his bearings, order a hot drink.

"Ruth!" the cook hollered behind the grill while slapping a greasy slip of paper onto the counter and clanking plates of steaming eggs on top and around it.

"Got it!" A slender redhead rushed over. She loaded the oval plates onto her forearm and spun around to deliver the food.

James watched her curiously, remembering Sadie's friend by the same name. She fit the description. He took a seat on the bar stool near the cook's sizzling griddle and checked the address on the piece of paper folded in his pocket.

Ruth asked without looking at him, "What can I do for ya?" She fished in her apron pocket for a pencil.

"Can you help me find 411 Prospect?" He held up Sadie's letter with return address.

Ruth squinted at the piece of paper until she realized what it was and who he was. She dropped her tablet and pencil. "James? Sadie's James?"

"Where can I find her?"

She dragged him to the door. "She's on her way to the train now. You better hurry!"

"Which way is the station?"

"That way." Ruth pointed back toward the way he had come. "Turn left on Bryn Mawr Avenue," she yelled since he was already out the door.

"Thanks!" James yelled over his shoulder.

"If you reach Morris, you've gone too far!"

The wind had picked up and snow swirled around like the inside of a shaken globe. With every step he took, James felt lifted in the air ever so slightly, propelled faster by the wind on his back or some greater power. He wondered where she was headed. If he couldn't catch her, they may not see each other again.

At the station, a trickle of passengers was exiting onto the platform. Sadie wasn't among those awaiting the outbound train. He swore as he hunched over to catch his breath. He'd try the other side of the tracks. He ran down the stairs, crossed through a tunnel, and tore up a set of stairs on the other side, taking the steps two at a time.

Amidst the huddle of passengers waiting for the downtown train, Sadie turned just as James ran toward her. They flung into each other's arms, kissing.

"You're here!" She threw her white-gloved arms around his shoulders and neck, standing on her tiptoes. She peeked at him between kisses. James hoisted her off the ground and spun her around, his hold snug around her waist. When he stopped, the words he had spent the last two months imagining he'd say escaped him.

"What are you doing here?" she asked breathlessly. "Did you finish training? You're not hurt, are you?"

She searched his eyes.

He held her face tenderly. "I'm fine. Better than fine." He smiled smugly.

"But, how did you find me?" Swirling snow caught in her hair. He tucked a stray curl behind her ear.

"Ruth."

"I can't believe you're here. I knew you'd come though." She smoothed his jacket and fixed the collar the way a woman made a fuss over her man. This simple act of intimacy caused his heart to beat faster, his throat to thicken. He kissed her forehead. She beamed at him with the smile that had kept him going through basic.

The Pennsylvanian rolled in, screeching to a halt. People shuffled forward like herded cattle.

James pressed his lips to hers again, hardly believing this was all happening, and a little bit in awe of her just like the first time all over again.

"I have an idea," he said. "I want to take you ice skating in Rockefeller Center. I'll have you home by curfew."

"Are you asking me on a date?" Sadie teased. "Like a normal couple?" She looked at his outstretched hand, which was eager to lead her on an adventure.

"I am," he said with a glint in his eye as the crowd pushed past them forming a line in anticipation of where the doors would swallow them up. "Does this mean you're coming?"

"How much time do we have before you deploy?"

"One day, eighteen hours…" He looked at the station clock. "Fifteen minutes. Not that I'm counting."

"What about your mother and Anne? Paul? They'll want to see you before you deploy."

"Anne gave me strict orders to find you, and I have. Besides, I need to be on 42nd and Broadway when it comes time to—"

Sadie placed a finger to his lips. "Don't say it."

He grinned. "Do you need to tell someone you'll be gone that long?"

"Ruth already knows I'm with you. She'll cover for me."

****

James stowed their coats and settled into his aisle seat beside her at the window. "Where were you headed?"

A shadow crossed her face. "To see Henry. I should have returned the ring long ago. I wanted to do this before..." She turned to face him in her seat. "I suppose I have a lot of explaining to do. To everyone. Mostly to you."

"It's okay." James brushed the subject away. The last thing he wanted was for her to feel upset or for them to waste even one second more talking about Henry. "You're here with me now. That's enough for me. Let's live in this moment."

"I like that."

They sat in silence as the train chugged along, gaining speed.

"James, do you believe things happen for a reason?" she asked.

He considered the fortuitous events Anne called fate that had led him to where he was right now. "Before, I never believed in chance or luck, in heaven or hell. I made things happen through hard work and decisions based on facts."

It was true. When calamity had struck, James never

blamed God or searched for meaning in it. It just happened. In the same way people aged, teenagers rebelled, and babies sought to walk, life went on. Who could explain such things?

"But when we crossed paths again, I was forced to reconsider." He reached his arm around her and kissed her on her crown while she nestled into him.

"There's something I've never told you."

"Okay," she murmured.

"When I enlisted, I failed my physical exam."

She pulled away to search his eyes. "You did? Why?"

"I'm color-blind."

She tilted her head and crinkled her brow, probably not understanding what this meant.

"They said I have deficient vision. That I see colors differently. But here's the fascinating part. My decreased ability to see green means I can see through or detect camouflage."

"So, your color blindness is a good thing?"

He nodded. "I'll be in aircraft scouting enemy positions." He didn't add that it also meant he was disqualified from being a commissioned officer and that he could forget about a career as a pilot. "The way the doctor explained it to me is that camouflage only works by disguising an object using color. Since my perception isn't keyed to the same colors, the camouflage is defenseless against me."

"Does this mean you won't be on the front line—you'll be away from danger?" The lilt in her voice crushed him.

Nobody was safe. No way would he say that, though. Instead he skimmed over the idea. "It means

I'll fly over enemy lines to spot camouflaged troops, bunkers, weapons. Drop bombs. Fly in a Flying Fortress. You want to see a picture?" He pulled out his pack and found one.

While she waited to see the picture she said, "So, you do believe things happen for a reason."

"I do now." He stopped to study her.

He felt the charge between them. What he wouldn't do to wake up next to this willful, shining woman day in and out. Anything seemed possible with her by his side.

Chapter Nineteen

Shafts of light shone down from the three-story-high, half-dome windows of Grand Central Station. James led the way. Despite the crowds, with James' warm hand around her own, Sadie felt safe. On the busy city street, cabs honked and jockeyed for position in lunch hour traffic. They crossed the street, and a blast of warm, urine-tinged air wafted through the sewer grate. Sadie marveled at the energy and rhythm of Manhattan as they neared Times Square.

"Isn't this something?" James drew her to him without breaking stride, kissing the top of her head. "You and me, in New York City. No place to be, no one to answer to."

"It doesn't get any better." She beamed at him and they stopped to kiss, an island while the city rushed on around them.

"I love you." He lifted her off the ground in his embrace.

"I love you, too." It felt natural, the words spilling forth in the same way her lungs drew air. Effortless. Nothing was staged or forced when it came to James, no pretenses.

They passed a store advertising watch and jewelry repair, a barbershop and a man selling hot sweet potatoes out of a cart. An enormous Camel advertisement spanned six storefronts. In the picture, a

149

paratrooper held a lit cigarette, his mouth formed an O and real smoke came out of it. A pack of Camels was prominently displayed beside his face.

When they waited for the traffic light to change, she saw a man wearing a U.S. Coast Guard hat and uniform talking on a courtesy phone in the GI phone center in Times Square.

"Who do you suppose is on the other end?" Sadie nodded toward the man.

"I think it's his sweetheart. He's telling her he'll be home soon." James pulled her in for another kiss.

"Or maybe it's his weepy mother, asking if he's getting enough to eat," she said.

The image was so poignant it brought tears to Sadie's eyes. She swiped them away, embarrassed by her display of emotion when James noticed and stopped her.

"Say." He stepped in front of her and cradled her face in his hands. His gesture made her erupt with more tears. It wasn't like her to be so emotional. All of her senses were heightened like never before.

"I'm okay, I'm okay." She wanted to stay strong for him. He rubbed her upper arm as they rounded the block by Radio City Music Hall.

"I wonder if my mother ever performed there."

James seemed ready to say something, but didn't.

The lights at Rockefeller Center were dimmed to conserve energy and on this gray wintry day, it seemed much later than it was, which was disappointing. They rented skates, laced up, and made their way onto the ice, the cool air fresh on her cheeks. She was determined to let James take her mind far away from his pending departure. She focused only on the rhythmic slicing of the ice made by their skates and the sheer joy of James' tug of her hand as they rounded each bend.

"Not bad for a city boy," she teased. In fact he looked stiff and skated like he was running, not gliding, with his shoulders rounded like the hunchback of Notre Dame.

"I have many undiscovered talents," James joked back and then proceeded to slip and fall, but not before releasing her hand so he wouldn't take her down with him. "And none of them are on ice."

She turned and skated back to him, circling herself to a stop while he got up, grimaced dramatically, and then smiled.

"I can see that." She suppressed a laugh.

James was up, back to his awkward run-skating, and with his arms outstretched like he was juggling balls. "Hey, don't be so quick to judge. I'm a fast learner." James crouched into a turn, and then attempted to skate backwards, but failed, almost colliding with, and taking out, a boy and his mother. Fortunately the rink wasn't crowded.

A group of sailors glided past doing tricks in their white hats, leaping in the air. James frowned at them and whispered, "Show offs."

She decided to end his misery. "How about we warm up with hot chocolate?"

"Now? I was just getting the hang of it." James tried his best again but narrowly missed a pair of girls on his right.

She led him off the ice where they switched back into their shoes, entered the rink-side cafe and ordered hot chocolate.

While sipping their drinks, James grew serious, set down his mug, and took her hands. "Sadie, I wish I had money to buy you a fancy goodbye gift."

"James, you don't have to…"

"But I do have something for you."

"You do?" She studied his face, her glance darting from one eye to the other.

"I do. And I will help you with it, if you want."

"What do you mean?"

He reached inside his coat pocket and pulled out a piece of worn, wrinkled paper. He handed it to her.

"What's this?" She unfolded the paper and read it aloud, "McSorley's Old Ale House?" She looked at him confused. "East 7th Street between 3rd & 2nd?"

"It's the saloon where we…I mean you can begin your search." James suddenly sounded vulnerable.

"My search?"

"For Audrey McCall." He said her name evenly, studying Sadie's face for a reaction. "Formerly Audrey Harrigan. McCall was her stage name."

"My mother—you found her?"

Seemingly encouraged, he continued. "Not exactly. Remember my buddy, Langley? He grew up in Manhattan. When I told him I was looking for an actress from the '20s and showed him your picture, he asked his family about her. Turns out his aunt was in the theater crowd at that time. She knew all the major players including the playwrights."

"The playwrights?"

"Rex Wyatt is his name. The one who was involved with Ms. McCall. The one who may be your father." James' eyes poured into hers.

"And now she's a barkeep at a saloon?" she asked

incredulously.

"No."

"What does this address mean then?"

"McSorley's is for men only. Langley's aunt said Wyatt is a regular there. I'm thinking he may know where Ms. McCall is. It's a start anyway." James treaded lightly, probably unsure how to interpret the way she dipped her view down to her lap. He knew she'd been apprehensive about finding her mother and learning the truth about her. "I'm sorry, maybe this was a bad idea."

She leaned forward and silenced him with a kiss. "James, this is the sweetest thing anyone has ever done for me. Thank you." She kissed his hand and then held it to her cheek. Then she put the paper away in her clutch. "After we finish here, let's walk through Central Park."

"What about McSorley's?"

"Let's not complicate our time together with a wild goose chase."

"Why not? Aren't you curious?"

"Not any more."

"I don't believe you."

She bit her bottom lip and looked away. Her voice was shaky. "There was a time when I would have given anything to know her. But I'm an adult now and I think I made it out okay despite her. Don't you?" She tried to lighten the mood.

"I know you're afraid."

"I'm not," she insisted. "Maybe a little." She took out her compact mirror and lipstick.

"Sadie, it's your choice if you want to find her."

"I know. I've made my decision." She finished

with her lips and clicked her clutch shut.

"You're right." James pressed his warm lips to her hand.

"I am?" She eyed him. "I am," she repeated, this time with determination, biting her bottom lip.

"There's just one thing you might want to know…" James stood and reached for his wallet. "Oh never mind."

"Tell me."

"It's just that…" James let his arms fall to his sides. "Langley's aunt, she knew about the time you had the measles."

"She did? But that was well after Audrey left."

"She was close with Ms. McCall then. She knew about your love of ice skating. And your scar…" He rubbed her gloved hands.

She pulled away. "How did she know these things?"

"It doesn't matter. Like you said, she's not worth your time anymore." Out of the corner of his eye he studied her while withdrawing the cash to pay the bill.

"Wait." She saw the hurt in his eyes. He really wanted to do this for her. She understood now. "Let me get this straight. Langley's aunt knows my mother but isn't in contact with her any more? She gave Langley the address of the tavern where a playwright frequents who might know where she is? You'd rather spend our last day together hunting down the woman who gave me up?"

"More or less."

She gazed out the window and sighed.

"Just promise you'll think about it."

Finding her mother was James' goodbye gift. She

couldn't deny him the decency of at least seeing it through. The chance that an old address was even accurate was slim. She would make a concession for him because she loved him, and see where this led. Although finding her mother terrified her, disappointing James upset her more. And, she had to admit his plan was working. He'd piqued her curiosity. "Okay, where do we go from here?"

****

When they reached the East Village, a wave of nausea washed over her. Sadie ignored her nerves and plowed on. They passed a smokehouse where people lined up for their fish and an Italian bake shop called Angelo's.

"Langley's aunt found a New York Times article from years ago that covered Miss McCall's starring role in a Broadway hit. She was still unmarried."

"I still can't believe you tracked down all this information for me."

James gestured toward a coffee shop and they ducked inside, finding a small round table in the front window for Sadie to sit at and wait.

"Good luck." She tiptoed up to press her lips to his, squeezing her eyes shut. Her vantage point was just right. James loped across the street and entered the tavern.

The brick exterior of McSorley's was nondescript. Two big windows graced the front on either side of a double door entrance. A shadow from a fire escape grating covered the "McSorley's" part of the name but she guessed the legibility of the name didn't matter; regulars probably kept this place afloat. "McSorley's Established 1854" was painted on the window to the left of the front door and "McSorley's Old Ale House Restaurant" was painted on the right. Four wood barrels lined the sidewalk also labeled with the name of the bar. An American flag hung proudly out a window above the establishment.

Was today the day she would meet her mother and father after all of these years? She suddenly realized how much she really wanted this to happen. Especially with James by her side.

The waitress, trying to make conversation, asked Sadie if "her man" was hanging a wishbone in McSorley's to reclaim when he returned from the war like the soldiers did during the First World War. She shuddered to think how many were still hanging.

To distract herself, she replayed all that had transpired between them since they met in Pittsburgh. But her thoughts kept returning to her mother. Would she believe Sadie was her daughter? She had the compact mirror as proof. What if she was angry Sadie had found her, robbing her of the privacy and emotional separation she clearly preferred? The fact that her mother knew of her childhood illness both softened her but also angered her. Had nothing been enough to draw her mother out of obscurity to find her?

She was on her second glass of water, crunching on ice to fight her nerves, when James re-emerged and loped across the street, trailing sawdust from his shoes. He made eye contact with her through the window, smiling, and this eased her worry for the moment.

"You're not going to believe this." James was out of breath. "I have something better than an address."

"You met Wyatt?"

"No. He wasn't there. But the barkeep knows your

mother. Sees her every day in fact."

Sadie puzzled over this coincidence.

"Because she occupies the same building." James leaned over, draped his arm around her shoulders, and pointed to McSorley's through the window. "See that American flag, sweetheart? It's hanging out of your mother's window."

Chapter Twenty

Sadie stood in the drafty hallway in front of apartment 1B, grateful to the stranger who held the door for her to get into the building. She stripped off her gloves, shoved them in her coat pockets, and rubbed her clammy palms on her skirt.

According to Langley's aunt, Audrey had corresponded with someone over the years. Had it been with Nanny? Mrs. White? Knowing Audrey was interested in her life gave Sadie the courage to face her fears of being rejected. More than that, she needed answers. James was right about this. She took a deep breath and with a shaky hand, buzzed the apartment.

As she waited, she realized she was still wearing Henry's ring. She tried to work it off, not wanting to call attention to her own mistake, but there wasn't time. The deadbolt unlocked with a jolt and the door opened a couple of inches, held by a chain. A fair-complected woman with flapper-length dark hair eyed Sadie. The lady's cheeks were hollow with age, but her beautifully set eyes were even more striking in person than she'd expected.

"I'm looking for Audrey McCall," Sadie said, unprepared for the sight of her mother.

"Who wants to know?" Her voice was breathy and guarded.

Sadie couldn't get the words out. A whiff of

Chanel No. 5 caused her throat to restrict. She forced her shoulders straight and summoned the courage she knew she possessed. She could do this. "I... Well. You—"

"Spit it out, dear. I don't got all day." Audrey strummed her fingers on the door and spoke with the hurried arrogance of a performer who couldn't be bothered with a stammering fan.

Sadie met her gaze. "I came because..."

"Oh, yes, yes, of course," Audrey interrupted. "Why didn't you just say so? You were sent by the agency." She shut the door abruptly, wiggled off the door chain, then opened it for Sadie to enter. "They didn't tell me to expect you so soon. Please, come in." She motioned for Sadie to enter, shut the door, clicked the deadbolt, and jiggled the chain in place. "Can't be too careful these days."

"Of course," Sadie agreed, realizing the honorable thing to do at this point was to correct Audrey for mistaking her to be hired help. But the moment passed.

"You'll have to excuse me. Had I known you were coming I would have tidied up. Let me take your coat," Audrey offered.

The moment Sadie handed it over, she realized her mistake. She'd been more concerned with whether her mother would recognize her than with anything else and now the familiar coat rested in her grasp. Audrey hesitated, studying the coat with curiosity. "I had a coat like this many years ago."

She knew! Sadie swallowed and clasped her clammy hand to her throat, letting her mouth slack open.

Audrey spun to face her. "I'm sorry. I don't think I

ever caught your name, Miss…"

Sadie panicked. Was this a test? Was Audrey asking her to reveal herself? Audrey looked at her expectantly.

It was a simple question, really.

And one Sadie couldn't bring herself to answer. "Pasko," she replied, feeling James' name wrap her in confidence.

"All right, Miss Pasko. Nice to meet you. Audrey McCall. But you already knew that." She shook Sadie's hand.

If she only knew, Sadie thought. Or did she know? The woman was a goddamned actress after all.

Sadie wasn't sure if she should feel guilty for deceiving the mother she'd spent her entire life wondering about or anger toward the woman for walking out on her.

Audrey moved across the cluttered, unkempt apartment with the grace of a ballerina, leading Sadie to a high-back chair near a window that happened to be decorated in pigeon stool.

"Shoo! Evil things." Audrey waved her arms thereby sending a flurry of wings flapping against the glass.

Sadie was surprised how much taller she was than her mother. In her childhood fantasy, her mother loomed above her, lifting her up and carrying her away. It was the same feeling she'd had when she visited a childhood home as a young adult—the rooms seemed smaller, the ceiling lower, and the foyer less grand.

"Can I get you something? Coffee—tea?" She glanced at her watch. "Maybe not here, but somewhere it's time for a martini." Her laugh exposed the hint of crow's feet, which only added to her beauty in Sadie's mind—proof of a full, happy life. With the exception of her aged hands and angular face, having lost the plumpness of youth, Audrey looked very much the way Sadie imagined her from the picture in the attic.

"Have you decided?"

What *had* she decided? Part of Sadie now wanted her mother to discover who she was so that she could confront her the way she deserved to be confronted. Mothers did not just abandon their children. Shouldn't her mother recognize her? Was she not even worthy of the slightest pull of recognition?

Or was she faking it?

"Tea, please," Sadie said as calmly as possible, trying to squash the nausea rearing its ugly head. Her pulse throbbed into her temples. She had the right to deceive this woman who had disappeared from her life years ago—at least until she got the real story. This was her chance to see her mother for who she really was.

"Coming right up. Please, make yourself at home."

Home. Interesting choice of words, Sadie thought. She sat and glanced around what would have been her home while the stranger in the kitchen filled the kettle and clanked it on the stovetop to boil. The stranger who was her mother.

In her absence, Sadie gawked at the apartment's disarray. A full ashtray perched on the fingerprint-covered glass coffee table, alongside a tarnished silver serving tray and its contents. Clutter and knickknacks abounded. She had to smile when she imagined her aunt curling her upper lip in disdain. The apartment was comfortable, unpretentious and—most importantly—real. Sadie felt herself relax one notch, despite the strangeness of the situation.

Audrey returned with a tray bearing two Fiestaware cups and a matching sugar bowl and saucer. "Like I said, I would have tidied up. Then again, I've never been much of a housekeeper. But don't write that." She caught herself and laughed nervously. "Oh, who cares what you write about my clutter. I am who I am. Not ashamed of it."

She was nervous, Sadie thought, which humanized her. And she was expecting her to, what? Write a story for the paper?

"You have a lovely home. Cozy."

"Tell me you're a better stenographer than you are a liar," Audrey said with unintended irony, then, probably sensing Sadie's bristled reaction, quickly added, "That's a joke, honey! I live modestly, within my means. Proud of it. Now, are you ready to begin?" She pursed her lips. "Don't you have something to write with?"

"I must have left it at home." She could act the part, too. She'd had enough practice pretending with Henry and her aunt, people she'd spent her whole life trying to please. And now she deserved an answer to the question—why?

As Audrey retrieved a fountain pen from her secretary in the far corner, Sadie spied a framed picture of a baby, displayed on the marble-top table near the tufted chaise and her heart leaped into her throat. She craned her neck to get a better view of the picture, but her mother was back. And Sadie wanted to hide her identity a bit longer until she got the honest answers she was after. Once her mother discovered who she was, how could she believe anything the woman told her?

"Let's begin. You do know shorthand? And you're prepared to type this up?" Audrey asked.

It seemed like a silly question to ask a stenographer. Unless…she'd play it out.

"Yes, of course." Sadie sat up tall.

"Good. Where should I start?" Audrey asked.

"Start with your full name, date of birth, and occupation."

"I was born on New Years' Day, 1902, Audrey Ann Harrigan. I never liked my first name, but I was named after my father's mother and she had a set of lungs, according to our church choir. I suppose I lived up to my namesake. Oh, that sounds dreadfully pompous." She frowned. "Scratch that."

Sadie pretended to draw a line through the words. "Did your grandmother live to see you become successful?"

"Successful? Oh, honey." Audrey shook her head then stopped herself. "What does success mean to you, Miss Pasko?"

The use of James' name strengthened Sadie every time her mother said it. They were working up to her reason for coming, and she leaned in to her next question.

"Weren't you Broadway's top musical star of the twenties?" Sadie cleared her throat and perched on the tip of her seat. Despite the thrill of posing as James' wife, nausea returned; she willed it away. "Your first and longest success was Gloria, the story of a poor maid who rose to stardom as a ballerina."

"You're not as unprepared as I thought," Audrey mumbled. "Well, people probably still think of me as that frivolous girl of my youth with a bad attitude and nice gams." She crossed her legs. "The one who cares more for a petting party or a man with a car than the political boiling pot her country is in. Am I right? Do I look like that woman?"

"Yes," Sadie said, quick with the answer.

"Your job is to listen and take shorthand. Don't tell me what you think I want to hear." Audrey lit a cigarette on a long holder and played with the layered, beaded necklaces dangling against the bodice of her true red tea dress. Despite herself, Sadie admired Audrey's cavalier attitude. She had been a flapper at the height of her career, and carried the independent toughness with her.

Sadie tried to write it all down, but struggled to form the words. The high of being this close to her mother coursed through her veins and revved her hand to write faster.

"You may not believe it, but," Audrey said, flexing the heeled foot of her crossed leg then flicked the end of her cigarette, missing the ashtray, "these legs made Ms. McCall queen of the Charleston and the Bunny Hug." She chuckled to herself, lost in thought. "Yes, it's true. That was a very long time ago. But I am not her. She is not me."

"I beg your pardon?" Sadie grew sicker from the swirling cigarette smoke and waved it away.

"I am the daughter of a farmer and housewife in rural Pennsylvania. Did you get that? Is this how people begin their memoirs or is a portrait of my humble beginnings trite? Be honest with me."

"Are you asking my opinion now?"

"Touché." Audrey chuckled. "Yes, I am."

"I'm not the writer, but I think readers will want to

know your beginnings. Yes."

"No they won't. They want scandal, saucy tales of my time traveling with a touring troupe, rubbing shoulders with the elite, my torrid love affair, an unwed pregnancy. It's the stuff that sells."

Sadie cleared her throat. She was in too deep now to reveal herself. Her head spun. She had to think of a way to get Audrey to tell this part of the story. It's why she came here. "Let's back up. Your parents let you leave?"

"Let me? I never asked permission. After the audition, I wrote a goodbye note, promised to send money, and climbed out my bedroom window."

"How old were you?"

"Old enough to know better, young enough not to care." She sucked on her cigarette holder and then contorted her lips to blow smoke straight up.

Sadie flared her nostrils, hit with more nausea. Perspiration prickled her forehead. "Mind if I use your bathroom, Ms. McCall?"

"Go ahead." Audrey leaped to her petite dancer's feet and led Sadie to it. "You look pale, honey."

A sour taste in her throat gave way to watering as she dashed into the bathroom and vomited as neatly as possible into the toilet. On her knees, holding back her hair with one hand and grabbing for tissue with her other, she wiped the spittle from her mouth. She dabbed at the perspiration on her forehead with more tissue, resting her upper body against the porcelain bowl. She'd been in such a rush she didn't close the door all the way.

Audrey appeared in the doorway. "Here." She handed over a damp washcloth, wrung out and cool.

Carolyn Menke

"Thank you." Sadie placed it on her forehead.

Audrey disappeared, closing the door behind her.

When the feeling subsided, Sadie hung the washcloth on the towel bar, splashed cold water on her prickly hot face, then rinsed her mouth. She patted herself dry. What was wrong with her? Here she was inadvertently soliciting the untold, intimate details of her mother's life—a woman who, until about ten minutes ago, had been a vague and distant memory—all while the man of her dreams waited outside, and she could barely pull herself together. Well, now that she thought about it, she had plenty of reasons to be unraveled and sick to her stomach. When she returned to the living room, Audrey was pouring steaming water into their cups. Sadie settled in the chair.

"How far along are you, Miss Pasko? Eight weeks—nine?" Audrey asked matter-of-factly without looking at her.

Sadie froze. "Excuse me?"

"Come on. I'm not stupid."

"I'm not pregnant. Just a little nervous, I guess."

"Is there a Mr. Pasko?"

Well, yes there was, and he was three flights down on the sidewalk. All she said was, "I'm not married. And I would never…"

"We all say that!" She chuckled. "Don't think you're any different." Her laughter filled the small apartment.

No, you're wrong.

"Life can be tough for an unwed mother. I know," Audrey said softly and sipped her tea.

Sadie frowned. She decided to go with the assumption of pregnancy if only to get the information

166

she came here for. Pregnant stenographer—the lies were thickening.

"Are you in love?" Audrey gestured toward the diamond ring.

Yes. She imagined James pacing outside. But knowing Audrey was referring to Henry, she said, "No."

"Would he make a good father?"

The question of whether Henry would make a good anything made Sadie pause. Still, Henry was probably as prepared for parenthood as she was. "He has a good heart," she conceded to be fair. "And he could provide financially." She couldn't keep her negative feelings toward Henry out of her voice as she spoke this aloud. The reality of the situation weighed heavily, pressing down on her shoulders, shrouding her like the heaviness of waterlogged clothing.

"Ms. Pasko. There is no shame in wealth. And I have to tell ya, honey, it's not about you any more."

"You speak from experience?" Sadie's fury grew, the words she spoke, skirting the issue that hung in the air, pointing their scornful fingers at Audrey. Sadie added, "Tell me about the baby in that framed picture over there."

Audrey retracted in surprise and shrank in her seat. "This is off the record. I did fall in love once and became pregnant. I'm only telling you because maybe my mistake will help you…in your situation."

"Go on."

"This man loved me. Called me his ethereal starlet." She swept her hands overhead dramatically.

The man loved her. Was that man her father? Sadie's pulse drummed steadily as her little inner voice rattled oh God, oh God, oh God.

"Let me back up. While I was touring, I performed one night in Philadelphia. It was the biggest show I had done yet and I was so nervous I could barely remember my own name. When I got on stage, I saw this man in the audience. For some reason, he had this calming effect on me. I know it sounds crazy, but there was something very genuine about him and when he approached me after the show, and asked me out." She spoke quickly as if she needed to tell the story more for herself to reminisce than for Sadie's benefit. "He took me to this darling little Greek diner called the Plaza where you reserve your slice of pie before you order your entree. Anyway, it was the start of the greatest love affair of my life. With him, not the pie. Although I do fancy pie," she said. "Being with him was this completely cathartic experience. He made me feel safe, special, like I didn't have to be on all the time. Said I hung his moon. God, was I stupid." She lit another cigarette.

"To believe him?"

"No, to leave him. Around the time we met, I was offered a position with a cast based in Philadelphia where he was practicing law. When we weren't working we were inseparable, yet I saw that we were moving in different directions with our careers."

"What do you mean?" Sadie was desperate to absorb and reconcile this new story of her mother's past, and of her own beginning. In her head she felt she was drowning—everything she fantasized about swam around frantically without finding anything to cling to.

"He was conservative, with old-fashioned beliefs about women. Acting was all right for me then, but once we were married, he was on the fast track and would need a wife who filled a specific role. It became clear to me that to be his wife would mean giving up my dreams of stardom on Broadway."

Sadie leaned in. Aunt Bea had been right about one thing—her mother wanted to be famous. A roll of nausea threatened again as everything unfurled before her.

"I met Rex Wyatt, who at the time was an aspiring playwright working on a show and, I'll admit it, he fancied me, and I stupidly thought it would give me an edge. I ended the relationship and moved to New York."

"You weren't in love with Mr. Wyatt?" No! She didn't want to hear this. Maybe she'd made a terrible mistake trying to unearth all the truths here, digging and chipping away. Maybe disappointment was what she deserved.

"Of course not. And, unbeknownst to me," Audrey said sympathetically, "I was, like you, already pregnant. It was a very difficult time. I had horrible morning sickness and felt very alone. I wrote to my parents and they basically shunned me. I had to waitress to pay my rent when I started showing. Nobody in their right mind would employ a pregnant performer."

Sadie lifted her cup in an effort to appear nonchalant, as if she were a simpleminded, unaffected stenographer who had little to gain from this stranger's plea for remission. But instead, inside she was reeling, her blouse stained with the perspiration of fear. If the mysterious playwright wasn't her father, who was?

"What did your lover say about the baby?"

"I didn't tell him. It is one of my greatest regrets.

169

At first I wanted to be rid of it. In the early days I told myself it wasn't a real baby yet. Plenty of women conceive and then lose a baby without ever knowing it. Nature's way. I wished for that to happen. At first. I was struggling and alone, but something changed my mind and I wanted the baby. For all the wrong reasons. I wanted someone to give me comfort. Someone to belong to. I was very selfish."

Sadie kept her eyes riveted on Audrey, waiting for her to continue.

"After I had my baby, a girl, I landed the lead role in a show on Broadway." Audrey closed her eyes and hummed a tune. "I can't remember all the score, but I'll tell you what I do remember and it haunts me to this day. I remember the way my baby cried for me when I had to leave her constantly with actor and dancer friends. When I did have her with me, I was always unprepared, too caught up in myself. I was a terrible mother and she knew it. She sensed it. The show ran on Broadway for more than a year, then I took small parts that allowed me to pay the rent. It wasn't easy. I was a child myself, practically. I probably should have given her up for adoption."

"Yet you never asked the child's father for support?"

"He had moved on. I found out through a mutual friend, my ex-roommate from my time in Philly, that he was settling down. So, at first I tried to do it on my own. By the time my little girl was turning two, though, I was desperate. I wasn't able to pay the rent and my landlord threatened to evict us. There was no way I could face my parents. My agent wanted me to tour for a year and possibly star in an early sound version for

Hollywood. I only had one option at that point."

She had more than one option. She had the option to keep her! The same thing any sane, loving, fit woman would naturally want to do, especially one who was making her own money to support them. Sadie's blood boiled over when she said, "But you were a star! Why didn't you take your baby with you?"

Audrey frowned at Sadie's emotional outburst. "Touring was no place for a child. Trust me, it wasn't. I could barely stand it. It may sound glamorous but everything about it, the traveling, the demanding schedule, the instability was downright grueling. I also had to face the realization that it wasn't right for me to keep my baby from her father, who could give her a better life. In order for me to do right by my child, I had to forfeit a relationship with her."

Sadie swallowed hard and clenched her fists to keep her emotions in control. She struggled to make eye contact with Audrey. Speaking slowly and evenly she said, "Do you regret that?"

"You bet your cashmere coat I do! My career was stagnant, honey. The next fresh face came along and I was out. Been washing dishes for the past ten years." She cradled her dry, cracked hands in her lap and sighed. "I made mistakes and was foolish, but the one thing I did right in this world was to see right by my daughter." She set down her cigarette.

"But you never returned for her, did you? After you were done with touring?"

Audrey was quiet, hesitant. Had she figured out who Sadie was? No, she couldn't possibly have.

"You were poor, but why didn't you ask the father to help you financially? You could have worked while your daughter was in school, been away less."

"Many times I almost went to her. I had been in touch with that ex-roommate who knew the father and sent me updates. In fact, that gal had set her sights on his colleague and married him. At one point she wrote to tell me my baby girl was very sick. High fever, sore throat, and skin rash. Measles. I had heard of people dying not necessarily from the measles, but from related problems, like pneumonia. Or going blind from it. God knows I wanted to be with her then. But my friend assured me my daughter had the best medical care possible, and there was nothing I could do. It turned out my daughter had already been given a serum after being exposed earlier in her life. Her case ended up being milder than it would otherwise have been, thank God, and she recovered. I wasn't needed. Again, I was being selfish to want to be there. I realized it was more important for me not to disturb her life at that point. It would have been confusing for her. I had already done enough damage and decided to leave well enough alone. Besides, I was always hopeful that my next big break would be right around the corner."

Sadie cringed at her mother's last remark. She remembered her bout with measles. She didn't readily accept her mother's reasons for staying away, but found herself softening toward the woman who spoke her true feelings. Maybe this wasn't what she'd wanted to hear, but at least her anonymity ensured the story was authentic. Her mother had no reason to lie.

"I'm confused. What happened to the baby's father?" Sadie's heartbeat made its way to her temples and she had to focus to stay calm.

"I was on tour and we stopped in his town. I'll

never forget that autumn day. I pushed the buggy past his house, stopping to strip wet leaves collected in the wheels. He had done well for himself at that point and had a lovely home with a sweeping lawn."

Her heart palpitated. Her chest constricted. She was about to learn the identity of her father at last. If he were well off and settled down, why hadn't he raised her?

"I imagined the life my daughter could have there where she belonged. A stable, financially sound upbringing. The best schools. A mother who baked cookies, braided hair, threw the best birthday parties on the block. As I walked along, I saw a Negro woman ahead of me. I decided to follow her. She went to the park. I struck up a conversation with her on the bench and it turned out she knew my daughter's father. Knew everyone in town. She was so natural with my little girl. I stood there, rocking her on my hip in the breeze, not ever wanting to let go... But you know what? Like I told you before, I had to do the right thing for my baby and this Negro woman felt right." Audrey paused and her eyes took on a faraway look before she continued.

"I was embarrassed with how unprepared I was. No bottle of milk packed or even a blanket for her. A chill was in the air. So, I took off my coat and wrapped her in it, nestled her in the stroller like baby Jesus himself. Then I looked in that woman's sorrowful eyes; she knew. She placed one hand on the stroller bar and nodded at me. Like she could read my mind. Then I ran. I didn't look back. I was so full of self-hatred and fear. I swear I thought I was damned to hell for doing that to my own child. Because the truth was...the truth was...right at that moment I felt relieved to be free once again to do my own thing. I wasn't cut out to be a housewife or mother. I had wings and I needed to fly."

Sadie forced herself to breathe. Her worst nightmare was unfolding—her mother had wanted to get rid of her; she'd been a burden and caused her distress, plagued her with a lifetime of guilt. She could barely utter her next question.

"How were you so sure this woman at the park, this complete stranger, would deliver your child to its father and he would accept her?"

"She worked for my child's father. And he had promised when I left years before he would do anything for me. He'd always 'have a shine for me,' he said. And I knew he would make a wonderful father. I saw his true character in his reaction to my leaving him. I made a terrible mistake. Do you see where this life got me? But I had to get it out of my system, I suppose. Besides, I don't have a maternal bone in my body."

Sadie sat there stunned. Why hadn't her mother's ex-roommate told her she had been adopted by the governor and his wife? Did the Negro woman at the park not follow through or, Sadie shuddered, did her real father turn her away? How could Audrey not know the truth? Somehow she managed to meet Audrey's eyes and posed her final question. "But the father didn't take her, did he?"

"Of course he did," she replied, surprised by Sadie's question. "He raised her as his own."

Chapter Twenty-One

"No!" Sadie's cry ricocheted off the cramped apartment walls that seemed to be closing in around her. Her mother had to be mistaken. The governor was her *father*?

A sharp sting pierced the bridge of Sadie's nose as if she'd been struck and pain radiated across her face. As she leaped to her feet, she cracked her shinbone on the glass cocktail table, then stumbled backward before spinning around to run. But instead of getting the hell out of there, her forehead bumped into a floor lamp, rocking precariously onto two of the four lion paws at its base before Sadie steadied it.

She shot to the door.

"Wait," Audrey called. "Was it something I said?"

Sadie turned to see the woman's mouth gaping. She backed away still facing Audrey until her trembling fingers grazed the apartment door.

"It wasn't what you said," Sadie growled, her lips twisted down in disgust. "It was what you *withheld*—my entire life."

Audrey stood, but let Sadie go.

After an embarrassing struggle with the chain, Sadie got out and never looked back. She was too overcome to remember her coat. Well, *Audrey's* coat. Back in the dreadful woman's grip, where it belonged.

Tears blurred her vision as she stumbled down the

stairwell, bumping her shoulder against a middle-aged lady carrying a brown box by its handle. The real stenographer?

When she burst out the door, James was leaning against the cast iron lamppost where she had left him. The way he looked at her with those sympathetically peaked eyebrows caused more tears to spill—onto her hair, her fur lapel and the concrete sidewalk below. Outside of James, the sidewalk felt like the only solid thing in her life. It wouldn't change, lie, become something else. She dove into his open arms and let the racking sobs take over.

"What happened? Where's your coat?"

"*Her* coat. Let's go." She struggled to catch her breath and tugged on his arm, not sure what to do other than get away from there. Her shin smarted from knocking into the table.

"Hold on." James took off his coat and draped it over her shoulders.

The wind breathed life into trash along the curb lifting and tossing it haphazardly and unexpectedly like her mother's confession. She dared the wind to move her, but it only whipped at her hair, stinging her face raw from tears.

James led her by the hand until they reached the end of the block. "Here," he said. They climbed the steps to a stone church with heavy wooden doors and gothic spires, which had probably been here long before the concrete around it. Sadie found comfort in the idea of something else staying as it was meant to be.

The church was open. Sadie wasn't surprised by this. After the stock market crash, churches stayed open all day and night. A piece of ripped newspaper crossed their path then swirled into the vestibule as they slipped inside. The door closed and the trash was lifeless once more.

The sanctuary was cool and dark, ensconced in a reverent silence that drew them in and shut out the city's noise. It appeared empty. A magnificent stained glass depiction of biblical scenes ran from the altar to the vaulted cathedral. Sadie's eyes went to the Virgin Mary cradling her baby.

The smells of melting wax and incense clung in the air, growing stronger as they walked up the aisle. A homeless man lay on a pew. Sadie had never been this close to someone destitute. Saddened by the sight, but sure that he wouldn't want her to stare, she turned the other way and continued quietly. When she looked back, James was leaning over the man, one hand on his shoulder. He offered what she guessed to be a generous amount of cash considering he had little himself. The homeless man mumbled, shaking his outstretched hand, "God bless you, son. God bless you."

Sadie wished she had the coat now, because she would have liked to lay it over the man.

She slid into the second pew, her shaky palm steadying herself on the smooth, polished wood. James followed and sat beside her. "Are you okay? What happened?"

Her voice came out in raspy gasps. "What my aunt said was true. Audrey gave me up willingly."

"Sadie, I had no idea this would happen." He shook his head as if it were his fault.

"No, no. Please don't." She cupped the curve of his strong jaw, drawing his face toward her, and silenced his lips with a kiss. All of the anger melted from her hot temples. James had a calming effect on her, and suddenly she was terrified to let go of him.

"I don't know where to begin." With so many emotions at the surface, she wasn't sure which one to address first. The shock of meeting her mother and learning about her father? The fear of nobody being who they seemed? The deep-rooted pain of parting with James indefinitely, after they had finally found each other. Where would she seek solace if not in her past, her present or her future?

"It's okay." James waited patiently for her to continue. "Take deep breaths."

Sadie took one deep breath and exhaled. It did help. "It's true what my aunt said about my mother leaving me to pursue acting. But Wyatt isn't my father." Her voice broke on the word "father." She also realized this meant her aunt was actually her stepmother.

"Who is?"

Speech escaped her. She turned toward the pulpit, drawn to the rectangular pieces of golden glass that made up Jesus' body on the cross. "My uncle."

"The governor?"

"Yes." She searched his face for a reaction. When he only nodded in response she felt a calmness sweep over her. She recounted her mother's story in a forced whisper. "She didn't know she was pregnant until after she left him." Sadie would need to get used to saying "father." "She kept me a secret until she couldn't take care of me any more." Her voice trailed off. "When she didn't want to…"

"Sadie—"

"It's true. When she told me all of this she thought

I was the stenographer hired to write her story and I didn't correct her. At least, I don't think she knew who I am. Maybe she knew all along." Sadie pushed out a big sigh. "She claimed to leave me with Nanny so I'd have a better life."

"You did have a better life."

Of course he was right, but she was too angry to admit that anything her mother may have done was honorable. "Maybe, but I'd rather live in poverty and know where I came from than grow up thinking I'm a charity case."

"Really?" James glanced in the direction of the homeless man. "You'd rather be without the basic necessities of life?"

She frowned. She needed to make sense of everything. "I just wish I had known he was my father. All my life, I felt like an outsider, invading their lives. At least her life," she said of Beatrice. "Now it makes sense. But how could they keep it from me?"

"Hold on," James said. "You're assuming the governor knew."

"Of course he knew. He and my aunt told me that my mother was my uncle's cousin. When I found the photograph of my mother, Aunt Bea told me about Audrey fleeing to New York. She let me believe my father's identity was unknown. He said nothing."

James seemed to consider this chain of events.

"I bet the secret was my aunt's idea, not wanting that stain on her hands—mothering her husband's love child."

"You're assuming Nanny knew and told them about Audrey. Would she have delivered that news? To a white couple she depended on for her pay and keep?"

"Maybe not, but he had to suspect. Why else would he agree to raise me?"

James paused. "Because he thought you were an orphan. Because he is a good man."

Her next question tumbled out. "What man would do that?"

"Sadie, I know you're hurting and it doesn't seem possible right now, but there are good men out in the world, men who would take in an orphaned child. I know I would."

"You would?"

He nodded.

She let that thought settle over her. He would raise another man's child. Could she say the same? What if it were James' baby, conceived and birthed by another woman? Even if it happened before they met, it would be difficult. She ached with newfound sympathy for Bea, arguably a critical link in her turbulent young life. Had Bea denied her a place in her home, Sadie may have ended up in an orphanage or worse, living on the streets at the mercy of hand-outs by do-gooders. Regardless of Bea's reasons for taking her in—whether it was to please her husband or keep her image intact— she had taken Sadie in when her own mother wouldn't. And that meant something. Her mother's words echoed in her head, "and raised her as their own."

She whispered, "But he had to suspect at some point. Why not tell me?"

"Maybe he wanted to be sure first? Maybe he tried to find your mother and couldn't?"

She eyed him wearily.

James conceded. "Okay, so he had the means to find her. I don't know, sweetheart. Maybe he was afraid to? These are questions only he can answer."

"I know. And hearing the truth from my mother helped." It was true. Although so much was left unsaid, and she probably would always struggle with unresolved feelings, hearing her mother's real story firsthand had deeply affected her. As much as she didn't like what her mother had done, she had to admit that she'd done the best she could.

"Sadie, they all love you. Gave you a good home and many opportunities. Opportunities I never had." James closed his eyes. When he opened them he added, "I'm sure they had their reasons for what they did and never meant to hurt you."

She leaned into his shoulder and sighed. "I hope you're right. I really want to believe that." She bit her bottom lip. They should be spending their last afternoon at the top of the Empire State Building or taking in views from the Staten Island Ferry. Strolling through a vest-pocket park. But she knew James didn't bring her to the city to sightsee.

James wasn't finished. "You can't look back on the past and wish to change it. It happened. For better or worse. And it's over. Done with. But look at you now and take what you can from it. You're a kind-hearted, educated young lady with...your whole life before you. And I love you."

His earnestness stopped her. How could she berate her father for secret-keeping after all the love he'd shown her over the years? She rubbed her forehead then caught sight of Henry's diamond ring. Evidence of more lies on her part. When she looked up at James, she couldn't bear to think of his departure, yet her mind went there, torturing her with the pain of never seeing him again.

"I have an idea." He broke the somber mood. "You showed me postcards on the train of artwork you admired. But I never got to see your favorite. Matisse's 'Open Window'."

She melted, pleased he remembered. Before she had a chance to respond, the magnificent Angelus church bell sounded: bong…bong…bong. Silence. Bong…bong…bong.

"Let's get out of here," James said with a spark in his boyish grin, taking her hand in his warm, calloused one.

As the pattern in the tolling bell repeated, they fled the church hand in hand.

****

Sadie insisted on paying the cab fare and purchasing their tickets to the Metropolitan Museum of Art. The high-pitched banter of school children in plaid uniforms filled the glass-covered atrium. Chaperones corralled the wayward bunch toward the first gallery where a museum employee stood ready to curate their fledgling minds, shape their interpretations of life through art—or was it the other way around?

She tugged on his hand. "Come on." She led him through the museum past various galleries. A security guard stood watch outside each. She hadn't been to the Met for years, but it had made such an impact on her that she remembered the way. At one point she paused in front of a painting.

"Look familiar?" she asked.

"Bernhard?"

"Very good." She narrowed her eyes with playful suspicion. "You remember that from two months ago?"

"Guilty." He pointed to the plaque. "But I do remember what you told me about his work having a tapestry quality about it. It's even more clear in person." He smiled.

They found many of the originals she'd shown James pictures of including more Bernhards and Prendergasts. As they drifted through the museum hand in hand, she wished they could stop time and exist like this forever. As much as she wanted to blame Henry, she knew what he did—however poorly executed—was no different than what she'd done with James: love another in the only way they knew how. She could have put a stop to it. She had naively thought her indifference to Henry would make him lose interest, but all it did was make her just as deceitful.

"Here it is." James pointed at the painting.

The children they had seen earlier besieged the gallery, shuffling shoes and wiping runny noses on starched white sleeves. The museum employee forged on.

"Yes!" Sadie, ignoring the clamor, grew excited. "Isn't it wonderful? To think that during the time Matisse created this, the world was in such turmoil. Yet you see none of that here. What do you make of the distortion in color? See the flowerpots, the masts, the sails?"

James looked at it curiously.

"What is it you see?"

As the children surged around them, he stood behind her, wrapping his arms around her waist. "I see something beautiful."

She felt his warm breath on her neck. When she looked over her shoulder, he was staring at her. "You

183

must be referring to the reflections of the boats on the water," she teased. "Remarkable, aren't they?"

"This is remarkable." He dipped her body and gave her a dramatic kiss, as much for the kids' benefit as his own. The school children responded with a chorus of giggling that ricocheted off the marble floors, the lofty walls, the gallery's ornate, gilded ceiling. She crumpled into laughter, feeling like a schoolgirl herself, kissed for the first time. James smiled with everything he had, melting her in half.

"Tell me something." She led him to a nearby bench. "Are you scared?"

"I've had my training. So have the other men. I used to think about life in terms of length of time." He rubbed her fingers with his thumbs. "Now I know it's about making the most of the time we have."

"Don't say that. Like you're expecting the worst."

"I'm not. I know I'll see you again."

He seemed so confident. She wanted to believe it.

"My mother once said without fear, we can't be courageous."

"You're the most courageous man I know."

"Sadie." He looked at the clock. She knew what he was about to say and didn't want to hear it.

"Is it time? No…"

"Not for my train. I leave first thing tomorrow. But there's one more thing we need to do before I leave."

One more thing? She could think of a billion.

"How courageous are you?" He stood and drew her up with him, kissing one of her hands then the other.

Chapter Twenty-Two

"Are you sure this will work?" Sadie asked James nervously as they stood before a brownstone on the Upper West Side. Her fluttering insides were quieted by his embrace on the steps.

"We can only hope," he murmured between kisses. "We don't have forty-eight hours to spare."

A woman appeared at the door before they rang the bell. She ushered them into the vestibule, out of the cold. James greeted her then said, "Sadie, I'd like you to meet Langley's...I mean Peter Langley's aunt, Alice Sherwood."

"Nice to meet you." Sadie extended her hand.

Alice took both of Sadie's gloved hands and held them out, tilting her face. "Look at you. Every bit as lovely as I expected. I often wondered what became of Audrey's 'little dear'."

"Thank you." Sadie felt a blush flood her cheeks.

Alice shook her graying head and placed one hand on the hip of her stylish dress. "Has it really been sixteen years?" Then she winked at James. "Come in, you must be famished."

Sadie whispered, "Does she know why we're here?"

"Not yet."

Alice had the table set and suggested they eat. Sadie and James exchanged glances because there were only three place settings. Alice said she'd anticipated their visit ever since hearing through her nephew of the small world connection. In fact, she insisted they stay the night. Sadie decided if that was what it took to accomplish their goal, they would stay. But where was Judge Sherwood?

"Excuse me, Alice, I hope you don't mind me asking, but isn't your husband joining us?" Sadie asked as they arranged their napkins in their laps, with Sadie and James sitting next to each other and the third plate across the table from them.

Alice stopped cold. She set down a heaping serving dish and bowl of rice before responding. "Peter didn't tell you," she said to James. "George passed last month." She made the sign of the cross.

Sadie locked eyes with James. She couldn't help but feel disappointed that their simple, on-the-spot ceremony was not meant to be, but she also sympathized with Alice. To lose the love of her life—she couldn't imagine it. She sought James' hand under the table and squeezed it.

"I'm very sorry for your loss, Alice," she said.

"Yes, very sorry," James said.

"He'd been ill for some time. Anyway, can't have Cantonese without mai tais to wash it down, can we?" Alice dabbed at the corner of one eye as she excused herself.

They made the best of the circumstance, encouraging Alice to speak about George, seeing how it seemed to improve her mood.

"In Paris, before the war of course, we ate at this quaint out-of-the-way place called Camelot," she said, the first of many tales of their European travels.

Sitting beside each other, James' hands lingered on Sadie's as she passed a dish.

"No menu there," Alice said. "We were served whatever the chef found at the market that day."

James held Sadie's gaze longer than necessary until she released the dish.

"George told me I was eating rabbit's cheese," Alice continued, slightly slurring her words.

"Rabbit's cheese?" Sadie asked. When she squeezed James' thigh, he stopped chewing.

"And the next day he caught me writing in my diary that I'd eaten rabbit's cheese." She exploded with laughter. "I know it was ridiculous of me to believe that. Can you imagine, milking a rabbit?"

Sadie smirked at James who was redder in the face than Alice.

As they finished up, Alice told them she wasn't feeling well and wanted to retire to her room upstairs. It was getting late and Alice insisted they stay the night, apologizing unnecessarily for the cramped quarters.

She offered Sadie the first floor guest room off the living room, made up the couch for James, and climbed the stairs alone, the idea of which saddened Sadie almost as much as their thwarted mission. Sadie washed in the hall bath and changed into her borrowed nightgown and robe. She bid James a polite good night and caught him craning his neck to watch her retreat to the bedroom.

Later, she heard snoring outside the room. James? She puckered her lips into a pout at the thought that he could so easily drift off when she was here—on the other side of this thin wall—and they were finally unattended. She slipped from the bed, tiptoed to the door, and peeked through the crack. James wasn't snoring after all; the noises must have been coming from Alice upstairs. She drank in the sight of his body stretched out across the sofa, his feet hanging off, one bulging arm tucked behind his head. Eyes wide open.

Could she do this?

Her belly swirled in anticipation of his hands on her bare skin, but as she stepped into the room, shivering in the cold dark, she suddenly waffled. They weren't married in the eyes of God or state. Henry's ring was tucked in her purse. And, she'd lain awake waiting for him to rap on her door, but he hadn't. Why hadn't he, she wondered, pressing her lips into a frown.

She took a few more steps until James shot to a sitting position, the sheet falling from his bare chest.

"Sadie?" His lips parted—those full, warm lips of his—as she stood awkwardly in her sheer nightgown. A look of bewilderment flustered his features.

Sparks fired across her chest. Her skin shivered from the cold but a heat burned underneath, especially when his eyes tripped over her nightgown, resting on her breasts.

She folded her arms to cover herself up and whispered, "James…"

James what? How could she conceal the reason she'd come here? Maybe she could say she needed a drink of water. Or an extra blanket. She opened her mouth to explain, but before she could speak, he launched himself off the couch and suspended his large frame so closely before her that she felt his warm breath on her eyelids. He covered her open mouth with his.

This time he wasn't timid or asking or pleading.

This time he was taking what he needed.

His mouth seared into hers, opening and closing, and opening and closing—she, on tiptoes and clinging to his shoulders, he, grasping her waist with hungry hands. She let his lips lead hers in a delightful play, then he released to tug on her bottom lip while she gasped at the ceiling.

"Sadie," he whispered longingly, sparking more fire bursts that spread to her limbs. "I need you." His eyes had taken on a lusty, rumpled daze.

His desperation seemed to ripple from every pore as he pulled her body to his, spinning around and backing against the wall, with his shoulder blades taking the brunt of the force and the framed artwork rocking from its wire.

"I'm yours," she murmured.

He slid fire-hot hands up the flesh of her outer thighs, seeking their way under her nightgown until resting frustratingly shy of her breasts.

The wanting in his heavy breathing told her this time was different. This time when he fixed her with glazed-over eyes, she knew he wouldn't be exercising his usual gentlemanly restraint.

In a thrilling instant, he scooped her legs off the ground and lifted her. She tried not to laugh, feeling like a silly girl living out a fairy tale. She wanted desperately to be the seductive woman he probably preferred—but how? He shouldered open the door, and pushed it closed with his foot.

He smiled, but his eyes looked clouded this time and she worried suddenly about what was going to happen. He wasn't returning her to the bed alone, was he? As he lowered her body, her every nerve ending tingled with suspicion. Instead of joining her, he hovered, then reeled back to sit on the edge of the bed as if he'd come to tuck in a child.

"What is it?" She propped up on her hands.

"Sadie." He averted his eyes in the darkly lit room.

She knew what it was. She was too needy, too fragile, too pleading. She had to convince him otherwise.

"I don't want you to regret doing this," he said.

He was worried about her? "I'll regret *not* doing this. We both will."

He shook his head while rubbing his forehead. "No...don't you see? I'm leaving tomorrow. What if? What—"

"James, please." Sadie sank her teeth into her bottom lip. He was leaving tomorrow, but it didn't change any one thing. It changed *everything*. Of course in an ideal world she'd want to wait until they were married and do this the right way, too, but they didn't have time. What if they were apart for months? Years? Her body ached for his.

"I don't care." She knelt on the bed in front of him.

His face softened into amused crinkles as he pushed the hair from her eyes, and lifted her chin with his fingers. He sighed. Not exactly the sound she'd been hoping for. When he brushed his lips against hers, she knew he was winding down, and that she'd have to agonizingly forget the urgent love making session she'd longed for.

When he finally peered up at her with his eyes only, a strength she didn't know existed welled up inside her. Under his gaze, she fumbled with the buttons on her nightgown, marveling at how quickly he'd snapped to attention, his eyebrows rising. She noticed first that sexy indent in his jaw, then saw his lips parting. She hastily worked on the top three buttons while he watched, then she gathered the gauzy material in her sweaty palms, shimmied it over her bottom and pulled it over her head.

The only trouble was that a button got caught in a tendril of hair, and she collapsed into herself, covering up with her arms while working it free. And just as she decided her attempt at seduction had fallen terribly short, he filled the silence with his deep, warm voice. "I love you," he said simply and she knew it was his way of saying he was still with her in this moment. Still wanting this. Still wanting her.

She threw her nightie at his face for good measure, seeing a full smile tug at his lips. Then, eager to see him lose complete control, she settled back on her elbows, arching her back, allowing the moon's glow to spill forth across her milky-white breasts and pale pink nipples. She inched away from him, drawing up her legs to one side, hoping to lure and tease.

That did it.

He pushed her heated skin down to the cool swirl of sheets, kissing her full on the mouth while massaging her breast. She hooked her calf around him and wrestled on top, guiding their mouths into the give and take rhythm of the sea's tide.

He rolled her back down, his warm mouth trailing kisses along the side swells of her breasts, her rib cage that lifted and lowered in time with their breathing, her taut belly and beyond. Where had these hands been before and how had they learned what to do? She couldn't help wondering how many other women he had melted to oblivion under his work-roughened hands, yet despite the slow burning jealousy that creased her brow, she gave in to the currents gushing up and down her spine. However many there had been, she was the only one now.

When their bodies joined at last, she cried out, tears escaping her eyes. James deepened their intensity by looking deeply into her eyes as they moved together, building pleasure. When she felt spent by so much joy, he brought sheer ecstasy rippling across her by tilting her hips in just the right way. Waves of warmth engulfed them.

Pulsing.

Bursting.

Shuddering.

Smug with their achievement, they continued all night long, smelling of fresh-sweat and the salty summer sea. By early morning, she willed him to rest. They slept nestled like roots of a willow tree, entwined so deeply they were inseparable.

When they roused at the first early light, Sadie found herself wrapped in James' arms. She looked up into his eyes, wondering how long he'd been awake.

"Morning, beautiful," he said huskily, kissing her forehead. His fingers brushed the small of her back sending swells up from her belly to her throat.

"Morning." She closed her eyes and drew her lips into a satisfied smile. He kissed her on either side of her lips, over the now tender skin scratched raw from his stubble. She sucked in her breath at the deep stirring he awakened in her belly.

Today he was leaving. She tried to hide her sadness through kisses, but how could she hide anything from him now that she'd opened herself up so completely?

Her smile crumpled slightly as she fought back the sharp pain behind her eyes.

"Why don't you meet me at Luna Park on Coney Island next week? Just the two of us." He brushed tangles of her hair off her shoulder before pressing his lips to it.

She wrinkled her brow and forced her quivering lips into a smile. "All right. I'll pack your favorite bathing suit for the beach."

"The yellow one?"

She grasped the sheet to her chest and rolled on top, sitting. The room was aglow now, and she wasn't quite as willing to let him see her in the stark daylight.

"Yes, the one with the peephole here." She pointed to her cleavage over the sheet. "And the halter tie up here." Sadie drew her hand behind her neck where she'd tie the imaginary strap, her elbow erect.

He grasped her hips. "We'll swim in the ocean."

"I'd like that." She let the sheet fall away as she leaned over to kiss those warm lips some more while he ran his hands up and down her bare back.

"Don't forget your dress. And dancing shoes for the music on the pier."

She slid off to lie facing him while he caressed her curving hip and fixed her with those overcast eyes.

He turned her wrist to study a scar Sadie always hid under her glove. "I've been wondering…" He traced his thumb along the whitened, leathery skin, covered in patches of tissue paper, "what happened here?" He didn't cringe or recoil at the sight of it like she always assumed people would.

"I touched the stove griddle years ago. My uncle—" She caught herself. "I

193

mean...Edward...replaced it with the safer Hotpoint Electric." She'd need time before she could refer to him as her father.

James brought her scar to his mouth and brushed his lips along it. "I would have liked to have known you then. Really known you."

She was overcome by a wistful affection for him, and for the time they'd lose while he was gone. That burning along the bridge of her nose heated her whole face to the point she dropped her tear-filled eyes.

"The war won't last forever, Sadie. I'll be back before you know it and we'll be together." He smoothed her hair from her face and traced his thumbs over her lips. "Did I tell you I bought us that farmhouse in the country you've had your eye on?"

She gasped, forcing her quivering lips into a smile, grateful for his well-timed fantasy. "You mean the one with the pond and the weeping willow?"

"That's the one." He kissed her nose. "With the barn and more land than you can see from the porch. I already dug the holes for the fence posts." Now he kissed her lips while cradling her face.

"Not bad for a city boy." She pulled back to crinkle her nose. "Tell me more."

"We can teach the kids to ice skate on that pond," he said.

"Oh, there will be kids?"

He nodded, stone serious, his laugh creases now white lines marking each and every wonderful trace on his flushed face. "A bevy of girls like you. We'll be blessed with a house full of them—"

"Unless they happen to be sons. To help in the fields."

"Fields? But I'm just a city boy."

A smile rippled over her and she bit her trembling bottom lip to quiet that unease which kept creeping back.

"And long after the war is over, on hot July days, we'll swim in the pond and lay like this." He cupped her bare bottom playfully.

"We won't need much," Sadie murmured through kisses, determined not to ruin their last precious hours together.

"Just each other," he added.

Their fingers entwined, his kisses came faster, went deeper. Soon, his hardness stirred against her. Sadie cherished every nip and nuzzle, the weight of his body on hers, and the building intensity—never wanting it to end—knowing it had to.

Chapter Twenty-Three

At the train station, Sadie squeezed her eyes closed as James pulled her in for a long embrace. He'd insisted on escorting her here before he went to collect his things and leave. She still wore his coat; he fastened a button she had missed.

"I'll write every chance I can," he said.

Sadie swiped the tears from under her lashes. The train whistle blew a final warning as stragglers jostled past them to board. Life went on, yet everything outside of James and this moment seemed insignificant.

"When I return I'll find you. The first thing we'll do is get married." He reached inside the sleeves of his coat on her to find her hands.

"Okay," Sadie agreed eagerly.

"You know, your father once told me life is a lot like fox hunting. You have to think ahead and be hopeful. That's what we need to do. Think ahead to our future together." He released her hands and tucked his finger under her chin, lifting her face to meet his gaze.

She mustered a smile, barely holding herself together. "Hurry back to me, James."

"Promise me something?" he asked in between more nuzzles. "Whatever happens, promise me you'll go to my family if you need anything. Here's the address." He handed her a piece of paper that she put in her clutch.

"All aboard!" the conductor bellowed.

When she looked up again, he cupped her face in his hands and caught her streaming tears with his thumbs, wiping them away. Then he kissed her with such tenderness she never wanted him to stop. She had witnessed soldiers saying goodbye to their lovers on the platform before, never imagining she'd be doing the same.

She started to take off his coat, but he stopped her.

"Keep it. You'll be cold."

"What about you?"

"Don't worry about me." He melted her with a smile then pulled her into his embrace again. She could live in his hold. While they clung to each other, he whispered, "Sadie, may the road rise to meet you." She buried her face in his chest. "May the wind be always at your back. May the sun shine warm upon your face." He kissed her forehead, then searched her eyes. "Until we meet again—" He kissed her lips this time. "May God hold you in the palm of His hand."

"Oh, James, that's lovely."

"It's an Irish blessing." He rocked her in his arms. They were the last couple still standing on the platform.

"You have to go," he said, but held her more tightly.

"I don't want to."

She gave him one final squeeze. One last kiss. Then she forced her wobbly legs to climb aboard, scrambling to find a seat. She flung her body toward the only free window seat on his side of the car, threw open the window, and stretched out to reconnect with him from above. He reached for her hand. Their fingers just missed each other as the train's motion, working against them, carried her away.

"Look!" James loped along the train, motioning to the curtain of new snow that draped the covered platform. "The angels are proud!"

Sadie steadied herself on the edge of the window and then covered her quivering lips with a trembling hand. When James reached the edge, he had to stop, but Sadie kept her eyes on his shrinking figure. He held up one hand in a wave. Then his arms went limp at his sides, as if they had nothing more to do. She held her hair back from the wind, returning his wave, desperate to keep eye contact.

The old woman beside her said, "Miss, do you mind? I'm freezing."

Sadie reluctantly withdrew and closed the window, deciding she would never be grumpy when she turned old. She would be the road rising to meet the heartbroken, the wind at their back, the sun on their face. If she lived to be old. Then she thought sadly what if she were blessed with a long life, yet one without James? She would have nothing. She kept watching him through the window as he grew smaller and smaller until he was blocked from view by a curve in the track.

Chapter Twenty-Four

Hell week was in full swing at Bryn Mawr and students scurried around the campus like rats seeking cover in broad daylight. Though it began as a tradition to pass the doldrums of winter, Hell Week now provided a distraction from news—or lack of it—from brothers, boyfriends, and husbands.

Sadie and her friends were late for chemistry. Sadie maneuvered across the icy campus inadequately dressed, deceived by the sun's strength through her window that morning. She was numb to her surroundings, preoccupied with thoughts of James. And Henry. The deceit was gnawing through her, tarnishing what she had with James and mocking Henry, whom she'd never meant to hurt. It had been a month since she and James parted at the train station, four long weeks of pining over a shadow of their time together. And during those dark days when Sadie awaited his next letter, she allowed horrible thoughts to creep into her head. Had he been injured?

"Hey, I forgot my textbook. Anyone have a copy of the periodic table?" Ruth riffled through her bag as they burst into the toasty lecture hall.

"Take mine." Sadie pulled a folder from her bag and handed it over, scattering stray papers in the folder's wake. Maria helped her pick them up. Maria, Ruth, and Sadie found seats together in the middle of the lecture hall.

Professor Masters shuffled through a stack of papers at the podium as bundled stragglers entered with fogged glasses and flushed cheeks and smelling of cold air. The room filled.

When Sadie opened her book to their current chapter, she realized James' letter was gone. She had been using it as a bookmark, but had stuffed it in her bag loose after being woken from a nap at the library yesterday. The letter must have fallen in the aisle when she pulled out the paper for Ruth. She craned her neck to look up the sloping carpeted aisle all the way to the double doors where they entered.

Just inside the double doors two students from another class huddled over a piece of paper giggling. One girl pushed the other forward. It was Barbara West, a first year theater major. Miss West giggled to her friend and then cleared her throat loudly. Barbara wouldn't dare.

"My dearest Sadie."

She dared.

"I'm sorry for the delay." She splayed a hand on her chest. "With the long days it has been hard to write to you."

The lecture hall quieted with confusion; Sadie wasn't sure if they were more alarmed for herself or Barbara, the latest victim of Hell Week.

Miss West was undeterred by the intimidating silence. "Please know I don't think of you less…in fact, you're all I think about."

The girls erupted in laughter. Sadie lunged out of her seat, stupidly giving herself away, and bolted toward Barbara to get the letter back. Quick and as agile as a ballerina, Barbara flitted across an upper row, speaking louder and faster now. Sadie followed awkwardly.

"Take your seats, both of you," the professor demanded. For the first time this school year, Sadie was grateful to be nameless among a sea of faces. She hunched over, seeking an empty seat to crawl into and hide.

"Excuse me. So sorry," she said to the girls whose legs she brushed past and whose coats she accidentally trampled. "Terribly sorry!"

"Now then," Masters boomed. "Where is Sadie Stark?"

Sadie froze. This was not happening.

"Sadie Stark?" he asked louder.

This was happening.

While debating which end of the row was nearer so she could at least free herself from this awkward stance, Sadie tripped over someone's shoe and fell right into the lap of none other than Emily herself.

"Right here!" Emily trilled, pointing to Sadie in her lap.

Sadie collected herself and rose, prepared to explain the hazing ritual and then apologize for the mockery they had made of his classroom.

The professor frowned at her. "Sadie Stark? You got the highest grade on the exam." He slapped the stack of papers that decorated his podium.

Hesitant applause rippled across the room, breaking the silence that Masters commanded. Sadie hung her mouth open, dumbfounded. She tried to ignore the heat radiating across her wind-burned cheeks and a sudden wave of nausea. She nodded at Masters and stumbled into the aisle.

"If your circus show is over I suggest you take this available seat in the front row," he said and began the day's lecture.

****

"Where's Maria?" Sadie asked Ruth after checking for her in the library. She'd missed lunch.

"I don't know. I didn't see her at the literature review," Ruth replied.

"I'm worried. Do you think everything's all right?"

They scoured the campus before deciding she had to be at the house. On their way back, Ruth cried out, "She's here! I found her."

Maria was sitting in the Blanca Noel Taft Memorial Garden near the sunken reflecting pool, almost as frozen as the water.

"Good God, what are you doing out here? You'll get frostbite!" Sadie wrapped her arms under Maria's armpits to help her up.

At the house, Maria lay on the sofa, covered with a mountain of blankets, as stoic and ashen as stone.

Sadie clicked on the Bakelite radio in the living room while Ruth boiled water for tea. She turned the dial to WIP. Uncle Wip's "Kiddie Club" had just ended and Sadie expected an update on the war. Someone had brought home a copy of "The Philadelphia Record" where a new list of casualties was reported by state. Sadie scanned the report quickly for Maria and adjusted the volume.

"Don't bother," Louise said from the doorway. "I was here when she got the call."

"What?" Sadie lurched toward Maria and sat on the edge of the sofa. "Is it true?"

Maria dissolved into sobs. "He's gone..." She covered her face with shaking hands. "Oh God, oh God." Maria's weeping shook her tartan-draped shoulders.

Sadie pulled Maria's face toward her chest. Ruth knelt beside Maria with her hand on her back and asked softly, "What happened?"

"His mother told me." She choked on the words. "It happened during a night maneuver. He was so brave. He left his foxhole to help a friend who lost both legs in an explosion and couldn't move. Tony carried him out. The friend survived because of Tony. My Tony—" She sobbed.

"He's a real hero." Sadie hugged her more tightly.

"Tony, sweet Tony," Maria said over and over. "We were going to be married." She sniffled and wiped her nose with the back of her hand.

Ruth got the tissue box and brought it over. Sadie felt helpless. They huddled in silence for a long time. At last she said, "Can I do anything for you? Draw you a bath?"

Maria shook her head and lay back down. Their housemates shuffled in and stood around saying their condolences. Maria nodded and pressed tissues to her swollen eyes and reddened nose. In time Louise called them in for dinner. When all the girls had left except Sadie, she bent to kiss Maria's cheek and cover her with more blankets.

"They say he's in a better place now," Maria whispered, her face still white and sunken. "Do you believe that?"

Sadie hesitated not knowing what to say and then thought of James and his late night encounter at the boarding house. "I believe he's your angel now," she said confidently. "And he wouldn't want you to suffer for him any longer."

Maria nodded like a terrified yet obedient child. Seeing Maria like this was too much to handle. When Sadie stood up, she had to grab onto the arm of the sofa to steady herself. The blood rushed from her head and an overwhelming nausea flooded her body again.

"Stay with me." Maria reached for Sadie's hand.

And Sadie did.

Chapter Twenty-Five

My lovely Sadie,

I hope this letter finds you well. How's the studying coming along? They transferred me to an airbase in Tibenham, England so you can send your next letter to the address on the envelope. They're treating me just fine here in Tibenham. I'm the bombardier for a crew aboard a B-17 Flying Fortress. Remember the picture I showed you on the train? A real heavy bomber, she is. Flies high and long and as tough as a tank. I'm on milk run missions, sweetie, and flanked by allied fighters, so please don't worry. Always happy to see the airfield control tower coming into view though. Sure is a sight. Keep sending the pictures. No matter what happens to me, know I love you with all my heart.

Yours,

James

James folded and stuffed the letter into an envelope and licked it.

"What do you think of Frances so far?" asked Chuck Forester, a radio operator from Cincinnati, of their nicknamed B-17 Flying Fortress. "She can jar you something fierce."

"As long as good ol' Frances stays up in the sky—I'll like her just fine," James teased.

Chuck lifted his cot's mattress. "Look at that. Instead of springs, we've got twine holding us up."

"No wonder I can't lift my chin without pain shooting down my spine," James said.

"Is that a letter to your girl back home—Sadie?"

James nodded, wanting to tell Chuck about her, but afraid his voice would crack. He fingered the envelope. Then he dug into his bag for the picture she sent him at Fort Dix. He handed over the tiny square for Chuck to see.

Ruth had taken the picture. Sadie was leaning against a brick wall, cradling an armload of books. Her mouth was open in laughter. Over Chuck's shoulder, his eyes met hers in the grainy image.

"That's her," James said proudly, his forehead creasing as he studied the way her hair was gathered over one shoulder. What had she been thinking about when this picture was taken? Had it been a memory of him? Who knew what had amused her in this moment and he suddenly wished there had been more moments, a lifetime more, of them together, for her to recall.

"She's a keeper." Chuck handed the picture back. "When I get back to Dolly and our three boys..." He settled on his cot and kicked off one boot. "I'm buying us a car."

James tucked Sadie's picture safely away and pulled off his undershirt that was dampened from sweat. "Sounds like a fine idea, Chuck. What kind?"

"A Ford." Chuck leaned over to untie the other boot, exposing his thinning hair on top. "My boy, the youngest, he's a fine ball player, did I tell you? Built like you." Chuck rubbed his face, pushing up his glasses to work his knuckles over his eye sockets. "They say God has a plan. You think that's true? Or are we still alive because of some unexplained fortuity?"

His voice dripped with sarcasm.

"Keep your mind on your boy," James said, as he eyed the older man.

James withdrew his journal to write. But as he turned the page from yesterday, Chuck interrupted him. "Don't write about the missions, James. They'll be easier to forget that way."

"I don't have a choice, but to remember it all. None of us do. Besides, wouldn't you want your family to know what happened to you? The whole personal story, rather than a one lined telegram?"

"That's what you're doing?"

"Look—these men," James said of the fallen heroes, some of which he'd sat shoulder to shoulder to during their last harrowing moments. "I'm writing for them. I'm writing for their girlfriends. Their widowed wives. Their children." And maybe, James admitted to himself, he was also writing to rid himself of the guilt. Because when he wasn't careful, and when he let the anger simmer through his chest, he cursed their maker. What God would rip those men from their families? Why them and not him?

"James," Chuck said. "You were ordered to take a two-day break. For the love of God—put the journal away."

****

James muddled through the next day in a hazy fog. He'd played cards with Chuck and Frank and a few others who were new until they all grew tired of losing to him.

"You want to catch a ride out of here?" Frank wrestled into his uniform jacket. His eyes danced with mischief. "See what kind of trouble we can scare up?"

James chuckled at his friend. "Not this time, thanks." He rubbed at the aches along his shoulders from his last mission in Frances. Boy could she toss a man around inside that shell.

Not long after he ran drills with a new gunner from Wyoming, the two men stopped to watch the bombers come in near the tower.

Here came one now.

James planted his feet apart on the frozen ground, warming his hands by rubbing them together. His skin was numb, the same way it always felt while flying. He felt as cold as the freezing air through the gunner's open windows, or the ice on the men's guns. He carried the chill everywhere he went, and especially now that he'd stained his shirt with sweat from a workout.

The familiar stench of cordite hit his nose; he froze in place looking for the source of the smokeless explosive.

The bomber they'd been watching suddenly burst into flames.

"Christ!" James grabbed at his hair. When the plane started losing altitude, he collapsed to his knees.

"They'll get out," the new gunner said, helping James to his feet.

James pushed him aside and squinted to see signs of survival, desperately counting parachutes aloud as he pointed. "I see two parachutes there...three...four, five, six."

"There's another two," the gunner said.

Eight men floated toward safety, their legs dangling like Christmas tree ornaments. And James found himself laughing uneasily through his gaping mouth, his face burning from the heat in the sky. But only eight?

Ten men had been aboard, but he only counted eight.

Where the hell were nine and ten? The vomit surged up his throat when he saw that one man's parachute had caught on the plane's wing. He was still struggling with it but the flames lapped at his arms, searing him alive. It was probably a man James had passed the saltshaker to yesterday. Or the lucky bastard he'd lost a pile of bills to while playing cards with last week. Maybe he'd been the one who shouted something about the pin-up girl he was going to marry.

Now James was watching him die.

Later that night James jolted awake, again chilled by his own sweat. As he took deep breaths to slow his heartbeat in the dark, he couldn't help but notice how empty his corner of the barracks had become.

Take a break.

That had been his order.

But it was impossible here.

"Chuck," he whispered in the darkness. "You awake?"

Chuck rolled toward him. "No. I'm asleep. You should be too."

"I can't..." James' voice quaked in the darkness and he fought against it. "I can't get these visions out of my head." Death was around every corner.

"You'll be fine, kid. A few more missions to go and you'll be heading home. Home to your girl."

"Seventeen missions." But James had seen the men who'd beaten the odds of combat in the sky, only to have most of their bodies burned, or pieces of metal lodged in their jaws, spines, or shoulders. Unable to walk or feed themselves or use a toilet. Hospitalized, then sent home.

"Fine. So focus on seventeen more."

"It could have been us on that bomber today. Our bodies disintegrated." Fear seized James' prone body on the cot.

"But it *wasn't* us," Chuck said.

"No amount of firepower can save us up there, Chuck. No amount of training. No amount of skill or intelligence. Nothing."

"Shut the hell up and go to bed. You'll be home soon."

Home. But in what capacity? Returning broken was quickly becoming James' greatest fear. How would he take care of Sadie if he couldn't take care of himself? He pulled out the stationery and pencil.

Sadie my love,

I miss you, honey. I need to tell you some good news. Bomber crews are granted a cap on missions. Twenty-five. That means after I complete all twenty-five, I'll be coming home to you. I've been working steadily now. I'm on mission eight. Sometimes we fly out a few times a day. It won't be long now. Study hard, sweetie. Do a good job, okay?

Yours,
James

Chapter Twenty-Six

"My brother-in-law's pay came in," Ruth told Sadie as they trudged home from campus. "And my sister paid me a Lincoln over break to watch her kids. Let's go out to eat. My treat."

"No, save it for your next date with Jack. I'm not feeling so well lately. Maria said the flu's going around."

She could only hope it was the flu. And, she could use a break from schoolwork and fixating on her empty mailbox cubby. Waiting for James' next letter was crushing her to bits. But this nausea—please dear God let it be the flu.

"Jack won't let me pay for anything." Ruth eyed her skeptically. "How long have you not been feeling well?"

"Never mind about me." Sadie stuffed away what she had been terrified to reveal to anyone. "How is your sister faring with Bobby being overseas?"

"She manages. Last week she won a bag of sugar playing cards with her gals. Before that, a pound of butter. Usually they just try for food ration stamps. Hungry?"

"Not really." Her stomach turned at the thought of food. "But it is lunch time."

"That's right. I insist." She directed them toward the sandwich shop near the Main Line.

Inside their booth, Ruth ordered soup and toasted cheese sandwiches for both of them with victory garden slaw. "All you need is a hearty meal. Cherry pie for dessert, too. Didn't you say that's James' favorite?" she needled, obviously trying to perk Sadie up.

"It is." Sadie was pleased that Ruth remembered. She had to tell Ruth what she suspected, as soon as she found the right moment.

When the soup was delivered, Sadie nibbled first on the saltine crackers nestled inside the lip of her soup saucer. She drew a spoonful of broth to her mouth. The hot, salty liquid burned her throat as it went down but felt good within seconds of her swallowing. Miraculously, she started to feel better. Maybe she had been hungry after all. Lingering in the back of her head was the other reason she'd been ignoring.

"Here, have mine, too." Ruth slid her untouched cup across the table.

As Sadie dunked crackers in between spoonfuls, Ruth settled back in the booth and bit her thumbnail. "I was beginning to worry about you." She took off her hat and adjusted the pin on a stray curl. "I thought you needed to see a head-shrinker or something."

Sadie laughed, something she hadn't done in some time, then the fingers of doubt snaked up and wrapped around her throat. Pretending she was fine was growing harder to do—especially with Ruth worrying about her.

"I don't know what's come over me. I guess I just needed a hot meal with my best gal." Sadie held her bowl on an angle while ladling the last of the wonderfully salty dregs into her spoon. As soon as she swallowed, her lips quivered and she set down her spoon. "Or maybe…"

"Maybe what?"

Here was her chance to tell Ruth. Why couldn't she bring herself to confide in Ruth?

"It's been six weeks since my last…full moon." Her eyes dipped to the bowl.

"Six weeks?" Ruth clanked her forkful of slaw to the plate.

Sadie pushed the bowl away and lowered her head in defeat, dredging her forearms across wet spots of spilled broth and cracker bits.

"What in the world, Sadie?" Ruth pierced her with wide eyes.

"It's nothing. Not really." Sadie wrung her fingers, sniffling and then taking the napkin Ruth offered. "I mean, it can all be explained away. The vomiting and nausea feels just like the flu, I swear it."

Ruth sat up tall and tilted her head as if seeing Sadie in a whole new light.

"Don't look at me like that. The tiredness could be from staying up so late studying, right? Tell me that's all it is. Tell me I'm overreacting." Sadie's eyes welled up with tears.

"Wait, wait, wait." Ruth waved her hands around. She glanced around at the booths near them and then leaned in to whisper. "Hasn't your female calendar always been a little off, Sadie? It wouldn't be unlikely for you to miss a cycle here and there. How about here…" She gestured to her chest. "Are they tender?"

"Painful," Sadie squeaked and crumpled into her quivering fingers.

"Say—I have to ask when. During your trip to New York?"

"Shhh…keep your voice down." A hot surge

warmed Sadie's cheeks, and it wasn't from the soup.

Ruth looked up while she tapped her fingers, probably doing the math that Sadie had gone over in her head too many times already. "Why didn't you tell me sooner? I could have…" Ruth trailed off. There was nothing she could have done. What was done was done.

Ruth's eyes widened in fear.

Dear God, Sadie thought, even Ruth believed it. And now that she'd told someone, it was that much more real. A knot formed in her stomach while the creeping acid soured her tongue, making her want to gag. Not only was Ruth a nursing student, she was wiser to the ways of the womanly world—probably because she'd been raised by a mother. And unless Ruth could miraculously come up with a plausible reason for Sadie to be feeling the way she was, she had to face the truth.

"This is probably the worst thing that could have ever happened to me," Sadie said. She rubbed at the throbbing pressure at both temples. "Ruth, if this leaks to the press, I'll be doomed. They'll write it up all over the papers. Newsboys on every corner."

"Listen—if you're pregnant, which is probably likely…I'm so sorry," Ruth said. "Maybe James will be home soon, and nobody would have to know. Have you even talked to the governor since finding your mom?"

Sadie held her face with both hands while cringing at the foul whiffs of the passing bus boy's dirty wash bin. "No. I've been in hiding."

"I have the feeling your aunt will want to keep it all quiet." Ruth lowered her voice to a whisper.

Sadie looked up to the ceiling, then covered her face with quivering, sticky fingers. "Oh God, she'll try to ship me off to a maternity home." Ruth was right. Her aunt would consider Sadie's indiscretion a disgrace to the family who'd raised her.

Sadie struggled to breathe evenly while her waistband dug into her belly. Between deep breaths, she said, "Ruth, what have I done? What if I have to leave school?"

"That's not going to happen."

But they both knew it could. And probably would.

"I'll have to hide this as long as possible," Sadie said, yet already her wool skirt felt pressed more tightly around her bloated belly than when they'd arrived less than twenty minutes ago. It was all in her mind, Sadie kept telling herself.

"Remember that girl who concealed her pregnancy right up until the birth?" Ruth asked. "Or the one who claimed she didn't even know she was pregnant until she went into labor?"

"Yes."

"You can do that. I'll help you."

"Thank you." Sadie held her friend's hand and smiled through shiny eyes. Sadie leaned back in her seat and let the thought of the truth fall over her. How would she face her family? She'd been avoiding the break-up with Henry because she hadn't wanted to disappoint them.

Now this. What would her father think of her now? That his own daughter had been so wanton. She couldn't bear it if her immorality reflected on him and their family. Yet even if she hid her pregnancy, she realized, placing her hand gently on her belly, at some point she'd have to take care of the baby growing inside her.

Not just a baby—James' baby. Excitement fluttered in waves over her belly, but quickly flattened into a queasy churning that made Sadie cover her mouth with her napkin. What did she know about babies? Not the first thing. Babies terrified her.

"Does James know?" Ruth asked.

"Not yet. I wanted to be sure first. I'll write him today." She cast her eyes downward, and pinched her big toes together. At least he'd support her. She knew he would. He only had thirteen more missions left and then they'd get through this together.

Just as quickly as the idea buoyed her mood, she swung the other way, sagging her rounded shoulders like a beaten-down barmaid. "But what if my family disowns me, Ruth? My aunt…she'll…"

"Everything will work out, don't worry. The important thing is that you take good care of yourself, okay?" She slid her slice of cherry pie toward Sadie while bearing a lopsided grin traced more with concern than celebration.

"What if I can't hide it? What if they find out?"

"One step at a time, okay?" Ruth said.

Thank God for Ruth.

Sadie nodded. Her quivering bottom lip was just the start of the blubbery mess about to follow. But she couldn't do that here. People would notice and speculate. Like that neighboring booth full of juniors who were whispering and then caught Sadie's staring eye. They wrinkled their noses, probably in disgust at what she'd done, turning their backs to her as if the silent shunning had already begun.

As they walked to the door, Ruth swiped a handful of mints from the glass candy jar near the diner's register and handed them to Sadie.

"Peppermint helped my sister with morning sickness," Ruth whispered.

Sadie nodded and shoved them into her pocket, except for one. She tried to untwist the candy, but it stuck to its wrapper. Sadie sighed. She couldn't get anything right these days. Not with Henry, not with her mother, and not now.

Her aunt had warned her.

James wanted to wait.

An unmarried, educated woman from a well-off, refined family—like herself—did not get into this predicament.

Apparently she was her mother's daughter.

Chapter Twenty-Seven

"You want in?" asked Conn, a cigarette dangling from his lips.

James nodded and took a seat. He wasn't exactly interested in playing the odds around this table any more than he was in playing the odds in the skies, but he needed a distraction. And although he was relatively new to poker, he'd been able to win enough to be harassed for it. Chuck used to say James won so much because he could read people. A good poker-faced opponent never fooled James.

Conn dealt.

"Whatcha got for the pot, Pasko?" a radio operator asked.

James felt his pocket for the black crackle lighter Sadie's father had given him, the one with the governor's insignia. It was impressive, and the men had their eyes on it. James had never used it to bluff before, which is why it might work this time. Nobody would be expecting it from him.

He fanned his cards close to his chest while leaning back. He'd been dealt a good hand, not a great hand. As he arranged his three eights, the jack of spades and the two of clubs, a plane flew overhead. His pulse quickened while he checked to see if it was an enemy aircraft. He'd learned how to differentiate the enemy planes by the picture on the military-issued cards they used. False alarm. He tossed some cash in the pot.

Seated next to him, Lenny fidgeted. The plane must have gotten to him, too. He whispered, "Whatever happens to me, you remember what I told you to do?" His facial tics put James on edge.

James frowned and shook his head in disbelief. "Don't talk like that, Len. But yes, I remember." Lenny's wife and daughter lived in Louisiana. Lenny wanted everything sent to them.

"Jus' checking." Lenny's round face looked as pale as a full moon. His eyes kept flickering around and James knew if he didn't stop, he'd be accused of cheating.

It was James' turn to play so he discarded the two and drew. Five of hearts. If he could match the jack of spades, he'd have a great chance of winning with a full house. When placing bets, he always did some basic math to understand his odds. Then he knew his chances of improving his hand. He also considered who was gathered around this table. Lenny, for example, often raised a certain amount and bluffed, so it was likely he'd repeat that.

Last time James played, he'd won with a straight he caught on the draw. But he didn't want to sit around playing cards. He wanted to complete more missions, help end this godforsaken war, and get back to Sadie. Back to living again. Being here felt like death row except worse. He never knew when his time might be up. Then again, maybe that was God's mercy.

After a few rounds, he decided to bluff. Everyone at the table with the exception of Conn had recently been bled dry and wouldn't want to take another risk. James banked on Conn folding. He strategically placed his lighter in the pot.

Conn, eyebrows raised, fingered his chin in a thinking gesture. "Tell us about last week's bomb run."

Damn. Conn's entreaty for James to talk meant he wasn't going to fold. Not yet anyway. Conn continued. "Those Jerries didn't stand a chance, did they? Tell the boys what you did. Don't be bashful..."

James shifted in his seat, uncomfortable with the attention. He discarded a card and drew—of all things—a two of clubs. He hid his disappointment. At least he hoped he did.

"Dropped all 'em bombs in the right place, you did," Conn continued. "They never saw it coming, did they, Pasko?"

"I don't know about that, but we took them off course probably," James said modestly. He didn't want to relive it—the sound of shells bursting when they'd been hit. But the men were all staring at him, and stories of survival gave them new hope.

James continued. "First we lost our escort." The fighter plane accompanying their bomber had been shot down, making them an easy target. "We got hit in the left wing, and in the engine."

"You bailed then?" the radio operator asked.

"No. But we probably should have...we'd been hit hard..." James trailed off because Lenny looked like he might vomit.

"Could you have made it back to base?" Conn asked.

"Doubt it. The plane was too damaged. Then another engine was hit. Everything happened real fast." The air had rushed through the cabin making a terrible sound. That's when James had screamed in horror as

Roger, their ball-turret gunner, had been hit and his ear was gone. The vomit had gushed up and out, choking James. He'd braced himself with his heavy flying boots against the vibration of the plane and then collapsed down to hold Roger's convulsing upper body.

"Where was I hit?" Roger had gurgled while the blood seeped out the corner of his mouth. James struggled to keep his panic inside.

Please, God, have mercy.

James said, "Stay with me, buddy, okay?" His tongue burned from the bile acid. He realized his vomit was covering his chest and had spilled onto Roger. James wiped it off Roger, fighting to breathe. Wiping and shaking and screaming.

They could've been shot down at any second. *Why weren't they parachuting out?* He strained to look through the waist window while still holding Roger and screaming, "Hold on, buddy. Keep holding on. I'm here, I'm here." The vast expanse of water below approached.

"We're clearing the water," Captain Marshall announced. "But we can't make it back to base."

Then Roger's body went limp. His quivering skin relaxed while his body quaked and convulsed a few gruesome times. Roger's eyes froze in place. "Jesus!" James shook him and shouted through sweat-blurred eyes, "Roger, Roger! Don't!"

The group around the card table were all looking at James now, the game nearly forgotten.

"When did you parachute out?" a radio operator asked.

James shook his head. "We never jumped. We landed, but it was risky, and we're lucky the Jerries didn't get us on the ground." He remembered bracing for impact in their crash landing position, his knees pulled to his chest and against Chuck's back. All he'd been thinking about was Sadie and her soft skin in the hollow under her jaw. If he fixated too much on losing her though, it just might have killed him before the Germans did.

"Landed in the middle of a frozen field. Then the British arrived to help," James said.

They went around the table discarding and drawing one more time before anyone spoke. James still needed another jack.

Ralph, a hot head navigator from Iowa cleared his throat, his eyes gleaming like a proud new daddy. But before he could show his cards, the sirens sounded. James looked up with the rest of them and watched as a formation of enemy planes soared ominously overhead.

The Germans were back. It was show time.

Chairs toppled as the men scattered in every direction, to collect gear and climb into planes. A controlled mayhem unfolded—men darting to get to position as quickly as humanly possible, probably praying to God the same way James was, that they wouldn't get hit from above in the scramble.

The last thing James remembered was seeing Ralph swipe the lighter out of the pot and stick it in his pocket. He shouted as they ran alongside each other. "Straight flush, Pasko. I had a straight flush!"

As empty as his pocket felt without the lighter in it, James couldn't help almost smiling as he thought about how crushed poor Ralph would be when he had to give it back. Because there was no way Conn would ever believe Ralph's story of the straight flush.

Chapter Twenty-Eight

Sadie hurried to answer the door before the persistent knocking woke Louise in the parlor. With every step, she grew increasingly irritated. There had better be a fire somewhere, she thought, curling her lips down.

A wave of nausea reminded her that she had bigger issues to be concerned about. She flared her nostrils against the next queasy ripple while swinging the door open. A uniformed messenger boy held a tan Western Union envelope. His bicycle was propped at the bottom of the steps.

"May I help you?" she asked him.

"I've got a telegram for a"—he read the name through the envelope window—"Miss Sadie Stark?"

A telegram for her?

Sadie's heart thudded like a ticking bomb. Each beat notched up her throat. She stared at the envelope before nodding. Then her breath caught as she touched the crisp vellum, trying not to look at the recipient's name in typewriter text located in the top corner.

Her fingers ripped open the envelope in jagged pieces, slicing her finger. She winced at the prick.

"Come inside." Ruth guided her back into the foyer.

Sadie ripped the tan paper out and unfolded it. Her eyes scanned the chunks of words in fits and bursts.

All she could think was: this wasn't an army telegram.

James was alive.

She collapsed onto the piano bench and exhaled, blowing loose strands of hair from her hot face while sucking her finger. Her next thought was how foolish she'd been to assume she was James' next of kin. She wasn't his wife. Technically, she was nothing to James on paper, in the eyes of the military.

That thought settled in her gut like a brick. Then she reluctantly read the economical message for the first time.

SADIE STARK

411 PROSPECT PLACE BRYN MAWR PA

DOLL COME FIND ME AT ZETA PSI at 3337 WALNUT STREET NE CORNER OF 34TH AND WALNUT SOON AS POSSIBLE PACK AN OVERNIGHT BAG I'LL EXPLAIN LATER HURRY

HENRY MCALISTER

Pack a bag? What for? And why had he sent a telegram? Her mind raced back to the recent calls Henry had made to the rooming house. The ones she'd missed while holed up in the library, and hadn't returned. But a telegram? It seemed dire, even for him.

Maybe he knew about her pregnancy. She shuddered. What if someone had overheard her conversation with Ruth at the diner? Or one of her housemates had caught her vomiting in the toilet before class? Anyone could have passed along a suspicion through a friend or boyfriend at Penn. It wouldn't have taken much—as Henry's social circle spread far.

But he wanted her to go somewhere with him, which was strange.

To elope?

She wouldn't put in notice for this trip, thinking wistfully of her last adventure—with James—and how she hadn't hesitated for even one second before breaking curfew that weekend to run off without permission.

Curfew. That gave her an idea as she flew up to her bedroom. She dressed, pinned on her hat, and slipped Henry's ring into her purse while deciding she'd tell Henry she wasn't allowed to go anywhere with him. She had to be back on campus or else take a tongue-lashing and demerits from Louise.

Downstairs Louise was still nestled in her favorite high-back chair in the parlor, covered from the waist down by her fringed wool blanket, an open book in her lap. An eagle guarding her nest, Louise had intended to keep tabs on the girls' comings and goings. Sadie thanked her lucky stars the woman was pretty awful at it. She had to return Henry's ring. In person. Nothing else would do.

She inhaled deeply and held that breath while descending the last few rickety stairs, avoiding the wood plank that creaked.

****

On the train to Philadelphia, Sadie sat next to a middle-aged woman and across from a young mother holding a wailing infant. The young mother's broad hips were flanked with a toddler on each side. Where Sadie had hardly paid any attention to babies before, now they seemed to be everywhere and she couldn't peel her eyes away from this one. The mother turned the baby so he could see Sadie, who sat facing him. He stopped crying, apparently interested in his new view.

He seemed vulnerable, barely in charge of his own body. His mouth formed a little O. One ear turned out, and his head, the size of a grapefruit, displayed tiny hairs like the stick-like trees atop Pennsylvania's winter hills.

Could she do this, Sadie wondered, while studying this tiny, yet incredibly demanding little bundle with curiosity, but mostly, fear. She'd have to. She sank her teeth into her cracked bottom lip. Her eyes darted to the woman's dull wedding band. What would people think of her when they saw her bare fingers holding her baby?

The baby seemed to be trying to make sense of this world. He flung his head back into his mother's chest, infuriating himself at his sudden loss of control. He screamed something dreadful and his eyes turned into little slits surrounded by dimpled, pink flesh.

Sadie smiled sympathetically. Suddenly, he stopped, and through a toothless grin, he cooed at her. Sadie's smile widened. They had made a connection.

But the idea of trading places with that baggy-eyed mother across from her smothered Sadie like hands holding her under water. She gasped against the ebbing nausea, struggling to breathe normally. She could barely take care of herself at the moment—how would she expect to take on anything else?

If only her sickness had been caused by the traveling motion and would stop once she stepped off the train. Suddenly the inside of the train car seemed to be closing in around her as she sought some relief from the constant need to vomit. If she thought Henry's diamond ring had weighed her down earlier, it was nothing compared to the acid creeping up her throat and the queasy waves flooding her hunched body.

"They grow up fast," said the middle-aged woman to the new mother. "No matter how hard you try, you can't keep 'em forever," she added, adjusting her headscarf. "That's a good thing," the young mother replied, bobbing the infant, and ignoring the toddler who burrowed under her arm.

The scarf-clad older woman continued. "When my son was a boy I made sure he ate well, did his chores, said his prayers. At night when I tucked him in, I covered him with extra blankets so he wouldn't be cold. I dreamed of his future. Then he grew up on me. They do that you know. When you least expect it, they're gone."

"I'm sure he's a fine man today," Sadie said.

"Was. It'll be six months today since he died in the war." The woman made the sign of the cross, then laced her fingers together in her lap.

"I'm terribly sorry," Sadie said. Her eyes moistened at the idea of losing someone she loved. Losing James.

The young mother straightened in her seat, and glanced at her children ever so subtly. She said, "Yes, very sorry for your loss, ma'am."

"They don't belong to us. We think they do, but they don't. Still, it ain't right for your child to go first. Ain't right…"

Sadie gazed out the train window, recalling a favorite Bible passage Nanny liked to paraphrase: 1 Corinthians 13. "When I was a child, I spoke like a child, I thought like a child, I reasoned like a child. When I became a woman, I put away childish things."

She was going to be a mother. It struck her like a

slap to her face. Whether she liked it or not. She had to put away childish things—stop blaming others, stop letting life happen to her, stop living passively. Maybe she had no control over her baby's future, James' safety, God's plan, but she could be responsible for her actions right now. That much belonged to her. She needed to get her life in order.

Although she was exhausted just thinking about what she had to do, and struggling with the nausea that was now a constant companion, a newfound clarity lifted her spirits.

First, she'd find Henry. She'd ask what he knew and why he'd wanted her to come. And then she'd give back the ring.

Henry couldn't possibly love her, not with the way a parade of girls distracted him as easily as the wind changed direction. Maybe once he realized she didn't love him, he'd move on to find the right girl. Would he help Sadie then? He was an unlikely ally, but she had to try.

She saw a farmhouse through the train window. Smoke curled out the chimney into the darkening sky. Each shuttered window held a lit candle. A black lab leaped through the deep, white snow to greet a pickup truck moving up the lane. A woman keeping vigil on the front porch fell to her knees. The train moved on before Sadie could see what happened next and this bothered her. Sadie needed to know what happened to bring the woman to her knees in prayer. Had she just realized she'd lost her son?

The mother on the train cradled her baby. His eyelids grew heavy and fluttered, resisting the inevitable. He wailed, fists clenched in tiny balls, then surrendered, hunkering down into deep sleep.

Sadie reached inside her purse for the piece of paper James had given her with his Pittsburgh boarding house's address. A part of her wanted to reverse the train and disappear to Pittsburgh, take a job at a factory, construct a new reality. Women were needed in the factories. But this was a selfish, cowardly plan that didn't account for the people who cared about her or the innocent life growing inside her. In fact, she began to doubt her letter to James had been a good idea at all. He certainly didn't need further reason to worry about her wellbeing.

Henry's stop was next.

She put the note away and took a deep breath. She could do this. She had to.

Chapter Twenty-Nine

"Jesus, doll, where on earth have you been?" Henry dragged her in for a rough hug that squeezed the air from her lungs and assaulted her nose with the pungent stench of rubbing alcohol. The fraternity room smelled of liquor and wet dog. Glenn Miller's big band music drifted down the hall.

Henry went on. "I've been worried sick. Why haven't you called? Why have you been ignoring me? It shouldn't take an emergency telegram to get my fiancée's attention. Are you trying to give me a heart attack?"

"Calm down, Henry." She marched across the room to throw open the window before the reek of dirty socks forced the contents of her stomach into her throat. He'd been on another bender, she thought, noticing the bloody roadmap riddling his eyeballs. A suitcase lay open on the bed, half-filled.

"You know what his problem is—your uncle?" Henry's forehead vein bulged as he launched into one of his unexplained rants. So, this wasn't about her pregnancy. Sadie placed a protective hand over her belly. If he knew, his fury would have met her at the door.

"He's 'new money.' New money doesn't get it."

"Get what? That it's wrong to work for a living? It's beneath you?" Sadie's anger flared to the surface.

Henry jerked his head at her quick outburst. Then he dumped the contents of a drawer into the suitcase.

She narrowed her eyes and grabbed at his pale, thick forearm. "Henry, what's going on?"

He didn't respond, but his eyes flickered to the dresser. That's when she saw the crinkled paper. She lunged for it and scanned the opening line. "We regret to inform you..." It was a suspension notice from the department head.

"How long have you been lying to me?" She shook the paper in the air.

He snatched it from her hands and crumpled it.

"Doll." His face contorted and he swatted her words away like pesky gnats. "You have to believe me when I say I was going to tell you. I was. I just needed to figure out some things. And now I have." He wiped his upper lip with his sleeve.

"What things?"

"Listen, I need your help." Again he changed the topic back to himself and what he needed. Always what he needed, Sadie noted.

He strapped on his watch and checked it. "Come away with me. What do ya say?"

Had he gone mad? She swallowed the lump in her throat. "Are you in trouble with the law?"

"No." He laughed awkwardly. "Don't worry your pretty little head." He closed the suitcase and latched it.

How dare he talk down to her like that, she fumed. A fever hot anger boiled. "Are you expecting a draft letter?"

"Okay, you want to know the truth, baby? I've always tried to shelter you, not upset you with...with things you don't understand. But you give me no other choice here. If you have to know, you have to know. We're leaving. You and me. Now." He looked around her then waved his hand away. "Forget your bag. I have cash. Lots of it. We'll buy whatever you need there. Anything you want, doll."

Leaving? With lots of cash? She sank her teeth into her cheek.

"We have to leave soon so make yourself useful and hand me those papers over there." He opened the top desk drawer, took a revolver from it, and tucked it into his trousers under his coat. Then he hustled around removing other traces of his sham of a life.

"Go where? And why do you have a gun?" She seethed through gritted teeth, tasting the iron sourness of the cuts her teeth had caused.

"Canada, doll. Hurry up with those papers, will you?"

She feared what he might do next based on the erratic way his voice vacillated from high-pitched angst to his normal urgency. But she needled on. "Are you dodging the draft, Henry?" She backed away with shaky hands, feeling the grooves of his dresser along her spine as she inched toward the door. "That's against the law."

He grabbed her by the wrists and pulled her so close to his face that she smelled the pine needle breath of his gin fix. "Keep your voice down, okay? It's just for a few weeks, months maybe."

She tore away from him, her nostrils quivering, trying desperately to keep it together. She wouldn't go anywhere with him. And, she thought, as panic crawled over her flesh, he could be arrested for defection.

She stopped moving and rooted her heeled boots in

their spot. "I'm not going." Her voice was steady and firm.

"What the hell are you talking about?"

"You heard me." She met his eyes with a steely stare, standing as still and as strong as a statue.

"Do you want me to die in the trenches over there—like an animal? I'm not expendable. I've got big plans for our future."

"For your future." She stabbed the air between them with her pointer finger.

He glowered but didn't argue—which told Sadie he planned to flee with or without her. She suspected nothing she said—that he would disgrace his family, worry them sick, possibly tarnish his future career— would change his mind about Canada. If only she hadn't come here today or had arrived minutes later, after he had already left, then the decision would have been made for her. But that's not how it was unfolding. Part of her knew this was her moment to tell him all of the things she'd been too scared to say before.

"I can't marry you."

There, she thought triumphantly. She'd said it.

Henry stood frozen, staring at her, for once, speechless. Then he sat on the edge of the bed. "Oh fuck," he said, his head in his hands. "You're breaking it off with me?" He looked up through splayed fingers. When she nodded, his face fell and he groaned. "You don't mean it."

"You don't get to decide what I do with my life." She winced, holding her belly as a cramp seized her lower abdomen. The feeling alarmed her, but she pushed through it. She opened her clutch and handed him the ring.

His brick-red face blended into his hair. "Jesus, Sadie. You spring this on me now? Do you have any idea how hard this is for *me*?" He paced, the hurt emanating from every pore in his barrel-chested, thick body.

"I'm not in love with you."

Another cramp peeled away inside. She grimaced and steadied herself on the bedpost. What was happening to her baby? Was he in trouble?

Henry spun around to face her, scaring her with what he might do. He snatched the ring and at the same time squinted at James' coat she'd hung on the doorknob. "I get it. You were with him when I came to see you that weekend. But he's gone now, isn't he?" He chuckled sadistically. "Who will have you when that son-of-a-bitch comes back in a box?"

She looked away from his intimidating glare inches from her face and focused on James' words penetrating her woozy head. The words he'd spoken and written flooded back to her now.

The war won't last forever.

I'll be back before you know it.

I lost you once—I won't lose you again.

"You'll never be happy." Henry puckered his cheek in disgust as he dug the ring into his deep trouser pocket.

He was wrong. He was too caught up in his own selfish world. If he truly cared about her, he'd never ask her to help him break the law. She heard James again.

No matter what happens to me, you deserve to be happy.

You make me want to be a better man.

I want to make you proud.

She doubted Henry had any desire to make her proud. She reached for James' coat and slipped it on, letting Henry see for himself who she'd chosen. Then she inhaled and puffed her chest, threw back her shoulders, and lifted her chin. "Henry McAlister. You…" She pointed at his chest. "You are a frightened spoiled child who never grew up." She blew the air from her lungs. When he walked toward her, she stopped him with both hands up. "You picked the wrong woman. I won't play your charade any longer. I have indulged you, and I regret that. And I've been dishonest. But there's no greater crime than what you're doing."

"What I'm doing?" He gestured to himself with a hooked finger.

"Turning your back on responsibility. You're a fraud. You are not a man of your word. You don't have a clue what it takes to work for anything. Not for your country, not for your family, not for yourself. Certainly not for me. You wouldn't know the true meaning of love if it crossed that threshold and slapped you in your pompous, self-seeking face."

Henry retracted his face into a double chin, rolling his eyes.

She wasn't done. "You think you're better than everyone because your family has money? Because of your last name? You're wrong. You've never helped the poor, never rolled up your shirtsleeves for anything. You've always taken what was given to you and then asked for more."

Her heart hammered against her chest, blood and adrenaline pumping her alive with confidence, yet more cramps tugged at her insides. She needed water, to lie down, something. Instead, she continued. "This is your chance to make things right. I'm asking you to do the honorable thing and stay. For once. If not for your family, for yourself."

She held her breath, waiting.

Henry grabbed his suitcase handle, glared back, and turned on her the way she had feared he someday would. As he walked out the door, he said, "You'll never find what you're looking for."

I already have, Sadie thought smugly. *I already have.*

As the coward fled the room, she held onto the door while watching him go. Her chest heaved with the delicious feeling of triumph. She buttoned up James' coat with fumbling fingers, and tucked her purse under her arm. Then she marched down the creaking hall.

She'd done it. It was just as she'd planned.

But then a warmth spread down her inner thighs. She peered down. A pressure gave between her legs and she watched the black-red blood pooling at her feet, slowly spreading like molasses. Oh God! What was happening?

Afraid to move, she watched in terror as the thick syrupy blood coated the floor, and seeped under her boots. She picked her feet away, and groped along the grimy wall toward the stairwell. She felt woozy and funny, as if her head were unattached to her body. She had to get out of there before anyone saw her. Before anyone found out that the governor's daughter—and Henry's ex-fiancée—was bleeding out her illegitimate child on their fraternity floor.

She swayed in slow motion and then everything went dark.

Chapter Thirty

When Sadie opened her eyes, she lay in a metal hospital bed, a thin white blanket pulled taut across her body, the lights dimmed. How she got here, she had no idea.

"Sweetheart, thank God." Uncle Edward hovered, appearing out of nowhere, taking her hand and rubbing it between his own, a worried expression aging his handsome face, ruffling his calm demeanor. "You gave us quite a scare." His voice was deeper than usual, hoarse, as if he were coming down with a cold.

When Sadie propped up on her elbows, her head pounded in protest. "Oh…"

"Lie down, sweetheart, I don't want you to strain yourself."

She eased back down. A curtain whipped open revealing the pursed-lip glare of a nurse in uniform, hands on hips, white hat secure. A less mature nurse may have buckled in the governor's presence, but not this one.

"Visiting time is nearly over, sir," she announced. "No exceptions."

Edward nodded, turned his full attention to Sadie, and offered to raise the head of her bed so she might be more comfortable.

"I'll do that," the nurse said. When she finished, she padded on to the next patient, and left them alone.

Edward seemed to be at a loss as to what to do next. He picked up a vase full of pink rimmed pale roses off the windowsill and scanned the room as if looking for a better spot for them. When he couldn't find one, he placed them back on the sill.

"The doctor told you then?" she asked meekly, unable to meet his gaze.

"Yes." He settled in the chair beside her bed, patting her hand. He had never been one to display affection—toward her or Aunt Bea. A hand pat was significant.

"Is the baby okay?" was her next question.

"The doctor thinks so, yes, but you need to stay in bed for a few days. Plenty of fluids and rest."

"Really?" She settled down in a daze, surprising herself with her need to know about this baby who days ago she hadn't known existed. An IV was taped to her hand; the tube that strung from it ran up to a bottle hanging on a metal hook. She concentrated on her body for a moment and when the fingers of nausea needled her, she knew her baby was indeed okay. She welcomed the feeling, thanked God for it. She anxiously awaited Edward's reaction to her pregnancy, but he said nothing.

"Aren't you…upset with me?"

He stood and strode to the window. "You're an adult," he said almost under his breath. Then he turned to face her. "And you'll be married soon. We can make that happen sooner if you want."

So, he'd assumed the baby was Henry's. She could tell he wasn't pleased, even with that assumption, and appreciated his brevity. Although she wanted to talk about what was happening, she felt uncomfortable discussing it with the man she admired. How would he react when he learned that she wasn't going to marry Henry? And the fact that the baby was James'?

"How did I get here?" she asked.

"Someone at the fraternity house called an ambulance. You were brought here a few hours ago. They said you fainted. Where the hell is Henry and why wasn't he with you?" He ran a hand through his salt and pepper hair. He loosened his tie with a jerk.

Sadie sighed, not prepared for this conversation. She figured he would not take the news of Henry's leaving well, especially now that he believed Henry's baby was involved, but there was no reason to beleaguer.

"Henry's gone. Went to Canada."

"Canada?" He stood, hands planted on hips like the nurse had done earlier. He stared out the window, mentally piecing together the puzzle. Sadie needn't explain further. Once more, Henry's actions revealed his true character, and this time she did not defend him.

"You know his leaving isn't your fault." He furrowed his bushy, gray brows. "He'll be back."

"I tried to stop him. He wouldn't listen."

"When has he ever listened?" He threw his hands up in anger and shook his head.

She grew bolder. "I called off the wedding, too."

"You did *what*?"

"I know how it must look."

He shook his head and began pacing again. "Sadie, honey, you're choosing a difficult path."

"I know, but aren't the best things in life worth it? I just know I can't go through with marrying Henry when I'm not in love with him."

He remained silent. Again, his reaction surprised her. She was expecting one of Aunt Bea's lectures, delivered far more tactfully through him, but none of it came. Little did he know she had planned to call off the wedding regardless of Henry's decision to leave.

"You support my decision to call off the wedding?"

"I'm not happy about it. But Henry never deserved you. I'd be dishonest if I didn't admit to that. I only supported your engagement because I thought it was what you wanted. I've always wanted you to be happy, honey. Everyone has to live their own life. I wanted to tell you how I felt before he proposed, but after it was done, your aunt wouldn't let me say another word on the matter. Convinced me of Henry's redeeming qualities. What redeeming qualities will she find now?"

He kept pacing the room, more agitated than ever. "You know who impressed me recently? That young man who came to our home to return your stolen handbag."

Sadie sat up again, forgetting about her headache and grimaced when the sudden movement caused her temples to throb. "You mean James Pasko?" Her heart sank when she realized whatever respect her father felt toward James might swing the opposite way as soon as he found out they'd conceived out of wedlock.

"Yes, yes. You remember him?" he asked. Then he studied her, as if seeing her for the first time.

"Of course I remember him." *I'm in love with him.*

"Reminds me of myself, that boy." He took a seat, pulled on his ear, and watched her. Then he smoothed her hair by running his hand from her crown to the base of her neck, another unusual display of affection.

"Sadie, everything's going to be okay. You know I'll help you. Beatrice and I both. We'll support you in any way you need."

"Thank you," she said. "I know you'll be involved, like you were for me." She searched for the right words to express how much his presence meant. Although he'd traveled often, when he was home, he'd always listened attentively, read to her in the library, and invited her to share her favorite passages or recite poetry while he smoked his pipe, pleased with her inquisitive nature. Not knowing her parentage, she'd always thought some part of her was missing when in fact he had been there all along. She likened it to the way people resist the church and seek solace in other ways, then fall on hard times and blame God for their hardships when in fact He had carried them through the worst of it.

"You're sure about this?" he asked.

She nodded.

"What will you tell your child someday?"

She seized this opportunity. She couldn't ask him for the truth unless she was willing to offer the same.

"This child will know who her father is. That James is her father." There. She'd pushed it all to the surface, now it was up to him.

"James?"

She nodded. "I won't keep any secrets."

He stared down at his shoes and pulled on his ear again.

"Sadie." His face was drawn, his voice fraught with remorse. He took off his glasses to rub at the bridge of his nose and brow. "There's something very important I need to tell you, sweetheart."

241

Here it was. At last. She tilted her head at him and furrowed her brow, afraid that her voice might squeak if she spoke.

"I've been meaning to tell you this for a long time. Please forgive me for not doing it sooner. I know you're an adult, but I still think of you as the little girl I need to protect. I know…" He waved his hand in defense. "You're a woman now." He struggled on the word "woman," forcing it out. "But it's time you knew the truth, about you and me."

"You and me?" It was an interesting choice of words.

"Your story is tangled up in mine, I suppose. I'm an old fool, Sadie. Terrible at this," he said, his bottom eyelids drooping. His extreme unease reminded her of the day he sat her down to have "the talk." She had started her period and thought she was dying. Nanny and Aunt Bea were away on a trip and there was nobody else to console her, with the exception of the maid she barely knew, and apparently it was important to him that she have someone to talk to, as uncomfortable as it must have been. Glossing over details, he simply said God made her this way, like every woman, and when she fell in love with a man who loved and respected her, she could have a baby. When the time was right. Then he warned her about the dangers of boys. He had used the word impulsive. "They don't think, just act. Will get you in trouble," was the message she had taken away.

He was acting as awkward now as he had been then, scratching at his temple and making a strange noise in his throat. She decided to spare him further agony.

"I know what happened."

He looked up, his mouth slack.

"I found Audrey. She told me everything."

His creased his forehead in wrinkled lines, raised his eyebrows. "You found her? Where?" The mask he had worn was at once transparent; in one look she saw what lay dormant all of these years. A hint of desperation had crept into his usually calm voice.

He had been in love with her mother. He was, quite possibly, still in love with her.

"In New York City. She lives above an Irish tavern." She wouldn't tell him the whole truth, that Audrey washed dishes and lived alone with a cat.

He looked up to the ceiling, and grabbed at his neck skin. "Oh, God. That woman brought me to my knees." His voice cracked. "I was smitten the moment I saw her perform on stage. I know it sounds unbelievable, this love at first sight business, but that's exactly how it happened…for us. I was crazy with infatuation, yet I never could pin her down. She had big aspirations of her own." He gushed like river water bursting through an open dam, all of his pent up emotion pouring through the floodgates. The same pride she felt for James now spread across his face but did not last.

Just as quickly he composed himself. "She was fresh off the farm and I feared someone would take advantage of her in her quest to become famous. I wasn't trying to control her—just help her. She refused to marry me, but I would not be dissuaded. I was so convinced she would marry me someday that I engraved her initial in that compact mirror you have. I planned to give it to her on our wedding day."

Her mother had never known about the compact. "But you never got the chance to give it to her, did you?"

"She had other plans. She skipped town with a playwright. I had no idea she was pregnant with you."

"I know…"

"I told her I would do anything for her and I meant that. If she ever needed anything, I would be there for her. And I was true to my word."

She thought of James and his exact sentiment on the train platform at their parting.

"Of course I was heartsick. Eventually I did move on though. I turned to work, burying myself in it, putting every ounce of energy into my political aspirations so that I wouldn't have anything left over to feel sad about."

Sadie understood this. She always thought highly successful people were motivated by some significant thing, be it severe loss, unattainable joy, a deep-rooted unfulfilled purpose. Although, it saddened her to realize it was extreme loss that propelled her father to greatness.

"Then I married Beatrice. Everything was easy with her. No discord, no ups and downs."

No passion.

"Beatrice has always been a good wife and I had feared I would betray her by telling you about your mother, because in telling you, I'd be admitting my deep love for another woman. And you were well adjusted. It didn't seem right to dredge up the past when so much was at stake. But I was prepared to tell you if you came to me and asked. I know now I was wrong, to expect a child to approach her parent with such a thing. I handled it all wrong, damn fool that I am." He fidgeted in his chair, but kept eye contact with her.

"Did you ever try to find her?"

"In the beginning, before my marriage to Beatrice, yes. I did try. I naively hoped she would reconsider a life with me, once she got acting off her mind, but I was being selfish, and I'm ashamed to admit it. You can't expect someone to give up on their dreams. I searched playbills and secretly followed her theater successes, but then she disappeared off the scene. I assumed she had settled down and had a family of her own. I figured she wouldn't stay single for long. I had no idea you existed." He sighed. "Once I was married, I put away hopes of a reconciliation. Although Beatrice and I couldn't have children, my political career was taking off and we were doing fine. We had our health. But I felt some part of me was missing. Later I realized that part was you."

"Me?"

"You'll see." He gestured to her. "When you become a parent, it's like nothing you can imagine now. Do you remember the stalk of curly willow I cut from a branch of our big tree out back? Remember how we planted it near your playhouse and it grew into a strong, wild thing? And you said it would grow stronger than my big tree? That's what it's like to be a parent. You watch your own grow stronger than you ever thought possible, stronger than yourself. It's like watching a piece of you walk around taking chances, making mistakes, succeeding, floundering—all separate from you. And there ain't a damn thing you can do about it." He chuckled. "You're at once amazed, fearful, frustrated. Proud. You can give your child everything, but her dreams, well, her dreams are something that belongs only to her. And the hardest part is letting go. The hardest, most selfless part—I believe that was how it was for your mother to let go of you."

Sadie's eyes welled and threatened to spill over. He wasn't one for emotional talks and, like an addiction, the more he shared, the more she craved. She hated to taint his pristine image of her mother; the truth about her not wanting to raise her child would hurt him. She decided to guide the conversation back to his story. "What happened when Nanny brought me back from the park that day?"

"That day...I'll never forget it." He squinted as he replayed the scene. "I came home from work early to surprise Beatrice with calla lilies for our anniversary. Instead, Nanny met me at the door holding you in her arms. I took in Audrey's perfume on you and knew at once that you were her daughter. Nanny told me your mother needed help and that I would know what to do. Beatrice had miscarried her second baby a few months prior, and was struggling, rarely left her room." He shook his head.

"I assumed that you were the playwright's daughter. It didn't matter to me, you were a piece of her and I wanted to raise you—in turn, help her as I promised I would. This is where it gets difficult for me to explain. The lies. In a moment of panic, I told Beatrice that your mother was my cousin. I did have a cousin in the theater. She wanted to believe me. You have to know that it was all my idea, not your aunt's. It was only natural for her to worry about scandal. Press speculation, you know. She showed great compassion toward you, honey. And she desperately wanted to be a mother. That night, after Nanny had you tucked into your new bed and asleep, I went to find Audrey."

"You did?"

"Yes, I wanted to see her and find out about you and the circumstances leading to her giving you to Nanny. All I knew was your name. A lovely name." He smiled. "But, I was too late. The cast had packed up, vacated their dressing rooms, taken to the road, it appeared. A security guard was about to make me leave when I broke down and told him my story. To convince me she was gone, he led me to the special dressing room at the back of the theater that she had occupied and he let me see for myself. All that was left was a row of perfume bottles along the base of the mirror at her dressing table—the same ones I had given to her on special occasions. At the time I had given them to her, we were so happy..." He paused sadly. "I didn't know if I should be happy that she had kept my gifts that long or if I should be disappointed that she had left them behind. Of course they were almost empty. As empty as I felt. The guard said she had left in a hurry. I slipped the bottles into my pockets, trying to gather what was left of her for you—a keepsake of sorts."

"You did that for me?" Sadie asked, surprised that in his own grief he would think of another man's cast-off child. She wasn't surprised, though. He had always made her feel special. "But what about the photograph?"

His face fell at the recollection. "Outside of the perfume, the photograph was the only thing I kept after she left me. I had forgotten about it, actually, until you found it in my office desk. Beatrice was deeply hurt when she saw that photo, saw that the woman had meant something to me, was obviously not my cousin, suspected I had saved the picture because I still loved her. I never meant to hurt her or you, but I inadvertently caused trouble between you both, I know it and I take full responsibility, even now."

"It's okay," Sadie assured him, although she couldn't help but wonder how her relationship with Bea might have been different otherwise.

"I told Beatrice about Audrey then. That you were her daughter. That she had left with the playwright."

Sadie nodded, remembering how her aunt relayed this critical piece of her past.

As if reading her mind, he said, "It was wrong of her to tell you that, dear, and I apologize from the bottom of my heart. I should have told you the truth sooner, but I couldn't do it. Another lie sprang from the first."

"Did you suspect you were my...father?" It was the first time she used this qualifier—the word "father" hung in the air on display, after sixteen years of glaring omission.

"Yes, I did, especially when you turned your face to a certain angle or used an expression from my side of the family. At first I convinced myself it was my imagination manifesting in what I wanted to see. I couldn't be sure. Had you inherited my mannerisms or inadvertently picked them up?"

She wondered if he had fantasized about Audrey coming back to him because he was raising her—their daughter. She imagined it must have been difficult to harbor a secret like this all of those years. Then a horrible thought crossed her mind. Did he blame her for

Audrey's leaving? And for her staying away? No, she decided. He blamed himself for that. She assumed that was why he wanted her to know Henry's leaving wasn't her fault—because he too had been left behind.

"I hope you can find it in your precious heart to forgive this old fool."

"I do forgive you," she said. "More than that, I owe my life to you. You saved me, don't you know that?"

He looked at her quizzically.

She drew on James' words. "The past is just that—the past. You can't change it. You shouldn't dwell on it. What was done was done. And you have always been wonderful to me, you have always made me feel important, been my soft place to fall. Like right now."

"Sweetheart, I can't tell you how much it means to hear you say that," he said, again choking on his words. "I don't want you and your baby to go through what happened with us."

She felt a tightness across the bridge of her nose. She reached for his hand. "For what it's worth, my mother did love you. She was in love with you, not the playwright. And she said leaving you, the father of her child, was her greatest regret."

"She told you that?"

"She did…" Sadie hesitated. "Father."

He leaned over and kissed her forehead. "Daughter."

He wrapped her up awkwardly in his arms and together they wept softly. She cried because she could never go back in time, never return to her childhood when she so desperately wanted to know who her parents were, where she came from, that they loved her. She cried because nothing stayed the same. Life went on. She had gone back to visit places of her past before. Once she visited their home before the governor's mansion. That nostalgic day was the closest she had come to going back in time, yet the place had changed and therefore wasn't the same anymore. Some changes were obvious, the white birch was taller, the painted picket fence had aged and faded, a crack had formed on the driveway, which seemed shorter than what she remembered of those sun-drenched afternoons playing hopscotch and riding her bicycle across the bumpy spots hear the sidewalk. Other changes were less obvious. Had the stone wall worn from nature's elements? Had the ceilings inside the house always been so low, the rooms so small? It occurred to her now that perhaps it was she who had changed, having grown in perspective, richer because of her life experiences, so that she saw this place differently when in fact everything was as it had been. Whether real or imagined, could anything, any place, any person really stay the same? Could you ever really return to a place of your past?

"Hand me my clutch," she asked him. When he did, she opened it and took out the compact mirror. Then she handed it to him. "She lives in apartment 1B above McSorley's."

He nodded, but wouldn't take the compact. "Thank you, but that part of my life is over. I have Beatrice to think about now."

Before leaving the hospital room, he kissed the top of her head, promised to check back in the morning, and he lay something across her feet, warming them. He smiled knowingly. It was James' coat.

Chapter Thirty-One

James said a little prayer as the bomber taxied down the runway for takeoff. They'd had no time for a briefing session, inspections, or final checks. Instead, he and the crew had hurriedly assembled their flight gear. Now the aircraft climbed and accelerated toward enemy skies.

Sweet Jesus, flak was flying everywhere. With visibility this poor, and enemy aircraft closing in on their escorts, they'd need a small miracle to stay on course to the drop point. The Germans meant business. Shrapnel penetrated the aluminum skin of the bomber, sizzling beside James' left boot. Out of the corner of his eye, he noticed that a German fighter plane was hovering on Frank's side of the bomber.

"Frank. Move here," he hollered.

Frank moved seconds before the shards of metal blasted through, marking more holes than James could count. Through the window a flock of enemy fighter planes stalked their formation like predators on prey. The smell of cordite, sweat, and fear hung all around him.

The crew looked numb, stoic and dazed, but James guessed they felt like he did on the inside, steeling for whatever God was about to hand to them. He'd never tell Sadie about the scene unfolding, especially while he was still here. Instead he'd written about his earnest feelings for her and his take on the war, though he was not honest about the danger. He kept his language upbeat.

Trying to get on with it, love, so I can see you sooner.

Eleven more missions to go and I'll be home.

We have a solid crew. The very best.

But in reality they dared the devil in this game of Russian roulette. James never knew when or where the next flurry of shrapnel would pierce the bomber—a few inches in either direction could make the difference between his returning to her in one piece or cold in a closed casket. Or never at all. All he had was faith, blind faith, to get through this hell storm.

"Christ!" A torrent of shrapnel hit them. The force jarred James' body and his metal helmet banged against the curved shell of the bomber. He looked over and saw their waist gunner slumped over another toppled body, both alive minutes ago. Vomit surged up James' throat and he choked it back.

Two of their four engines were out. Allied fighter planes came to the rescue, destroying the nearest enemy aircrafts, giving them a momentary reprieve. James' cheek flinched, and he half-collapsed in his spot from relief.

Captain Marshall maneuvered near their target, an important German transport facility, and then turned control over to James as bombardier. By now James had been rattled to his core. To witness metal chunks ripped apart mid-flight was one thing—body parts was another altogether. He convulsed, fighting back the urge to vomit again.

He kept shifting and moving trying not to fixate on

what might happen next. Sadie flashed through his mind—a vision of hope sweeping away as she glanced over her shoulder—like a silent movie outtake before the reel neared its end. Never in his imagination did he join her. Maybe he was too scared it wouldn't happen. And when he peered into the Norden M-9 bombsight to dial the calculated aim point, he kept seeing her eyes dilated in a panic that clouded his confidence. He'd prove his worthiness by getting this right.

He centered the bomb drop with trembling fingers and made final adjustments. All he had to do now was release the 500-pound explosives and then they could get back to base. Back to a respite from this hellhole only to wake up and do it all over again. Finally he was set.

But the damn toggle switch was broken.

It hadn't been the first time their crew faced a mechanical malfunction, but the toggle switch for Christ's sake! With a full bomb load onboard, they wouldn't be able to land. If they had to ditch the plane, he'd damn well make it count by turning the aircraft into a bomb itself.

James felt a heavy hand on his shoulder.

"What's wrong?" Frank asked.

"I don't know. Are the bomb bay doors stuck?" James asked.

"Let me—"

Frank seized, his eyeballs bulging as blood squirted from a gaping hole in his neck, splattering James' face. James recoiled, tasting the iron sourness of Frank's blood on his tongue. Then he flung forward to help Chuck, who held Frank's head in his lap, apply pressure to stop the blood. The lurching bomber tossed them about.

"Frank! Can you hear me?" James cried. "Come on, come on, come on…"

Both men tried to stop the blood and when they applied pressure, Frank twitched his arm.

"Frank! Hang on, brother!" James shouted, his upper lip a spasm of emotion.

Chuck was feeling for a pulse and shaking his head. "He's gone. Frankie's gone."

"He's not! I saw him move. He's still alive."

But Frank had gone rigid and James could tell with his own trembling fingers pressed to Frank's clammy skin searching for a sign, that Chuck was right. Frank was gone. Frank, who had cried in joy over recent news of his son's birth, now lay motionless, his eyes rolled back, lids snapped open.

They'd come this far. James had to complete this mission for Frank and for his wife and for their boy. He had to make it count. He used the interphone. "Captain, can we try again?"

As if in answer, the lumbering aircraft maneuvered around. "Pasko, one more go and then we're heading back."

James grated his knuckles together. "This one's for Frankie." He dialed the sight, forcing his hands to stop shaking, making minor adjustments. Sweat trickled at his temples. When everything was set, he reached for the switch, alternately praying and cursing.

It's not going to work, James thought. The goddamned mechanism won't deploy and they were going to get shot at again and again.

Then as if God answered his prayers, the bombs started falling before his eyes. James watched them explode right on target, sending bursting orange flames and smoke all over the railroad staging facility. His chest swelled with satisfaction. They'd attacked as planned.

The rest lay in God's hands.

They moved farther into the danger zone.

"There's no turning back," a crew member cried. "We're down two engines, boys. We need to lighten the load."

Captain Marshall's voice boomed, "Let's go boys, prepare to bail out."

Chuck was strapping on his parachute with the others.

James wouldn't do it. He dug his flying boots into position and shook his head no against the whistling winds streaming through the aircraft. How could anyone abandon the remaining crew? He sure as hell couldn't.

"Pasko—come! Now!" Chuck tossed him a parachute to strap on.

If there were some way to survive together, James would stubbornly go down trying.

The bomber rocked back, knocking everyone off their feet. James slammed his shoulder against the curved shell. He'd barely sat up when the bomber lurched the other way. The shrapnel penetrated the bomber. Chuck grabbed at his arm and calf. Then James knew the aircraft had spiraled out of control—the lurch in his gut told him they were losing altitude.

He panicked and grabbed the parachute at last. He struggled to strap it on as the forces of gravity tugged on his body, now on all fours. Through the open bomb bay he saw glimpses of sky, then land, sky, land—all spinning before him.

It was now or never. He swallowed more blood and gulped for air, wondering if this was it. Was he going to die now? Without seeing Sadie again? Would he take his final breaths in this godforsaken, doomed bomber?

He helped the remaining crew jettison the bottom hatch. The jump bell sounded. When it was his turn, he stood on the bomb bay and gave a final salute to his captain. He heard Sadie's raspy voice singing, *We'll meet again. Don't know where. Don't know when. But I know we'll meet again some sunny day.*

And he jumped.

Chapter Thirty-Two

Beatrice Stark stormed into the spartan hospital room as if she'd rehearsed it. Sadie watched from the bed with wide eyes as Beatrice, wearing a fox fur stole draped around her shoulders, flicked off the Murrow Boys' war update broadcast on the Bakelite radio. Her hired driver deposited a hard shell tweed suitcase on the floor, awaited his tip, then left them.

"Darling, you look dreadful."

Beatrice had changed, too. Puffy bags under her eyes and deep creases around her mouth aged her. Sadie drew the starched sheet and blanket up under her chin. Beatrice lit a cigarette. "Well? Do you have any idea what it took for me to get here?"

"Thank you for coming," Sadie whispered.

"I know you're thankful." She tilted her head to blow smoke in a singular stream. "I mean, who else would have come? Certainly not Henry. Not now." She took another long drag. "Anyway, the travel was awful, even with the hired car and I'm exhausted."

Of course she had to sneak Henry's name into the conversation, Sadie noted. She wanted to believe her aunt was just upset that Sadie had broken off the engagement. That she wanted Sadie to be happy and thought Henry could give her the life Bea thought she needed.

Sadie asked, "Where's—"

"Uncle Edward?"

Uncle Edward? Hadn't they talked? Didn't Bea know the gig was up? Sadie squinted in confusion while Bea took a long drag on her cigarette and walked to the window.

"Your *uncle* has been pulled away on business in New York."

Sadie wasn't sure if her emphasis on the word "uncle" was to let her know that she intended to keep up the charade. Or did she not know the real story? That couldn't be. In any case, her father's absence explained Bea's irritation, Sadie thought. She knew how much the woman loved to shop in New York City and now she was stuck here, in a hospital, with her.

"Over there." Beatrice pointed a maroon-gloved finger to the suitcase. "I packed a few things you'll need. I'll be back in the morning to collect you," was the last thing she said before leaving, barely making eye contact.

Curiosity spilled out of Sadie. The moment the door closed, she threw back the blanket and scrambled from her bed, wincing ever so slightly from the woozy rush of blood from standing suddenly. The nurse had ordered her to keep her feet up, but she couldn't help herself.

She set the trunk on the bed, unlatched both clasps, and opened the hard shell top to explore the contents. Clothes, neatly folded, never worn. When she slipped her hand past the elastic strap and into the bulging satin pocket, her fingers discovered the silky softness of her favorite dressing gown. She beamed, pressing the gown to her face. Also inside that same satin pocket, Sadie's hands found the cushy pillow that smelled of home.

Nanny. Thank heavens for her Nanny, Sadie thought, replacing the hospital's starched, flat pillow with her own.

The rest of the items that she "needed" came out next. What was this? She held up the first item to her chest, a swing-style maternity top. The dress under that looked like a tent. Each maternity outfit came in varying sizes to allow for a burgeoning girth and expanding ribcage. Sadie gave up before she reached the bottom, disgustedly throwing them back in, one by one, shoving until they filled the trunk back up and she could shut the top.

This was Bea's doing. Sadie tasted her aunt's manipulation in the thread of every article of clothing. It wasn't nurturing or thoughtful, and not the slightest bit maternal. The woman had no idea how to be a mother.

Even she, at eighteen, would have known better than to thrust the situation into the face of a girl like her, barely hanging on. A navy skirt had fallen off the bed. She picked it up, noticing the trail of buttons along the waistline. That couldn't be, Sadie furrowed her eyebrows while she adjusted the band to its farthest buttonhole and held it up. Terrified by what she saw, she squinted in disbelief. Her aunt had to be loony if she thought Sadie would ever fit into that. She'd have to swell to the size of a watermelon!

When she heard the nurses talking in the hall outside her door, she jammed the skirt in the trunk, locked it back up, and slid it to the floor. Then she slipped under her covers. At least her throbbing head now rested on a familiar cushion.

The next day, Sadie dressed in the starkly lit, cold-tiled bathroom, fumbling with the buttons on her old blouse. The material pulled across her chest. She tugged on the gaping areas with trembling fingers then ripped it off and tossed it to the floor. Through blurry tears, she looked at the maternity shirt hanging on the doorknob. She'd have to wear it. Everything had changed. Her body. Her life. There was no romanticizing it.

Overnight, it seemed, her body had become a vessel, with the sole purpose of bringing a new life into this world. But already she doubted herself. What if she started bleeding again? The doctor had said bleeding wasn't uncommon during the first trimester of pregnancy, and since it had stopped, she would be able to resume her school schedule. But Sadie was terrified. She moved about slowly, as if being careful with her body might lessen the chances of it happening again. If she couldn't even manage without needing medical attention this early in her pregnancy, how was she to survive the months ahead?

She took a deep breath and gripped the bathroom doorknob. Before turning the handle, she let her memory rest on what James had said before they parted at the station. *Without fear, we can't be courageous.* She could do this. Despite or maybe because of her fear, she could be brave. She had to. She took a deep breath and emerged from the bathroom.

Beatrice was staring out the window, holding the thorny stem of a pink rose from the bouquet the governor had given Sadie. She dropped it as if pricked, all warmth gone, "We need to talk."

"About?"

"About your options."

Here it came, the conversation Sadie had been dreading. She stepped back while feeling for the wall with her hands and leaned on its cool surface until a dizzy spell subsided.

Beatrice studied her with the practiced eye of a middle-aged matron and then closed the door and lowered her voice. "I mean your options as an unmarried mother-to-be." She sat on the end of the bed and invited Sadie to join her by patting the taut industrial sheet. Sadie remained where she was. It was hard to defy her aunt, even in this small way. But then again, she couldn't top an unexpected pregnancy, could she?

"There's nothing to decide." Sadie straightened and held up her chin. "James and I are going to be married."

Beatrice shook her head ever so slightly. "You're an intelligent girl, but you're not thinking clearly now. Uncle Edward and I—"

"You mean *my father*." Sadie braced for a backlash by folding her arms across her tender, swollen breasts.

Beatrice closed her eyes for two beats of the heart, and then opened them. "All we ask is that you go to a maternity home. We'll pay for the very best."

Never. Sadie placed a protective hand on her belly.

"You can carry out your pregnancy in private there. You've always preferred privacy, haven't you?" She stood and reached out to take Sadie's hands, but Sadie tucked them behind the small of her back and pressed to the wall.

No amount of reclusion would prevent people from judging her. They'd likely still call her promiscuous or naive, and that was something she'd have to tolerate. She had more pressing concerns now. And come to

261

think of it, why should she hide the product of the love she and James shared?

"To hide my pregnancy will make it seem like I'm covering up a mistake."

"Not hide...protect. Your reputation." Beatrice's eyes narrowed. "And *your father's*."

Sadie tensed from her jaw on down. Of course she knew how a scandal could affect her father's public career, and for Beatrice to use that threat now meant she must have been feeling desperate herself.

"Besides," Beatrice took full advantage of Sadie's reaction, "you'll be more comfortable at a maternity home. And the peace will give you clarity. A chance to think about how you wish to proceed."

"Proceed?"

"Think of it as a temporary solution," Beatrice said, her posturing thinly disguised. She busied herself by folding Sadie's clothing into the suitcase. Then she held up a maternity girdle. "I bought you this to conceal your condition," she said without inflection and Sadie knew it must have pained her to shop for such an item. What lies had she already told people? "See the outlet pleats for expansion? I'm sure you'll find it...useful."

It looked as comfortable as a steel vise.

"This will correct your look without being too restrictive." Beatrice packed it in the suitcase. "Wear the girdle under your normal clothes for now. The maternity wear is for later."

Sadie bit her bottom lip and stayed silent. Her aunt seemed to interpret this as her agreement.

"Remember to wear a sweater—unbuttoned. And no pencil skirts." She removed the one that Sadie had worn a few days ago when she fainted. She then lifted and wrinkled her nose at James' coat. "This won't do, either."

A knock sounded at the door. Beatrice laid the coat on the bed and moved to answer it. Spying her opportunity, Sadie lunged for the coat, hugging to her chest the only physical trace of her former life. What she wouldn't give for James to fill his coat now, so that she could escape her newly altered reality in his embrace.

A nurse handed paperwork to Beatrice to sign and then disappeared. Discharge papers, no doubt, and Beatrice's signature was yet another indication of her regained control. Or so Beatrice probably thought. Sadie had plans of her own, but she'd have to be careful.

Beatrice turned to face her, the papers in her grasp while she rested her fist on her tailored waistline. "I'm not trying to tell you what to do, dear. You're too young to realize it now, but I do have your best interest in mind."

She pursed her lips, waiting for Sadie to respond. When Sadie didn't, she added, "I'm not saying you shouldn't keep this baby." She paused and Sadie detected in the narrowing of her eyes an emotion that Sadie had never witnessed before. Fear? Beatrice recovered and continued. "But I don't think I have to tell you that a financially established couple could provide for your baby what you can't."

The way she and Edward had provided what Audrey couldn't. Or hadn't wanted to.

"You make it sound as if James' commitment means nothing."

"Soldiers don't always return. If you care for your

baby, you'll want the best for it, right?"

Sadie sighed. She wasn't really surprised. No way would her aunt stand idly by and support her. No, she suspected Beatrice wanted her to disappear in the middle of the night, a disgrace and embarrassment to the family, and then surrender her baby to strangers. Return as if nothing happened. As if James had never happened.

The nausea peaked again, but Sadie wouldn't let it weaken her. She had to stay alert. Beatrice didn't care about her; she hadn't even asked how she was feeling. What she cared about was her *own* reputation.

"It will only be a temporary setback," Beatrice said.

"Like having my tonsils removed?"

"And nobody has to know. We'll tell everyone you are…traveling? Whatever you wish."

How considerate of you. "For months? During the war?"

"Visiting family."

Sadie guessed Beatrice had agonized over this plan, and had perfected the story just like her tightly curled victory rolls. They reminded Sadie of the exhaust strips that remained in the sky from the fighter planes that James described in his letters.

"And when I come back?"

"You'll have a fresh start at marrying well," she said with such verve Sadie could spit.

Beatrice seemed encouraged by Sadie's questions. She closed the suitcase lid and clamped the locks shut, signifying that their conversation was over and the matter was settled.

Sadie stood tall, mustering the courage she needed.

She had leverage of her own after all. Hadn't she unearthed one of Beatrice's own secrets? Now that Sadie's identity was known and proven, Beatrice had more to hide than this out-of-wedlock pregnancy.

"Is this how it was for you? Did you hide your pregnancies like this until you were farther along?"

Beatrice's eyes showed more white than beady black. She tugged on a black glove, her fingers filling their holes. "I'll pretend I didn't hear that."

"You're good at that—pretending, I mean. Just like you pretended all my life."

"Do not blame me for what that woman did to you."

"You mean when she dumped your husband's child in *your* lap to deal with? A constant reminder of the woman who'd slipped away..." Sadie hadn't meant to take it so far, but she was desperate. Let her slap my face, Sadie thought, knowing she never would.

"When this is all over," Beatrice said, "you can return to Bryn Mawr and finish your degree. I know how important that is to you." She worked on the other glove. "Your life will be just as it was. Before Henry's proposal." She mumbled the last part as if the words were poison on her tongue and then fixed a stare at Sadie. "Isn't that what you've always wanted? I'm sure you'd hate for an ill-timed pregnancy to cause you to be expelled."

And there it was.

Sadie's heart sank. She had been hoping otherwise, but Beatrice spoke the truth. If it were known that Sadie was with child, school officials would excuse her, under the guise of concern for her health while on campus. She couldn't help but think of that girl Ruth had mentioned, the one who claimed she didn't know she was pregnant until the baby was being delivered. It seemed obvious now that she'd concealed her pregnancy to stay in school.

According to the doctor, she was six weeks along. Her due date was November 22nd. She would agree to spend the summer and fall term at the maternity home, but with any luck and the grace of God, James would be back before she had to make further decisions.

"I need to finish out the school year first. I only have two months left." Sadie fingered the suitcase's brown leather handle.

"Fine, darling." Beatrice curled up the corners of her lips. She'd won for now.

While James was fighting the war in Europe, she'd soon wage a war of her own here. One thing was certain. Nobody could make her surrender her baby.

****

Beatrice's hired car pulled up to the curb outside Sadie's rooming house on Prospect. It was mid-morning and no one was around. Sadie guessed most of the girls would be in class on campus. Ruth stood waiting on the front porch. She helped Sadie up the steps, gently reminding her to avoid undue exertion, as the driver carried her tweed suitcase trunk to the porch. They sat at the table for soup and a hunk of crusty bread. Sadie stared off in a daze hardly able to believe how quickly her life was changing.

"She's sending me away," Sadie said. "To a maternity home for unwed mothers."

Ruth set down the pot and stared at her. After a long pause she asked, "Where?"

"St. Joseph's downtown."

Ruth nodded. She opened the icebox and fetched the glass bottle of milk. "Say," she said, refilling Sadie's glass. "Just you wait for James' next sugar report and you'll be feeling more like yourself in no time."

Sadie nodded, but could barely lift the spoon to her lips. Her mail cubby had been empty for a week now. Ruth knew because when Sadie had called her from the hospital to tell her when she was being discharged, she'd asked Ruth to check for mail. Unless Beatrice had gotten to it first.

"Mail gets held up overseas all the time," Ruth said. "Once my sister didn't hear from Bobby for weeks because he got reassigned."

Yes, James could have been reassigned like Bobby. Or transferred. She couldn't bring herself to consider anything else. Slivers of worry took hold. Why hadn't James responded to her news of the baby? Surely he'd consider it good news.

The next day her prayers were answered. She received word.

The knock came at the door as Sadie was washing breakfast dishes before heading out to her philosophy lecture. She wiped her hands on the dishtowel and made her way to the door. The courier set a box at his feet to hand her a slip of paper to sign.

"Ma'am, I'll need the signature of Sadie Stark?"

Sadie signed and took the box with curiosity. It was definitely from the Army, but she didn't recognize the handwriting. Postmarked by a Leonard Dixon? Leonard. Lenny?

She scaled the stairs to the refuge of her room, a flutter of nerves choking the air from her lungs. She set the box on her bed and stabbed at the packaging with her metal letter opener.

Why would Lenny be sending her a package? Had this been a prank? Please let this have been a prank. Or there might be a simple explanation. If James had been injured and couldn't use his right hand to write. Unable to write, my God!

The letter opener wouldn't penetrate the tape so she slumped to her knees, attacking the box with her nails, clawing and scraping. At last it yielded to her frenzy to reveal the unacceptable.

James' journal.

This couldn't be happening. Not to her James. Her James was safe from it all, somewhere else. He had to be. So why wouldn't his journal be with him? Unless he'd asked Lenny to send it to her for safekeeping?

She picked up the accompanying letter with shaking hands. Her eyes scanned the contents of the box, avoiding the letter with Lenny's impending news. She saw personal items in the box. Pictures of herself that James had asked her to send.

Then she unfolded the letter. Lenny's opening line stopped her cold.

James asked me to write if something happened...

Her breath caught. She couldn't read the rest from left to right, top to bottom. Instead, fragments jumped off the page at her.

His bomber got hit.

It went down too fast.

And the final blow.

No body has been found.

She threw back her head and let out the sound of a tortured animal, her arms outstretched and fists clenched in a rage that she'd never known before. Her cry was part moan, part sob, and vibrated from her insides out, scratching her throat raw and heating her skin to a feverish high. Like a puncture wound that cut to the bone, it ripped her apart so deeply she was sure it would never let up. Ever. She'd continue to wail long after she went hoarse, or mute, or unconscious.

Footsteps sounded. Someone folded over and around her, enveloping the hunch of her back in what was intended as comfort, but Sadie shook the person away.

"No! No! No!" she screamed, her voice staccato and detached.

Still kneeling, she scratched at her forearms, letting the same nails that had clawed open the box now draw blood from her skin, needing to feel something other than the anger and absolute grief that threatened to swallow her whole.

Someone stopped her, clamping gently on her trembling fingers to quiet them, then released her. It was Ruth. Maria was there, too, patting her face with a cool towel.

Sadie refused to believe this was real. She ran her hands over the worn leather-bound journal and eyed more closely the personal items Lenny included in the box. The letters she had sent James. More pictures. His half of the train ticket from their trip to New York. The postcards they'd purchased at the Met in Manhattan.

She forced herself to read more of Lenny's note even though she imagined nothing could bring her comfort.

We don't know what happened.
It was an emergency mission.

I am so sorry.

She bowed over the box, weeping with the journal James had loved pressed to her chest. Why would God do this? Was He punishing them for what they'd done?

I'll pray for you.

It was a merciful end to a letter that must have been difficult for Lenny to write. She was grateful to him. But those last four words he'd written? The God who had taken James from her wasn't worthy of prayer anymore. If He could do the unthinkable, she told herself, why should she care what He'd do next? What did she have to live for?

A wave of nausea was all she needed to remind herself. She placed her now-reddened, scratch-riddled arms across her lower abdomen, recognizing God's reply. There, still and small and yet unannounced was the only reason to keep on living.

Chapter Thirty-Three

When Sadie first arrived at St. Joseph's Home for Unwed Mothers, the nuns gave her a new name to hide her identity. Using the alias Rose, she sifted through her first few days in a stew-like fog. The only bright spot was her roommate, a quiet girl with wide-set eyes and a tiny gap between her front teeth. She was further along in her pregnancy, and therefore in the know, even demonstrating how to mop without straining herself.

"They call me Mary, but my real name is Lois. No fooling," she whispered that first night when Sadie wiped her tears along her pillow.

"I'm Sadie," she whispered back.

She'd been away from her family before, but as the governor's charge, she'd always been treated with utmost respect. Here, none of that mattered. She was just Rose—another unwed pregnant girl paying for her sins.

They left her alone her first day. Then the chores began—mopping, cleaning, and laundering. By her third day at St. Joseph's, Sadie felt captive. The first chance she had to slip away she bolted outside into the brick-lined courtyard to get some fresh air. The high-pitched voices of children came from someplace nearby. Through the iron gate at the end of the hedgerows, she saw the adjoining orphanage. A chorus of laughter surrounded the children playing in the yard, but their absentee mothers cast a shadow that only she could see, and it weighed on her. A curly-haired blond boy waved and limped toward her.

Sadie gripped the iron bars and smiled eagerly, but before they could exchange words, Sister Margaret came up out of nowhere and placed her robed arm over Sadie's shoulders. "We need you inside, dear."

As they entered from the back door, she couldn't help but notice from this vantage point that Holy Cross Cemetery was located across the street. And she thought to herself how disturbing it was that she now lived on a metaphorical crossroad—at the place where life began and where it was laid to rest. Where did that leave the orphans? A living purgatory? Already she was becoming jaded.

After receiving Lenny's package, she'd written to James' mother in Pittsburgh. Mrs. Pasko confirmed the news that James was missing in action. She also had news that Lenny hadn't shared yet. A few of the crewmembers who had bailed early from James' bomber that day had survived and were rescued. That a few had survived gave her hope. Hope that he might be a prisoner of war somewhere. That her James was alive.

After some time, Sadie delved into James' journal, hoping it would reassure her. But the content differed vastly from the letters he'd sent home, and she hesitated to continue. She'd always pictured him safe from it all. Within pages that blurred from her tears, he'd carefully documented each combat mission, the men who died, leaving behind girlfriends or wives, siblings and children. At times she had to stop reading and slip it back into the satin pocket inside her tweed suitcase in the wardrobe. But not for long. He'd written: *I'd give*

anything to see my Sadie now. Sweet Sadie, wait for me.
****

"Rose?" Lois called for the passing nun's benefit. "Sister Margaret needs us in the maternity ward now."

Sadie padded toward maternity in the adjoining women's hospital, one hand on her lower back to support the pressure of her eight-month belly. A swirl and jab near her ribcage nearly dropped her to her knees. She grabbed Lois' hand and placed it on the spot. Within seconds another jab answered their anticipation.

"My! Isn't he a strong one!" Lois remarked.

"Was that his heel?" Sadie asked, hopeful he wasn't breech.

"No question about it." Lois was due any day now.

They entered the maternity ward and got to work. An institutional brightness set the tone. A long row of hospital beds lined each wall, eight in all, most of which were occupied with women who'd recently given birth. *Married* women. For the next week or so, these housewives were confined to bed rest, focusing on recovery, feeding their newborns, and primping for their husbands.

"Rose, please take my son back to the nursery. And I could do with clean sheets," a new mother ordered while filing her nails, her eyes never leaving her task. Sadie went to the baby, who was still swaddled the way the nurses had wrapped him in the nursery. As soon as she lifted the precious warm bundle, careful to support his head, the mother lit up a cigarette.

"I need clean sheets, too," the woman in the next bed said. "And my menu was never collected." She removed hairpins and rollers.

Sadie spoke up. "Could you please refrain from smoking until we've taken the babies to the nursery? The rule is clearly outlined in your pamphlet, based on the laws and regulations of the State Department of Health."

Sadie met Lois' gaze and they silently celebrated with smug smiles. She'd spoken up not only for the newborn's sake, but also to exercise what little authority she could over these women they were forced to wait on. It was these small victories that kept them mentally able to carry out their last trimesters.

The woman snubbed out her cigarette, pouting.

"Rose," said the woman in curlers with the menu. "Be a dear and let me know when my husband arrives, will you? It's almost viewing time." She brushed her curled hair into rolls on top of her head.

"Of course," Sadie said, stabbed with jealousy. The idea of James visiting her and holding their baby launched her recurring fantasy. She often pretended she saw him at the other end of the long corridor, still well and handsome the way he looked when she'd last seen him. Always in her daydream, she sprinted toward him and he lifted her into his arms, and all was right in her world again.

"And, Rose?" the first woman asked, still holding her prematurely snuffed cigarette between two fingers in wait.

"Yes?"

"Quickly, please."

Most of the unwed expectant girls did their work as required and kept to themselves. They seemed to believe the nuns and social workers who told them their babies deserved better.

Sadie busied herself with work, tedious and degrading as it was, but still, she felt restless and out of control. Then she got an idea. She approached Sister Margaret. "Sister, could the orphanage use some extra hands with the children?"

Sister pursed her lips. "That isn't the way we do things." She walked away.

"But…" Sadie followed. "I just thought that they might benefit from an extra helper or two."

"Doing what?" she asked, still walking.

"I could help with meal times and get them ready for bed. Play in the garden?"

Sister snorted. But then she stopped and turned to face Sadie. "You know, Rose, perhaps that is a fine idea. Might be a good lesson for you."

Sadie wasn't sure what she meant by lesson. That implied Sadie had done something wrong and needed correction. Besides, the orphans were children, not savages.

"You'll see what a lot of work they are. Well, I'll consult with Irene over there, and if they can use the help, you can go. Remember, this doesn't replace your other chores."

"Of course not. Thank you. Thank you, Sister!"

****

Sadie doled out the meager portions of stew with unsteady hands, her eyes welling up at the sight of the gaunt little bodies with hollowed eye sockets peering at her. She swept up and down the long table refilling cups with water, because the milk had run out.

"Hold on, little ones. I have a treat!" she gushed, winking, and flitted to the kitchen to grab the two loaves of bread she'd spied and set aside while the cook

275

had been chopping vegetables. Those and a thick slab of butter.

But when she got back to the table, nearly out of breath with excitement, she turned the loaves of bread to slice them and saw that the undersides had gone splotchy and furry with mold. "No," she gasped. She tried to hide the frustration in her voice.

"It's okay, children. I'll find the good parts, okay?" she said as calmly as possible, and she set out to do just that, carving off what she had to.

"They can have my share," said Phillip, the curly-blond boy who'd caught her spying that first day. He was the oldest, and probably the hungriest, yet he didn't hesitate.

Sadie melted, her eyebrows drawn up in the middle, her mouth a puddle. She tousled his hair with her hand while fighting to steady her quivering lips.

Working with the children soon became the one bright spot in Sadie's life at St. Joseph's. Sister Margaret was right—the experience was eye-opening, just not in the way the sister had hoped. If anything, it made Sadie more sure about her decision to keep her baby. She was willing to bet that each orphan's long-gone mother had been told her child would be placed with a loving, stable couple. So why were they still in the orphanage years later?

One night Sadie drew the quilt over Phillip's small body in the last cot in the row, like she often did. He said, "Miss Rose, will you tell me a story?"

She couldn't lie to him about who she was. "Call me Sadie, Phillip."

"Okay, Sadie." He beamed up at her through his sleepy eyes.

"It's late." Sadie smoothed his hair.

"Please. Just one? And I'll promise to look out for your baby if he comes here someday."

Sadie's breath caught, and she smiled uneasily. "That's very kind of you, Phillip." She leaned down to kiss his forehead. "I think you'd make a wonderful big brother." She paused. "Have you washed up and said your prayers?"

He nodded.

"All right," Sadie said. "Tonight I'll tell you a story my Nanny used to tell me when I was a little girl. It's about a brave young slave and her baby. But first let me check on the others."

Sadie threaded through the rows of cots and cribs, checking in on the sleeping children. She pulled the blanket over young Patty whose legs had kicked it off. She readjusted little Richard so that he wouldn't fall off the edge. A little boy she didn't yet know looked like his pillow would give him a crick in his neck, so she adjusted it for him. Before she knew it, she found herself mothering these motherless children. Children who were waiting for their lives to begin without knowing it. In each of them, she saw herself.

Then she settled onto Phillip's small cot, pressing on the cover to form a cocoon around his legs, careful of his stiff, turned-in foot. "Now, where was I? Oh, yes. This brave young woman was running away."

"Why?"

"She wanted to be free." Sadie hesitated to say more about what this meant, unsure if he would understand. She'd try. "You can take everything away from a person, Phillip, even their freedom. But you can't take away their spirit."

277

"Or their *song*," he said, and Sadie was taken aback. Wasn't that just like Phillip to be wise beyond his years? Sadie had learned about the power of song, too. When Nanny had taken her to church and sang from the pew with rich reverberation, Sadie felt the love from her tautly wound bun to the tips of her shiny patent shoes. She'd believed the whitewashed walls of the chapel were likely to burst. She often sang to the children here.

Sadie continued. "And nobody during those days of the Underground Railroad broke the code of silence."

Phillip's eyes widened.

"Even the youngest child, probably Richard's age, was sworn to secrecy. That's how it worked for these people who wanted to escape. And they always feared betrayal." She paused to emphasize this fear. "Can you imagine being dressed in rags, walking barefoot, and carrying a baby strapped to your chest?"

Phillip shook his head.

"And running at night so you wouldn't be seen," Sadie added, to complete the visual image in his mind.

"Where did she go? How?"

"That's a very good question. They went north. She learned the way by listening to secret lyrics in the songs. This scared, brave mother learned about a promised land in the North. The songs told the slaves to follow the Big Dipper north where they would be free." Sadie pointed outside the rattling window. "If you look closely, you may see the stars that form the shape of it."

He sat up and looked. "I see it."

Sadie smiled. He was probably confusing the city's twinkling lights for stars, but she didn't correct him.

"So this brave mother trekked from Alabama to the Tennessee River and then downriver to where the Tennessee and Ohio rivers meet in Kentucky. All by following the stars, and with a lot of help from kind people along the way."

Phillip hunkered back down, curling onto his side under the covers. Sadie handed him the soft bear that he liked to sleep with.

"Where did she sleep?" he asked through a yawn.

"She stopped at safe houses along the way. At each safe house she and her baby were given a hot meal, clean clothes, and a place to lie down. They hid by day in an attic or barn. Traveled by night. She was given directions to the next safe house. She lived in the fear that she'd be caught by her slave owner, or a bounty hunter. If caught, her baby would be taken from her."

Phillip hugged his bear to his chest.

"One night while she carried her baby into the woods, she heard sticks cracking nearby, probably from a horse's hooves. She found a place to hide while watching a bounty hunter dismount, grateful he didn't have a tracking hound with him. She gently covered her baby's mouth so he wouldn't give them away and rocked him to sleep. Then she held her own breath. By some miracle, the man never found them."

"Did she get away?" He gripped the sheet with his fingers under his delicate chin.

"Yes she did."

"Good." Phillip formed a tired little smile and seemed satisfied by the outcome of the story. "Tell me another one."

"Not tonight." Sadie stood and smoothed her skirt. "But tomorrow I'm going to tell you about Peg-Leg

Joe."

"Peg-Leg?" he asked through heavy lids. He rubbed his eyes.

"That's right." Sadie got up to close all of the curtains and turn out the light. "Ol' Peg-Leg taught the song: *Follow the Drinking Gourd.*"

Looking around the quiet nursery while she drew curtains, Sadie saw the future of a war-torn country. Just as James had detailed all the horrors of war, she decided she'd record notes about each child—their quirks and what made them laugh. Were they happy? Did they feel loved? Yes, and she'd note that. No detail would be insignificant. She'd give a voice to these children, documenting milestones and personalities the way she would have wanted it done for her child. It was almost overwhelming, the task Sadie set for herself, for each of them were special in so many ways.

"Peg-Leg went ahead of them, marking the trail with his peg leg," she whispered, back at Phillip's bedside.

Phillip had fallen asleep. She kissed his cheek in the illumination of the light coming from the other room. Then she realized Sister Margaret was watching from the doorway.

Sister nodded at Sadie with grim respect and left.

Chapter Thirty-Four

Slivers of light shone through the cracks above him. He was lying on the cold, hard ground—but where? As James focused his view, all he saw was a gauzy veil of nothingness. He inhaled the musty clay odor of a cellar, all earthy and damp.

Then footsteps. Heavy, clunky footfalls as someone traversed the hardwoods in a steady, even plod, stopping on a creaky floorboard. A floorboard that happened to be inches from his face.

"*Hast du amerikanische Flieger gefunden?*"

Pain seared across James' leg as he tried to move it. He flexed his fingers and toes. Good, he wasn't paralyzed. All his limbs were intact. But his leg. He couldn't move it.

"*Ein Bomber stürzte in der Nähe.*"

Bomber. It was the only word he understood.

"*You müssen die Gestapo an Ihrer Tür.*"

That, and Gestapo. They were searching for him.

If it weren't for his injury, he might have been able to take on the German. He only heard one speaking, but how many more were up there? The floorboard groaned under the soldier's weight, and James was sure he wasn't the only one concerned that it might yield to its occupant. James closed his eyes.

A man responded in a cool, even tone. Although James couldn't understand what was said, he sensed the words had defused and satisfied the determined German soldier because the footfalls moved away. The voices faded too. Finally, door hinges squeaked.

After the dust settled on the floorboards and the area above the crawl space was devoid of sound, James assumed the enemies had left. He didn't dare move; he barely allowed himself to breathe. Surviving shrapnel in the sky and then a plummeting aircraft had been his greatest concerns. Now, a new set of fears had taken hold.

The events of the crash unfurled in his mind.

Leaping from the bomber, freefalling through the sky, fumbling with the parachute release. As he hung like a Christmas tree ornament like he'd watched countless do before him, drifting in the fierce winds, he'd observed under his dangling boots his own aircraft crashing to the ground. Had his crew survived the fall? Had Captain Marshall made it out?

Then he remembered landing on the farmer's field, writhing in pain from his leg, but thinking that all that mattered was that he'd survived the fall.

That at that moment, he was still alive.

Now he was here. But where was that exactly?

He must have drifted off because when he came to again, he was startled to find a hole above him and the dirty face of a little girl staring down at him curiously. Her mother appeared next.

"Ma'am? Where am I?"

She pressed her lips tightly and cried to the person behind her. "*Faire sortir de ma maison!*"

James cringed at her outburst, knowing the danger his presence here was causing this poor family. A man gently pushed her from the opening and reached his hand to James. Slowly, he pulled James up and out of the dank crawl space.

"*Merci,*" James said, barely able to put weight on his leg.

"*Difficulté lui quelque chose à manger, femme. Regarde-le. Venez maintenant,*" the man told the stout, portly woman. She started throwing her pots and cookery around the kitchen. The man, whom James guessed to be her husband, kept gesturing for her to calm down, following at her heels. James noticed a boy watching him with a hint of admiration in his eye. He held out his hand and guided James to the table.

After he was seated, James said through cracked lips, "*Merci.*" He reached out with a shaky, weak arm to pat the boy's hand. "*Water? S'il vous plaît?*"

The farmer's wife clanked a bowl of stew onto the table before him and sloshed a glass of water. She glared at James as if she'd wanted no part in this plan. James kept trying to thank her and began spooning the soup into his mouth faster than he could swallow it. Overcome with a desire to consume, he lifted the whole bowl to his mouth.

When he had finished and wiped his face, he looked up to find the entire family of four staring at him. Even the hotheaded wife was silent. The husband elbowed her and she went to ladle out more stew for James.

The farmer studied James for a while and then he sat down. He glanced at his wife who stormed from the room.

When the man shook his head, James placed a hand on his arm. "I should go." Every day that he was there would put the farmer and his family in danger.

James knew that. As soon as the German soldiers had searched the surrounding farms, they'd be back looking for him again until they found him.

"*Vous restez.*" He pointed to the crawlspace. "*Il…*"

James nodded, wincing at his leg pain.

The man then pointed at James' bad leg. "*Lors de la récupération, vous devez quitter.*"

James wasn't sure what he was trying to say, but he thought the man meant he could stay hidden until his leg recovered. "*Merci, sir, merci,*" James groveled, falling onto his folded arms on the table.

He'd get back to Britain somehow. And then, back to Sadie.

Chapter Thirty-Five

Sadie entered the long, cool hallway to wash laundry and iron linens, grinding her teeth with every step. She'd been having false labor pains on and off for a week now. Near the utility closet she ran into Lois, whose limp hair stuck to her crown and temples. Her overdue state showed in her puffy face and swollen fingers. It was just the two of them so Sadie spoke freely, using her real name.

"Are you using *Lois* on the legal documents after you give birth?"

"No."

"And you're sure about—giving your baby up for adoption?"

"I think so, but I'm not sure. My head says yes, but my heart says no."

"What if your baby wants to find you someday and you haven't used your real name?"

"If I don't keep my baby, I don't want him to find me."

Sadie wanted to argue the point, but she resisted.

Lois spoke in hushed tones even though nobody would hear them. "I was told by one social worker that they already found a married couple who wants my baby. They can't have one of their own. I saw on the chart that the social worker wrote I'm...unfit." She cracked on the word then caught herself.

"That's a lie," Sadie said.

"The social worker told me my child is better off with two stable parents and I agree. Anyway, the couple doesn't care that I'm...I'm..."

"What? Don't listen to them. You love your baby. You're very capable."

"But I'm poor."

"These couples come here because they think we're desperate and wouldn't ever come back for the baby," Sadie said.

"Sadie, I am desperate. I have nothing. My own mother won't have me."

She wasn't sure what was more torturous—that they were stripped of their dignity, judged by others who had never been in this situation themselves, or the fact that they were told lie after lie. Estranged by their own families.

"Don't worry. I'll think of something," Sadie said.

****

The adoption agency was conveniently located a block behind St. Joseph's and the orphanage. Sadie slipped on a fake wedding band from the small bowl in the foyer—as the social workers had instructed the girls do during any public excursion. She headed out the back door armed confidently with new information, grateful again to Ruth for bringing her the books she'd requested from Bryn Mawr's library.

She found the man in charge. Mr. Cowley, who ran the agency, also had his hands on the maternity home. "You do realize that your baby is at a severe disadvantage?" he told Sadie, while poking at his yellowed teeth with a toothpick.

"How so?"

"Financial. Physical health. You didn't receive any care during the early stage of your condition, did you?"

"Like the married women bearing legitimate babies were afforded?"

"Your baby may have suffered without you knowing it. With no exams. And, many of these women here," he said behind a hand to his mouth as if he were confiding in her, "are poor, miss. These women," he said, flapping his hand about, "are unable to earn their own wages to support a baby. It's unfortunate, but that's the facts. It's my job to be the advocate for the unborn child." He looked smug.

"Mr. Cowley," Sadie said, trying very hard to keep her cool. "We do not need condemnation. What we need is the same treatment as every other mother in there." Sadie stood and pointed in the direction of the maternity ward for married mothers. "Women who have financial assistance at their beck and call. Why, I ask you, has federal aid been denied to those of us who happen to be unmarried?"

"I don't have the foggiest..."

"I think you do. Or should. Are you saying we don't deserve the same public benefits afforded to widows and wives?"

"Not at all. You're mistaken."

"You say you advocate for the child? How could it ever be in the child's best interest to separate him from his mother? Surely some kind of aid exists?"

Mr. Cowley cowered, but only briefly. "Well, I don't know, miss. But you should have thought of that before you..."

Sadie wanted to pound her fist on his desk, but she held back. It was useless. This man held neither the power nor the inclination to help her and the others. And the worst part was that Sadie knew she was smarter than him. Yet she had to listen to him tell her what to do with her child.

"You'll have to excuse me now. I have work to do. As do you," Cowley said.

"Very well, Mr. Cowley is it?" *You sorry little man.* "Perhaps you'll find the time to take action on behalf of the unmarried mothers on-site if, say, the governor were made aware of this indecency?"

"The governor?" Cowley frowned at her and chuckled nervously, hardly believing her.

She'd warned him. She spun to leave before he could respond.

Later that day, after news of her speech made its way around the home and the young mothers-to-be were encouraged to know that it may be possible to receive federal aid, Lois came to find Sadie while she was feeding the orphans their dinner.

"I heard what you said to Cowley," she said excitedly. "And I've changed my mind." She placed a protective arm across her belly. "I'm keeping my baby, too."

****

During the next few days, Sadie felt tension from the authorities at the home and kept a wide berth when they passed in the hall. They left her alone, as long as she kept to her unpaid domestic duties, but her time would come.

Ironically, that night after Sadie had finished sewing the final stitches on the sweater and hat set for Lois' baby, she heard the harrowing wail and screams of a woman in labor. She heaved herself up to help.

Lois' bed was empty. Could it be? She shuffled down the hall, stopped by a nurse who ordered her to go back to her room. By three o'clock in the morning, Dr. Wood had been called in. The screams from down the hall kept Sadie on alert for what seemed like hours until Lois' suffering went eerily silent, replaced with only the intermittent low baritone of Dr. Wood's voice and his attending nurse. Lois was in her twilight sleep no doubt.

Then she heard the most beautiful sound in the world: the bleating of a newborn. The worst was over. Lois' baby had come.

Relieved, Sadie lay on her side in bed, supporting her low-set swollen belly under a bundle of blankets. A singular stream of tears ran the way of gravity, across the bridge of her nose and down toward her pillow from home that supported her head, tickling her cheek in its wake. She didn't remember anything about what happened next, not even that she wiped away the tears, because she'd drifted off into such a deep slumber, as if she'd exhausted herself just by witnessing the labor through the thin walls of the dreadful place.

But the next day, she heard the news from Lois herself. "Sadie, he didn't make it." Lois sniffled through red-rimmed eyes, curled in a ball in her bed. "He was stillborn." She stuffed her face into the pillow and sobbed.

"But I heard his cry." Sadie lowered her swollen body onto the edge of the bed. In her hands she clenched the sweater and hat set she'd brought to give Lois.

"No." Lois' quivering voice rose a few octaves. "They said it was God's plan at work, and to make peace with it."

Sadie slipped into the bed with Lois to hold her trembling body. Lois' sobbing wracked them both. They'd been told that their pregnancies were meant to bring a child to a couple, Sadie reasoned. How would they explain this? Sadie marched back to Sister Margaret and demanded answers, but instead she got blank stares or averted eyes.

Days later, Sadie looked out the window at the Holy Cross Cemetery where Lois had been told her infant would be laid to rest. There were no freshly upturned mounds of earth. No, Sadie knew full well what had happened to Lois' child. Cowley had given him away without her consent. It was the same thing that would happen to her if she weren't careful. Unless. Unless she had somewhere to hide.

Appearances. The shame and scorn wrapped up in illegitimacy was written all over the faces of the people here and everywhere. Sadie had tried to ignore it, had tried to fight it, but in the end, she'd fallen prey to it. She was here, after all. It suddenly occurred to her that perhaps she was going at it all wrong.

She sat wanting to write the letter she'd drafted over and over in her head many times, but knowing it would be censored and probably torn to shreds. Too risky. If there was one person on earth who knew everything about appearances, and how significant they were, she was it. And Sadie had Ruth willing to help her. First she wrote a letter to her father and Beatrice, placed it in an envelope and put it under her pillow where they'd find it later.

Her due date loomed. She couldn't just pray and trust and wait any more—sewing baby clothes and knitting baby shoes and bonnets. If she gave birth to her baby here, she'd risk losing him like Lois had lost hers.

Something had to be done. And soon.

The next day after Sadie hung clean linens on the line, she noticed the nuns all walking together to the chapel. Her heart leaped. This was the chance she'd been waiting for to make a private telephone call. There was no opportunity for privacy at St. Joseph's, likely by design. All communication with the outside was usually monitored and the mail was censored. She rushed inside and dialed Ruth's exchange on the hall rotary phone, then nervously wrapped the black cord around her fingers until little red indents appeared.

"Hello?" Ruth's voice chirped across the line, churning up feelings of homesickness that Sadie fought back.

"Ruth, thank God you're there."

"How are you getting on, Sadie?"

"I'm fine," she said in a small voice. "You?"

"Good now that midterms are over." She stopped, probably not wanting to upset Sadie with news of what she was missing, even if it were something as grueling as exams.

Sadie wanted to tell Ruth that she didn't mind hearing about school, because in a way, she didn't. School was the place where she yearned to be. But then again, if she were to be honest with herself, she really didn't want to hear about it. Regardless, she needed to keep the conversation going because she had a difficult question to ask Ruth. So she said, "Good," with as much false enthusiasm as she could muster.

"Have you made a decision?" Ruth asked.

"Yes."

"And you're okay?"

"Yes," she said and thought of the irony of Ruth's question. To keep her baby felt selfish. To leave her baby felt selfish as well. Then she considered the unwed mothers who had returned to the orphanage desperately wanting their baby after they'd already left. They'd found work or financial help or for one reason or another, had changed their mind. Often it was too late. Their baby was adopted. Never to be found.

Sadie's heart squeezed as she thought about those broken women who came to the orphanage, begging for information about their children. Now that James was missing, she understood how devastating it was to not know where their loved one had gone or how they fared. And she couldn't help but reflect on how her own mother must have felt after leaving.

"Are you still helping the orphans?"

"Yes." Sadie smiled. "They need me here."

"If you ever need anything, I'm only a train ride away," Ruth said.

"Thank you. That's actually why I called. I need you to do something for me." Sadie hesitated but couldn't bring herself to continue. She wanted to tell Ruth how she suspected none of the women had given up their children willingly. Maybe they'd done it—like Audrey had—to give their child a better life. But Sadie also saw what was happening to the children who weren't placed.

She didn't need to convince Ruth of anything. Ruth was on her side.

"Anything," Ruth said eagerly. "Go on."

Chapter Thirty-Six

"Rose, there's a gentleman in uniform here to see you," Sister Margaret told Sadie after she'd come inside on that cold November morning from visiting the orphans. "But he's not on the approved contact list." The nun held a clipboard of papers.

Sadie frowned, her cheeks flushing for a reason other than the indoor heat, and she fixed a few pins in her hair as they walked toward the front room where visitors were received. She'd been cleaning all morning and her fingers had swelled despite the falling temperatures. The first flurries of the season flickered outside the windows.

"Were you expecting someone?" Sister Margaret asked while on her heels.

She wasn't sure how to answer the question.

The man standing in the foyer, nervously fiddling with his hat in his hands didn't look the way she'd expected. This man had a blank stare on his sober face, dressed in full uniform, shorn of his wiry cognac-colored hair.

"You came," she said. She'd been prepared to unaffectedly play the part, but the lilt in her voice revealed underlying emotion, taking her by surprise. Apart from Ruth, nobody else had visited. Nobody could, for appearances sake, she supposed. She leaned into Henry's embrace, and held it longer than necessary, even for the nun's benefit. Again, surprising herself. She hadn't expected to feel so emotional in the presence of a familiar face.

"Of course I came," he whispered in her ear, holding her gently by her elbows while he kissed her on the lips. He kept himself in check, though, maybe realizing he was under scrutiny for his visitation.

Another nun came around asking for Sister Margaret to unlock the medicine cabinet using a key that only she held in her possession, leaving them alone.

Henry whispered, "You mind telling me what the hell is going on?" His voice was gruff, but she sensed any irritation wasn't directed at her. He was here, after all. And the sterile home, although adequate, spoke for itself.

"I'll explain. Come." She led him by the hand to a loveseat in the far corner of the cozy front room, as far from Sister Margaret's prying eyes and ears as possible. She wasted no time. "I need to get out of here. Tonight."

"Why? And why didn't you tell me about your condition?"

She cupped her hands together and placed them in the space that was left of her lap. She sighed. "I didn't want to hurt you further."

He rubbed at his face and hung his head. "Sadie, I'm—"

"It's okay. We both did and said things I think we're not proud of. But thank you for coming. You have no idea…" Her voice broke. *Of her desperation.*

She noticed he didn't smell of gin and his eyes weren't glazed over or bloodshot. He hadn't used sarcasm or nervous laughter to conceal whatever pain he'd previously numbed with the bottle.

"Two days after I left you, they got me at the border. I would have gone to the joint and ruined my record if it hadn't been for the governor. Whatever it was you said to him on my behalf, I thank you for that. Even though I feared he'd toss me in a ditch on the way home. Anyway, the deal was I had to enlist. At least I got to choose my branch. It's been humbling to say the least."

Sadie placed a hand on his, feeling her pulse race. Her father had believed in him even when she didn't. That day in the hospital eight months ago, she hadn't pled anything on Henry's behalf. And yet, her father had helped him. Now that she saw the effect of her father's actions on him, she regretted her shortsightedness.

Henry leaned closer. "When Ruth said you needed me..." He looked into her eyes, revealing the real Henry for the first time. Not the boastful, pompous Henry. The one who had been hidden beneath layers of insecurity. But the hopeful glimmer in his eyes also twisted at her conscience. She hadn't meant to mislead him, but now she was afraid she had.

He continued. "When I heard you wanted me to come here, I put in notice for the emergency furlough. Did Ruth tell you I'm driving a truck back and forth to the training camps?" Sadie heard a flicker of pride in his voice. "Anyway, it took longer than I expected to get away." He hesitated then added, "I heard what happened to James and I'm sorry for your loss."

She bucked against his sympathy. Why did everyone believe the worst had happened? She would never give up hope for James, and she couldn't imagine that anyone could give up hope for a war hero, prematurely assuming they were gone. But she had to keep her emotions intact to carry out her plan.

"Thank you. You look well." There was no time to finesse the situation. "I cannot stress enough that we need to leave. Now."

"Sadie, if I've learned one thing, it is that running away isn't the answer."

"No." She panicked. "You don't understand." Was he trying to punish her like the rest of them?

Sister Margaret loomed, crossing her arms under and lifting her torpedo-shaped bosom that normally hung near the invisible waist of the habit. "Your time is almost up. Visiting hour is nearing its close." She narrowed her eyes at Henry while tapping her shoe.

Sadie placed her hand on Henry's arm. "Sister, I'd like you to meet my fiancé. He's come to get me. So we can be married." She choked on the last words because of the effect it had on Henry. He probably thought he had a chance now that James was presumably gone and her illegitimate child's birth was imminent.

"Leaving now?" Sister flipped through her chart.

"He had to wait for his furlough papers and we didn't know when they'd come through. Isn't that right...*darling*?" She fixed a stare on Henry, begging with her eyes that he go along with her plan. "We can't be apart another minute, can we?"

His stare was stone cold. He must have now understood her intended purpose for him being there. Just when she feared he'd give her up, he reached into his pocket and withdrew the ring. The ring! He still had it? He'd brought it? The ring that had once weighed her down would now set them free.

The proof was before Sister Margaret's pale, saggy face. Sadie couldn't help but beam when the old woman puzzled over the size of the diamond, the cost of which could probably pay their collective salaries for a year. Or feed the orphans. Then Sister narrowed her gaze at Sadie as if wondering how this wanton girl had lucked into such an undeserved end to her suffering. Ever since Sadie's outburst with Cowley, they'd treated her differently. Cautiously. Like the mouse they'd taken in had grown fangs.

"You will need parental consent." Sister planted her stout legs decidedly as if challenging them to get past her. Had Cowley already found a couple to take her baby? A ringing telephone distracted Sister Margaret from further interrogation, and Sadie thought about running. She was fairly certain now that they wouldn't let her leave without a fight.

A cramp burned in her belly. Another false labor pain. She was still in disbelief that a human being—her own flesh and blood—would soon find his way into her arms. And frighteningly soon. Lois had been sewing mittens mere hours before her labor began, and Sadie wondered if she'd known when she'd woken up that morning that her baby would come that day. She couldn't imagine being in-tune with something as mysterious as giving birth, even though it involved her own body, and this made her more sure that God had his hand in it.

"So, this is why I'm here?" Henry propped his elbows on his thighs, his eyebrows drawn up in the middle.

"I was afraid you wouldn't come if you knew. I'm

sorry." She paused briefly to let that settle in. "Henry, they're going to take my baby away from me. I'll never see him again. Henry, *please*."

Henry eyed her like she was crazy. "I can't believe they'd do that."

Another cramp rippled across her lower abdomen, as if her baby's movements were mimicking her restlessness. Maybe her plan to run away had been poorly timed. If she was starting labor, she didn't want to leave the very place where she and the baby would receive the medical care they needed. The idea of labor and delivery was scary enough *with* a doctor to help guide her through it.

"Well, I don't know for sure," she whispered, "but I have every reason to believe they're planning to take him. You have to trust me."

Henry stood, looking to the ceiling and cursing softly. She feared he'd have a fit like usual. But instead, he sat and pressed his hand to his brow. "I had hoped you went to such lengths to get me here for another reason."

"Henry. When you walked out on me that day I fainted, I almost lost my baby. You just left me there." She would claw at any thread of guilt if that was what it took.

"I made a mistake, doll. I know that now. But this will only make things worse for you. I'm trying to live an honorable life now."

Now? He'd chosen now to suddenly do the right thing?

Another cramp pushed her to action. "I think...something is happening to me." Her voice quivered in fear. She felt a warm gush between her legs and froze. Was she bleeding? She pulled herself up and looked back to see the cushion wasn't stained with blood. Her water must have broken. Lois said that might happen. She covered the spot with a sofa pillow.

"What are you doing?"

"We have to go now," she said.

"Where?"

They couldn't go to the governor's mansion, no matter how much Sadie might want to hide there. The mansion had been a safe house at one time, and Dr. White lived nearby and could deliver her baby. But it was too public. She couldn't subject her father to that scandal.

She hunched into another pain ripping her insides.

Henry panicked and ushered her to the door. "Where are your things? Your coat?"

"Never mind that," she said although she hated leaving James' coat and journal behind. She could only hope her father would bring everything to her later. There wasn't time now. She burst out the front door with Henry trailing behind. He'd hired a car, thank God, and she limped to it, chilled by the wetness between her legs.

As Henry helped her to the car, they saw their driver had fallen asleep and now fumbled to start the engine. Sister Margaret appeared at the front door of the maternity home yelling after them to stop. "You can't do this!" She ambled down the front steps and stood in front of the car door. "I'm calling the constable."

Sadie had an idea. As much as Sister Margaret cared about the rules, she cared about the maternity home and the orphanage even more. She turned to Henry and held out her hand. "You want to do something honorable? Give me that ring."

Henry stared at her. Then a flicker of understanding lit his features. He seemed to read her thoughts as he'd never been able to do before. But he didn't give her the ring. He gave it to Sister Margaret. "Take this and leave us." He opened the back door for Sadie. "Use the money however you see fit."

The nun relented, backing from the curb, making the sign of the cross.

Sadie reeled at Henry's sympathetic smile, but just as quickly, another cramp distracted her focus, and she ducked into the car. Henry slid in beside her. She told the driver the address, all of her other options exhausted. It was her only hope.

She winced as another labor pain wracked her belly.

"Are you okay?" Henry asked.

She reached out to bear down on something and Henry's arm was the closest thing.

"Drive!" Henry tossed additional bills into the front seat, and for once, Sadie was grateful that this man always got his way.

Almost two hours later, slick with sweat, Sadie braced for bumps in the road. She grasped Henry's meaty forearm with both hands, fingernails digging into his skin to ward off the merciless pains piercing her insides round after relentless round.

"It's gonna be okay," Henry kept repeating. Then he rolled down his window for her. "You can do this. Hold on." Henry tried to make her comfortable, but seemed at a loss. The simple fact that he was with her and that he believed in her was comfort enough. She wondered if her presence through letters to James had brought him similar solace.

This man Henry, who had dodged the law and avoided the draft for as long as he had, was now the only person capable of getting her what she needed. She briefly considered stopping off at the closest hospital. But she knew if they did that, her identity would be revealed, and all of the time she'd spent isolated at St. Joseph's would have been in vain. And she'd still risk losing her baby. No, she was determined to give birth in private. Her way. Ready or not, it was time to execute her plan.

When they reached their destination, Henry helped her out of the car and up to the door. "Are you sure about this?" he asked.

"No, but what choice do I have?" She growled through another contraction, placing her hands on Henry's barrel-chested torso for support. Henry rubbed her back with the hands that had once branded her as his property.

As he maneuvered her to the building door and looked inside, probably for someone to let them in since there was no doorman, she screamed through a contraction that seemed to persist longer than any that had preceded it. Her insides felt stripped apart while her body was torturously stretched. And then she felt pressure. An intense pressure down low.

"Help, someone!" Henry banged on the door again, all the while never removing his hand that was still wrapped around her, as if letting her know he would never again desert her in a time of need.

She doubled over and vomited on the sidewalk, ruining her only pair of shoes. He rubbed her back, pounded the glass again, and then held her hair off her face. It was a surprising gesture, and she would have thanked him, had she not been in such a traumatic state.

She caught a glimpse of Henry's ruddy-complected face from the corner of her eye. He looked like he'd seen a ghost and she guessed it had something to do with the person who appeared to help them.

The unmistakable former starlet opened the door and raised one pencil-thin eyebrow. She looked from Sadie to Henry to the vomit and back.

"I've been expecting you, honey, but not like this."

Chapter Thirty-Seven

A persistent rapping on the door to apartment 1B interrupted Sadie's nap. She suspected who had come, but why had it taken five days? She eyed Ruth while sitting in the over-stuffed chair near the window, her legs drawn up and covered with a blanket. When the rapping persisted, Sadie nodded. Ruth went to the door, released the chain, and opened the door.

It wasn't her father. Instead, Beatrice appeared, filling the one bedroom apartment with a nervous energy—the scowl on her face causing Sadie to stiffen. Ruth took the tweed trunk from her and stood there like a clothes tree while Beatrice draped a snow-dusted coat over Ruth's arm, then handed her the pillbox mink hat and muff as if she were hired help.

"Mrs. Stark, so nice to see you. Would you care for a coffee? Tea?"

Brandy, Sadie thought.

"Tea, please," she said without eye contact.

Sadie flinched at her dismissive treatment of Ruth who—just days earlier—had left her family's Thanksgiving table to deliver Sadie's baby. Beatrice couldn't have known that, but she guessed Ruth's presence was cause enough for her to be considered an unwitting accomplice.

After Ruth slipped away, Beatrice scanned the room like an alley cat before pouncing.

"Audrey's at the market," Sadie said then straightened protectively. Cradled in her arms, her newborn's eyelids flickered, as if the baby sensed her trepidation. But Sadie had weathered childbirth. She could handle anything now.

Beatrice slithered into the room wearing a belted rayon crepe dress, her purse dangling from its chain on her arm. "I've been worried to death, dear. When St. Joseph's called…" She hovered in front of Sadie, still not acknowledging the baby, and lit a cigarette. "Was Henry behind this?"

"No. It was my idea. I asked him to bring me here."

"But we had it all arranged. Do you have any idea what damage you've done?" She wouldn't even look at Sadie now, but instead rested one dainty arm across her chest, her fist a ball in the crook of her elbow, and blew smoke toward the ceiling.

A rush of anger flooded Sadie's cheeks. Beatrice seemed more upset that she'd breached their unspoken contract than genuine concern for her or the baby. This woman who claimed to have everyone's best interest in mind, had only herself in mind.

"I don't know why you refuse to let me help you." Beatrice perched on the couch to flick her ash in the tray. "Now you'll never be able to place it."

It. That's all the baby was to her, just a thing to be erased from their lives. While Sadie peered at her peacefully sleeping child, she began to understand how everything had shifted while she'd been gone. When Beatrice sent her away, the lies had begun, and now Beatrice would have to maintain those lies. What would it cost them?

"Where is my father?"

The simple question seemed to slice through Beatrice, cracking her impeccable facade. She took another long drag on her cigarette and then snuffed it out. "That's part of the reason why I'm here."

"Does he know? That I'm here?" Well, it was a silly question. Sadie figured her father knew and that was how Beatrice had found the apartment. But why hadn't they come together? Was he angry with her? Or did Beatrice not tell him that she ran away? Because if she had, if he knew, surely he would have been here by now.

Before Sadie could fire off another pointed question, Beatrice hung her head, placing both hands over her face. Her shoulders shook. She made no sound at first and then a low agonizing moan mixed with controlled sobs. Sadie recoiled in surprise. Was she finally acknowledging her mistake?

Beatrice looked up, fixing Sadie with beady, accusatory eyes. "Edward has suffered a stroke."

What? "When? Where is he?"

"Days ago, I don't know. I've lost count. He's receiving round-the-clock care. The very best. When this leaks out, it's going to be all over the news. You can imagine what it's taken for me to be here." She fiddled with her necklace.

"Why didn't you tell me sooner?"

"But how? You were Lord knew where. I found this address on a note in his dresser box the day before he…"

Oh God, maybe Sadie had brought this on. "Will he be okay? I need to know he'll be okay."

Beatrice didn't respond and Sadie wanted to shake

her shoulder-padded arms to life.

"We're not sure yet. He's stable and has improved somewhat. But," she choked on the word, "the doctors don't know if he'll ever fully recover. The damage was extensive. He can't speak or move."

The bottom fell out from under her. How could this be happening? The happiest time of her life, but also the most devastating.

"I need to tell him." Sadie drew back the brim of the pale pink bonnet Ruth had knitted to unveil her baby's profile. The child's mouth made suckling motions in her sleep that caused Sadie to smile even as she blinked away tears. "I want him to know that I had my baby."

Sadie couldn't peel her eyes away, still in awe that this human being came from her. And from James. Their daughter may have inherited her dark hair, but she had James' strength. She ran her pointer finger across the newborn's dimpled hand that reflexively clung to a lock of her hair. She'd give her life for this warm bundle nestled in a swaddled cocoon.

"A granddaughter," Sadie specified, when Beatrice didn't respond.

"Is she healthy?"

"Oh yes. Her lungs! Not that you'd believe it at the moment," Sadie gushed.

"And she was full term?"

"Yes."

"Good. They might be able to place her after all. If you're lucky."

That's what Beatrice had been getting at. And she was acting as if Sadie didn't have a say. If her father were here, he'd be gazing at the baby with the same wonderment she felt. He would understand.

"Except that I'm keeping her."

"Is that right? What's your big plan now, dear? You're going to live here?" She frowned while scanning across the cramped, haphazardly kept apartment. "You'll need a job," she added while gripping her purse in her lap.

"I can work at a factory. I already filled out an application."

"And give up your dream of a college education? What about your daughter?" Sure, Beatrice acknowledged the child when it suited her. "Do you really want this life for her—a life that includes..." she whispered, "...pigeon stool on the window?" She swept her arm in the direction of the studio's clouded source of natural light.

"Everything's different now. I wouldn't expect you to understand," Sadie said. Becoming a mother had changed her perspective already—all the fight had left her in some ways. In other ways, she'd never felt more capable or driven. "And my child has a name. I've named her Priscilla."

"Priscilla," Beatrice repeated. It had been Edward's mother's name. "Priscilla," she said again as if a name made her all the more believable.

"I've always wanted to use a family name." Sadie checked Beatrice's reaction. Could Beatrice accept this child who was related to her beloved Edward? Sadie wasn't sure, as she'd never felt accepted herself.

"Well, I guess it's a good thing you named her for her baptism. But her adoptive parents will likely change her name, so it doesn't really matter." She lit another cigarette. "And Sadie, if you don't follow through with the placement as arranged, you'll owe that Home for their contribution toward your expenses. We had an agreement with them. And if this is your decision, you're on your own."

Sadie couldn't believe Beatrice would threaten her like this, as if her situation weren't dire enough. There was no agreement—at least not one she ever saw. But she was stronger now. Her time at the maternity home with the other women—women like Lois—who shared her plight, made her feel less alone. Now she appreciated how scared her own mother must have felt years ago. And if she had never gone to St. Joseph's, she wouldn't have met the orphans. Someone had to help those children and the expecting women. If only she could.

"For Christ's sake, if you can't think about your poor father's reputation at a time like this, think about your child's. Do you have any idea what she will go through her whole life if you selfishly keep her?"

"No, I don't. But I do know what it's like to grow up without knowing where you come from. She deserves to know." *Like I deserved to know.*

Ruth appeared and set down a tray on the cocktail table. She busied herself by arranging the cups and demitasse spoons while tension thickened the air. "Who will care for this child while you're working?" Beatrice asked.

"I found somebody." She hadn't really, but the war widow down the hall needed money and Sadie suspected she'd do it. But leaving Priscilla with anyone other than Audrey or Ruth terrified her. Audrey said they could stay as long as they liked, but she had to keep her day job washing dishes at McSorley's to pay her rent, and Ruth was leaving the next day for Bryn Mawr. Sadie would work the night shift.

She had but one hope now. "When James comes back…" She trailed off, not wanting to reveal anything further that Beatrice would find fault with.

Beatrice waited for Ruth to leave before replying.

"There's something else you should know, dear." She fumbled with the locking clasp on the brass fastener of her purse. Then she withdrew a monogrammed handkerchief and handed it to Sadie. "I'm not sure how to tell you this, darling, and Edward certainly didn't want to. Before he…" She trailed off. "Before the stroke. He said he'd promised you from now on, he wouldn't keep anything from you."

"What is it?" Sadie's voice squeaked, her vocal chords strained with worry. Had something happened to Nanny? Henry? She sat up quickly, rousing Priscilla, who twisted and, like an inchworm, hunched her spine into the palm of Sadie's hand.

"I'm not sure what this means." Beatrice withdrew something from her purse, and clinked it on the glass oval table. A black crackle lighter. The one with her father's governor insignia.

"Where did you get that?" Sadie shot. She peered more closely, sucking her breath in short little gasps. "James has one like that."

"I know. Edward told me."

Her head pounded. Her nose stung. Did James send it back? She snatched for the lighter in one hasty swoop, grasping the cold steel and flipping it over. Her father did have several of these in circulation.

Etched into the paint was proof she couldn't ignore.

Her name.

As if anticipating her next question, Beatrice said, "An allied soldier mailed it to Edward. He found it in the wreckage."

Chapter Thirty-Eight

James glanced around the French stone farmhouse where he'd been in hiding. Fully recovered and eager to leave, he pulled back the kitchen curtain to see the farmer, Marcel, and his wife, Severine, standing near the barn. A wagon creaked in time to the clop-clop of hooves as it pulled up in the nighttime darkness.

It was time to go.

He slung the crudely mended pack over his shoulder. The civilian shirt Severine had sewn for him pulled across his shoulders and chest. James couldn't help but smile at the way she'd reached for a stool to stand on while measuring his body, and when the stool wasn't tall enough, she'd said, "*Merde*" and then climbed onto a kitchen chair with the tape measure gripped between her teeth.

"*Gros!*" she kept saying over and over, shaking her head, and "*Quoi ils vous nourrir,*" which left him wondering what it meant.

As luck would have it, the *pantalons*, as she called his trousers, had turned out to be the right length, with ample room where it mattered. He wasn't sure what had happened with the shirt, unless she'd run out of material, he thought, chuckling. In any case, he was grateful for the clothing that would help conceal his identity during the journey that lay ahead.

It was late and as James passed the dark bedroom

the children shared, he wished he could have told them goodbye before they went to sleep. But what was this? The boy appeared in his doorway, rubbing his eye. James walked over and crouched in front of him.

"Brave." He pointed to the boy's chest.

The boy shook his head. "Brave." He pointed to James.

James stood and palmed the boy's mop of hair with one hand, sending the little fellow into a toothy smile. His little sister hid behind him, peeking around.

James gestured for her to step forward. Then he reached into his pocket for Sadie's ribbon. It was still there. Always with him. A bit soiled and limp, but still as satiny smooth as the first time he'd touched it. He handed it to the girl.

"*Bonne chance*?" he said.

Her cheeks flushed a bright pink as she took it with a small hand and bit her bottom lip the way Sadie often did. His eyes welled up thinking of her, so he turned to leave. As he opened the door with the squeaky hinge for the final time—the hinge that he'd come to recognize during his forced seclusion—he knew he owed this family his life.

Marcel and Severine Paul were waiting for him near the wagon by the barn. James wasn't sure how to properly thank this couple. They'd put themselves in jeopardy on German-occupied soil. The language barrier left him feeling frustrated. But he knew even if they spoke the same language, no words could express his gratitude.

"*Merci*." He clasped Marcel's hand in both of his. "*Merci*," he told Severine, bending low to kiss her cheek. "*Vous très aimable*," he said, having learned the words for "you" and "very" and "kind."

Severine nudged her husband then. When Marcel reached out, James at first thought he meant to shake it. But that wasn't it. Marcel gestured to James' neck. He wanted his dog tags? Marcel gestured quickly, eyes averted, for James to give them up. For his own protection or for that of the wagon driver? James wasn't sure, but he removed them anyway and handed them over.

"*Merci*," he said again. He happened to glance back at the house and catch the faces of the children staring at him through the window. He planted his feet and brought his hand up in a salute.

"James," Marcel said quietly. "*Jean vous emmènera à la maison d'hébergement.*"

James shook his head to show he didn't understand.

"Jean." Marcel gestured to the driver. "*To sécurité.*"

James nodded. Marcel had already mentioned the "Comet line," which James recognized as the Belgian resistance group made up of families who offered their homes as safe houses to soldiers like him. He was hopeful that another family might be as generous as the Pauls, and could help him on his way to safety.

Safe houses.

Like Sadie's governor's mansion had been for runaway slaves. He never would have believed he'd be seeking one for himself. He climbed into the wagon on the dirt lane and hid in the back, his heart beating a thousand beats.

He was on his way.

One step closer to Sadie.

A journey awaited. There would be risks. As the wagon lurched and bumped along the ruts in the road, pitching James forward and back, he said a prayer that he would reach the Allied-occupied neutral territory before anyone discovered him.

Chapter Thirty-Nine

Dime-sized hail rained down; the wind whipped Sadie's face. She liked the sting. It temporarily shifted the pain from one place to the other. When she was close to the apartment, the wind picked up, rattling the American flag that hung outside the window. It had become a welcome beacon in the same way James described the airfield control tower coming into view. *Home again.*

Sadie entered the apartment. Her mother was cradling Priscilla and humming a show tune. When Audrey looked up, Sadie saw her splotchy skin and reddened nose. She set down the bag of groceries, passed her mother a handkerchief, and took the baby.

"Are you okay?" Sadie asked Audrey while drawing Priscilla to her shoulder and patting her warm back.

"*I'm* fine. It's you I'm worried about."

Sadie sank onto the sofa holding Priscilla so they faced each other. The little girl's cherubic face lit up and Sadie couldn't help but try to match it. A dribble of milk pooled in the corner of her plump mouth, so Sadie dabbed it with the tea towel on the table.

"How was your shift at the factory?" Audrey headed for the galley kitchen. She tied an apron around her svelte figure and then banged around for something in the lower cabinet.

"It's over. That's the best part," Sadie said wearily. "Did Priscilla sleep well for you? How's she been eating? She's had the sniffles and I'm worried she's catching a cold." She gently rocked her torso from side to side, helping Priscilla drift off for a full-bellied slumber.

"She'll be fine, honey."

Sadie reluctantly laid her in the cradle, and went about setting the chrome table with plates and silverware for breakfast.

"Why do you do that?" Audrey asked.

"Do what?"

"Set three places?"

"Well, I-I..." She couldn't bring herself to say his name. It hurt too much. But one of these days, James just might occupy his rightful place at the head of their table. At least she could hope he would.

"Honey. I'm concerned about all this. This routine. It's exhausting you."

Her mother was right. Sadie's body needed more sleep than the intermittent catnaps she took between feedings, during feedings, after feedings. At first their routine had seemed manageable. During the day, while Audrey worked, Priscilla slept often, allowing Sadie to wash, clean, and, when darkness settled in, prepare a simple dinner. During dinner she and her mother marveled over their blessed little one who conjured warm memories of Sadie at the same age. Then, after dinner, Sadie stepped into a pair of trousers—trousers!—and headed off to her first paying job, swinging a pail for her break. But something had to give.

Audrey guided her into a seat to sit down. "You're

doing the job of two people, mother and father. It's more than I attempted, and I'm proud, but this isn't the life I wanted for you." Sadie saw the irony. Although she had become a mother herself, she'd always be Audrey's daughter. And therefore, subject to her concerns. "This can't continue. I made my share of mistakes, and I wish I'd had someone in my life who cared about me as much as that woman cares about you."

"Beatrice?"

Audrey crouched in front of Sadie the way a young mother lowers her body to see eye-to-eye with her child. "I'm being selfish in letting you stay here, where I get to hold my granddaughter and have you too. But I chose this hard life, not you. Certainly not Priscilla. You belong elsewhere." She stood and walked back toward the stove. "And, honey, this terrifies me." She held up the scorched teapot Sadie had forgotten on the burner the other day when she drifted off to sleep after breastfeeding.

It terrified Sadie, too. Lately Priscilla was more demanding, crying every time Sadie set her down. While Sadie held her and paced the apartment, the sleep deprivation ate away at her patience, dulling her good senses until she felt like Henry probably did after too many guzzles from his breast-pocket flask.

Audrey swept back and clamped her hands on Sadie's upper arms. "I mean look at you. You aren't happy, honey. I can tell. What kind of life is this for you? For your baby?" She peered down with watery eyes.

"I am happy." Sadie smiled thinly.

Sadie had tried to hide her despair, but her mother

had seen through her false cheer. And to be honest, Sadie felt a little relieved that her mother had noticed.

Worst of all were her mood swings. One minute she'd be humming Boogie Woogie Bugle Boy by the Andrews Sisters while sweeping the checkered linoleum, and the next, she'd be in a rage because the bread bin was bare. Or the jam jar had been left a sticky mess. Once, she was so fatigued, she actually tripped on the steps leading up to the apartment, dropping the eggs and ruining the last bit of meat the butcher gave her on loan until her next paycheck. She'd bruised her shins. The right one still smarted with every step.

When the percolator gurgled and hissed, Audrey went over and poured two cups. She walked them to the table.

"Beatrice does love you. Maybe she shows her love differently, but it's there. Nobody pursued me, sought me out after I gave birth to you. Nobody paid my way to school. Sadie, don't waste an opportunity because of pride. The hardest thing I ever did was to take you to them, but I can see they raised you well. And you do have a choice. Make it a good one."

Sadie considered all this while wrapping her hands around the hot mug. Her mother took the seat beside her. The shame Priscilla would endure was one thing she hadn't considered when she fled St. Joseph's, but it followed them everywhere they went. Just the other day when she took Priscilla on a walk, Dorris—the widow next door who lost her husband at the start of the war—pretended not to see Sadie even though they made eye contact. When Sadie approached, neighbors huddled in conversation on the street corner, casting sideways glances. The protective arm of one woman shielded her daughter from even looking at Sadie, probably afraid the girl would get ideas.

"I am so scared," Sadie admitted to her mother, slumping in a chair. Audrey flung to her and they hugged, with Sadie's weary arms tight around her mother's waist and hips. Sadie sobbed into her starched apron, her mouth gasping for air. They stayed like that for some time.

Then Sadie pressed her cheek to her mother's stomach. "I'll see if I can switch to the day shift. Maybe Dorris can watch Priscilla while you and I work. I'll get my sleep at night." She'd consider it at least.

Audrey stroked her daughter's head. "That's a start. When was the last time you washed this hair?" Her hands rested on the headscarf permanently knotted at the top. "May I?"

Sadie nodded and let her mother untie it. Underneath, a limp, stringy mess matted together and hung at her neck.

"Come." Audrey pulled her to a standing position, and dragged the chair backwards to the sink. "Let me help you."

****

Sadie trudged into the factory for her first day shift. A new poster hung in the break room. The woman featured in the picture wore her hair tucked under a red and white polka-dotted headscarf. She held a wrench and a machine part Sadie didn't recognize. She was looking back over her shoulder at her soldier in the distance, who was crouched and holding a gun. The slogan read, "The girl he left behind is still behind him."

Sadie knew the poster was meant to motivate

women like her to support the war effort. Frankly, all Sadie cared about was her daughter and James. Her world had become that specific.

As Sadie walked by the other women also wearing trouser jumpsuits, she wondered if they missed being home baking bread and embroidering cushions. One waif of a girl wielded a torch while working on the structural steel in front of her. Sadie leaned away from the flying sparks.

"I'm Wanda," said a woman. She lifted eye goggles to reveal deep purplish-red rings around her eyes. "You new?"

"No. I used to work the night shift," Sadie said.

"Say, really? I was at the shipyard. Sure glad I'm not in the bottom of a boat welding seams any more. They needed me here to fuse them steel caldrons. Why'd you change shifts?"

Sadie hesitated, but she was eager to talk about Priscilla—who she already missed dearly. "To get my sleep. But my baby doesn't let that happen too often anyway," she joked. As soon as she said the word baby, her eyes welled up. She yearned for that wonderful weight in her arms. Her breasts suddenly felt heavy, as if she were carrying two massive torpedoes slung around her weary shoulders.

"A baby—that so?" Wanda was fastening on her tool belt.

"I tried to work nights so she and I would have the days, but…"

As Sadie recalled her baby's sweet smell, her breasts tightened and ached. She felt something hot and wet on her chest. When she looked down, she couldn't believe her eyes. She'd leaked breast milk onto her shirt! The twin dark spots looked like two bomber nose turrets side by side.

"Get used to the lack of sleep, honey." Wanda collected the tools they'd need.

Sadie panicked. She hadn't known her breasts could leak that easily. All she'd done was think about her baby.

"I've got five children at home myself," Wanda said. "And I like this job. Gives me a break from them." Then she eyed Sadie's milk-stained shirt. "Try some cabbage leaves when you get home. They'll help with the swelling and pain until your milk dries up. Come on, give me a hand now. Like they say, 'We've gotta keep them flying.'"

Cabbage leaves? Dried-up milk? But she couldn't afford to exclusively feed Priscilla formula. Sadie bolted away. Tears streaming, she pushed past the glaring line workers and found the bathroom. She locked herself in a stall and collapsed, grasping at the metal dispenser to break her fall onto the foul-smelling linoleum. She buried her sore eyes and snot-covered cheeks in the crook of her arm. Hunched over the toilet lid, Sadie shed enough tears to fill the Hudson.

****

Her scuffed boots slogged along the unshoveled walk in slushy steps. The balmy street was lit with Christmas lights and the street lamps were wrapped with garlands and bows—decorations she was too poor to purchase for Priscilla. Who needed it all anyway? Sadie sighed, blowing out one long stream of hot breath.

After she rounded the last corner, she stopped short, gasping at the sight of him leaning on the stairs to her apartment. Henry. Henry could buy her all the twinkling lights she'd ever wanted. He wore civilian clothes this time—a crisp, tailored suit that gave off his usual well-heeled appearance. And he held a bouquet of flowers.

If she distorted her vision by narrowing her eyes, she could pretend that the man standing there was James—that the war had ended and he'd come home safely, and that Priscilla—maybe an older child now— was running toward him as he kneeled. Her fantasy continued as she saw Priscilla fling her tiny arm around his neck, as he scooped her up with one arm and stood. The idea of Priscilla in the arms of a man who wasn't James, weighed heavily on Sadie.

Yet, Henry's presence piqued her interest.

"Hello, Henry," she said when she drew near.

"Sadie." He beamed. "These are for you." He handed her the bouquet of star-shaped poinsettias, her favorite. The polite thing to do was to invite him for dinner, but she wasn't sure that would send the right message.

"Thank you. They're lovely."

"I'm not here on furlough this time." He gestured to his suit and tie.

"I see that. Why did you come?"

He looked away, as if contemplating how to answer. It was a simple question, Sadie thought. He must have a practical reason for being here.

"I've never stopped loving you." That caught her off guard.

She shifted her lower jaw and looked down at his flawless wingtips.

"Sadie, there's something else. I wanted to tell you

I got a job with the governor's office in New York. I'll be living here permanently." He kicked at the crumbling bottom step. "Aren't you going to invite me in...doll?"

"I don't think that's such a good idea." She couldn't help but feel a little surprised that he hadn't moved on to someone else by now.

"Your mother called me," he said.

"She did, did she?" Sadie narrowed her eyes in disbelief. She closed her collar to the cold.

"You don't have to do this alone, you know." He fixed her with eyes that reminded her more of caramel candy than the liquor he used to abuse. "I'm sorry Edward hasn't improved. I think he would like to know that you're in good care. I can take you to see him..."

She gasped into her cupped hand. To see her father! She'd barely been able to afford a warmer bunting for Priscilla let alone a ticket to Harrisburg.

"If it's Priscilla you're worried about, don't be. I would raise her as my own. The way the governor raised you."

"Oh, Henry...this is all so sudden. I don't know what to say."

He searched her eyes and took a step closer, but didn't touch her.

She peeled her eyes away from his and shifted her weight, "You still want a future with me? After I told you I don't love you?"

He rocked back on his heels, looking skyward. His adam's apple bulged as he swallowed. Then he cocked his head at her. "When the war ends, Sadie, we can be a family."

A family. Sadie looked up at the window where

Priscilla lay in her cradle just out of view. What would she be depriving Priscilla of if she refused Henry's involvement in their lives? As much as a girl needed a mother, she also needed a father.

"Sadie, look at me, will you?" He gently cupped her face with one hand and redirected her gaze. "After all this time. Why don't you see me?"

How could she possibly answer that? She'd never let go of James. But lurking in the recesses of her mind, when she wasn't careful, was the harrowing reason James hadn't contacted her by now. The only explanation was that he didn't survive the crash. Or that he didn't survive as a prisoner of war. That was her new reality.

Henry knew it.

Her mother knew it.

Even she knew it. She just couldn't accept it.

"I don't blame you for hesitating. That's why I also came to tell you I'm sober now. Haven't touched a drop. I swear it. I have my own apartment right here in the city. I want to take care of you and Priscilla. You can quit the factory job. And when you're ready, you can finish school. Maybe Columbia?"

Sadie bit her trembling bottom lip. Her whole life was about Priscilla now. She would do anything for her child. She desperately wanted a better life for them both and here Henry was offering her a way out.

He pressed forward. "The war will end and then what? Will you ever be ready to move on?"

She knew what he meant. Would she ever let go of James? Henry was asking her to make an impossible choice. Could she learn to love Henry, for the sake of her daughter? Could she do the right thing out of obligation and for virtue? Or would it be too great of a betrayal to James? She felt like it would be, but she also knew James would want her to find happiness again.

"Say…" He spoke with uncharacteristic softness and folded his arms across his barrel chest. "When are we going to end our battle, Sadie?"

Faulkner came to mind and she quoted him: "No battle is ever won. They are not even fought. The field only reveals to man his own folly and despair, and victory is an illusion of philosophers and fools."

Henry cocked his head and eyed her quizzically. "You don't have to decide now. I wrote down my new address here." He handed her the folded piece of paper.

She tentatively took it and held it in both hands. And when he covered her hands with his, she was surprised to find they felt like a comforting blanket on a cold winter's day. She didn't pull away.

Chapter Forty

While climbing the stairs to the apartment, Sadie heard Priscilla's cries before she reached the landing. Frantic, she banged on the door. "Dorris! Dorris! What's going on?"

No answer.

She fumbled for her key and finally opened the door to an empty living room. Empty, except for Priscilla, screaming in her cradle. She ran to her child and lifted her. The heat that radiated off Priscilla was far too hot to be caused by a bout of fussiness. Her skin was as red as the cherries on the curtains behind her.

"Dorris! She's feverish! Where are you?"

She flew to the kitchen and ran cold water over a dishrag while holding Priscilla tightly to her shoulder with her left arm and bounced her gently. "Dorris!"

Had she left? There was no note. Sadie smelled smoke and saw that a lit cigarette still burned in the ashtray on the kitchen table. The cherry motif curtains she'd sewn from an old tablecloth rippled from the opened window.

She squeezed the rag in her free hand and then draped it over Priscilla, fighting back her own smoldering rage. Then she went back to the center of the living room and stood there, dumbfounded. Out of the corner of her eye, she spied something through the partially opened bedroom door. An arm dangled off the bed, limp at the wrist. *How dare she.* Sadie searched for the telltale empty bottle.

"Get out! Get out of here this instant," she said through clenched teeth, careful not to lose her temper while trying to sooth Priscilla. She stormed into the bedroom to deliver the tongue-lashing the woman deserved.

Dorris was sprawled on her side, an image that would haunt Sadie forever.

Beyond the bed, fresh blood had splattered the wall and dripped in red rivulets to the baseboards. The revolver was still grasped in her other hand.

****

"Goodbye shabby old place," Audrey sang in her usual sardonic wit while tapping the doorframe the neighbors had kicked open in response to Sadie's screams. "Honey, you never belonged here anyway," she told Sadie, her lips forming a sad smile.

"Where we live doesn't define us." Sadie brought Priscilla's forehead to her lips. "Right?" She inhaled her daughter's sweet, milky breath, but in the back of her mind she feared what would become of them. Priscilla still felt hot and Sadie worried about what was causing her fever. Did she have another ear infection? What if she needed medicine Sadie couldn't afford?

Audrey wrapped her arm around Sadie's shoulders, but they didn't linger. Sadie wondered: if her mother had kept her, and they'd struggled all her life, would she now be directing her anger and hurt toward her? Of course not. Then again, she didn't want Priscilla to ever struggle. And no amount of factory work would improve their situation. A loveless marriage to Henry certainly wouldn't either. But his money—she felt ashamed for even thinking it, but she desperately could use his money for her daughter.

Sadie took one last wistful look before vacating the only home she'd known with her daughter and mother. It occurred to her as she gazed around that cherry printed curtains and the polished knobs she'd worked hard to clean weren't enough to make her daughter a home. As she held Priscilla to her chest, the infant's raspy breathing came in small fits and her tiny ribcage labored. She thought Priscilla needed a doctor.

At the pay phone a block away, Sadie dialed the exchange at the governor's mansion.

"How's my father?" she asked Beatrice.

Silence stretched between them. "The same. I don't know how much he understands, dear." Then Beatrice switched topics, probably sensing there was no other reason for Sadie's call other than to check in on her father and if she didn't corner her soon, she'd lose her chance.

"Have you come to your senses yet? About the child?" It was always *the* child, not *your* child. Not Priscilla. A defense mechanism, perhaps.

Sadie noted the desperation in her aunt's voice. Beatrice expected her to flounder, but was it possible that she also missed her, especially now that her father wasn't well?

"My mother is helping me." And she was. At Alice's brownstone on the Upper West Side, Audrey had showed Sadie how to make a hot compress to relieve Priscilla's ear pain.

"Now you listen here. I was your mother all those years. I was the one who kept you, not her. She gave you away."

A realization swept over Sadie. This feud had deeper roots. After all this time, she suspected Beatrice still envied Audrey. She had a strange way of showing her feelings, but for the first time, Sadie saw how her newfound relationship with Audrey was affecting Beatrice. It wasn't just about Priscilla.

"Maybe I haven't been entirely fair to you," Sadie said. "But I want you to know that I'm not here with Audrey to hurt you. I know you did your very best, and I'm grateful for that. Our relationship has been more than just obligatory. But can't you understand that I love my daughter and I want to keep her?"

"It's not about what you want any more, Sadie. A real mother knows that. I want you to listen to me. And listen well. Stop being selfish and give that baby a proper home. The one she deserves. The one *you* deserved and you got. Don't you want the very best for your baby?"

Sadie was shaking. Her hands were trembling. She stopped breathing. All she really wanted Beatrice to say, she hadn't. She wanted to hear her say, "*Come home. Bring Priscilla. I love you both.*"

Priscilla writhed in her arms and started screaming again. Sadie dropped the phone and ran out.

Chapter Forty-One

They traveled through the night. When daylight crept over the horizon, spilling through and blinding James as he folded open the back flap of the wagon's canvas, the wagon pulled to an abrupt halt. Jean turned and whispered frantically in French, forming deep creases in his forehead, and motioning for James to get out. Confused, James grabbed his pack and crawled over the ribs of the wagon. When he jumped onto the dusty road, his heart was already pounding. Then he saw the enemy standing there near the horse. Three German soldiers with guns.

One had Jean by the arm. Another one shouted to James, "*Zeigen Sie Ihre Identifikation!*" while moving toward him with a bow-legged gate, pointing his gun at him. James couldn't even try to make a run for it, not with Jean at risk. Not with the gun in his face. He dropped his pack and held up his arms. Were they asking for identification? Once they knew he was an American soldier, they would take him prisoner. Ripples of fear slid under his skin. His eyes jerked from German to German, trying to figure out what they were after.

James guessed the third German was an officer, because he spoke in flawless English. "Show us your identification." He was almost too smooth, too much enjoying this. James wanted to take him down. He could have if it weren't for the other Germans and Jean.

He reached for his tags around his neck out of habit, to prove he was an airman for the United States Army, but Marcel had taken them. They were gone. He closed his eyes.

The soldier stopped inches from his face and waited, but only for a few seconds.

"I am an American—"

He kneed James in the groin.

James' legs turned to water. He dropped to one knee, and hunched in pain while the Kraut continued to pummel him until he fell to the ground. Everything grew hazy as James tasted the blood and foreign soil in his mouth.

The third one asked, "Where are the others?"

The others? James had no idea what he meant. Obviously they thought he knew more than he did. A gun jabbed James to get him up and moving. Jean was released. They wanted him. With one last look around for help that wasn't coming, James climbed into the truck. He prayed that maybe, once he talked to their commanding officer, they'd take him as a prisoner.

After a long, silent ride in the back of the dark truck that smelled like mold and musty hay, James was shoved into a cell. Now he winced at the swollen bump on his head and licked his dry lips. He jerked to attention when he heard the boots clicking down the aisle. A Kraut stopped in front of his cell. The man was young, with a ruddy complexion and skinny neck and barely any chin at all. His eyes drooped into bags that sank into his gaunt cheeks.

He clicked the lock and thrust the door open. "*Komm mit mir.*"

James followed him, seized by panic, the worst possible thoughts swirling in his head. Where was he taking him? After all that he'd been through—was he being marched to his death by this feeble prepubescent boy?

They entered a small room that held a desk and a pale, light-haired soldier sitting behind it. James guessed this was the commanding officer. A guard flanked the officer, legs shoulder-width apart. The officer smiled sadistically and gestured for James to sit in the chair across from him.

"Name, rank, and serial number," he said.

"James Pasko, Flight Officer, 29347823."

He wrote that down and handed it to the young kid, who left the room. Then the officer asked, "Company?"

James looked at him and shook his head. He repeated, "James Pasko, Flight Officer, 29347823." He wouldn't say anything more than he already had. He knew, according to the Geneva Convention, he had certain wartime rights.

"Terror flier!" barked the guard behind the officer. "*Spion*." He spit at James.

The officer defused the guard with a raised hand, speaking calmly in German with his eyes averted but facing James all the while. Then his eyes met James'. "Do you know the penalty for spying?" Outside of his raised white eyebrows, the rest of his face looked disinterested.

James knew the penalty. It was execution.

"I am a legitimate airman," James insisted, but without his dog tags as proof, or his uniform, he didn't know what else to say.

The first man returned and handed the officer a

loose-leaf binder, opened to a certain page. "Ah, you're from Pittsburgh." He let the word drip from his heavily accented tongue. "Home of Carnegie and steel. You enlisted?" With his finger still on the page, he looked up at James.

James stared but didn't nod. He knew the officer was trying to build a rapport with him so he could extract certain information. Information James would never reveal.

"And is this correct—you're...color blind?"

Ice-cold shivers traveled up and down James' spine. How had they known that—from his serial number? What else did they know? His thoughts jumped to Sadie.

The officer wrote something down. "Who's your captain?" he demanded impatiently.

James saw what was in the binder. Names. Names of all of the commanders. All typewritten.

"Your captain is Marshall. Am I right?"

James flinched and hoped they hadn't noticed.

The officer smirked. "Tell me your mission details and base location. They were using you to spot what— bomb where?"

He wouldn't let them force these details out of him. He'd never jeopardize his own men. Blood rushed to his pounding head as he leaned forward, squinting squarely into the officer's cold pale face and repeated the words, "James Pasko. Flight Officer. 29347823."

The officer slammed his fist on the table. His face flamed red and James knew he was madder than hell. He grunted something to the guard behind him, causing the guard to leave them.

"Listen. Listen well. You'll never get this out of

your head." His voice was calm, but there was fury in his widened eyes like a madman about to snap. "Remember you caused this. He's going to get the spies we found last week. They failed to cooperate with me, too. They were depending on you and you let them down."

James twisted in his chair. A single file of three beaten-down men passed by the door—American soldiers! The last one, with a face as flushed and as round as the moon like Lenny's, turned to make eye contact.

Seconds later, one shot rang out. *Bang!*

James heard the thump of the body falling and he screwed his eyes tight. After a few seconds, he opened his eyes and looked at the officer.

Bang!

James jerked in his seat at the thump of another body. He looked at the door while the vomit welled in his throat. He told himself this wasn't really happening. They were trying to get to him. He wouldn't let them.

Bang! the third and final shot rang out, followed by a thump. The screaming for mercy had pierced James' insides. The silence made him want to climb over the desk and claw off the officer's cowardly face.

"Will you tell me what I want to know now?"

"James Pasko—"

"Enough!" He motioned to the guard looming in the doorway, the barrel-chested one with a swollen looking bull neck. The one who'd called him a spy.

James was shoved out the door. The hallway smelled dankly of blood and an odor James recognized—fear. He was sent back to the same cell he'd been in earlier. A knee to the groin dropped James to his knees. A backhand to the jaw sent him sprawling on the cold, clay floor. Blows kept coming. Rifle butts to his back. Boots kicked into his ribs. James' ribcage seared with shooting pain and he thought his jaw might have snapped or teeth broken. He sprayed blood on the Kraut's face and spit-polished boots.

"Terror flier!" The guard punched him one last time, turning James' vision into a tunnel of darkness.

****

James peeled open his eyes to mind-numbing pain all over his body. Where was he? All he remembered was the pale, smirking Kraut and those shots ringing in his ears.

They couldn't break him. He was an American soldier. One who had been well-trained, well-prepared. Not like so many of the other poor souls who'd already been captured. He had to serve as an example. He had to be strong, to act with honor. He wouldn't let them take that from him.

A jab in his side made his eyes flutter all the way open. A kick to his back made him arch in pain. The blurry shape of someone hovered over him as the barrel of a gun pressed to his forehead. Someone mumbled in German while James fought to breathe.

One pull of the trigger and everything James had dreamed of would be gone. He hadn't come this far, survived against these odds, and made the promise he had to the woman he loved—for this to be the end.

He clenched his jaw and inhaled.

Chapter Forty-Two

The coughing and rustling sounds coming from Priscilla's crib roused Sadie. Little grunts escaped Priscilla as she tossed and flung her arms and legs. Sadie dragged herself from bed and placed one hand on Priscilla's forehead and the other on her chest. The child's skin radiated a burning heat. As Sadie stripped off the blanket, Priscilla's body started convulsing. Horrified, Sadie drew her up to her shoulder. The warm sour vomit spewed all over Sadie's silk dressing gown and in her hair, dripping along her arm.

Sadie rushed Priscilla to the bathroom to clean her up. She lay her on the soft rug and turned on the water, all the while telling Priscilla everything would be all right, hardly daring to believe it herself. After she stripped off the bunting, she was alarmed to see Priscilla's neck and chest were bright pink and covered in tiny bumps. A rash! The rash was spreading down her chest and to her back.

Her mother appeared beside her, rubbing her eyes in the light. "What's wrong?"

"I don't know." Sadie panicked at her baby's red eyes that were glazed over with a lethargy she had never seen before. "This is more than an ear infection." Something was terribly wrong.

"That looks like scarlet fever. Or maybe that's a heat rash. Is she still coughing? Could be whooping cough. You have to get her to a doctor." Audrey wiped Sadie's hair with a towel.

Whooping cough. Oh God, what if the condition worsened and she developed pneumonia?

"She needs medicine. Here, let me take her while you get yourself together."

But Sadie didn't have money for medicine or hospitalization, she thought, quivering. Her mother didn't either. She'd used what little was left to move them out of the apartment.

"I'll come with you," Audrey said.

"No, let me do this myself," Sadie said.

Minutes later, Sadie had her coat on and she was rushing out the door with Priscilla bundled in her arms. As she raised her arm to hail a cab, she recalled the last time she'd been in such a dire situation. The night she went into labor. Henry had been there for her. As she climbed into the taxi, the memory of that night flooded back. She held a curled hand over her quivering lips at the idea swirling in her head. She found herself needing to find Henry in this moment of crisis. His apartment in Morningside Heights wasn't too far. It was closer than the hospital. Priscilla's breathing was growing more labored and her little body shook with every rattling wheeze. It was two o'clock in the morning, but Sadie had to try.

"Where to, lady?"

"182 Claremont Avenue." Sadie recalled how Henry had used his dough to motivate the driver last time and wished she could do the same. She barely had enough to pay the fare, let alone an extra tip for speed.

As the taxi surged through the quiet city streets hugging Central Park, Sadie rubbed Priscilla's back and prayed to God that she would survive this. She cursed herself for being too proud to accept a handout sooner. At this point, she would do whatever it took to get her baby out of danger. And if that involved committing to Henry, although it felt wrong in every way, if it meant she could save and keep her baby, she would do it. Even if it meant living out her days on earth with a man who could never have her heart the way James did.

At Henry's apartment, her head in a frenzy, Sadie pressed random buzzers, not knowing which was the right one. The window on her right flew open and an older man's bald head popped out. "Lay off the buzzer, lady! You'll wake all of Morningside!"

"Please, sir. I need Henry McAlister. It's an emergency!" She pictured Henry fast asleep, and she suddenly wondered if this was such a good idea. She was wasting time. Did she need Henry? She felt like she did, and wasn't sure why. Maybe, in the absence of James, she'd confused things.

As she torturously waited, she peered down at her fretful little girl, spilling her tears onto the baby's heaving chest and then wiping them away with her glove. She was failing…failing…at this. Under the portico light, Priscilla's face looked redder than before and the rash seemed to be spreading to her arms. Or was that her imagination? When Priscilla wailed, Sadie saw how raw and angry her tongue and tonsils appeared. Then her tiny body convulsed again and the milky brown liquid projected onto Sadie's front.

"I don't know what to tell you, miss," the man called down. "Mr. McAlister's not answering his door. Where's your husband?"

As Sadie turned to leave, she heard the boisterous

crew slogging up the sidewalk. Dead center, held up by his friend, and with his arm snuggly around the shoulders of a pin-up look-alike, was Henry. Bleary-eyed Henry stumbled on the cracked cement.

"Sadie!" he boomed, having enough sense to pull his arm off the girl. He smiled foolishly and stretched out his arms to her. "You came!"

Priscilla whimpered and torqued her body as if reacting to the scene playing out before them with as much disgust as Sadie felt. Here, she'd been willing to give Henry a chance, mostly out of desperation, and this is what she found.

"You!" she shrieked.

The others fell away until it was just Sadie, holding her sick little one, and Henry.

"What's wrong?" His words slurred together. He couldn't even pretend to be sober, she thought.

"How could you!" Sadie pounded his chest as hard as she could, careful not to jostle Priscilla. "This is how you call taking care of us? This is your new life? In your new apartment? Paid for with your own money? It's nothing! It's all a lie. I can't believe I even thought for one second that you might be the father Priscilla needed. You aren't. You'll never be!"

Henry's mouth dropped open. He held both hands on his head with his elbows pointing to the sky as if he had no idea how this mess had happened. Then he ran his palm back and forth over his bangs that had fallen loose around his forehead. "I didn't know you were coming. How was I supposed to—"

"I can never be with you," Sadie growled, the anger bubbling up and out of her mouth. "Don't you see? It's not just about me any more. *She* deserves better than you. We need someone who doesn't turn it on for appearances, but someone who lives his life with honor every single day."

"Someone like James?" he said, his face twisting.

"Yes!"

"Where was James when you dropped out of school? Or the night you went into labor? Where is he now?"

That's when she crumpled a bit realizing that Beatrice had been right—that Priscilla did deserve better than what Sadie could give her. And she was angry at herself for coming this close to giving up on James.

"James never had a choice," Sadie said. "You always have."

"Come on," Henry said, softer now, guiding her by the elbow. "Let me help you get to a hospital."

"No!" She wouldn't take his pity now. She stormed for the corner curb. He was right on her heels and after she flagged down a taxi, she turned to see him pulling cash from his wallet—lots of it, more bills tumbling out than he intended in his drunken state. She hunched over her baby and wept. She wept because she had no choice but to accept his charity. She wept because the money did matter—here and now it did—and she wept because no amount of her love could save her daughter.

She leaned to the ground, holding Priscilla to her chest, and grabbed at the money that had fallen at his feet. She snatched at it like a chicken pecking corn. Like the pauper she'd become. Dragging Priscilla down with her.

Henry knelt to help her. Her ribs wracked with more sobs. Even if his money helped her this time, what about the next? And the one after that? She couldn't keep going back to him. Not like this. She was in no position to take care of this precious human being in her arms. Maybe God was punishing her for being so prideful, so petulant, so short-sided. But she saw it now—she saw the terrible, horrible decision she'd have to make.

"Sadie, I don't know why I ever thought it could work with us. I'm sorry, dol—" He caught himself. "Sadie. I never meant to hurt you or your baby."

She was sorry, too. Really sorry. Because the one thing that was clearer now than ever before was that she didn't deserve to be Priscilla's mother. As she stepped toward the waiting taxi, her vision blurred.

And then she turned around to face him one last time. "You asked me why I don't see you. I do see you, Henry. And the thing is..." She gasped, her lips quivering, "...the thing is, I still don't know who you are."

Chapter Forty-Three

Six weeks later, Sadie hovered in the adoption agency's doorway. She shivered as she held Priscilla more tightly, shielding her from the bitter February cold.

"Forgive me, little one. Please, forgive me," she whispered into the baby's dark curls. She'd never cut the precious wisps in the hopes that James would someday see them. A lump formed in her throat. She closed her eyes while nuzzling her sleeping child and inhaling her milky baby scent.

The antibiotics had restored Priscilla's health after her hospitalization. If she hadn't survived the pneumonia, or if she'd suffered irreparable damage because of it—because of *her own* negligence—she never would have been able to live with herself. The apartment was musty and old, and Dorris had been a heavy smoker.

Her mother's words had echoed in her head that night in the hospital and throughout Priscilla's recovery, "You have a choice, Sadie. Make it a good one."

She'd known it was time to be honest with herself at last.

As if God were testing her, a car pulled up near the main entrance. A man emerged and turned to help a woman climb out. A couple. They faced each other and embraced in a natural and easy way, his arms cradling her in the lovely red swing coat. Because they held their embrace for some time, Sadie peeled her eyes away so that she didn't invade their private moment, and when she looked back, she saw their fingers entwined as they approached the door.

Her stomach turned. Why couldn't she be here to rescue a brand new life like they were instead of the other way around? With James instead of alone? Strangely enough, something Beatrice said had been the driving force behind her decision to come here. "It's not about what you want any more..." Sadie wanted so much more for Priscilla than she was able to give.

As for Henry, she couldn't lie to herself. She would never love him, or any other man the way she loved James. Priscilla deserved honesty. Maybe, just maybe, if the adoption agency guaranteed she would be placed in the right home, Sadie would have the courage to sign the papers.

Inside, Cowley's office door was closed, and she breathed a sigh of relief. They hadn't left on the best of terms. A new adoption worker she didn't recognize herded her and her precious bundle into another room.

"You're doing the right thing, miss," the social worker said.

If she was, why did it feel so wrong?

"It's Sadie Stark. Please call me Sadie," she said. They'd have her name eventually, she decided, so she might as well use whatever influence the Stark name carried while she could—for Priscilla's sake.

The woman squint-stared but said nothing. She seemed professional.

"I have conditions," Sadie said evenly, willing

herself to stay strong.

"Of course you do. Please have a seat and we'll discuss everything."

Patricia Blackwell was the woman's name, at least according to the nameplate propped beside the papers for note taking. It was important to Sadie that she knew the name of the woman who wielded the power to place her daughter.

"Ms. Blackwell, do you have children?" Sadie asked.

"Yes." She spun around a framed picture of a young boy. She lowered her voice. "My husband and I adopted William from the orphanage." She seemed to understand why Sadie had asked.

"Then you know why I need you to guarantee my daughter a good home."

"Miss...I mean Sadie. I'll be honest with you. Nobody here can guarantee anything."

Sadie's heart sank, but she knew what the woman said was true. Even if the perfect couple walked through the door, and they answered everything honestly and to Sadie's high standards, their lives could sidetrack through no fault of their own. People got sick, died, fell out of love. And then what? No guarantee. When she thought about what kind of mother she wanted Priscilla to have, a version of herself emerged, but a more patient, more stable, more substantial version. More mature. And of course the parents in her fantasy could only exist as she and James had—together. As a couple.

"Maybe guarantee is the wrong word. I'd like them to be kind-hearted, financially stable, loving. I want them to know who I am and who the father is so that someday she can…" She broke off.

"I understand," Patricia said warmly, and Sadie had to believe she meant it. "I'll include all the information you want in her confidential file. A sealed file here until she turns eighteen."

"Okay," Sadie said feebly while cradling Priscilla, unable to look in her eyes because of the guilt. Instead she focused on her daughter's little mouth, making suckling motions, a dimple exposed in her chin. Yet her conscience chanted, *You're weak! You don't deserve her!*

"Will you be able to sign the papers today, Sadie?"

She wasn't sure. She could tolerate Priscilla judging her later, blaming her, even hating her for what she was about to do—just as she'd felt toward her mother—but she could not live with herself if through her own inadequacies, and her own selfishness, she ever put Priscilla in danger again.

Still, could she take the greatest risk of her life?

Each time she inhaled, her upper body trembled. At last she withdrew a wrinkled piece of paper. Here she'd written all of the information she wanted Priscilla to have. Her family history and James'. Their birth dates and places. Their circumstances. Why she was here. Their story. It was all in a letter that she'd hoped to never have to write.

It was little comfort, but she kept telling herself that unlike Lois, who'd been stripped of any choice, the very fact that she was here on her own volition had to benefit her somehow. Yet while she imagined all the children in the orphanage and the files upon files that existed in the cabinets filling this office, she doubted she even had the right to demand special treatment.

Forgive me, God.

"We will do our very best. Excuse me for just a moment." When Patricia left the office, she left the door ajar. At first Sadie considered fleeing. Maybe this was a terrible mistake. It didn't feel right. But she assumed it never felt right, even under the best circumstances. She realized no woman would do what she was about to do without it affecting her on some profound level.

She paced the small office. Muffled whispering from the hallway brought her up short. She hid along the wall, listening.

"Yes, they want him," one woman said.

The other woman's voice was muffled and so Sadie moved closer to the door and turned to press her back along the wall.

"Which one?"

"I don't know his name. You spoke with him yesterday though."

"You mean the one with the club foot?"

"Yes, that's him."

Phillip? Sadie perked up.

"But why? They don't want a baby? I would want a baby."

"Well they did, originally. And Cowley kept trying to steer them that way. To one of the newborns. But when they heard about that one…that he's been here so long, I mean. The wife was beside herself when she learned that he hadn't been placed and that it's because of his foot. The husband is a physician, I think. Did you see how handsome they are together?"

"I did. They—"

Approaching footsteps interrupted the women. A

knock sounded on Cowley's door across the hall and Cowley's distinct voice welcomed the guest in. Although Sadie strained to hear anything else, the door shut and the hall was silent once more. Her mind raced. Had she seen Phillip's future parents entering the adoption agency? Sadie figured that any couple who requested a child on the basis that he would most likely not be placed otherwise must be kind-hearted. Her relief for Phillip almost overshadowed her current terror.

When Patricia returned, she looked flushed. "Well, Miss Stark, as much as I would like to help you, I don't know that I can. Most couples do want a newborn such as yours, but we don't have any interest at the moment. And I just don't think when…"

Sadie wasn't sure if she should rejoice or cry. Was this good news or bad? She couldn't decide.

"What about the couple in Cowley's office? The ones who just arrived?" Sadie asked, hardly able to believe she was actually campaigning for these people who, for all she knew, weren't right at all. But she couldn't think like that. *If they wanted Phillip…*

"Who? Oh, they've already made a decision."

"Yes, but, might you ask them if they would be interested in a sibling?"

"Well, I suppose it wouldn't hurt to ask. Is that what—"

"Yes." She answered too quickly and felt the need to explain. "Mrs. Blackwell. I know this must be unconventional, but you seem—caring. I overheard the social workers in the hall saying this couple intend to adopt Phillip. I know Phillip. I cared for him while I was in the mother's home. And if my daughter were to be adopted into the same family...it would be...she would be...it would just give me the greatest comfort to know they had each other."

Patricia Blackwell inhaled deeply and nodded. "It is unconventional, like you said, but they do seem like good people. Like you are."

"Can I meet them?"

"No, I'm sorry. No. But if you were to sign these papers now, to show your intent, I will propose your idea."

Sadie began shaking and rocking and hugging Priscilla, so relieved that God had granted her this small token of opportunity, yet at the same time mourning her loss already. She scribbled her name before she could change her mind.

"If you'll wait here, I'll be back."

"Wait." Sadie placed her hand over Mrs. Blackwell's as the woman reached to scoop up the pen and paper. "Can you please place this in her file along with the information I've given you?" She handed her a sealed envelope with James' lighter inside. "It's something of her father's. He's missing in action."

Patricia nodded and tugged on the envelope. Sadie reluctantly let go.

Chapter Forty-Four

Bryn Mawr, 1945

On her way to the diner, Sadie noticed that a crocus had pushed through the frozen earth. She'd forgotten how resilient the dainty flower could be, and this one spoke to her.

Persevere.

When she neared the Main Line on the corner of Prospect, she saw a woman lowering a fussy baby into a wicker coach across the street. She resembled the woman from the adoption agency, seared into Sadie's memory, wearing the same red swing coat with the padded shoulders and sash belt. Sadie tore down the sidewalk to get to them, accidentally bumping into a Bryn Mawr student walking with a friend and knocking the books that were cradled in her arms.

"Sorry!"

She kept running.

Near the stroller, she shouted, "Wait!" like a crazy person, causing the red-coated stranger to stop in her tracks.

Sadie collapsed to her knees on the cold concrete, and searched the eyes of the baby. The child seemed ready to giggle or cry, but hadn't decided which.

It wasn't Priscilla.

Of course it wouldn't be—logic had temporarily

escaped her. Priscilla would be three years old now—running, hopping, dawdling. Laughing. She'd never heard her own child laugh. No matter how much time passed, she'd forever remember Priscilla as the pink-fleshed baby held tightly in the bunting Sadie had made her, standing in Patricia Blackwell's office on that bitter day in February.

"I'm sorry. Really, I am." Sadie clasped a gloved hand to her distorted mouth and pulled herself up. "I don't know why, but I thought she might be..." She couldn't bring herself to utter Priscilla's name. Nobody was supposed to know she existed.

"Who?" the woman asked.

Ever since her surrender, Sadie had lied to everyone. Lying through omission. Only her aunt and Ruth knew the truth. But she couldn't mourn the loss of the most precious being in the world without ever saying her name.

"I had a daughter," she whispered breathlessly. "I named her Priscilla." And once those words tumbled out, a waterfall followed. "She made this wonderful coo when I sang to her, and the weight of her body in my arms was...well...delirious. You understand, I'm sure. She even had a dimple here." Sadie pointed to her chin but her mouth twitched against her will, her nostrils flared.

"I'm sorry for your loss," the woman said.

It occurred to Sadie that this woman assumed Priscilla had died. That death was the only reasonable explanation for their separation.

"Oh no, she's alive!" She clung to the woman's forearm. "I just don't know where..." As she spoke the words, a terrible thought passed over her. What if something had happened to her daughter? She would never know. She didn't even know if her name was the same.

On that pivotal day in the hospital room, when her aunt suggested she hide her pregnancy, Sadie's greatest fear outside of losing James had been expulsion from school. Later, everyone—her aunt, Sister Margaret and the other nuns, Mr. Cowley, even Patricia Blackwell, had said her life would go back to the way things were. Someday.

They were wrong.

Like an oak tree ripped from its place in the ground, its root system severed and exposed, a part of Sadie had died that day. And that part of her—the greatest part—that kept her close to James in his absence—was out there in the world, reliant on some other mother and father for her everything, probably never knowing how special she was to Sadie.

Although she'd promised herself she wouldn't go back to the adoption agency, she had. Many times. Until they fed her a story that might have been a lie. Or not. She would never know.

Was she happy? Was she well? Was she loved by her parents? Did she know how much Sadie loved her?

Yes, they said. Move on. Carry on. Get back to living.

But how?

The guilt never subsided. And when she scoured the *Times,* her breath caught each time she swore she saw James' face in the nameless soldiers in the pictures. On closer examination, it was never him. Not knowing what had happened to him—and now Priscilla—clung to her every fiber, the agony never far from her mind.

Even as she threw herself into her studies, finishing her college degree a semester early, visiting her mother in Manhattan during school breaks, she could never be that girl again, the one who stepped foot on campus eager to do great things. No, she had lost everything great in her life, even the need to persevere. What did she have to fight for now?

"I kept her booties," Sadie rasped. "Her very first ones. They're in a little box in my desk drawer and I pull them out now and then to remind myself that she was real. I can still feel her. I thought if I never talked about it, the hurt would wane. But it hasn't. I don't know what to do."

The woman stared at her. A lone tear streamed down her frozen cheek. Then her face became a puddle like Sadie's. "I have a secret, too. This is my sister's child I'm raising. She has nowhere to turn. Nowhere to go."

A rage simmered—the familiar rage that had started to burn the very day she opened the box from Lenny and in the days and weeks and months following her separation from Priscilla.

Sadie knew what she had to do—she had to rescue other women like herself. She never wanted anyone to experience the harrowing days leading up to their delivery like she had. Nobody had sat her down and explained what to expect with her pregnancy or how to manage the pain of childbirth. She'd survived the scary, lonely months leading up to her escape with only the other desperate women like herself as company. She had been one of the lucky ones to get out, and to have a place to go. She at least had a fighting chance. That it didn't work out still hurt. But for other women, maybe it could. Maybe, if they had a safe haven, they could get their feet on the ground and make it work.

She turned to the woman behind the baby coach. "What if your sister did have a place to go? A place where she'd have support while she finished school or looked for a job?"

"Does such a place exist?"

"I don't know," Sadie mumbled. "But if it did?" Sadie suddenly saw her path out of this tremendous hopelessness. She'd help women like herself who, through no fault of their own, were being judged, punished, and cast off—left to deal with their grief in silence.

She'd give them a voice.

"Here's my number. I'd like to talk to your sister," Sadie said.

Chapter Forty-Five

One year later

Sadie wiped the sweat beading her upper lip with a patch of exposed skin outside her dirty work glove. She knelt to greet the calico cat that had taken residence in the barn. Her barn. The same one her mother had caused mischief in, swinging from the loft rope Sadie had found still tied to the cobwebby rafters. Sadie couldn't help but smile when she pictured her mother, a young starlet, climbing out of the farmhouse window to catch a train to New York City. It seemed almost fitting to Sadie that she would find her way back here.

She pitched the soiled straw into her wheelbarrow. Sally would be along soon to visit with her son, who had just taken his first steps. She could hardly believe it. Sally, who'd lumbered up the porch steps that sweltering August day as Sadie had been nailing the Springhaven plaque over the circa sign near the door. Sadie remembered looking over her shoulder and taking in the sight of Sally, swollen from her fingers to her toes—the girl's face pinched in fear. The next girl came a week later. And another after that, until the hollow existence that Aunt Bea was sure Sadie would suffer out here in "no-man's land," was filled with new purpose.

Sadie had opened Springhaven—a mother's home

for young women that was safe and secure. Here, Sadie helped new mothers make informed decisions. She'd devoted her life to it, but nothing would bring Priscilla back.

One day, when a uniformed man knocked on the door, Sadie's heart had drummed out of her chest, until she discovered it was Sally's boyfriend, home from the war, there to marry her. Although Sadie had wept with joy for them, she couldn't help but plunge further into her own grief at what might have been.

The war had ended, but Sadie's sorrow only worsened. The returning soldiers, although a blessing and answer to prayers everywhere—each and every one—also served to remind her of her own loss.

"Sultry day, isn't it?" Sadie asked the cat nestled on top of a bale of hay watching her. The calico tilted her triangular head, exposing a weepy eye. Sadie had seen her underside bloated with a litter of kittens, probably due soon. "Poor mama." She stroked the fur that slid across lumpy ribs. She'd pick up fresh cream at the Dalton's market after her chores.

But as she lifted the pitchfork, someone slid the wide barn door all the way open, startling the calico, who hissed, arched her back, and leaped off. Sadie frowned. She liked to keep the barn cool by cracking the door.

A silhouette appeared.

She glared into the streaming light, through dust dancing in the sunlight's wake. An eerie coolness swept through the barn's central corridor.

"Sadie." His deep, unmistakable voice cut through the air. "Aren't you a sight." His outstretched arms beckoned her, but her legs, calf high in urine-soaked straw, wobbled in her muck boots. Could it really be James?

"I lost you once—I won't lose you again," he said, echoing the very words he'd told her at the train station that cold winter day.

She tore off her gloves as she ran. "James! Oh, James!" They melted together.

He lifted her in his arms. She wrapped her legs around his waist, and clung her arms over the decorated shoulders of his starched uniform. He grasped her in a familiar hold, one that she'd yearned for the entire time they'd been torn apart. She cried out as the space blurred around them. "I thought I'd lost you, I—"

"You could never lose me, Sadie—I'll always find you."

His lips were on hers. Salty, burning, nips and nuzzles interrupted her breathless words—as desperate as she was to sink in and cling, she had to know what happened. She slithered down to stand, still embraced in his arms, sneaking peeks between kisses. "How did you find me?"

"It wasn't easy. In New York I went to your mom's apartment. Some man answered the door, said Audrey didn't live there any more. So I went to Bryn Mawr and Louise gave me this address." He brushed the hair back from her face. "Dear God, I thought I'd never touch you again," he whispered breathlessly.

They fell into the hay. She ran trembling fingers over his face, tracing his cheekbones and jaw, ears, and neck. His hair was shorn close and his uniform crisp, but she knew he'd been to hell and back on the inside.

"When Lenny…sent me the box…with your journal." She pulled back and grasped his face with her hands. "Let me look at you. What did they do to you?"

She kissed the scar over his eyebrow and then each pained crease on his face, those familiar and those that were new to her, he talked at last—allowing her to rediscover the subtleties in his mannerisms that her single photograph of him had failed to capture.

"It doesn't matter. I'm here now." His voice was gruff with tenderness.

"But what happened? Your letters stopped coming and I didn't know what to think and then the lighter… Someone wrote to my dad and said he found it in the wreckage. Beatrice gave it to me and I thought…I thought…"

He squeezed his eyes shut and rubbed at his face with one hand, the other firmly planted on her hip. "That was a mistake. I am so sorry. My bomber also crashed, but I parachuted out. This kind farmer and his wife took me in. After I was well enough to travel on, the Germans caught me and accused me of being a spy. I was incarcerated at Buchenwald, a German Nazi concentration camp. So many people helped me. I can't even tell you how lucky I am. Once I got out, and back to England, I was in a hospital recovering, before they sent me here. When I was captive, did they ever send word?"

"No."

He stroked her back. "Sadie, we've lost a lot of time, but we're together now. We have the rest of our lives together. We can put all that behind us and start fresh now."

Start fresh. If he only knew. Their separation marked her darkest days, and little did he know how motherhood had both saved and haunted her. Hearing that James had perished would have killed her had it not been for the baby who needed her. His baby. The child that he would never know.

Sadie pulled away, ashamed. She climbed off James and sat beside him. James propped himself on his elbows. "What's wrong?"

Sadie blinked back tears. James sat up beside her and took her hand tightly in his own. He squeezed and released her hand, then cupped her face and tilted her eyes up to his, brushing Sadie's tears aside with his rough thumbs. "Don't cry. We're together now."

The pain cut too deep this time, her earlier fears of single parenthood seemed feeble in comparison to telling him about the terrible thing she'd done.

"I had your baby…a little girl." She dove into his chest, unable to meet his gaze. "I wrote to tell you. I was so scared." Her voice caught.

James' face softened. "Oh, Sadie." He hugged her hard and fast. She sobbed into his uniform. The rough material chaffed her skin, but she couldn't stop.

"I made a mistake. A terrible, awful mistake. I gave our little girl away…"

He continued to hold her. "You did what you had to do."

After a long time passed, the calico appeared and licked her paw lazily. Then she attacked James' untied bootlace. Despite whatever Sadie had done, life cruelly carried on.

He said, "We'll go get her and bring her here. To our home." He kissed the top of her head then scooped up the feline and placed her across their laps.

"We can't do that, James. She's gone. How could I have let her go?"

"Because you loved her. Like your mother loved you."

"So, you don't hate me?"

"I could never hate you. I love you like I always have, and always will."

Chapter Forty-Six

Springhaven, 1972

Sadie dipped her head and covered her mouth with quivering fingers. "Not a day goes by that I don't think of it…"

She'd waited thirty years to reunite with the daughter she'd surrendered, but now that the day had arrived, she panicked. Her arms hung helplessly as she awaited her daughter's next reaction. Anger?

The young woman clenched her fist around the lighter, but said nothing. Sadie noticed how the curve of her ear mimicked her father's. Although she stood taller than Sadie, she had Audrey's delicate wrists and her dancer's physique.

When she finally met Sadie's gaze, her eyes weren't the steel-gray hazel Sadie had always imagined, like James'. Instead she saw a salty blue ocean and the depth to match it.

"It's really you, I can tell," Sadie said, desperately wanting to hold the young woman standing on her porch, but refraining from doing anything hasty that might frighten her off.

"It's me," the young woman squeaked, folding Sadie into the hearty hug she needed, both women intermittently sobbing and smiling and wiping at their faces.

Sadie guided her daughter inside to the sitting room off the kitchen and they crumpled onto the checkered sofa, inches apart, facing each other. "James!" she cried.

The sound of his heavy work boots clomping down the stairs made Sadie even more emotional. And then he filled the small-framed doorway with his great presence. One look in the room and he dropped the socket wrench he'd been using onto the hardwood floor, a confused look melting into recognition.

"She's the very image of you, Sadie." He sank into the room while both women embraced him. They held like that for a while. Sadie lost perception of time. Then Sadie and James watched their daughter settle on one sofa, waiting until she seemed comfortable before sitting together on its flanking twin. James kept wiping at his eyes and gaping against the emotion. Sadie rubbed his back.

"Thank you. Thank you for coming." James folded Sadie's free hand into his and rubbing it with his other.

"Thank you for welcoming me."

That her daughter ever doubted a welcome reaction pulled at Sadie's insides.

"I have to tell you I was apprehensive about all this." The young woman gestured with her hand. "I wasn't sure you wanted to be found."

Sadie remembered how she'd felt when after buzzing apartment 1B that day she'd suddenly been face-to-face with her estranged mother. The fact that Sadie's daughter was here meant something, but what? Was she simply curious about a genetic health history? Or was she interested in a relationship? Single tears streamed down each cheek as she tried to reconcile the lovely vision before her with the baby she had once held. She was all grown up now, certainly—her adulthood evidence of the time they'd lost.

"My parents told me I was adopted and that they'd help me find you when I was ready."

"The doctor and wife?"

"No. My parents run Carmine's in Philadelphia. Didn't you know that?"

"I was told nothing, but I think I saw your parents at the adoption agency. At least I hope I had…" Sadie said, surprised to learn she'd clung to an inaccurate fact about the very people she'd entrusted the care of her first born child. Confusion colored her memory. Had the loving couple who asked for Phillip not been the same people who raised her daughter?

"They were told I'm Italian, like them. And that I came from unmarried teenagers. Destitute, but intelligent."

Sadie and James looked at each other, surprised by the misinformation, both seeing the unbelievable humor through the tension.

James said, "You're English on Sadie's side and Ukrainian on mine."

"No wonder I can't cook," she joked.

Sadie laughed, adding, "I imagine you have many questions."

"I do."

"And I know you must feel apprehensive, but please don't feel that way. For thirty years we have been waiting for you to knock on the door. I've never given up hope. Neither has James. I imagine if you didn't know that we're not Italian, you must not have read my letter?"

"There was no letter in my file. All I have is my birth certificate that I sent away for and the lighter, which is what ultimately led me to you. But I want you to know that I did have a wonderful life, raised by good people who love me very much. A big, boisterous, cantankerous Italian family. And that was part of the reason I never pursued a relationship sooner. Outside of a conversation when I was young, when my parents told me about you, we never talked about it. But once on my birthday, I overheard my mother telling my aunt how brave you must have been, and that left a lasting impression. You see, you were my hero because of my mother, not despite her. Because she revered you, so did I.

"When I turned eighteen, they sat me down and gave me the envelope, still sealed, and I was the one who first found the lighter inside. I was intrigued, that of all things, this would be my only clue to you. I researched who was Pennsylvania's governor at the time of my birth, but I was afraid to look any further. I wasn't ready. And I was worried how my search might affect my adoptive parents."

James kept rubbing Sadie's hands, probably sensing the waves of emotion rolling inside her.

"After college while I planned my wedding, I thought—I wonder how my mother might have worn her hair on her wedding day. What had been her first thought when she walked down the aisle? I was curious. I went back to the adoption agency and asked if there was anything for me. There wasn't."

Sadie raged at herself for being too trusting—she'd written letters she never sent because she was certain the original letter had been in the file, where she had included her full name and James', their families' locations and how to reach them. But she was too choked with outrage and sadness to even speak.

"My husband kept encouraging me to write away for my birth certificate. Together we would dig through the records, whatever it took, to find you. I wasn't sure how you were related to the governor, but I assumed one of you was somehow. My birth certificate simply stated 'girl' and under father, 'unknown.' But I had your signature, and I saw that your name matched the governor's."

"I named you Priscilla," Sadie said through the burn in her nose, thanking God for this husband of her daughter's who, like James, had persevered.

"Priscilla?"

"Priscilla was your great grandmother's name."

"Priscilla," she said again slowly, as if contemplating the sound of her given name through her own voice. "I was named after my Italian mother's mother, Theresa. Growing up my nickname was Tree."

Tree. They sat in silence as Sadie thought how fitting the nickname was for hers and James' willowy child.

Just as saplings turned to trees, their trunks widening, their branches scraping at the sky, children lost their innocence, sought repentance, spent the rest of their adult lives trying to make wrongs right—always growing, learning, changing, sometimes for the better, sometimes not. Her father had said it best. Everyone had their own life to live.

Sadie leaped to her feet. "I need you to see something." In two strides she reached the antique secretary and unfolded its wooden closure. Inside a little drawer, she withdrew the sole relic that proved her daughter's existence. With child-like eagerness, Sadie placed the baby booties on her daughter's lap.

"I made these for you."

They cried together at the sight of the tiny handmade booties, knitted by Sadie's imperfect teenage hands, stretched where Priscilla's pinky toe had once been.

James was beside Sadie, helping her back onto the sofa with his arm around her.

"I tried...God knows I tried to keep you. I was so determined at first. James—" she said, turning to him and rubbing his thigh, "—was in the war. I was sent away to live with strangers. I ran away and tried to work a factory job at night, but it was too much. I worried with your every little sneeze that someday you might need medicine I couldn't afford. I could barely put food on the table. And then that lighter was found at the crash site...I thought I'd lost him. I wanted you to have a mother and a father."

Theresa shook her head, tears streaming down her face as she reached out to Sadie and held her hands. They sat there like that for some time, just holding hands and it felt like the most natural thing in the world, as if lost time had been restored. "You must have been very scared. And alone."

"I wanted to find you. My arms ached for you. I didn't want to intrude on your life. But I did call the agency and ask. By law, I had to wait until you were eighteen. And I thought you'd find my letter that explained why."

"I've always wanted to know why. Thank you for sharing this with me—it's even better coming from you in person. I realize how painful the decision must have been for you."

"So…you forgive me?"

"I never blamed you," she said, and Sadie knew to have such empathy her daughter had been raised by a loving, secure family.

Theresa continued. "I've also wanted to know if you were very much in love, and I can tell that you are, and I'm guessing you were, but if you could tell me…" She kept breaking with emotion. "I'm curious if my existence is proof of your love?"

When Sadie and James gazed at each other, Sadie saw the same rugged young soldier who jumped off the train to retrieve her stolen clutch. "Really, he was all wrong for me," she deadpanned.

"She was engaged to someone else," James said with an impish grin.

"Hold on." Sadie went to retrieve the letters, also in the secretary. "When we were separated during the war, this is how we communicated." She placed the box on the coffee table, took off the lid, and held up a stack of yellowed envelopes and post cards rubber-banded together. "Many months' worth of our lives apart are documented here. During the war, these letters kept me going. I often bypassed the mailbox and waited on the curb."

"This is wonderful. Truly," Theresa said.

Sadie was lost in her reverie, saying things she'd never even told James. "I thought I'd lost him during the war. I loved him, you see. He was part of me, and I was a part of him. I had a new life here, but I missed him. I dreamed of the day he would return. That would be a happy day! I imagined his strong arms around me at the train station. In my fantasy he held you in his arms and saw your curls—did you know you had the sweetest curls?"

Theresa shook her head.

"Theresa." She mentally replaced the name she'd chosen with this one. "I have tried to avoid dwelling on my past. I thought what's done is done. I can't change it. Before you came along, James once told me to look to the future. I tried to follow his advice, but at first I thought I wasn't capable of doing that, of being hopeful, I mean. When I was pregnant with you, all I could think about was how I would never surrender you. But then the first few months of motherhood clouded that up. I began to see through your eyes. I had dreams for you. I knew James would have dreams for you, too. And those dreams involved something neither of us could give you at that time."

"Did you have other children? Do I have siblings?"

"You have a sister, Anne. She's a painter." Sadie motioned to the framed artwork that hung throughout the cozy den.

"A sister? I've always wanted a sister."

"And three brothers," James added.

"Make that four," she said. "My parents adopted a boy at the same time they adopted me."

"Phillip?" Sadie squeaked.

"How did you know that?"

"When I was pregnant with you, I took care of him in the orphanage. Your parents are the couple I saw that day at the agency…"

.   Theresa nodded and added, "We're very close. Always have been. He's a surgeon now."

Knowing her plan had come to fruition helped

Sadie and would give her the strength to continue healing. Another of God's ironies swept over her. "Did you say you were raised in Philadelphia?" That her daughter had been living so close all those years, and that they had probably even been to the same places, maybe at the same time, was groundbreaking.

"I was. When I worked at the restaurant as a teenager, I used to wonder if I'd know you if you came in the door. I wondered if I'd feel a connection to you and just know...I know it sounds silly." She brushed the idea away, not realizing that Sadie had done the very same thing with countless babies over the years.

"How did you come to live here—at Springhaven? Is this the former home for unwed mothers where I was born?"

"No. But," Sadie said, a smile drawing up her lips, "you could say Springhaven was born because of you. After I said goodbye to you, I had a terrible time with the guilt. My mother inherited this property and I decided to open the doors to other young women who were, like I had been, pregnant and alone. When my father passed, his wife, Beatrice, with whom I'd since reconciled, sent me the inheritance. I used that money to keep the home afloat. Around that time, I kept thinking about how I could honor James and all the other fallen heroes of our country. He had kept a journal. A beautifully written journal that depicted his time in combat and the stories of all of the men he fought with. I thought, why not share this and dedicate it to those brave soldiers and airmen? So I sent it to a publisher in New York. The book helped fund Springhaven."

"Really?"

"It became the start of my writing career," James said.

"A very prolific career," Sadie added proudly while James wiped at his eyes. "He completed college on the GI Bill and went on to publish countless novels, an anthology, and his memoir."

"What a legacy," Theresa said before an extended silence.

Sadie rubbed at her temples not wanting their reunion to end, fearful that after her initial curiosity was satisfied, her daughter might leave. She had that distinct feeling—the same one she had every time she reached the end of one of James' novels, when on turning the page and seeing just a few paragraphs dangling unanchored on what had to be the last page, she instinctively slowed down her reading, not wanting the story to end.

James said, "I once told Sadie that the past is just the past. I was too young to realize it then, but I was wrong."

"The past is not just the past," Sadie agreed.

"It stays with you," James added, "is part of you, as much as you don't want it to be sometimes, it is."

"It makes you who you are. Like this burn scar on my palm and these wrinkles that crease my face that I forget exist until I look into the mirror," Sadie said. "But maybe it's time we look forward and appreciate what we have before us. What do you say?"

Theresa hunched over, her body wracked with sobs. "I'm sorry. I'm extra-emotional these days and what you both just said is really touching." She placed a hand to her stomach.

"Are you pregnant?" Sadie asked.

"I am," she said through a teary smile. "My first. Nobody told me how sick I would be!"

"I know just the thing to help you." Sadie led her to the kitchen while noticing that her daughter still grasped the baby booties in her hand.

She took James' hand. In that moment, the three of them connected at last, she became whole again.

A word about the author...

Carolyn Menke is a graduate of Carnegie Mellon University. A professional blogger, creative writing teacher, and award-winning flash fiction writer, she enjoys horseback riding and geocaching with her three daughters, husband, and goldendoodle.

http://www.carolynmenke.com

Thank you for purchasing
this publication of The Wild Rose Press, Inc.

If you enjoyed the story, we would appreciate your
letting others know by leaving a review.

For other wonderful stories,
please visit our on-line bookstore at
www.thewildrosepress.com.

For questions or more information
contact us at
info@thewildrosepress.com.

The Wild Rose Press, Inc.
www.thewildrosepress.com

Stay current with The Wild Rose Press, Inc.

Like us on Facebook

https://www.facebook.com/TheWildRosePress

And Follow us on Twitter
https://twitter.com/WildRosePress

Made in the USA
Middletown, DE
24 September 2015